The Twisted Gate

By Matt Glicksman

Copyright © 2017 Matt Glicksman

All rights reserved.

ISBN: 9798483226130

DEDICATION

To my amazing wife, my first audience. This would not have been possible without your unwavering support.
Volim te uvijek i zauvijek

ACKNOWLEDGMENTS

A special thanks to those who read through the early drafts. Your feedback and encouragement have always been invaluable to me. I'm honored that you took the time to read through the story and share your impressions:

My wife, Ivana
My sister, Kristina
My father, Howard
My close friends, Will and Kevin

Thank you to my editor, Laura, for not only improving this manuscript, but for the lessons you've taught me in writing that I will carry with me forever.

And to my cover illustrator, Nele, thank you for your beautiful cover design. You've captured the essence of this story wonderfully.

CHAPTER 1

As the sun shifted to red in the late-afternoon sky, a young boy walked through the forest with his dog and hoped to reach home before dark. His loose, dirt-stained clothing indicated the effort of a long day's hunt, albeit a successful one. The limp body of a rabbit swung from his belt. Enjoying the sound of the leaves crunching below his feet, the boy realized his hunting companion was no longer following him. He came to a stop and found the auburn-coated dog a few yards back.

"Come on, girl. We're almost there. We have to get back before dark," the boy beckoned. Normally an obedient pet, the mutt completely ignored her master. Her muscles were tense as she stared into the woods. The youth retraced his steps until he was next to his dog, which came up to his waist. Patting her head, he dropped to his knee and looked in the same direction as the animal. The boy made do with the little light that peeked through the trees. The area appeared to be empty and quiet, and so he squinted, hoping to see what had hooked his friend.

"What is it, girl? What do you see?" he whispered.

The dog's floppy ear twitched, and she let out a low growl, followed by a bark. The boy strained again to see what he was missing, but all he noticed was how the shadows around them grew larger and began to consume them. The sun was dropping below the horizon. Before he could take her collar and lead her back to the village, the dog bolted and barked intermittently. The boy cursed his companion as he took off after her and shouted for her to stop. His short legs were no match for the speed of the canine as she darted between trees and hurdled over brush. Dusk settled in, and if they didn't head back now, they would be outside the village after dark. This was not only dangerous for them physically, but the boy imagined his mother waiting for him at the edge of town to punish him for disobeying such a fundamental rule. However, he refused to abandon his friend. Within minutes, the youth found his dog motionless and silent, save for the panting. He leaned on his knees as he peered into the forest, using all that remained of the faded sunlight. The dog's ears perked up, and the boy listened as well. A soft groaning steadily grew louder.

 The ground beneath them shook violently, and a thick vine burst forth from the dirt beside them. The boy recoiled in fear and grabbed a hold of the dog's leather collar. The beast barked at the intrusion as she was slowly pulled back by her master. Another vine shot up from the ground on the other side of them, which caused the pair to stumble as they retreated. The boy heard the ground fracture and scrambled to get a safe distance from the terrifying event. Sensing that they were finally on solid ground, the boy clung to a nearby tree to stabilize himself. He clamped his eyes shut and prayed for it all to stop. As the earthquake became less intense, he cautiously lifted his eyelids. Over a dozen vines had emerged from the ground, growing thicker as they grew taller. They twisted together, spiraling to form an even larger structure that resembled the trunk of a tree. The formation surpassed the treetops, and yet the structure continued to rise. The whole incident only lasted a few minutes, but it felt much longer to the boy.

And then, as suddenly as it all began, the earth became still. The youth released the support he had been clinging to and marveled at the structure before him. The newly woven tree trunk towered over any other tree in the forest. At the top, the tips of the vines curled back and hung a few feet from the ground, gently swaying back and forth. After such a major disruption, the boy found the situation eerily serene.

"What the—stay," he commanded his pet as he tiptoed toward the tree. Full of awe, he watched one of the dangling vines swing harmlessly. He inched his hand forward to feel the mysterious structure.

A loud yell came from the trunk. The boy recoiled before he could touch the vine. A second shout followed, and he was not about to stick around and find out who or what was making the noise. The sound of furious scratching from inside the massive tree was the last thing the boy heard before he sprinted toward the village. His dog followed closely behind him. The boy wildly waved his hands in front of his face to move aside branches that hindered his escape. He still heard the roars, urging him to run faster. His companion matched his pace. Too terrified to even glance over his shoulder, he only had one goal. He no longer cared about the potential punishment awaiting him in the town. In fact, he would welcome it if it meant he survived the night.

****

A voice called out in his mind, *It's time now. Go and fulfill your purpose. Kill King Batar.*

Agony consumed him. Trapped in a confined space, he howled, grabbing and pulling at his hair. After a few quick breaths, he cried out again. He clenched his fists, and his long nails pierced the skin of his palm. The physical pain did little to distract him from the indescribable anguish that tortured his mind. Wishing to break free, the captive clawed desperately at the walls of his prison. He felt pieces tear away which motivated him to scratch more furiously. Another wave of agony swept in, and he stumbled back. He squeezed his head and screamed at the top of his lungs. He could barely think, but something drove him to break free.

In the darkness, he frantically patted the walls. His fingers found a crease in the structure, and he traced it to its deepest point. He plunged his sharp nails into the crevice. His hand slid through and felt the cool air of the night beyond the wall. His breathing was erratic as he tried to tolerate the pain long enough to get his other hand through, but it was too overwhelming. With his left hand, he clawed across his chest, ripping through his clothing. Blood oozed from the fresh wound, and the physical pain provided temporary relief to his mind. Without wasting another moment, he forced his left hand through the opening to join his right. The captive gripped the two sides of the hole and pulled the wall apart. As the agony rushed back into his brain, he bellowed and stumbled out of the tree trunk. Unfortunately, his prison hadn't been the origin for his suffering. He sucked in air through his gritted teeth and buried his nails deep into the earth. He tried to combat the torment with sheer willpower, but it was useless. He raised his head and howled to the night sky.

His claws tore recklessly at his chest and abdomen, further shredding his shirt and vest so that his torso was completely exposed. He felt the flesh being torn away and the blood pouring from his body. The pressure in his skull intensified as another wave of mental torture washed over him. His breathing quickened as he brought his right hand up and dug the nails deep into his forehead. He bared his teeth as he raked down the right side of his face and over his eye. The agony receded.

He fell on all fours and gasped for air. In the moonlight, he could only see with his left eye as the blood—dark red, almost black—pooled on the ground. The cumulative injuries he had endured seemed to relieve the inexplicable mental pain he had first been exposed to. There was still a tingling in the back of his head, but he paid it no attention. He was finally capable of creating coherent thoughts. He examined the long, sharp nails of his claws. He didn't remember having such beastly hands. He analyzed his clothing and found the pieces to be surprisingly well made and extravagant, despite the new rips. His ornate vest hung in place thanks to a few resilient threads. As he rolled over to sit, he found his expensive linen pants soaked with blood. He noted the massive tree made of vines. How did he end up trapped inside? But, it all led him back to his grotesque hands. The blood rolled down his wrists as his claws began to shake.

 He wiped away the blood running down his face and spotted a soft glow in the distance. The light was faint but oddly inviting, and so he felt compelled to move toward it. He journeyed through the woods and wiped his face each time the blood invaded his eye. But as he made it to the forest's edge, he discovered he was no longer bleeding. On the opposite side of a clearing stood a village, the source of the light. Encouraged by the sight of the street lanterns in the distance, he hurried across the field. He desperately needed help. The agony was slowly seeping back into his mind.

CHAPTER 2

A young priest in his midtwenties strolled down the corridor of the rectory. He was dressed in a long brown robe with a black scarf that hung around his neck. The most tantalizing aroma filled the air, and he followed it all the way to the kitchen.

"Smells great!" the priest said with a smile.

The cook peered over his shoulder. "Don't even think about it, Don Millan."

Millan feigned innocence. "What?"

"You know what. You don't get any until it's ready, and certainly not before Don Skully's here. I swear, you and Tyro are just a couple of scavengers."

Millan chuckled softly. There must be something he could snack on until dinner. He considered rifling through the pantry when a loud knock came at the front door of the rectory.

The cook lightly banged his wooden spoon against the lip of the pot. "You best get that."

Millan left the cook in peace and made his way to the entrance of the priests' home. The rectory only contained six small bedrooms, a kitchen, and a common area, extremely modest by the guild's standards. The young priest held his side as his stomach grumbled. The knock came again.

"Yes, yes, just a moment." Millan swung open the door to reveal a woman. In one hand she held an envelope, and in the other, she gripped the reins of her horse.

"Is Don Skully in?" she asked.

"Yes."

"This letter is for him. Can you give it to him?"

"Of course." Millan reached for the envelope, but as he grasped it, she didn't let go.

She locked eyes with him. "It's very important you get this to him right away."

Millan pulled a bit harder on the letter. "Yes, I understand."

"Good." The courier released the envelope and led her horse away.

"May the angels watch over you," Millan called to her halfheartedly. When she didn't respond, he shook his head and shut the door. As he made his way to the room of his superior, the young priest inspected the blank envelope. Since Nesinu was such a small village, it didn't have its own Scriptorum. However, the scribes from Nolka, the nearest city, would send couriers to deliver any letters intended for Nesinu residents. The odd thing was the couriers never made any deliveries this late in the day.

The young priest arrived at his destination and knocked softly.

"Enter."

Millan pushed open the wooden door to find Don Skully, an elderly man, seated behind a desk. His attire mirrored that of the young priest. The nearby candles gave off such a heat that beads of sweat covered the old man's bald head.

Don Skully reclined in his chair and dabbed the moisture on his forehead with the end of his black scarf. "Oh, Millan, is it dinnertime?"

"Unfortunately, no. This came for you just now."

"A letter? At this hour?"

As Millan crossed the room and handed the envelope to Don Skully, the entire room began to shake. Millan stumbled to the wall and used it for support as his superior stayed put in his chair. The contents of Skully's desk trembled but remained in place. The heart of the young priest pounded away as he thought back to his studies. As far as he knew, there was only one thing that caused the ground to shake.

The small tremor ceased, and despite the serenity that followed, Millan made no attempt to move. "Are you all right?"

"Heh, I may be old, but I'm not helpless."

The young man held up his hands as if to indicate he meant no offense. "Of course. I'm just watching out for our head don, that's all. So, what do you suppose that earthquake was?"

"Perhaps it was just a natural tremor." Skully unfolded the letter.

Millan rolled his eyes. "Right. Natural. What do you think we're up against?"

"I don't know, but I suggest we go find out. Let's see what the watchers say. With a shake like that, the pods should be close enough to see."

"Understood." The young priest headed for the door. "Are you coming?"

"Uh, yes. You go ahead. I'll be out in a moment."

Millan left the old man and set out for the rectory entrance. He needed to figure out what sort of threat might be coming, and the watchers would be his best source of information. Watchers were tasked with policing the citizens and guarding the towns or cities. At this hour, they would be patrolling the edge of the village on the lookout for any suspicious activity. Nesinu only had a few watchers because of its small population, but cities like the kingdom's capital, Light's Haven, employed thousands.

The young priest exited the building to discover he

wasn't the only person in the street. Although the sun disappeared for the night, people were leaving their homes to discuss the tremor that had shaken their town. Millan was searching the crowd so intently for Captain Pirok, the head watcher of Nesinu, he didn't notice the old priest had joined him.

"Any sign of the watchers?" Skully asked.

The young priest wasn't much taller than the average height of a villager, but compared to his hunched-over superior who leaned on a walking stick, Millan felt like a giant. He bent to speak directly into Skully's ear. "Captain Pirok's coming to us now."

A middle-aged man dressed in select pieces of armor weaved between the bystanders. His appearance may have been considered dashing if not for the abundance of unkempt facial hair. The man approached the two priests and politely bowed. "Don Skully, Don Millan."

"What news have you?" Skully asked.

"No visuals yet. I can't imagine it will be long, though. A quake like that? They'd have to be close. Probably a few pods just inside the forest's edge. Maybe a dozen fray or so."

"Really? A dozen fray?" The preliminary report excited the young priest. This would be his first opportunity to fight demons, and the fray were the weakest class, barely intelligent.

Skully cleared his throat. "Don Millan, why don't you go find our squire? This could be excellent practice for the both of you."

"At once." The young priest darted back into the house in search of their student. Activity outside of Nesinu was rare, and save for a major event more than ten years ago, there was scarcely any cause for concern. Millan scurried through the rectory, even though he knew finding Tyro would be easy.

He paused outside the squire's room but continued on when he heard voices in the kitchen. Opening the door,

Millan found the cook and the squire picking up food and broken dishes off the floor.

"Ah, Don Millan, good. Can you lend us a hand?" the cook asked.

"I'm sorry. I actually came to get Tyro."

"Me?"

"That's right. There could be fray upon us at any moment." Millan tried to hide his smile, but he had been waiting forever for a chance to fight demons.

Tyro made no move to stand up.

Millan noticed the panic on the squire's face. "Come on. You'll be fine. You've been doing great in class. And you'll be with me and Don Skully."

Tyro got to his feet and wiped his hands on his plain clothes. As a squire, he was not yet inducted into Candelux, the priest guild, and therefore, he didn't wear a robe. The only indication that he was connected to the priests was the short brown scarf that hung around his neck.

The cook sat back on his feet. "Fine. Go. But, I better not see any demons in here or no dinner for either of you."

As Millan led the squire back down the hallway, he began to recite some of the blessings in his head. Which one would he use first?

When the pair joined Don Skully outside, the old man turned his back to the crowd. "Ah, Tyro, good of you to join us."

"Thank you, Don Skully."

Barely able to hold back his excitement, Millan clapped his hands. "So, any news?"

Skully lowered his voice. "Unfortunately, there's been a change in plan."

"A change? What's happened? What's out there?" Millan cast his eyes toward the edge of town.

"I'm not sure yet, but I have a terrible feeling. We can't risk an attack on the village."

"What is it? An iymed?"

"I don't know. I wish it was easier for me to explain."

"Please," the young priest begged. "Whatever it is, we can kill it together."

"No, I'm afraid it's too dangerous. I need you to listen to me very carefully. You must evacuate the town."

"Evacuate? Is that really necessary? The sun's already down. What about the Blessing of Marked Defense?"

This was one of the spells the young priest had been practicing in his mind. After a short incantation, all the homes in the village would be protected with light energy. It wouldn't help too much against a strong demon, like an iymed, but for fray, it would do just fine.

"Millan, please trust me," Skully insisted. "There isn't much time, and for the sake of all these people, you need to get them out of here. I want you and Tyro leading them out of Nesinu in ten minutes. The watchers can help you."

"Ten minutes? What about you?"

"Don't worry about me. I can handle myself. Once I discover what's out there, I'll catch up to you. Head south toward Nolka. You should be able to make it with everyone before midnight. Millan, I'm counting on you."

The young priest understood the gravity of the situation and quietly nodded.

Skully faced the townspeople and lifted his hands over his head, silencing the murmurs of the crowd. "Everyone, please, may I have your attention? I would like for everyone to remain calm. In light of recent news, I believe the potential threat is too great."

"What is it, Don Skully?" a voice called from the sea of people.

"I cannot say with complete certainty, but I believe our lives may be at risk if we remain here. I'm taking a precautionary measure and calling for an evacuation of the town." His statement was met with outrage and panic, but Skully quickly subdued the crowd. "Please. Please. I understand this is an unusual request, but I'm afraid there's no time to argue. If I'm right, you will need to get as far away from here as soon as possible."

"And what if you're wrong?"

"If I'm wrong, and I pray to the angels I am, you come back to your lives tomorrow. I would rather err on the side of safety, though. Please grab only what you deem to be absolutely necessary. Don Millan, with the help of Tyro and the watchers, will escort you all to Nolka. You are leaving in ten minutes. Get moving!"

As some people scattered to their homes, others headed to the south part of the village. Millan was frozen as Skully hobbled toward the east side of the town with the support of his walking stick. For nearly a decade, Don Skully was the only priest in Nesinu. Anyone who wished to join Candelux went elsewhere to study. Despite his parents' wishes, Millan became the first squire to train with Don Skully. The old man was more than just a mentor to him. Skully's presence at Millan's Acceptance, his official induction into Candelux, meant more to the young priest than the attendance of his own parents.

Though Millan had been reassured that Skully would rejoin the group, he had an unsettling feeling in his stomach, something beyond the normal hunger pangs. Officially, the guild encouraged precautionary evacuations for very small towns that might be defenseless against a sizable attack, but most priests never instituted such drastic measures. Trusting the judgment of his superior, though, Millan reentered the rectory to pack his bag, after which he followed orders and led the villagers toward Nolka.

****

In his head, the voice echoed, *If you need help, seek out the Brotherhood.*

He made his way across the open field. He concentrated on his breathing as he quietly endured the physical pain of his self-inflicted wounds. Although they

The Twisted Gate

had already healed, he was still covered in blood. The agony in his mind was only a nuisance, but he felt it slowly returning. He rubbed his temple to alleviate the pounding in his head, but there was little relief. The village wasn't much farther, and he pushed himself to keep going. As he neared it, the town appeared abandoned, save for a single person in the middle of the thoroughfare. Hunched over, he hung his head and his long white hair fell over his face.

When he arrived at the town, he used his left hand to pull his hair back behind his ear, exposing only the left side of his face. Before him, a short old man leaned gingerly on a walking stick. The villager, dressed in brown garb with a black scarf, lifted his hand, indicating the visitor to stop. He complied.

"Who are you?" the old man asked.

The visitor groaned. He felt the villager's eyes scrutinizing him. He straightened his back and towered over the old man.

"Did you hear me?" the villager asked. "My name is Don Skully. What's yours?"

He grimaced as his headache worsened. He did his best to focus on a response. "Onto djja."

His own words startled him. What he had meant to say and what his tongue produced were not one and the same. He was afraid to speak again.

"Well, that's too bad," the old man said. "Maybe I can help you there. Do you at least know you're a demon?"

There was no way he heard that correctly. He wasn't a demon. And, did this old man really understand the jargon he had spoken? The growing pain pressed him to speak. He needed answers. "Ajjes ujjditov?"

"Those words you're speaking. They're Kisejjad, the demon language. That would make you a demon."

"And are you a demon too?" the visitor asked in his twisted dialect.

Skully tapped his walking stick on the ground. "No, I'm a priest. I stop demons."

"If you're not a demon, how can you understand me?"

"All priests must learn Kisejjad."

He studied his claws and turned them over. He didn't want to believe it, but it seemed to make sense. He had to be certain, though. "And you're sure I'm a demon?"

"Yes," the old man said. "The dark energy is a dead giveaway. I guess the question now is how bad are you? You're not showing me everything."

"Showing you?"

"In a manner of speaking. I can see you're definitely not fray. I would pray you're a lesser iymed, but I doubt I'm that lucky."

He winced as his headache thumped louder in his head. *Fray? Iymed?* The words seemed familiar, but it was difficult to remember where he'd heard them. Was he really a demon? If so, how did he become one? No, it wasn't possible. He pushed past this train of thought to address the more pressing issue. "How do I stop the pain?"

"Pain? That's not good. Verago sent you here with a purpose, didn't he? What is it?"

The agony was getting worse. The demon threw his head back and yelled as loudly as he could, trying to expel the pain through his mouth. His nails dug into his palms as he tightened his fists. Fresh blood trickled down his arm. He leaned forward into a staggered stance and rested his hands on his knees. A few strands of his long white hair dangled over his exposed face. A bright-yellow aura surrounded the priest. Where had that come from?

Skully pointed at him. "Who did that to you?"

The demon felt the claw marks that ran down the right side of his face. "It was the only way to stop the pain."

"I can help with that. Knowing your name would make it easier, though."

"I already told you. I don't know. I don't remember anything."

"Not even your purpose?"

The demon recalled the voice he'd first heard in his

prison. He may have forgotten everything before his arrival, but amid the torment, he knew this. His breathing became uneven as he tried to cope with the agony. "To kill King Batar."

The demon fell to his knees and cradled his head in his hands. With the heel of his palms, he pressed firmly against his eyes.

"Angels, help us," the old man said. "They were right."

The demon ignored the ambiguous statement. "Please, help me."

"Yes, of course. There's only one way to stop your pain."

It felt like daggers were being pushed through his brain. As he squeezed his head even harder, his nails punctured his scalp. He barely made out the words of the priest.

"May the power of the angels flow through me. Grant me the strength to fortify my soul and summon the light to— "

When Skully failed to continue his blessing, the demon opened his eyes. A silhouette behind the priest guided the old man to his knees. The shadowed figure slowly withdrew a dagger that had been plunged into the priest's side. The newcomer inched toward the demon and stepped into the light. The blood dripped sporadically from the tip of the knife.

The man crouched beside the demon. "My name is Pirok. I'm the watcher captain of this village. I'm also a Brother of Prevarra."

The agony was unbearable. "What? Who?"

"The Brotherhood of Prevarra. We're the devout followers of Verago, the one who sent you. I'm here to help you."

"The pain. It's getting worse."

"I know how to stop it. You must use your energy to kill that priest."

CHAPTER 3

Plagued by mental torture, the demon targeted the injured old man. He leapt forward and reached for the priest's throat. An intense flash of light burst from Skully's hands, and the energy seared the torso and face of the demon. The pain was welcomed. The demon took hold of the priest's neck and squeezed. The old man struggled to breathe as he grabbed the claw with his blood-soaked hands.

"Angels, watch over him," the priest managed to utter.

The demon glimpsed at his chest. Needles of light protruded from his torso like a porcupine. He snarled and tightened his grip on Skully's neck. His talons pierced the elder's skin and crushed his throat. The demon's chest tingled and pulsed with pain from the priest's attack. It felt as if he'd fallen onto a fire, but he made no attempt to touch the affected area. Skully's body went limp, and the light faded away. As the priest slipped from his grasp and collapsed, the demon closed his eyes and reveled in the peace of the night. The agony had retreated just as the other human had promised.

"Oh, Dark-Hearted One. You are truly a powerful being that has been unleashed on our kingdom. I am at your service." The remaining human knelt with downcast eyes.

The demon noticed a difference in this man when compared to Don Skully. The priest had a glow that was bright-yellow and impressive, while this man's aura was gray and underwhelming.

"Mijjen rujj zovtov?"

"Pirok," the watcher said.

"Pirok," the demon repeated in his twisted tongue. "Why am I speaking this way?"

"Kisejjad is a distortion of normal language. Although you understand and think normally, when you speak, your words are translated by your demon tongue."

"And you can understand me?"

"Yes. All Brothers of Prevarra must learn Kisejjad before becoming full members of the sect." Pirok glanced at the beast towering over him. "And how shall I address you?"

The demon growled softly. The question got more frustrating every time. "I don't know. I don't know my name. I don't remember anything before tonight. The pain has distorted my thoughts and memories."

"You're referring to the agony. That pain you feel is connected to your strength. If you don't use it, it builds up and hurts you. Most demons never encounter it, but some of the lesser and greater iymed are known to suffer. They're much more powerful than the fray."

"The fray. The fray." The demon struggled to recover the term from the recesses of his memory. "They are the weakest?"

"That's right. Not too bright either. The lesser iymed are stronger, smarter, and appear more human. And the greater iymed, even more so, but there's only a few of those. You should know the Brotherhood can help you fulfill your purpose."

"What do you know of that?"

Pirok lowered his head. "My apologies. I overheard you

speaking to the priest. We can help you kill King Batar. We're all loyal servants to the Devil, and we're at your disposal."

The demon shuffled his feet through the dirt as he circled Pirok. He wasn't sure how, but he sensed the watcher's fear. "Very well then. Where can I find King Batar?"

"He lives in Light's Haven in the castle."

"Light's Haven. The name is familiar."

"Right. Your memory. Light's Haven is the capital of the kingdom. It's a few days by foot. Horse would be faster, but unfortunately, they were all taken when the town was evacuated. The capital is heavily guarded. Many years ago, Verago sent all the demons in the kingdom to attack it, but they were unsuccessful."

Wrinkles appeared on the demon's forehead. "If Verago's entire army couldn't conquer Light's Haven, then what hope do I have by myself?"

"I think you were sent here to tip the scales. But, you won't be alone. You'll have the Brotherhood by your side. You just need to gather the other demons."

"And how do I do that?" the demon asked.

"Well, uh, um," the watcher stuttered. "You, uh, you have to summon them, but I don't know how to do that. You'll need to speak with an overseer. They're the leaders within the Brotherhood. The closest one lives in Nolka, a few hours walk to the south. She'll be able to answer all your questions and help you contact the other demons."

"Good. Then let's go."

"Uh, yes, of course." Pirok hastened to his feet and brushed the dirt off his pants. "But before we go, we'll have to replace your clothing and cover your eye. We don't want to draw any unnecessary attention to ourselves. I think I may have something you can use."

The demon followed his new ally down the main thoroughfare of the village. Deep in his mind, he felt the sting again. Killing the priest had pushed aside the pain for a while, but he realized it wasn't a final solution. It was only a matter of time before he would be tearing at his flesh once again. In front of one of the houses, Pirok looked furtively up and down the street. He pushed open the door and beckoned the demon to enter.

The large demon crossed the threshold. "Is this your home?"

The watcher lit one of the indoor lamps and hurried into the adjacent room. "Yes. Come."

The demon leaned against the wooden frame of the bedroom, blocking the only exit out.

Pirok pulled clothes out of his wardrobe and threw them on the floor. "I can't describe what an honor it is that you showed up just outside of Nesinu. And, to be your first contact. This is truly an honor."

The demon was only half listening, more interested in his hands.

"So, you must've met Verago then. I couldn't even imagine what it's like to meet him. What a mighty presence he must have, awe-inspiring and breathtaking. Is that what it's like?"

"I don't know." His voice was flat. He didn't care.

Pirok popped out from the wardrobe. "You don't? Surely, a powerful demon like yourself would've met the Devil in his throne room."

The words of his companion bored him, but they also brought vague images swirling into his head. He had met Verago, but the details of the encounter were hazy. The room was dark with hints of light given off by tame fires. A figure he believed to be the Devil sat before him on a throne, and on either side of him rested two massive, indistinguishable shapes, one red and one black.

When the demon didn't speak, Pirok filled the silence. "Yeah, any Brother would give anything to meet Verago. We've pledged more than our lives to him after all. And we can't wait until his glorious return. It's so unjust what happened to him, and we're all fighting and doing our best to secure the Talisman of Zavi. But the Prima is very powerful. You'll probably have to defeat her before you can get to the king. She lives in Light's Haven as well. But I'm sure you'll have no problem dealing with her."

He stared blankly at Pirok. Not much of what the watcher said made sense to him.

The man returned with an armful of clothing. "The overseer can explain everything better than I can. Here. Best to change it all. This long shirt is actually a sleeping gown my parents gave me years ago. Never used it. With your height, it should fit you well. And the pants, well, they'll probably be a little short."

The demon removed what remained of his shirt and vest. The tattered fabric crumpled to the floor. The demon slid his arms through the sleeves of the white sleeping gown. The ends barely passed his elbows, and the bottom of the gown hovered above his knees. Dissatisfied with the length, the demon tore away enough material so that the tattered ends hung by his waist. Next, the demon lifted up the pants and surveyed the length before tossing them onto the bed. "Mine will do fine."

"Oh, um, sure. I also got you this, for your eye."

The demon examined the long piece of fabric. "For the scars?"

The watcher hesitated. "Uh, no, for your eye."

"What's wrong with it?"

Pirok waved the demon over to the wardrobe. The watcher pushed back the closet door to reveal a mirror. The demon was stunned. His right eye was far from human. The iris shimmered with shades of orange and red, and the pupil was long and thin, like that of a cat. As he fixated on his reflection, the iris receded, and the brilliant colors were replaced with the black void of the pupil.

"What…what is this?" His claws, his speech, his pain. Everything pointed to the fact that he was a demon, but he refused to believe it. He went to touch the demonic eye, and when he felt the scarring, he bellowed at the watcher.

"What is this?!"

Pirok stumbled backward and dropped the white cloth. The demon snatched the mirror and flung it against the wall. The watcher covered his head as the glass shattered into thousands of pieces. Then, he scrambled to his feet and darted out of the room.

The demon steadied his breathing. The floor was covered in shards that glimmered faintly in the lamplight. As he crossed the room, he winced with each step. At the threshold to the bedroom, he stooped to pick up the white cloth. He gripped it tightly in his quivering claw. "This is a mistake."

"What is?" The watcher peeked from behind the doorframe.

"All of it. And the pain. It's still there."

"It'll only get worse. Come on, we should hurry. The overseer can help you better than I can."

The demon shook the cloth free of glass shards before wrapping it around his head to cover his eye. As he stepped back outside, he noticed that the gray aura around the watcher had vanished.

"It's this way," Pirok said. "This road heads south. It's a bit of a walk, so if you have any questions, I'll do my best to answer them."

The demon had a multitude of questions, but the agony was scratching at his brain. They had only gotten as far as the edge of the town when he started to drag his feet along the ground. "How far did you say this was?"

"A few hours at a decent pace."

"Impossible." The demon halted. There was no way he would survive a few minutes, let alone a few hours. He gnashed his teeth as the pain grew steadily.

"It's…it's…it's going to be all right. You just have to keep moving."

The demon's knees struck the ground, and he began to pant. He heard the doubt in Pirok's voice.

"No, no, no, get up. Come on, you have to keep

moving."

The demon curled his lips as his body tensed. The pain swelled in his head. He shoved his claws into the dirt, trying to keep them under control. He barely made out the pleas of the watcher.

"You need to use your energy! Do something, anything! Are you listening? Cast a spell! Use your energy!"

The demon had no idea how to fulfill Pirok's request, but soon, the shouts stopped. The agony grew at an alarming rate and before long, his body was convulsing. He made every effort to keep his claws buried, but it felt like pokers used to stoke a fire were being driven into his skull. He roared as the pain came to a head, and then he lost consciousness.

CHAPTER 4

Millan woke up with a start. The details of his dream were mostly faded, but the trembling in his heart was not so quick to leave. For a moment, his surroundings were unfamiliar, but then he recalled his location. As Don Skully had ordered, Millan had led the villagers of Nesinu to Nolka. With the help of the town's watchers, he and Tyro kept guard as the party of a few hundred traveled through the darkness. To his relief, there was not a single disturbance during the entire trip. Millan prayed Skully's night was just as peaceful. Many of the citizens in Nolka were kind enough to take in the refugee families. Millan had been given a small bed in the Candelux rectory while Tyro was placed in the squire quarters.

On his way to the archdon's office, Millan passed many Nolka squires until he found Tyro. "Any word from Don Skully?"

The squire frowned. "Sorry, Don Millan."

The priest pressed on to the office of Archdon Feranis, the head priest in Nolka. As he traversed the halls, he couldn't help but notice how much larger the Nolka rectory was than the one in Nesinu. However, it was no match for the Sanctuary, the massive rectory in Light's

Haven that even rivaled the royal castle. The wood floor beneath his feet gave out a hollow sound, and a creaking board greeted him every few steps. When the Nesinu priest finally reached the office of the head archdon, he gave a quick knock.

"Yes?" An elderly man opened the door. "Ah, Don Millan, won't you come in?"

"Thank you, Your Grace."

Feranis was dressed in his rank's standard black robe and white scarf. In terms of age, he was about a decade younger than Skully, but even so, the years were much kinder to the Nolka archdon. For one, Feranis still had all his hair. He offered Millan a seat before taking his place behind the desk. "How are you this morning? Did you sleep well?"

"Yes, I did, thank you. It was very kind of you to take us all in."

"Please, please, it was the least I could do. Tell me. Do you have any idea why Don Skully ordered the evacuation?"

Millan cast his eyes to the side. "No, I'm afraid not. He just said it would be safer for us all to leave. It was supposed to be a precaution. During the trip, though, one of the watchers told me a boy in the village spoke with him right before he called for the evacuation."

"Yes, I was told the same. Do you happen to know what was said?"

"No, Your Grace."

Feranis placed his elbows on the desk and interlaced his fingers. "Well, don't worry about it. I'll speak to the boy myself."

"I take it Don Skully didn't arrive in Nolka last night?"

"Not that I'm aware of. That is to say, I haven't received any such notification from the watchers. I'll have to speak with them to be sure. They'll know who's come in and out of the city."

Millan perked up. "If you don't mind, I can go speak

with them right now."

"Very well. You'll find their post near the city fountain. Do you know where that is?"

"Yes, I believe so. I've been here once before. I think I remember the way."

The archdon reclined in his chair. "Speak with Captain Lufira. You can tell her I sent you. Please let me know what you find out."

"Of course. Thank you." Millan hopped up and bowed before exiting the archdon's office. The Nesinu priest retraced his steps and headed toward the entrance of the rectory.

As he joined the citizens on the bustling street, he observed the sun's position in the sky. The day had started a few hours ago. Skully would have to be in Nolka by now unless something went wrong. Millan walked briskly as peddlers and pedestrians offered courteous bows to the priest. His title was clear by his robe and scarf. Normally, he would take his time and admire all the different people and shops, but he was on a mission.

Millan did his best to remember the way to the city fountain, but it had been three years since he had been to Nolka. Soon, he was confronted by an unexpected split in the street. The young priest reviewed each path silently, too shy to ask for directions, before pressing forward blindly. Minutes later, he ended up down an abandoned alley where he finally admitted to being lost. Millan noticed a man in beggar's clothing seated on the ground. The young priest cautiously approached the lonely man from behind. He was about to crouch beside him when he heard the poor man whimpering. Millan reevaluated his decision and quietly took a step back, hoping the destitute man wouldn't detect him. But, guilt suddenly overcame him. As a Candelux priest, he had basic healing knowledge, and if the man was injured, Millan could help him.

The young priest took a deep breath and closed the gap once again. "Excuse me. Are you hurt? Do you need some help?"

The poor man whipped his head around. The beggar's face was deeply creased, and his droopy eyes accented his frown.

"My name is Don Millan. Do you need help?"

"Priests won't listen. They're blind."

Millan was stunned by the response. He opened his mouth, but no words came out.

The beggar covered his face with his hands. "I lost him. No one believes me. No one will help me."

"Who did you lose? What's his name?"

The poor man separated his fingers and dragged his dirty hands down until they rested under his chin. "My friend. My friend. He was in a big empty field. Hurt, I think. I went for help and…and…" The man's dark-brown eyes drifted to the side, and he froze like a statue.

"And? What happened?"

A tear rolled down his face. "I…I can't remember. I don't know where he is."

"Where who is?"

The beggar sniffled and wiped his cheek. His face tensed, and his lips moved as they tried to sound out the name.

"Erynion!" he finally shouted.

Millan twitched, startled by the sudden outburst.

The beggar grinned and revealed what remained of his teeth, but the smile disappeared. "Erynion. And I'm sure he needs my help."

"And your name?"

"I had a name once. My parents gave it to me, but it's long been forgotten. People call me Dulo."

Millan placed his hands on his hips. "Well, Dulo, I will help you find your friend. What do you think of that?"

The beggar's eyes widened. "Honest?"

"That's right. I'm headed to the watcher office to ask about a friend of mine, and I'll ask about yours as well. Would you be so kind as to point me toward the center of town?"

The destitute man sprang to his feet. "Oh, thank you, thank you! I've never met a priest as kind as you. You must be new. No one ever pays me any attention. But, of course, I'll direct you. The fountain is my favorite place. I'm not allowed in it, but sometimes when the watchers aren't looking..." He scouted the area and stifled a giggle. "I jump in anyway."

Upon receiving directions from the beggar, the Nesinu priest thanked him. As he resumed his journey, Millan thought about the poor man and found it odd that this civilian in need had not been helped. If his friend was truly in danger, then someone should be able to help locate him. Millan walked into the town square and marveled at the beauty of the fountain. It was still being built when he had visited a few years ago. He and Don Skully had passed through on the way to Light's Haven. The angel statue was made of gleaming white rock and spit gracefully into the pool below it.

"Don!" someone hollered from near the fountain. A middle-aged man wearing a brown scarf was waving at him. Millan looked around, not sure if there was another priest nearby.

"Don Millan," the squire said again as he jogged toward the Nesinu priest. "I'm Gheron. Archdon Feranis thought you might need some help, so he sent me to assist you."

"Oh, how nice. It's a pleasure to meet you, Gheron."

"And you as well. Were you able to speak with Captain Lufira?"

Millan scratched the back of his head. "Uh, no, I'm afraid I got a little lost and ended up on some backstreet."

"I'm sorry to hear that. If you'd like to follow me, it's right this way."

"Thank you."

As the pair crossed the square, Millan decided to delve into the issue of the beggar. "Gheron, may I ask you something? Have you heard of a man by the name of

Dulo?"

"I have. He's a beggar. Everyone knows about him. Why do you ask?"

"I ran into him on my…detour. How about a man by the name of Erynion?"

"I don't believe so. Another beggar?"

"I don't know. Dulo claimed his friend, Erynion, was in trouble but couldn't seem to remember where he was. He also said no one would believe him."

The squire snickered. "Well, I'm sorry to tell you this, but Dulo is special. A bit of a *Dardan fool,* and I don't mean that in a cruel way. I'm just speaking the truth. A few horses short of a full stable, if you catch my meaning. He's been in Nolka for some time now. Fifteen years maybe? I remember I was just a teenager when he showed up. He's always been known for fabricating people, events, places. Folks around here have learned to just ignore his claims. But, the watchers keep an eye on him and the other disturbances around the city. Maybe they'll be able to tell you more."

****

A little girl screamed, *"Help me, please!"*

He jolted awake. The brilliant rays of sunlight beat down on the clearing where he lay alone and forced him to shield his eye with his hand. Images from the night before flashed through his mind mixed with the strange dreams of his slumber. As he tried to piece the fragments together, his thought process was broken by the sight of his hand, covered in blood. It wasn't the blood that shocked him, but rather the fact that it wasn't a claw anymore. He sat up, held his two hands beside each other, and wiggled his fingers. They were identical. They were human.

He carefully touched his face. There was a cloth wrapped around his head. His fingers traced the scars that ran down his right cheek. He undid the buttons of his shirt and cautiously exposed his chest to the daylight. The wounds had healed, but the scarring was unsightly. He suddenly remembered the little light needles sticking out of his chest, but the memory only lasted a moment.

Differentiating between what had happened the previous night and what he had dreamt was no simple task as both events were hazy at best. The village, the old man, and the little girl blended together. He remembered his hand around the old man's throat. Perhaps that was why the girl was screaming. Or maybe she met a similar fate. The thought sickened him as he looked at his stained fingers. Out of all of it, though, he clearly recalled the suffering he had endured. But, now there wasn't even the faintest tingle. Sensing he had a companion from the previous night, he searched the immediate area, but there was no one. He sat in the middle of a large expanse. The earth was blackened and lifeless, except for a small circle of dirt with patches of grass beneath him.

None of it made sense. He got up and looked around, hoping to find something he recognized, but it was all empty. The village was gone. He felt alone. His friend had apparently abandoned him. He closed his eyes and concentrated, but he wasn't able to conjure up a name or even a face. However, there was a voice.

You should know the Brotherhood can help you fulfill your purpose.

The words revealed a blurred outline of his companion in his mind. And though the speaker was clearly different, his words mimicked the unexplained whispers to kill the king and seek out the Brotherhood.

What a mighty presence he must have...the Devil.

The one-sided conversation was coming back in pieces. Opening his left eye, he observed his surroundings again.

I also got you this, for your eye. It's this way...south.

South. He squatted and touched the black ground. The soot clung to his fingertips, and he rubbed them together to remove the dirt. He used the sun to determine his bearing and headed south. As he trudged across the black desert, the warmth radiated from the earth. At the edge of the charred soil, he found it particularly odd how the trees beyond the black field were so lush and green. They were untouched and stood in stark contrast to the empty wasteland he was about to leave behind. He discovered a road that divided the forest. It appeared to head in the direction he needed to go, and so he followed it.

CHAPTER 5

Gheron and Millan exited the watcher headquarters. In the short time they had spent inside, the city had grown busier.

"So, Don Millan, would you like me to accompany you to see Watcher Hyron?"

"No, thank you, Gheron. I can take it from here."

"As you wish, Don. I hope you find your friend."

"Thank you. So do I."

The two parted ways, Gheron toward the rectory and Millan in the opposite direction. The Nesinu priest had been given detailed directions to the home of the lead watcher of the night shift. Typically, this was information not available to the public, but a member of Candelux could hardly be regarded as an average citizen. Since the appearance of demons centuries ago, the priests rapidly grew to be the most influential guild in the kingdom. And because of that, the leader of Candelux has always been the top advisor to the royals. Some citizens believed the priest guild was more powerful than the monarchy and used its position for its own benefit, but most dismissed these notions as conspiracy theories. Millan joined Candelux to make the kingdom safer and to help others, and so he fell within the thinking of the majority.

Millan quickened his pace as fast as his flowing brown robes would allow. The people who passed closest offered him a courteous nod. Outside the home, he surveyed the exterior briefly to ensure it matched the description he had been given. As he rapped his knuckles on the door, Millan heard frantic movement inside. The locks slid out of place, and the entrance opened just a crack.

A young woman peered out. "Yes?"

"I'm sorry to bother you, but I was wondering if Watcher Hyron lives here."

The woman scrutinized his clothing. "Well, you look like a priest, but I don't recognize you."

"Of course, how impolite of me. My name is Don Millan. I'm from Nesinu. We evacuated the town last night, and a friend of mine, a fellow priest, Don Skully, stayed behind, planning to rejoin us later. I was wondering if Watcher Hyron knew if he came through late last night."

"Of course. I apologize, Don Millan. Come in." The woman opened the door. "Perhaps you don't have such problems in your small town, but in the city, some will use the brown robe for deception. And with Hyron asleep, I must be cautious who I allow in. My name is Fiela."

"I understand. So Hyron lives here?"

"Yes, he's my husband." Fiela led him into the living area. "But as I mentioned, he's asleep. You see, he doesn't get home until very early in the morning, just as the sun comes up. Can I offer you anything to eat? To drink?"

"No, thank you. That's very kind. It's quite urgent that I speak with your husband, though, if it's not too much of an inconvenience."

Fiela bit her lip. "Of course, I'll be right back."

As she left the living area, Millan took a seat. He felt a little guilty for using his influence as a priest to get the result he was seeking. She was only gone for a few moments before she returned.

"He'll be out shortly." Her smile appeared forced as she

took her place across from the priest.

In the ensuing silence, Millan placed his hands on his thighs. Moving each finger like the leg of a spider, his hands crept to his knees.

"May I ask you something, Don?"

"Why not?"

"Why was Nesinu evacuated?"

"That was the order of our head don, Don Skully. It was just a precaution."

"A precaution for what, though?" Fiela asked

"Well, we don't really know yet. We're still trying to figure that out. That's one of the reasons why I came here to speak with your husband."

"Oh?"

"You see, Don Skully stayed behind while the rest of the village evacuated. I just need to know if he made it to Nolka or not."

"What's all this then?" came a raspy voice. The man was similar in height to Millan, but his build was more muscular. His jet-black hair was tousled from his brief sleep.

Millan rose to his feet and cordially extended his hand. "You must be Watcher Hyron. My name is—"

"Yeah, I know who the *fangle* you are." The man ignored the gesture and sat next to his wife. He rubbed his eyes with the heels of his palms before running a hand through his hair.

Millan quietly cleared his throat and retook his seat. "I appreciate you taking the time to speak with me."

"When a priest from the glorious Candelux graces your home with his presence, you don't really have a choice, do you?"

"Hyron!" Fiela scolded in a sharp whisper.

The watcher rolled his eyes.

"I'm very sorry for waking you," said Millan.

"Mm-hmm. Let's get on with it then. What can I do for you?"

"I'm looking for a friend of mine, another priest. He was supposed to follow us to Nolka. I was wondering if you saw him enter the city last night. He's an elderly man, bald, gray beard, brown robe, black—"

"Yeah, yeah, I know what you fangling look like. And no, no priest came through the gates all night after you all arrived."

Millan's heart sank. Something must have gone wrong. He'd have to return to the rectory and report his findings to Feranis.

"Was that it?" Hyron asked. "May I go back to sleep now?"

Millan sadly nodded. As the watcher got up to leave, the young priest remembered Dulo. "Wait! There is one more thing."

Hyron motioned for Millan to continue. "Do you know a man called Dulo?"

"Yeah, sure, the beggar. He's a lunatic."

"Did you see him at all last night?"

The watcher folded his arms across his chest. "Sure, so what? He comes and goes all the time. Sometimes he's gone for days. And he always comes back ranting about some friend that he's lost."

"Erynion?"

"Yeah, I think that was the name this morning. But I have to warn you, Don. The name's different every time. He goes out and meets travelers, hunters, salespeople. And then when his 'friends' part ways from him, he has a fangling fit and comes back saying he's lost them. People around here just stopped listening to him."

"And he always goes out alone?"

"Always goes out alone. Always comes back alone. You know, we have a running joke that he meets up with demons, but he's such a Dardan fool that they don't bother killing him." Hyron chuckled. "Some people think he's possessed."

"I see." Millan pitied the poor man.

34

The Twisted Gate

"Look, Don, don't worry about him. He's harmless. If he gets too bothersome, sometimes we'll lock him up for a bit until he's calmed down."

"I see," the young priest repeated. "Well, thank you for your time. I'm sorry that I woke you for nothing."

Hyron's voice softened. "Don't worry about it. Look, I hope you find your priest friend."

"Thank you. Sleep well."

The watcher departed, leaving his wife with the priest. Fiela escorted Millan to the front door and stood in the threshold as he entered the street. "Don, I'm sorry about my husband. He's not normally so impolite, especially to a priest. He's just very grumpy when he's woken."

Millan smiled kindly. "Think nothing of it. May the angels watch over you."

****

The whispers swirled in his head. *Humans in general cannot be trusted.*

As the sun crossed the sky and hovered over the treetops, the end of his path came into view. The city ahead was surrounded by walls, the entrance guarded. For the hundredth time on his trek, he checked his hands only to find that they were still human. He made sure his shirt was buttoned and then adjusted the cloth covering his eye. As he neared the gate, two watchers converged on him.

"Welcome to Nolka. Who are you and what is your business here?" one watcher questioned.

Nolka. That was the name of the city he was seeking. His spirits lifted, pleased that he'd wound up at the intended destination.

"Please state your business," the other watcher insisted.

He opened his mouth to speak but was interrupted by a voice.

"Erynion!" A man in beggar's clothing rushed past the guards. "Wow, you've gotten bigger. Or maybe I got smaller. I'm so glad that you're all right. No one believed me." The beggar shot the watchers a nasty look. He took the demon by the hand and led him past the guards and into the city. As they moved farther from the gate, the demon caught bits of the watchers' conversation.

"Should we tell Don Millan?"

"I don't think that was Don Skully. He certainly wasn't dressed like a priest."

"Wasn't there a watcher missing too?"

"Captain Pirok. I actually knew him before he moved to Nesinu. That wasn't him, though. Did you see that scar on his face? Must've come from fighting something nasty. Looks pretty fresh too."

"Yeah, I bet he's missing that eye. Maybe we should tell him where he can find the Pink Leaves."

"Eh, he seems fine. And a missing eye couldn't be half as bad as spending time with Dulo."

The laughter faded as the demon turned a corner. The beggar guided him down back alleys and away from the busy streets. Their path narrowed before coming to an end at the city wall. A tattered canopy hung haphazardly overhead, and a nice rug with a large gash was sprawled on the ground. The wall blocked the sun, but remnants of light still illuminated the sky.

"Well, here we are. Home sweet home," Dulo said.

"Ujjra—" the demon cut himself off.

"You know, I just had this feeling."

"Imdana sterdana ujjnek?"

"Right, and there you were. You remember me, right, Erynion?"

"Raujju hajji djja on vejja."

"Haha, of course. You wouldn't forget your best friend, would you? I'm glad you're back, Erynion."

The demon watched as Dulo scurried about to put his things in order. The beast was unsure about plenty, especially his past. Perhaps the beggar had some idea of who he was. And so, he decided, for now, he would keep the name Dulo had given him. The demon casually inspected the quiet corner and considered how he would contact the Brotherhood. His new beggar friend was harmless, but he was going to be useless too. Because if there was one thing Erynion knew for sure, it was that Dulo had no idea what the demon was saying.

CHAPTER 6

Millan walked into the large dining hall of the rectory. Tables with occupied benches were arranged randomly throughout the dining room, except for the largest, which ran parallel with the front wall. This table of importance was slightly elevated and occupied by Archdon Feranis, along with four priests. A loud hum filled the room as conversations meshed together. Tyro gestured to Millan to join him, Gheron, and a few other squires from Nolka. As the young priest took his seat, the others became awkwardly quiet. There was still no word from Don Skully.

Millan stared at his food as the others dug into their meals. The clanging of forks against plates joined the hum of the room. He had spent much of his day at the north gate, hoping each time he looked out, he would spot a lone figure in the distance. The road only led to Nesinu, and no one appeared. An hour or so before the sun intended to set, his stomach scolded him for paying his hunger no heed for the entire day. The watchers assured him if the elder priest arrived, they would send word to the rectory immediately. Reluctantly, Millan had returned to his new home.

As the Nesinu priest took a couple of bites from his

dinner, a watcher approached the head table. The man bowed before Archdon Feranis, who motioned for the watcher to step forward. Millan kept a close eye on the interaction. Before he spent the day at the north gate, he had reported his conversation with Watcher Hyron to the archdon. Concerned with the fate of Nesinu and Don Skully, Feranis had requested a scout head north before noon, giving the rider plenty of time to return before nightfall. Millan wondered if this interruption was news from the scout.

Feranis stroked one side of his chin before turning to the priest next to him. The female don leaned in as the archdon whispered into her ear.

Millan nudged Gheron with his elbow. "What's going on?"

The squire glanced up at the head table as the female priest wiped her mouth with her napkin and excused herself. Gheron swallowed his food. "I'm not sure, but it's rare that an incident would require immediate attention during dinner, especially from Don Yatiga."

"What's so special about Don Yatiga?"

"She's the highest-ranked don in Nolka. She's already started training in her specialty for Ascension. In a few more months, she'll be an archdon."

Millan lifted his eyebrows. "Really? What did she choose?" Once approved to begin the process of Ascension, there were a few different paths a don could decide on, and with any luck, Millan would be allowed to start in a few years.

"Restraint. She's been training with Archdon Volko in Light's Haven." Gheron took another bite of his dinner. "Aside from history, she's also been teaching the senior squires the Blessing of the Holy Prism."

Millan knew the Nolka squire was bragging. The Blessing of Divine Restraint was the introductory spell for squires, and the Holy Prism blessing was normally taught after Acceptance, a squire's induction into Candelux.

"Gheron!" Yatiga said as she strode by the table. "You're coming with me. You, too, Benedoli."

Gheron hopped up, as did Benedoli, a female squire from a different table. "Yes, Don," they said simultaneously.

Millan sprang to his feet, and his end of the bench squealed as it skidded across the floor. "Please, Your Grace, can I be of assistance in any way?"

"Don Millan, please sit down," Feranis said sternly. "You are a guest in our city. Enjoy your dinner."

The young priest sensed some annoyance in the archdon's voice, and so he quietly sat back on the bench. Millan watched Yatiga leave with Gheron and Benedoli before returning to his dinner. As the squires began clearing the plates, Millan suggested to Tyro that they excuse themselves to check on the families who had taken refuge in the city. As the pair prepared to depart, Feranis called from the head table. "Don Millan, may I speak with you in private, please?"

Millan blushed as he promised Tyro he'd catch up with him later and then hurried to the hall exit. As Millan matched the footsteps of his superior, the hollow sound of the boards reverberated in the small hallway with a soft creak here and there. Feranis opened the door to his office and allowed Millan to enter.

The archdon sank into his chair behind his desk. "Please, sit down."

Millan obliged. "I apologize for the interruption at—"

Feranis raised his hand. "This is not why I called you here."

"It's just that I thought with the scout—"

"Don Millan, please," Feranis pleaded. "Believe me. I understand your concern for Don Skully. This is why I've asked you here. There's been no word from the scout that was sent this morning. He should've returned some time ago. And there's something else. I spoke with that boy. I think I understand why Don Skully ordered the evacuation."

Millan's leg bounced with anticipation. "You do?"

"He said vines had burst from the ground and wrapped around one another to create a massive tree. Does that sound familiar to you?"

A chill swam up his spine. "A twisted gate?"

"I think so. Even though he's just a boy, I can't imagine he would describe a pod in that manner. The fact that both Don Skully and the scout from earlier are missing also lends credence to something more sinister than a few fray."

"By the angels, he knew," said Millan.

"Most likely. To what degree, we won't know until we find him. But it seems like he made the right decision by calling for the evacuation."

Millan wanted nothing more than to go search for his mentor, but the prospect of a powerful demon lurking in the area put him on guard. "So, what do we do now?"

"Now? We stay here in the city behind the walls. Night is when the demons gather their strength. In the meantime, though, I've sent a letter to Light's Haven to inform them of my suspicion and that we'll be investigating the matter."

"We?"

"You, me, and the other priests in Nolka. Naturally, we'll wait for morning so that the demons will be at a disadvantage. After the squire classes, we'll all meet in front of the rectory and head to Nesinu together."

Millan dreaded another walk. "By foot?"

"No, by horse. Don't worry. I've already spoken with Kona Magara. She runs the stables here in Nolka. She's allowing us to borrow some horses for those priests who don't own one, including yourself. You should get some rest."

Millan covered his face. "A twisted gate. He didn't have to stay behind. Or I should've stayed to help him."

"You shouldn't think like that. Don Skully did what he

thought was best for the village and for you. Trust me. I knew him long before you did. He's always been stubborn. When he thinks he's right about something, he never wavers at all. You really think you could've convinced him to let you stay?"

A smile crept across Millan's lips. "He is a bit stubborn, isn't he?"

Feranis chuckled. "Yes, he is. He and I were close friends when we lived in Light's Haven."

"That's right. You were an advisor to Primus Ayristark while Don Skully lived there."

"Well, yes, but—" The watchtower bells clanged irregularly. Although Nesinu was a small town, it also maintained a watchtower with a single bell. The young priest had only heard it ring in this manner one time.

Feranis fetched an ornate staff from the corner of his office. The long piece of wood featured a golden four-pointed star at the top. Millan recognized the shape on the end as a replica of the Talisman of Zavi. Clear like crystal, the real artifact was passed down through the generations and worn by the reigning Prima or Primus.

"Come," instructed the archdon. "It appears I may need your help tonight after all."

Millan and Feranis hastened down the halls and out of the rectory, where they were joined by other priests, as well as the senior squires approved for combat. As they stood in the courtyard, a watcher rounded a corner and sprinted toward them.

"What news?" Feranis asked.

The watcher gasped for air. "Your Grace, it's the north gate."

"Let's go!"

The group dashed toward the city gates. Millan stayed close to Feranis as the watcher explained the situation. "They came out from the woods. They were at the gate before we knew it. We weren't able to shut it. We couldn't even get a signal off to the tower."

"What? Where was your seeker?" the archdon asked. "I specifically asked your captain for one to be posted."

Dons like Millan were trained with a basic ability to detect different types of energy. The seekers were watchers who shared this skill with the priests. While fray demons were always easy to spot from their physical appearance, the iymed sometimes looked human enough that it wasn't so obvious. Only by detecting their dark energy could a priest or seeker know the difference.

"We had one, but I don't know where he is." The watcher did his best to keep pace with the old man. "There was some situation in the city. He was called away to help investigate."

"Depths!" Feranis cursed, a mild swear compared to some of the language of the commoners. "So, are the gates still open?"

"I believe so. We rushed to shut them, but we were sabotaged. Someone uncoupled the gear mechanism. When we tried to close it by hand, we were attacked from inside the walls. Two of our company were shot with arrows; one died and our lead was injured." The watcher struggled to catch his breath. "Your Grace, I think it was the Brotherhood."

Feranis clenched his jaw. "So, after all these years, they're finally coming out of the shadows."

"I was ordered by the lead to run to the watchtower to alert our captain, then go to the rectory to bring help. I don't know how my comrades have fared in my absence, but the sooner we get there the better."

"I agree," the archdon said.

The Candelux group finally arrived at the north gate where the battle was underway. While a handful of watchers were engaged with some of the larger demons, other fray scampered past them into the city. The priests spread out and began to restrain the beasts.

"Where did you put your wounded?" Feranis asked the watcher.

"He's alone in the guardhouse over by the gate."

The elder priest noticed Millan beside him. "Don Millan, I assume Don Skully taught you how to heal?"

"Yes, Your Grace, the basic blessings."

"Good. Treat the wound and make sure his life's not in any danger. He doesn't have to rejoin the fight, but you do. Get back out here when you're finished."

"Understood." Millan ran to the guardhouse. As he weaved between the fighters, his pulse thumped in his ears. He'd never had an opportunity like this to use all the blessings Don Skully had taught him. He was eager to put his slaying and cleansing skills to the test, but he knew his healing was equally important.

The Nesinu priest reached the guardhouse uninterrupted. He flung open the door and spotted the watcher lying on the floor in the shadows. Millan knelt beside him.

The watcher groaned in pain. "Oh, it's you."

"Watcher Hyron, how are you feeling?" Millan removed the blanket covering his shirtless patient.

"Like I was shot in the shoulder with a fangling arrow."

Despite Hyron being fully awake, Millan couldn't help but notice that his demeanor was not all that different from earlier in the day. The priest studied the injured shoulder and determined that he had been hit from behind. The tail end of the arrow was undoubtedly broken off so Hyron could lie down. Millan examined the metal tip of the arrow that protruded through the front of the watcher's shoulder. The young priest briefly hovered his hands over the injury. "You've lost a lot of blood."

Hyron scoffed. "Brilliant assessment."

Though he had learned triage and blessings of healing, Millan had never healed a wound like this before. Standard practice was for a second priest to soothe the patient and numb the pain during the procedure, but there was no time for that. The arrow had to come out before he could do any healing.

As Millan pinched the tip of the arrow, Hyron gripped the priest's wrist. "What are you doing?"

"I...I need to pull it out before I can heal the wound."

"Are you kidding me? No sleep? You're just going to pull it out?"

"I'm sorry. Sleep requires total focus. I can't do both. I'm sorry, but it's the only way. It needs to come out."

The watcher tightened his grip on Millan's arm. "If you touch that arrow while I'm conscious, I'm going to rip your fangling head off."

The young priest was paralyzed. Although not a large man, Hyron seemed like the type who could make good on his promise with his one good arm.

"Depths! Fine." Hyron scanned the room. "There. Pull on the bottom of that table leg. Rickety thing should snap right off."

Although the watcher released his wrist, Millan stayed put.

"Come on. Just do it. Hurry!"

The young priest shimmied to the table and yanked the foot of the leg. It snapped with considerable ease. Wiggling it back and forth a few times, he freed it from the final splinters that clung to the table.

"Good. Good." Hyron pointed to the right corner of his forehead. "Now, hit me right here as hard you can."

Millan was still, except for the tremble in his hand. This didn't seem like sound healing advice.

"Come on! You have to knock me out somehow. Now hit me!" the watcher ordered.

Taking in a sharp breath, the priest raised the table leg and swung down with all his might. The impact landed in the middle of Hyron's forehead and fractured the wood. The watcher collapsed, and his head struck the floor. Believing his patient to be unconscious for the moment, Millan quickly knelt and secured the arrow tip between his thumb and index finger.

Eyes half closed, Hyron barely lifted his head. "Ugh,

what the—"

The flesh tore and the blood flowed freely as Millan dislodged the arrowhead. The watcher sat straight up, clutched his shoulder, and howled. Millan retreated out of fear for his safety. What followed was a slew of curses as Hyron flopped around on the floor. Millan tossed the arrow aside and prepared to subdue his patient. The young priest tried to calm Hyron as he positioned the watcher flat on his back. Pulling back the watcher's bloody hand, Millan placed both of his hands over the wound. Quietly, he mumbled the Blessing of Rapid Recovery. The energy flowed from his body into the watcher's. Hyron's breathing steadied, and the bleeding came to a crawl.

The door opened behind him, and Millan glimpsed over his shoulder to find a man in a pink robe embroidered with green vines. The young priest had heard of the Pink Leaves sect, but he had never met a member before. Rumor had it their healing abilities rivaled even the best archdon healers.

"Thank the angels. I heard the scream and assumed the worst." The man hovered over Millan. "But it looks like you've already closed the wound. Well done. I'll tend to him from this point on, Don. Thank you."

Millan politely nodded and left his patient with the pinkleaf.

****

Be wary of the Candelux priests. They are your greatest enemy, the voice faded in and out.

The sun set as Erynion, the demon, observed Dulo closely. It appeared as though the beggar was conversing with the demon, while in reality, he was only talking to himself. Sometimes Dulo would stop and wait for a response, to which Erynion would respond with any phrase to appease the poor man. While Dulo chatted nonsensically to himself, the demon contemplated how he could complete his purpose. How could he seek the Brotherhood when he couldn't speak the language? The thought perplexed him.

As the last rays of sunlight dwindled in the distance, Dulo lit a broken lantern hanging on the wall. Erynion barely noticed how the flame did a poor job illuminating the area as a high-pitched ringing caused him to wince. He closed his left eye, but the sound persisted. Panic set in as he recalled a similar feeling from the previous night. If the pain was going to come again, he needed help to stop it. The demon had listened to the beggar's ramblings for long enough, and his company wasn't helping.

As Erynion got up to leave, Dulo slid in front of him. "Hey, where you going?"

"Duredar bed njja fut."

"Oh, um, want to go together?"

"Zjja venu zited aknitjja." Erynion held up his hand since he knew the beggar didn't really understand him. His fingers tensed as his nails grew into talons.

Dulo's eyes widened. "Whoa, how did you do that?"

Erynion flipped his hand over. "Onto djja. Njjas dugatons titaba."

"Hmm. I might be able to help. Where did you say you were going?"

"Duredar bed njja fut. Rejjis revoa dinjja."

"Oh, I know where that is. Why didn't you say so earlier? But we really shouldn't leave here. Bad things can come out in the dark, especially outside the city. I should know. And you're still hurt from last night."

As Dulo rambled on, the ringing in the demon's ears grew worse. Erynion found it hard to concentrate on the beggar's words, not that they really mattered. The pain grew steadily, and he fell onto one knee. The agony was still bearable, but he knew what was coming. He placed his right hand on the ground for support. The sight of the claw distressed him. No, it wasn't true. He was human.

Dulo crouched beside the demon. "Hey, what's wrong?

See, I knew you were still hurt. Let me help. Tell me what to do."

Erynion could only grit his teeth as the memories of the last night seeped into his mind.

The pain you feel is connected to your strength. If you don't use it, it builds up and hurts you.

He eyed Dulo like a predator stalking its prey. The beggar shuddered, then ran screaming down the alley for help. The agony was becoming more painful, yet still manageable. Erynion knelt alone for some time. For how long, he had no clue. Had he really been abandoned to suffer through all this again? Distant footsteps of a small group drew closer. He stood up to leave, but they were already upon him.

"I brought help!" Dulo exclaimed.

Next to the beggar stood four people. One wore a brown robe and black scarf while two others wore regular clothing with brown scarves. The fourth wore no scarf and spoke first.

"Wait a second. I remember him."

"What do you mean you remember him?" asked the woman in the brown robe.

"He came in through the north gate."

"You're telling me you knowingly let a demon into the city?"

"Of course not. He was completely human earlier. Or, at least he appeared to be."

"But you sense the darkness now, don't you?"

"Yes, there's definitely something there, and it's growing. Something isn't right."

As if needles were gently poking at his mind, the demon spoke Kisejjad through his teeth. "Are you with the Brotherhood?"

The woman wearing the brown robe stepped forward. "No, we are not."

An image of Don Skully flickered in his memories. "You're like the other one. You're a priest."

"That's right. I'm with Candelux. What's your name?"

The demon cradled his head in his hand. "Erynion. Who are you?"

"Don Yatiga. What is your purpose here?"

"Leave me be." He didn't want to talk to her. Candelux priests were, after all, his enemy. Erynion closed his eyes as the pain worsened. The conversation continued without him.

"Well, he speaks Kisejjad, so he's definitely a demon. You really didn't see this energy earlier? Not at all?"

"No."

"Was he speaking normally before too?"

"I don't know. He never had the chance to speak before the idiot brought him in."

"He has no clue what kind of danger he's had in his company."

"His physical form seems to indicate he's probably an iymed, even though he doesn't appear all that powerful."

"Powerful enough to suffer from the agony. Look at him struggle, holding his head. The signs are there."

"So, what do we do?"

"We need to make sure he's not a threat to the city. Help me put him in a prism, just like I taught you."

Feet shuffled through the dirt, and when Erynion opened his eye, Don Yatiga was standing over him. The demon barely saw her face in the faint light of the lantern hanging in the corner of the alley.

Erynion snarled.

Yatiga didn't retreat, and her voice was calm. "It hurts, doesn't it? It'll only get worse."

"Can you stop it?"

"Yes." Yatiga redirected her gaze. "Gheron. Benedoli."

Three voices began to chant, but the demon wasn't listening to the words. The voice in his head had cautioned him about Candelux, but the prospect of losing the pain forced him to ignore the warning. A yellow triangle glowed on the ground beneath Erynion. A flash of light blinded him, and when the demon was able to see again, he was trapped inside a prism of energy.

The radiant prison of light put Dulo's lantern to shame. The demon clearly saw the priest's face. "I still feel the pain."

"And you will continue to if you don't answer my questions," Yatiga said. "In order to help you, we need to know a few things. Understand?"

The demon barely nodded as he fought through the torment to listen to her words.

"Erynion. Is that a real name?"

"Real enough," he muttered.

"Knowing your name will greatly help us in stopping your pain."

"I don't remember."

"What about your past life?"

"I don't know."

"Where were you from?"

"I can't remember any of that!" Erynion glared at the priest through the wall of light. As the agony struck again, his body tensed. The demon grabbed his head and dug his nails into his skull.

"Then what do you remember?" Yatiga asked.

His jaw was clamped shut, and he sucked the air through his teeth. "My purpose. That's all I know."

"And what is your purpose?"

Bells clanged loudly in the distance. Erynion ignored them.

"We're under attack?" Yatiga stooped so she was at the same eye level as the demon. "What do you know of this?"

"Nothing." Erynion felt the blood drip down his hands.

"Don Yatiga," one of the others interrupted. "What should we do?"

"Focus, Gheron. The others will deal with the attack. We'll join them when we're done here. You two just get ready to cleanse."

"Yes, Don."

"Looks like we're out of time, Erynion," Yatiga said. "Tell us your purpose and we'll take away your pain."

"You claim to help, but the agony only grows worse." The demon reached for her, but as his claw hit the barrier, he withdrew it immediately. The sting of fire enveloped his finger.

The priest rose to her feet. "Whatever Verago has planned, he will fail. You tell him that when you see him."

Erynion stretched his arm toward the barrier again, but this time he pushed his hand through with little effort. He cringed as the flesh around his wrist burned. His arm quivered, but he held it firmly in the light. The agony's growth stagnated, and the demon stood up inside the cage of light. He took cleansing breaths, but the agony refused to recede.

"Don?" the woman in the brown scarf called out. *"Don?"* she repeated when the priest gave no answer.

"Move away! Now!" Yatiga instructed.

The group retreated outside the demon's range. Erynion stepped halfway into the barrier and stopped. The light seared everything it touched, and black wisps of smoke floated from his skin. But instead of crying out, the demon smiled. The mental anguish was fading, and his mind was experiencing a much needed reprieve.

"I have to thank you," Erynion said. "This feels wonderful compared to what was in my head. And since you finally helped me, I will answer your question."

In the glow of the prism spell, the demon saw the fear written on the priest's face. However, Yatiga stood her ground. "My question?"

"My purpose. I am here to kill King Batar."

CHAPTER 7

Millan slipped out of the guardhouse where his patient was left in the care of the healer. The watcher numbers had grown dramatically, and the majority of the invaders around the gate had already been dispersed. As the large metal door was pushed shut, the Candelux ranks took their cue and restrained or imprisoned the remaining demons. Millan moved forward to help, but a screech from behind stopped him in his tracks. A stray imp, poised atop the guardhouse, flew at him. Millan reflexively swatted at the demon and made contact with its ribs. The imp sailed through the air, kicking up dust as it landed. The Nesinu priest promptly rattled off the prayer for the Blessing of the Holy Prism. A triangle lit up under the fiend and light rose around him. Off to the side, there was a loud *thud*, followed by a cheer from the fighters in the area. The front gate to the city was finally slammed closed. Their efforts could now shift toward cleansing the invaders.

As Millan focused on the fray demon he had imprisoned, he thought back to his lessons with Don Skully. He had been taught how important it was to cleanse demons when given the chance. Physically killing a demon simply returned them to the Depths, an underground network of caverns that the Devil called home. On the other hand, a cleansing ritual would purify the demon's soul, preventing it from ever being infected by dark energy again. Unfortunately, though cleansed, those souls were still bound to Verago. And so, their fate would be to remain in the Depths forever, never to return to the Surface, a term which comprised anything aboveground.

Millan quietly chanted. The demon launched himself forward to break through the blessing, but he was too weak and ricocheted back into the prison of light. The spell steadily shrank and restricted the movement of the captive. The little demon shrieked as the light wrapped around him, conforming to his body and freezing him in place like a statue.

Millan held his hand over the fray's chest. "By the power of the angels. Let the holy light free your soul from the darkness, so that it may be pure and incorruptible."

The demon's heart ignited as the holy energy dissolved the source of its power.

"Be at peace!"

The blessing faded away, and the demon slumped to the ground. Its body melted into the dirt, and its soul was sent back to the Depths indefinitely.

"Don Millan! That was great!"

The young priest spotted the squire from Nesinu. "Tyro, you're out here too?"

"Yeah. Turns out I know a lot for a second-year."

Millan noticed a nearby Nolka priest was having some difficulty restraining a greater fray. The fray, less intelligent than their iymed brethren, came in all sizes. The larger ones were just as thoughtless as the smaller ones, but their size made them physically stronger and more formidable.

"Come on. Let's go help him," Millan said. "Replace his divine restraints."

The squire summoned a chain of light that burst out of the ground and wrapped tightly around the wrist of the greater fray. As the slack was removed, the beast was pulled to one side. Millan took his position on the opposite side and mirrored the blessing. His holy chains caught the other wrist and forced the greater fray to his knees.

"Thank you." The Nolka priest released his own restraint spell and held his hand over the demon's chest. The large fray thrashed about to no avail, and soon the demon shared the same fate as his impish comrade.

With the area free of enemies, Millan patted Tyro on the shoulder. "Not bad."

"Gather up!" Archdon Feranis waved the priests over. "We may have cleared the gate, but many of these fray have escaped into the city. We need to get the Blessing of Marked Defense up to prevent further harm. We'll be doing a group incantation to protect the entire city."

The archdon put his back to the gate and placed his staff on the ground. The priests, including Millan, stood in an arc behind Feranis. With outstretched arms, they prepared to recite the group blessing.

"By the light!" Feranis shouted.

"By the angels!" the priests answered.

"We call upon all that is holy to consecrate the marked."

"May the light be a beacon of hope."

"To protect those within."

"May the angels guard them with fortitude and honor."

"And to repel the evil that infects our land."

"May the demons be cast into oblivion."

Millan felt the energy surge within his body. He had never used so much of his power in such a short span. And though it tired him, he also found it warm and soothing. The energy flowed from him naturally.

"Grant this Blessing of Marked Defense," the archdon concluded. The city lit up as the homes marked with a four-pointed star, the symbol of Candelux, became protected from the fray demon attack.

The watcher captain sheathed her sword as she approached Feranis. Lufira offered a polite nod. "Thank you, Your Grace. This should make it easier for us to clear out the stragglers."

Save a few left to guard the gate, the watchers scattered into the city. The priests began to socialize, congratulating one another on a job well done. This was the first time in years that demons had attacked the city, and spirits were high. The celebration was short-lived, though. A sharp whistle penetrated the night air, and one of the Nolka priests pointed to a rooftop. "Up there!"

On a nearby building, a lone figure stood with his arms folded across his chest. A hood rested loosely atop his head and a cloth mask hid most of his face. The light from the streets illuminated him just enough to make out his tightly wrapped clothing, which peeked out from under the long cloak. Based on his attire, he appeared to belong to Anoctis, the infamous guild of thieves and assassins, but his voice betrayed him.

"Nemlit nejj dnezil djjel!" The demon extended his arms outward. "Nasujj kesken aud etjjav nilara ujja!"

"Get him!" Feranis exclaimed.

Streaks of light whizzed through the air toward the demon. The target dodged the attacks and bolted toward the center of the city. As the archdon picked up his staff, the priests and squires sprinted past him in pursuit. They tried to close the gap to the demon, but its movements along the rooftop were too quick.

Tyro ran alongside Millan. "My Kisejjad is still rusty. Did he say execution?"

"It certainly sounded like it."

At the town square, the group found their assassin-dressed adversary standing at the top of the fountain. Around him, outside the retaining wall that enclosed the angel statue, were five citizens on their knees, bound hand and foot. Beside each person was a demon, distorted and mangled. An outer circle of fray encompassed the group at the fountain and acted as a barrier between the priests and the residents. Despite manifesting in all forms, the fray were always more repulsive than the iymed. Verago never spent much time on aesthetics for his lowest-ranked soldiers, which resulted in misplaced bones and organs. As long as they could wreak havoc, they were good enough.

The iymed raised his hands high into the air. "Stay back! Any closer and they die."

Millan saw no other choice but to obey. He was politely pushed aside by Feranis as the archdon made his way to the front of the group.

The demon threw back his cloak. "Welcome to this special performance!"

Feranis subtly gave orders to the priests near him. "On my command, we need Blessings of Holy Prism around the hostages."

"You all are just in time for the beginning of the end. You may call me Reaper. I will be your host this evening." The iymed gave an exaggerated bow. Millan found the theatrics odd for such a morbid event.

Archdon Feranis took a step forward, and the demon yelled, "Come no farther, pig!"

The archdon complied. "You have your audience, demon. There's no need to harm the innocents. Say what you must before I return you to your master."

"The old pig is deaf. You clearly wish me to cut down your friends. Call me Reaper."

"I will call you no such thing. If you'd like to offer your real name, then that would be another story."

The iymed sneered. "Do you believe this to be a game? Do as I say, or I kill the fat one."

The overweight Nolka captive cowered as the fray beside him inched closer.

The archdon relented. "Fine. Reaper. What do you want in exchange for the release of the hostages?"

The demon was silent and motionless on the head of the angel statue. A breeze wafted his cloak ever so gently.

Time slipped away in silence until the archdon spoke again. "Are you as deaf as I? What are your terms?"

Reaper grinned deviously. "I have none."

"Prisms! Now!" Feranis hollered. The blessings manifested around the hostages and knocked back the fray. The executioners struck at the barriers but failed to break through. The archdon lifted his staff. The four-pointed star glowed brilliantly and blinded the demons around the fountain. Feranis swung the staff across his body, and the path of the star made an arc of light that flew toward the enemy and cut through the entire group of fray. Some of the demons were incapacitated, but most were killed instantly.

Feranis reached for the iymed on the angel statue. "Blessing of Divine Restraint!"

Chains of light shot from his hand and hurtled at the demon. Reaper sprang backward and threw off his cloak to cover his trail. The blessing pierced the fabric and chased after the demon. While midair, Reaper put both hands behind his head and pulled forth a scythe. As the light chains were upon him, he swung his weapon down and deflected them away.

Millan was impressed by the acrobatics of the iymed as he gracefully landed outside of the priest's range. Reaper turned tail and made a run for it.

The archdon's star glowed once again. "Blessing of the Lumenail."

A spike made of light fired from the artifact and streaked across the plaza. Reaper spun around and struck the spell with his scythe. The holy energy made contact and fractured the blade. The iymed released his broken weapon and resumed his retreat unarmed.

Feranis motioned to pursue, and Millan and Tyro broke out into the lead. But as they passed the fountain, the entire group halted. A flash of light at the other end of the plaza launched Reaper backward. The demon tumbled through the dirt and came to rest near Millan.

The demon groaned as he struggled to get on all fours. Millan's eyes shifted from Reaper to the priest who had knocked the demon down. His blond hair was tied back into a tail that bounced with each step. In his right hand, he carried a small kite shield, a strange object for a priest to bring into combat. The glow from the shield lingered from its recent blessing as the newcomer slung it across his back.

A couple of priests behind Millan cast their divine restraints. Reaper grimaced as the chains wrapped tightly around his arms and pulled him back into a kneeling position. His jaw trembled, but the demon refused to call out in pain.

"You know what comes next," said Feranis. There was a hint of sadness in his tone. Despite ridding the Surface of another demon and making the kingdom a safer place, it was clear Feranis took no pleasure inflicting pain on another soul.

Reaper took a few swift breaths. "Then my purpose is fulfilled."

The archdon cocked his head. "And what purpose is that?"

The demon glanced at the angel in the fountain.

Feranis placed the end of his staff on Reaper's cheek and delicately forced the iymed to make eye contact. "Suddenly you don't want to talk? Come now. You said your purpose was fulfilled. That means there's nothing we can do about it, right? What was your purpose?"

"To allow him to escape."

"We've captured only you. Whom have you allowed to escape?"

"The one who will bring an end to all you know," Reaper said. "One who can walk the Surface. He will usher in the era of Verago, and the living shall be wiped out once and for all."

"We've defeated all of Verago's soldiers before, and we'll do it again."

The demon spit at the ground. "You will stand united before him, and even your precious Prima will fall."

"It may surprise you that you're not the first demon to make such a claim. Anything else you'd like to tell us before I send you back to the Depths forever?"

"No. He's with her now. And in the end..." Reaper eyed everyone standing around him. "You all die."

"Give my regards to Verago." Feranis positioned the four-pointed star at the tip of his staff over the heart of the demon. "By the power of the angels, let the holy light free your soul from the darkness, so that it may be pure and incorruptible."

Millan shielded his eyes as the star gave off a radiant light.

Reaper bellowed, then fell silent.

"Be at peace."

****

There are many like you, but none are your equal.

Erynion paid little attention to the voice in his head. He bathed in the warmth of the holy prism's wall as the light singed his flesh. The group of humans, including Dulo, slowly backed away from him. The prison flickered and faded, and visibility in the alley was solely the responsibility of Dulo's broken lantern.

Erynion felt the tingle crawl up his neck. "Wait, I need your light."

"Behind us!" one of the humans shouted.

A loud *twang* rang out from the darkness, followed by a thump. The body of Don Yatiga lit up, giving off just enough light to show the immediate surroundings. The priest and squires knelt beside the body of the seeker, who had an arrow protruding from his chest. Dulo screamed and sprinted up the alley toward the distant streetlights. Erynion edged closer to the group, but kept some distance so as not to disturb them.

Don Yatiga moved her hands around the seeker's wound. "It'll be fine. You're going to be fine."

The injured man took labored breaths until he exhaled one final time.

"Please," Yatiga begged. "Please, find refuge with the angels."

Two silhouettes neared the humans but stood just beyond the range of Yatiga's light. Based on the outline of their figures, Erynion assumed they were both women. The shorter of the two reloaded her crossbow.

A sweet and sensual voice spoke from the shadows. "Vjjal norujj tua badiro vromi du vjja."

Yatiga squared off with the new threat. "Who are you?"

"Patience, my child," the voice said in Kisejjad. The taller figure addressed her companion. "Your work is done here, Overseer. Thank you. You may go."

Erynion recognized the title. "The overseer? Are you two with the Brotherhood? I came to this city to meet her."

As the crossbow-wielding silhouette departed, the demon in the shadows giggled. "That may have been the case before, but right now, it's best if you come with me."

Yatiga stepped between the two demons. "He's not going anywhere. And neither are you."

"You have no idea who you're dealing with." The demon maintained her dulcet tone as she glided into the light. The lower half of her body came into view first. A long red dress spread out like a star on the ground and concealed her feet. The dress clung to her hips and thighs but flowed more freely as it extended from her knees to her ankles. The top half desperately hugged her body, giving shape to her curves. Despite the low cut of her dress, her breasts were obscured by the long, straight black hair that snaked down her neck. Yatiga's light finally revealed a face with stunning features, partially covered by her hair. The demon grinned slyly as she sashayed toward the priest.

Hands at the ready, the two squires joined their superior.

The demon in the red dress pulled back her hair like a curtain and tucked it behind her ear. She locked eyes with the male squire. "What a handsome squire. You've got a bit of age too. I like that. Come to your darling Sereyna."

"Look away, Gheron." Yatiga blocked his line of sight to the demon. "Benedoli, take Gheron and run! Go find Archdon Feranis."

Sereyna placed her hands on her hips. "Aww, don't go and ruin my fun."

"Leave them alone," Yatiga warned. She looked over her shoulder at the two squires. "What are you waiting for?! Get out of here!"

The two squires hugged the wall and passed the demon in the red dress, but Sereyna made no attempt to stop them. Erynion moaned as the agony became more than just a distraction. Remembering how physical pain relieved him the night before, he held his forearm in front of his mouth. The demon stretched his jaw and sank his teeth into his arm. He sighed as his claw hung lifeless at the wrist and blood flowed down his arm. He was relieved enough for him to watch the encounter unfold.

"I could've killed them, you know," the female demon taunted.

The holy glow around Yatiga's body shifted to her hands. "Yes, I know who you are, Seductress."

"Please, I do so very much prefer Sereyna."

"I don't think so," the priest shot back. "You made a mistake coming here. The archdon will be along shortly to deal with you."

"Sadly, I'll have to skip that meeting. More pressing matters to tend to." From her left side, Sereyna produced a staff that Erynion swore had not been there before. A small blade protruded on one end like a glaive with a large hook on the opposite end.

"Blessing of Divine Restraint!" The spell erupted from Yatiga's hands.

With a swift swing of her staff, Sereyna caught the

attack on her hook and twisted the weapon. Yatiga arched her back and heaved on the chains.

Sereyna was unmoved. "Adorable."

The priest grunted as she yanked with all her might, but the demon still didn't budge. Sereyna jerked the staff backward, and Yatiga stumbled forward. The bladed end of the demon's staff sailed toward the priest. The chains of light vanished as Yatiga barely had enough time to create a barrier of light to repel the strike.

As Sereyna steadily applied more pressure to force the dark blade through the holy spell, she brought her face within inches of the priest's. "Don't be afraid. You're too important to die right now."

Yatiga gasped for air. Her body went limp and the barrier of energy disintegrated, once again leaving only Dulo's lantern to light the area.

Still biting his arm, Erynion closed the gap with the demon in the red dress.

The corner of her mouth pushed up. "Stop that. You look ridiculous. You have a name?"

He released his bleeding arm and allowed it to hang by his side. "Erynion."

"Sereyna."

"I heard. Are you with the Brotherhood?"

The female demon snickered. "Do I sound human to you?"

"Well, I was told to seek them out."

"That was before I found you. Now, you need to come with me."

Erynion hesitated. "Can…can you stop the agony?"

Sereyna caressed his cheek. "Yes, but we need to leave the city right away."

The body of Don Yatiga twitched and rose to her feet.

"Are you ready to go, my child?" Sereyna asked.

"Yes, master."

CHAPTER 8

As the large bell rang out a single tone across Nolka, indicating half past ten, Millan sat quietly on his bed. The excitement of the night had been so exhilarating that fatigue was settling in earlier than usual. He replayed the events of the night; healing Hyron, cleansing the fray demon, and protecting the citizens in the square from Reaper.

"Don Millan," a voice said timidly.

Millan jumped up. He hadn't noticed someone entered his room.

Gheron stood at the foot of Millan's bed. The squire was pale and sickly. "Sorry, the door was open. Archdon Feranis has requested your presence in his office."

"Understood." Millan bit his lip. "You don't look well. Are you all right?"

"Yes. I just need some time and rest."

"What happened out there?"

"It was…the demon was unaffected…the seeker…and the other was so…powerful. My thoughts were clouded. I could feel my…my control slipping. Please, I don't want to discuss this further," Gheron begged.

"I'm sorry. I didn't mean to pry."

"I have to go now." The squire hurried away.

Millan picked up his black scarf from the bed and hung it around his neck. On his way to the archdon's office, he speculated what Feranis could possibly want from him at this hour. He reflected on the meeting before the attack. Perhaps, Feranis wished to continue it and discuss the plans for tomorrow. When he arrived at the office, Millan found the door already open.

"Ah, Don Millan, good. Come in. Please, close the door behind you."

The young priest was surprised to find another man in the office, standing off to the side. Millan recognized him from his shield. This priest had prevented Reaper from escaping in the town square.

"Don Millan, may I introduce you to Don Eriph from Light's Haven," Feranis said. "Soon to be Archdon Eriph, if I'm not mistaken."

"Please, that's not necessary," said the shield-bearing priest.

"It's an honor." Millan crossed the room and gave a slight bow.

Eriph returned the gesture. "It's a pleasure to meet you as well."

As he lowered himself into his chair, Feranis invited Millan to sit while Eriph stood against the wall. "Don Millan, I'd like to ask you, along with Don Eriph here, to accompany me to the Scriptorum this evening where we'll have an audience with Prima Mashira."

Millan's eyes widened. He had only met the Candelux leader once, at his Acceptance. Any fatigue in his body vanished. "An audience with the Prima? Me?"

"Yes, in light of the possibility of a twisted gate outside Nesinu, I had already arranged to consult with the Council regarding our expedition tomorrow. But due to the events of tonight, that meeting was delayed. It's now even more crucial we speak with the Prima and update her on the situation. I will need you to accompany me in case she has any questions for you regarding the evacuation of Nesinu."

"You...you think she wants to...to speak with me?" Millan stuttered.

"Calm yourself," Feranis said. "The Prima's human just like us. There's no reason to be nervous. You're not on trial. We just need to have all the information we can get. And whether you realize it or not, in Don Skully's absence, you are technically the head don of Nesinu."

"More like the only don in Nesinu."

"Even so, I want you to be there."

"Of course, Your Grace."

"Good. Collect your thoughts. The audience is in twenty minutes." Feranis leaned on his elbows and clasped his hands. "In the meantime, I have a favor to ask of you."

Millan briefly glanced at Eriph, who was quietly observing the discussion. "Of course. I'll help in any way I can."

"Don Yatiga has gone missing. The watchers at the north gate reported her leaving the city with two unknown figures. You'll hear more at the meeting with the Prima and her advisors, but I fear the worst. What I must ask of you may be difficult. I have considered asking one of my own priests, but with you here, seeking shelter, perhaps you can fill the void."

Millan fidgeted in his chair. Different scenarios ran through his mind. What if Feranis wanted him to search for Yatiga? At night? Alone? There were still fray out there, sure. And who were the figures leaving with her? What if they were demons too? Iymed? Verago? Millan's spine tingled, and he was barely able to nod.

"I need you to supervise her squire class in the school tomorrow."

The tension in his muscles melted away. "Excuse me?"

"Don Yatiga teaches a senior squire class. I imagine you must have been involved with teaching your squire in Nesinu. Is that correct?"

"Yes."

"Excellent." Feranis said. "Then I would like you to teach the class in her absence. Can you do that?"

"Um, uh, well, sure, I'd be happy to help. Tyro wasn't quite senior, so this will be new for me. What do I teach them?"

"Anything you like. This is only temporary for now, so I leave it in your hands."

"No problem." Millan had no idea what to teach.

"Thank you." Feranis placed his palms flat on the desk and stood. "Now that that's been taken care of, let's head over to the Scriptorum and prepare for the audience. We'll be using the Scribe's Mirror."

"The Scribe's Mirror?" Millan knew the Scriptorum delivered letters across the kingdom but was unfamiliar with this term.

Eriph pushed off the wall. "Don't get out of Nesinu much, huh?"

"Not really, no."

"You'll see." Feranis grabbed his staff from the corner and ushered the two priests out of his office.

As the three men walked out of the rectory and into the street, Millan studied Eriph in his periphery. The shield across Eriph's back had three points at the top and tapered to a single point as the bottom portion hovered around his waist. Millan was intrigued by the object. "Don Eriph, may I ask you something?"

"Ask away."

"What made you choose a shield as a conduit? I've never heard of a priest wielding a shield."

"Uncommon, maybe," Eriph conceded, "but certainly not unheard of. I wanted a defensive specialty. A shield seemed appropriate."

"So with whom did you specialize?" Millan pried.

"Perhaps," Feranis interrupted, "you two can discuss such matters after the audience. I would like to explain now how I want this to go. At the beginning, I'll introduce you both. Then I want to address the events in order. Don

Skully and the evacuation of Nesinu will be first. Don Millan, I have no doubt the Council will have some questions for you."

"Yes, Your Grace."

"Then I'll discuss the events that happened here tonight. Once we answer any questions concerning the attack and Don Yatiga's disappearance, there shouldn't be too much more to discuss. The Prima may have to speak with Don Eriph concerning his Ascension, but Millan, you may be excused at that time."

"There's no reason for him to be excused if he wishes to stay and listen," Eriph said calmly.

Feranis glimpsed at the shield-bearing priest. "As you wish."

Millan sensed there was something more behind their exchange but decided not to delve any deeper. The watcher headquarters came into view, along with the large clock tower, which housed the six bells used to signal the demon attack. The clock read five minutes to eleven. The city square was quiet as they crossed the area where Reaper had been defeated. It was the first time Millan had witnessed the cleansing of an iymed. Before long, the group entered a side street and came upon a building with a sign hanging above the door. The wooden plaque had an illustration of an unfurled scroll.

Feranis knocked on the Scriptorum door. "Someone should be waiting for us."

The door swung open, and an old man with white frizzy hair appeared in the threshold. His voice was hoarse from age. "Good evening, Your Grace."

"Good evening, Elder Scribe. Thank you so much for allowing us use of your services at such an hour."

"Of course, of course. Please come in. I see you've brought other guests."

The archdon held his hand in front of each priest as he introduced him. "May I present Don Eriph from Light's Haven and Don Millan from Nesinu. They will be accompanying me."

"Pleased to meet you both. I am Elder Scribe Pasiti. Please follow me to our Scribe's Mirror." Pasiti guided the three priests through the Scriptorum. "You have my assurance that both scribes conducting the ritual will be blinded and deafened for your privacy, as is customary."

"Excellent. Thank you," Feranis said.

As they arrived at a room, Pasiti paused in front of it and addressed the two dons. "I don't know how familiar you are with the Scribe's Mirror, but I request that you do not cross the lit candles or throw any objects at the mirror or the scribes. Such actions will result in bans from our Scriptorum and any scribe services, along with any lawful consequences."

"We understand the terms of your ritual, Elder Scribe," Feranis replied respectfully.

"Excellent. Please enter this room. Once you are inside, it will be locked, and only I hold the key. When you wish to leave, simply knock on the door. I will be right outside."

"Thank you."

Once inside, the Nesinu priest was in awe of the large, golden-framed mirror at the far end of the room. A pair of unlit candles stood in front of it. Facing the room with their heads lowered, one scribe was posted on each side of the looking glass. Both were fully garbed in large cloaks and hoods so that no part of their bodies could be seen. Pasiti walked up to the first candle and lit it. He calmly placed his hand on the first scribe's shoulder before crossing to the opposite side. The cloaked figure delicately grasped the frame of the mirror with both hands. Pasiti lit the second candle and performed the same gesture to the second scribe.

"I'll be right outside." The elder scribe passed them and closed the door.

Millan winced at the sound of metal scraping against metal as the lock slid into place. The reflection in the glass began to distort. Waves rippled out from the hands of the scribes, changing the image near the edges first. Feranis positioned his staff on the ground and used it to lower himself and kneel. Millan and Eriph followed suit and knelt before the Scribe's Mirror. The reflection of the three priests eventually faded and was replaced by the inside of the Sanctuary, the glorious rectory at Light's Haven.

In the mirror were five empty seats, including the modest throne for the Prima. Millan recalled kneeling there in person only a few years ago during his Acceptance. Silence hung in the air as the young priest wondered how long before the Council arrived for the audience. Surely, five minutes had passed by now. Or had it? He had always imagined that such high-ranking officials would be timely, but perhaps they had no desire to wait, and so they showed up a bit later than scheduled. Millan barely made out the sound of the clock tower striking eleven as the low-toned rings struggled to penetrate the thick walls of their room. Millan tried to count them, but it was difficult to make out each ring.

He abandoned his count as the mirror showed the arrival of the Council: the Prima and her four advisors. Each advisor wore a black robe with a white scarf, similar to the archdons, except each scarf had two red stripes at the end of it. Millan recognized the four advisors from when he was inducted into the guild. Advisor Deidok was clearly the oldest, and as he gingerly took his seat, he reminded the young priest of Don Skully. Advisor Ayristark was the Primus before Mashira and had aged well over the years. Advisor Razza Merona was the youngest and the only other female on the Council. And lastly, Advisor Cole was a short, middle-aged man who seemed standoffish to Millan during their only encounter.

In contrast to the advisors, Prima Mashira wore a pure-white robe with a red scarf. Atop her head she wore a gold circlet that most would consider modest given her power and authority. The humble crown kept her long, golden hair in place as it spread out along her shoulders and back.

When the Council had reached their seats, the advisors waited for the Prima to sit first before doing the same.

"You may rise, gentlemen," the Candelux leader uttered, and the three priests stood before their leader.

Feranis stepped forward. "Your Luminescence, I apologize for the delay in our meeting and pushing this audience to such an hour of the night, but these matters require your attention most urgently."

"It's no inconvenience, Archdon Feranis. If the events are as you have described in your letters, then we must address them immediately. Please continue."

"Thank you, Prima. To my right is Don Millan from Nesinu. He led the evacuation of the town as ordered by his superior, Don Skully. And on my left, you know Don Eriph, recently returned from his specialty training. He aided us tonight with the demon attack on Nolka."

"Hello, Don Eriph, Don Millan. It's nice to see you both again."

Millan's heart started racing. The Prima actually remembered him?

"And you as well, Your Luminescence," Eriph said confidently.

The Nesinu priest realized he hadn't responded and spoke quickly to catch up with Eriph. "And you as well, Your Luminescence."

"Don Millan, can you explain to me what happened yesterday?" the Prima asked.

The young priest interlaced his fingers. "Of...of course. W-what would you like to know?"

"Archdon Feranis has written his account, but I would like to hear it from you directly."

"Of...of course. W-where should I begin?"

The Prima smiled kindly. "I suppose from the beginning. Please take your time. Whenever you're ready."

Her reaction soothed him, and Millan took a deep breath. "Well, it seemed like any other day. Don Skully and I had breakfast with Tyro, our squire. This was before class. We were going to start teaching him—"

"Don Millan," the Candelux leader interrupted. "I meant the beginning of last night. Tell me what happened that led to your evacuation from Nesinu."

Millan tittered. "Of course. Um, well, I was in the rectory delivering a letter to Don Skully when the ground started shaking. He said we should speak with the watchers. We thought maybe they were fray pods. Based on the intensity of the quake, we expected there to be multiple pods close by. When we arrived outside, the sun was already down. Um, Captain Pirok informed us that no pods had been sighted near the village. Don Skully asked me to go into the rectory and fetch our squire. But by the time Tyro and I rejoined him, Don Skully had changed his mind. He wouldn't tell me why, but he insisted that we evacuate the town. I was to lead everyone to Nolka while he stayed behind to assess the threat."

"And that was the last time you saw him?" Mashira asked.

There was a lump in his throat. "Yes."

"In the letter, Archdon Feranis mentioned a boy who had seen something in the woods. Were you aware of this?"

"Yes, Your Luminescence."

"Tell me about that."

Millan nervously tapped his thumbs together. "That boy hunts in the area around Nesinu for himself and his mother. During the evacuation, I heard he'd spoken with Don Skully while I was in the rectory. Apparently, he saw something during his hunt, and whatever it was made Don Skully order the evacuation. Since I was leading the villagers throughout the night, keeping them safe, I never had the chance to speak with the boy. When we finally made it to Nolka, Archdon Feranis and his priests were very welcoming and helped find shelter for our residents. The only people who were missing were Don Skully and Captain Pirok."

"And your watcher hasn't turned up either?"

"No, Your Luminescence."

"Thank you, Don Millan." Mashira said. "Archdon Feranis, your letter stated that you spoke with the boy and his description leads you to believe we may be dealing with another twisted gate. Is that correct?"

"Yes, Your Luminescence. I understand if you have doubts. I had them myself. Children tend to exaggerate. But, what he described is just like what popped up during the Assault on Light's Haven and again at Devil's Breach."

The Assault on Light's Haven was a significant event where the full force of Verago's army failed to conquer the capital. Since Millan was only seven years old at the time and lived far away in Nesinu, he remembered very little of the incident. However, the mention of Devil's Breach reminded Millan of his visit to Light's Haven for his Acceptance. The stories of what had happened a month earlier were circulating throughout the city. Don Skully warned Millan not to put too much stock in the different rumors, but rather pay attention to the commonalities. All talk about Devil's Breach started the same way. A twisted gate burst forth in the royal gardens, and Verago himself emerged.

"Now, take into account that Don Skully is still missing." Feranis's mention of Millan's mentor brought the young priest back to the present. "This leads me to believe we are dealing with something very powerful, something that could only come to the Surface through a twisted gate. After all, Don Skully was no ordinary priest."

Millan was thrown by the statement. He knew Feranis had been friends with Skully, but what did he mean by "no ordinary priest"?

"True," the Prima said.

"And in light of what I had learned from this boy," Feranis continued, "I asked Captain Lufira to send a scout to Nesinu. To my knowledge, that scout never returned."

The advisors murmured to one another, but quieted

when their leader spoke. "I must admit this becomes more and more unsettling. Please, tell me about the attack on Nolka."

Feranis nodded. "In addition to requesting a scout to investigate Nesinu, I also petitioned the watchers to station a seeker at the gates for the day. As we ate dinner, I was told about a minimal disturbance within the walls detected by the seeker. He said it was faint, but definitely dark energy. I ordered Don Yatiga to look into the problem. Two of our senior squires, Gheron and Benedoli, accompanied her. I bring you this account secondhand from Benedoli."

"I understand. Please continue."

"The source of the dark energy was from a demon that was somewhat of a mystery. He was a large figure with cloth wrapped around his head to cover his right eye. His clothing was tattered, and his pants were stained with blood. Don Yatiga and the seeker discussed the strength of the demon, and how he appeared to be weak. But, he had a human form and seemed to be enduring the agony. When they tried to learn his purpose, he was not very communicative. And so, they surrounded him with the Blessing of Holy Prism for cleansing. As it turns out, he was able to walk right through it."

Mashira raised her eyebrows. "Through it?"

"That's right. But he didn't pass all the way through. He stood in the wall and allowed the light energy to burn him. He made no attempt to attack them. In fact, according to Benedoli, he was thankful for the blessing."

"Did he say anything to them?"

Feranis nodded. "He said his name is Erynion."

"Erynion?" Millan blurted out.

The archdon gave him a sharp look, and the young priest tightened his lips.

"Also, he said his purpose is to kill King Batar."

The advisors on the Council stared at Mashira. Aside from the subtle movements of her fingers, she was still like a statue. "What happened next?"

"Two women came up behind them," Feranis said. "One killed the seeker with a crossbow."

"Demons?"

"One was for sure. She spoke Kisejjad. But the one carrying the crossbow never spoke. However, her demon companion referred to her as overseer."

"Overseer? So the Brotherhood's involved as well." Mashira clicked her tongue. "This keeps getting better."

"After the overseer was dismissed, the other woman—the demon—approached them. And when she stepped into the light, she was very attractive. Red dress. Long black hair. She caught Gheron in a trance."

Mashira shifted uncomfortably on her throne. "The Seductress? What exactly is going on here?"

"I'm not sure. Don Yatiga ordered the squires to run while she remained behind. Not long after hearing Benedoli's account, I received a message from the watchers at the north gate. Don Yatiga had left the city with two unknown figures. Their descriptions matched that of Erynion and the Seductress." His voice quivered. "That...that was the last she's been seen."

"I'm so sorry, Feranis. I know how close you were to her."

There was a long pause as the Nolka archdon wiped the tear pooling in his eye. Millan wished to give the archdon some privacy, and so he focused on the floor.

Feranis sniffed once and then loudly cleared his throat. "While Don Yatiga and the squires investigated the disturbance, the tower bells rang to signal an attack. We were informed by the watchers that the north gate had been sabotaged. When they tried to close the gate manually, the Brotherhood attacked, allowing the fray to push through the city gates."

Mashira pursed her lips. "The Brotherhood again. I suppose they're not as disorganized as we'd like to believe. We must deal with them swiftly."

The Twisted Gate

"Of course, Your Luminescence," Advisor Ayristark said.

"Please, Feranis, continue."

"After the watchers managed to close the gate and we cleansed the fray, a lesser iymed calling himself Reaper appeared. He said the demons that had escaped into the city had taken civilians captive with the intent to kill them. He led us to the center of Nolka where a group of fray were in fact holding five townspeople hostage. We rescued them and dispensed with the fray. Reaper tried to escape, but thanks to Don Eriph, we were able to capture him and ultimately cleanse him. I'm afraid it was too late when I realized this was just a diversion so the Seductress could infiltrate the city unhindered and recover this mystery demon, Erynion."

"And did this iymed have anything to say before you cleansed him?" the Prima asked.

"You mean aside from the typical banter about how Verago will kill us all? He admitted his role as a distraction so another could escape. I can only assume he was referring to Erynion. He made it sound as though this demon was the answer to their prayers, as though he would be unstoppable."

"And do you believe him?"

"I don't know," Feranis said. "I'm suspicious. Usually demons scream about Verago being unstoppable and how if we stand against the Devil, we'll fail. I've never heard one of them talk about anyone else that will lead the demons to victory, not even the greater iymed."

"Thank you. Is there anything else?"

"Yes, Your Luminescence, there is. Tomorrow morning, I'd like to travel to Nesinu with my priests and Don Millan to investigate. At the very least, we need to destroy the twisted gate."

"We will consider your request, but first I'd like to hear from my advisors on this situation."

Advisor Deidok stroked his beard. "A demon strong

enough to pass through a holy prism must be a greater iymed. If what you say is true about his experience of the agony and his human form, then that only confirms it. It's possible Verago has created another and sent him to the Surface through the twisted gate witnessed by the young boy."

"Perhaps the Marksman," added Advisor Ayristark. As a squire, Millan had learned all about the five greater iymed that terrorized the kingdom. The Marksman was one, but he was killed sixteen years ago during the Assault on Light's Haven. Since he wasn't cleansed, the priests have been expecting him to reappear.

Advisor Cole nodded. "Yes, I was thinking the same."

"It's a possibility," Mashira said. "But why call himself Erynion? We know his demon name has always been Alejjir."

"The Seductress is known for changing names, why not the Marksman?" Advisor Razza Merona suggested.

The Prima rocked her head side to side. "Fair. What concerns me is how a demon that strong got into the city undetected. It makes me lean more toward the Shade."

Millan's eyes darted between the different Council members as they discussed the situation. He felt honored to witness such an event.

"No one's seen the Shade for over a decade."

"That could be said about all of the greater iymed."

"Fine, but why would the Shade be experiencing the agony? Why would he suddenly have no control over his energy?"

"Maybe he went to the Depths, and Verago gave him more."

"I think we're all forgetting that the Shade's power is to hide his energy, not to appear human. That requires some amount of holy energy. How would that be possible for a demon?"

"It doesn't have to actually be holy energy. It could just be an illusion."

"Putting aside this demon's inherent ability, I think there are more pressing questions to ask. Like, why walk into Nolka when his objective is to kill the king?"

"Confused by the agony?"

Feranis interjected. "According to Benedoli, he was looking for the Brotherhood."

"To what end?" Mashira asked. "Does the Brotherhood in Nolka have something of importance?"

"I don't know."

The Council again talked among themselves.

"Maybe he didn't know any better. Why else would the Seductress put herself at risk by infiltrating the city to recover him?"

"That's right. Even Verago knows how fragmented the Brotherhood is since the Assault. And our sources tell us they weren't even aware that Devil's Breach was going to happen."

"Fragmented, but not useless. As shown by tonight's events, they deserve our attention once again."

"And we will deal with them."

"But back to the Seductress. If she was sent to fetch this demon, Erynion, then clearly he's meant to play a critical role."

"Yes, that's true."

"A critical role in what?"

"Good question."

The Prima held up her hands. "I believe there's an important part of this no one has considered yet. The demon's objective is to kill King Batar, but the king wears the Talisman of Zavi. No demon can even come close to him, including a greater iymed."

"What if the demon lied about his purpose?" Razza Merona suggested.

Don Eriph raised his voice. "Or what if this isn't a greater iymed?"

Through the Scribe's Mirror, the Council gazed at the priest with the shield. Mashira folded her hands in her lap.

"What exactly do you mean by that?"

"If I may, Your Luminescence." Eriph bowed respectfully.

"Of course. Please explain."

"What about a demon lord?"

"Ha!" Advisor Cole exclaimed. "A demon lord? Everyone knows a demon lord is too powerful to survive on the Surface. The agony would dominate it. Look no further than what happened at the Assault."

"That's right," Razza added. "They say based on the scars, it nearly tore its own head off before killing all those demons."

Eriph pressed on. "Yes, but we also know that not all demons can be iymed because of the agony. And even less can be greater iymed. Wouldn't it stand to reason then that there are a very select few that could successfully become a demon lord? What if Erynion is one of those select few?"

Mashira narrowed her eyes. "Why are you so adamant this new threat is a demon lord?"

Eriph looked over at Archdon Feranis.

The Nolka archdon shook his head ever so slightly. "No good will come from this."

The shield-bearing priest addressed the Council. "Because that's the information we received. We sent Don Skully a short letter to warn him. I was on my way to Nesinu to offer my assistance. Unfortunately, I was too late."

Mashira placed her hands on the arms of her seat. "Warn him? Who's we?"

Eriph glanced at Feranis, but this time the archdon kept his sights fixed on the Council. "The founders."

The Prima's knuckles turned white as she gripped the throne. She straightened her back, and her nostrils flared. "Excuse me?"

Millan shuddered at the change in her tone, but Eriph's voice remained relaxed. "The founders, Your Luminescence."

"As in the Death Gods?"

"That's correct."

"And when exactly did you receive this information?" Mashira asked.

"A few days ago. Before I left Alovajj."

The Death Gods were a group of citizens from various guilds who were exiled from the kingdom for controversial reasons. They now resided south of the border in Alovajj. The mention of this city sent the advisors into a frenzy.

The Prima lifted her hands to quiet the Council. "Alovajj. You went to Alovajj? Without our permission?"

"Yes, I know how it sounds, but—"

Mashira sprang to her feet. "How it sounds? Don Eriph, you are on the verge of Ascension. And now, you have disregarded one of the most important rules of our guild."

"Yes, but that rule was put in place to—"

Mashira spoke over his protest. "No priest—don or archdon—is allowed to travel to Alovajj without express permission granted by the Council. This rule has been strictly enforced for three years now. Were you not aware of this?"

"If you could just listen to—"

"Were you or were you not aware of this? Answer me!" the Prima insisted.

Eriph grumbled, "Yes, I was aware of it."

"Then you know the penalty for it."

"Do what you must, but please, just hear me out. They know things that can change this war. They can help. They have information we can use."

"Oh, I'm well aware of that," the Prima said sternly. "There's a reason why they were exiled. This information you're referring to is dangerous. Pursuing it is what caused the incident at Deimor Outpost, the same incident, need I remind you, that is exactly why we enforce this rule with no exception. What possible reason could you have to go to Alovajj?"

"I went for my specialty training, to train with Founder Brahawee."

Mashira closed her eyes and lowered herself back into her seat. Millan looked around, trying to figure out what exactly was happening. The young priest knew the Death Gods had been exiled not long after the Assault on Light's Haven, but Don Skully never explained the details to him.

"Don Eriph," Advisor Ayristark said. "When you consulted with me about whom to choose for your specialty training, did you not ask whether the founders were eligible?"

"Yes, but—"

"And do you remember my answer?"

Eriph broke eye contact with the Council. "You told me that it would not only be disrespectful to choose a founder over an archdon, but it would also be viewed as treasonous."

Ayristark curled his lip. "You didn't heed my words at all. You spit on them and treated them like chaff."

"You must believe me when I tell you my decision was not out of disrespect but out of concern for our guild. Are we really supposed to turn a blind eye to the progress the Death Gods have made? Founder Brahawee was an archdon in Candelux and is the foremost expert on defensive conduit blessings. I was hoping to bring new ideas, abilities, and information back to our guild."

"I knew the shield reminded me of something," the Prima said with disdain. "Unfortunately, the only thing you've brought is shame upon yourself. We adhere to the rules of this guild for a specific reason. We must protect the people in this kingdom, and we must preserve order. Yes, there was a time when diplomacy was an option with the Death Gods, but after the attack on Deimor Outpost, we have no need to fraternize with them."

Eriph shook his head. "You're not listening to what I'm trying to say. We need them now."

"For centuries, we've survived without their help,"

Mashira said. "This is no different. I'll give my advisors the opportunity to defend your actions, otherwise I'm left with no choice but to exclude you."

"There's always a choice."

"If you think I'm pleased with this, you're sorely mistaken. But what would you have me do? Exclusion is the penalty for breaking this rule. If I show you leniency, what prevents the next priest from traveling to Alovajj without permission? What is the point of having rules if they can be broken with no consequence? Advisors?"

"The Death Gods are the worst of the worst. How could you believe they had anything good to offer?" Cole scolded. "If you side with them, then you are not one of us."

Razza Merona offered her opinion next. "Personal feelings for the Death Gods aside, I agree with Prima Mashira. We have rules in place to keep everyone safe. You knew that travel to Alovajj was banned, and yet you went anyway. How could anyone condone that?"

Deidok leaned forward. "There may come a time when the bond between Candelux and the Death Gods is reforged and the rule is done away with, but now is not that time."

Ayristark scowled. "You chose a founder over one of us."

Millan was dumbfounded as Eriph made no attempt to contest the Council's comments. The Nesinu priest was about to witness an expulsion from the guild.

"Don Eriph." The Prima addressed him officially. "For blatant disregard of the guild's policy with respect to Alovajj and the Death Gods, I, Prima Mashira, witnessed by the Council and all others present, hereby exclude you from Candelux and strip you of your title and all privileges."

"You're making a mistake," Eriph cautioned. "At the very least, listen to the warning. They've given me information on the Brotherhood as well."

"The Death Gods are renowned for their deceit. Any message you have from them will only hinder our activities. This leaves me with a heavy heart, but as of this moment, you're no longer a priest of Candelux. That means these affairs are no longer your concern. Archdon Feranis, are there any other matters we need to discuss?"

"Only our plan to travel to Nesinu tomorrow."

"Right, the twisted gate. I support that course of action. I trust in your abilities, and I know the priests will be safe with you. Even the Seductress wouldn't be foolish enough to attack in daylight. Are there any who are opposed?"

Advisor Ayristark raised his index finger. "Not opposed, but I advise exercising extra caution in your travels."

"Absolutely," the Nolka archdon said.

"Excellent. If there's nothing further to discuss, then this meeting is adjourned," Mashira said. "I will be expecting your report tomorrow evening. May the angels give us strength and guide us. May the angels watch over you."

Only Feranis and Millan replied. "And you as well."

CHAPTER 9

"Don Millan, please wake up. You're going to be late."

Three knocks came in quick succession.

Half awake, the Nesinu priest rolled over. "Hmm?"

"Don Millan, I was sent to get you. Are you up?"

"Yes...yes. Just a moment." Millan kept his eyes closed and before long he was fast asleep. Loud pounding on the door jarred him awake.

"I'm up!" He forced himself out of bed. The Nesinu priest yawned to the point his jaw nearly popped out of place. His robe hung from a nearby chair, but he lacked the motivation to move toward it.

"Don Millan?" The female voice was persistent.

"Yes, I'm awake. I am. Just let me get dressed." The young priest shuffled his feet and pulled the robe over his normal clothes. Then, he flipped the black scarf over his head and around his shoulders. He checked the area one last time to see if he had forgotten anything before he opened the door.

"Good morning."

"Good morning, Don Millan. My name is Benedoli."

He recognized her by her red hair, but he hadn't been close enough before to see her lovely freckled face. "Yes, I know. I saw you last night."

The squire scrunched her forehead.

Millan felt his heart skip a beat. "At the, um…the…the dinner. In the dining hall. When Don Yatiga called on you."

Benedoli studied his face. "Are you all right?"

Millan suppressed a yawn and wiped the sleep from his eyes. "Yes, I just had some difficulty falling asleep last night. Why? Is something the matter?"

"Archdon Feranis said you'd be teaching the senior squire class in Don Yatiga's absence."

"He did?" Millan gasped. "He did! Of course. Am I late?"

"Not yet. Follow me, please."

Millan shut the door to his room and strolled down the corridor after her. As they descended the steps outside the rectory, the clock tower rang out seven times.

The squire peeked over her shoulder. "Seven strikes. Now we're late."

"Not the best start, I suppose."

"I think given the circumstances, a few minutes won't hurt."

"So, you have your classes outside the rectory?" Millan asked as they journeyed toward the city center.

"Yes, the rectory is for offices, dining, and living. Our city has a large school that is shared by the guilds and sects for training. We reserve a few rooms for our squire classes."

Millan suddenly realized he had no curriculum prepared. "So, what should I teach the class?"

"I don't know. Whatever you like, I suppose. Whatever you want to teach us."

As they meandered through the crowd, Millan reminisced about what he enjoyed most from his time as a squire. The truth was that he relished everything Don Skully had taught him, from history lessons to blessings. As the pair passed by the fountain, Millan slowed his pace.

For an instant, he saw Reaper standing atop the angel statue. The so-called execution had all been a distraction so the Seductress, one of the most vile creatures known in the kingdom, could recover a new demon of unknown power and significance.

"Don Millan, over here."

The Nesinu priest discovered he had lost his guide, but it didn't take long to spot her by one of the side streets.

Benedoli waved at him.

Millan jogged up to her. "My apologies."

"No worries. We're already late as it is."

Their destination wasn't much farther up the path. Though the school was large like the Candelux rectory, the exterior was plain and matched the architecture of the surrounding buildings, making it relatively inconspicuous. Benedoli escorted Millan through the school until they arrived at the squire classroom. When the door opened, there was a hush, and the squires stood in respect. Millan's guide weaved between her classmates and took her place among them.

The Nesinu priest pushed the door shut before making his way to the front of the class. "Good morning."

"Good morning, Don," the students answered in unison.

Millan took a deep breath. His heart was pounding. "Please be seated. My name is Don Millan. As some of you may know, Don Yatiga has been missing since last night, so Archdon Feranis has asked me to teach your class this morning."

The class watched him in silence.

"So…um…well, I'm not exactly sure what Don Yatiga was teaching you all. Maybe we can start there. Who can tell me what you were learning?"

A girl with dark hair sitting next to Benedoli raised her hand. "Don Yatiga was going to administer a test today about the Assault on Light's Haven."

Groans came from the other students as the girl quietly

defended herself to nearby classmates.

"Hey now, that's enough," Millan said. "Everyone, please calm down."

The class fell silent again as the young girl crossed her arms in front of her chest.

"Look. I'm not your teacher, so I won't be giving any test. How about we just talk about the Assault a little, huh? We'll see how well you would've done if there were a test. You know, when I was a squire, the Assault was the most interesting history lesson for me because I was alive when it happened. In fact, I'm sure most of you were too. Who can tell me when the Assault on Light's Haven happened?" Millan pointed to a squire near the back.

"About sixteen years ago."

"That's right. And what other event, unrelated to the Assault, coincided with that day?" Millan gestured to a student who was timidly holding up his hand.

"Prima Mashira's Illumination ceremony."

"Correct," Millan said. "Some believe the demon attack was intentionally scheduled for that day so the Prima wouldn't have any time to learn how to wield her new power. But as we all know, the Assault failed. Right? Light's Haven is safe and sound. Who can tell me the two major incidents that contributed to our victory? Benedoli?"

The class laughed. Hers was the only name he knew. Millan blushed but hid his embarrassment by bringing his hand to his mouth and pretending to yawn.

Benedoli rolled her eyes. "Our victory was thanks in a large part to Shinigami's betrayal of the Brotherhood and the surfacing of the demon lord."

"Thank you. Now someone else. Tell me about Shinigami."

The dark-haired girl next to Benedoli bit her thumbnail between her smiling lips before she finally raised her other hand. Before Millan had the chance to acknowledge her, she spoke. "Shinigami was the leader of the Brotherhood of Prevarra. It's estimated that he held the rank of Grand

Overseer for over twenty-five years. There's no record of him having any family. No one knows where he came from. And before the Assault, no one outside the Brotherhood even knew what he looked like or where he lived. When the demons attacked, he surrendered himself to the royal watchers and gave up the demons' positions."

"And which—"

"Don Millan," one of the squires interrupted.

"Uh, yes?"

"Why would he do that?"

"I'm sorry?"

"Shinigami. He comes out of nowhere and leads the Brotherhood for a quarter of a century, helping the demons. He's the greatest human enemy in the kingdom. And then, on the day the demons come together to form one giant army, ready to lay waste to Light's Haven, he switches sides? Why?"

"Well, that's an interesting question. I suppose the person who could answer that best would be Shinigami himself. But since he's not here, what do you all think?"

"Change of heart!" someone called out, trying to stay anonymous.

Another squire scoffed. "Nobody just has a change of heart after twenty-five years."

"Well, then what do you suggest?" Millan asked.

"I think he and Verago had an agreement, and the Devil backstabbed him."

"What?" another student challenged.

"Sure. Once Verago saw his army on the verge of victory, he cut his ties with Shinigami, who in turn betrayed Verago in an act of desperation to save his own hide."

"That's ridiculous. Verago isn't an idiot. He wouldn't cast aside his most powerful ally until the Talisman was good and destroyed."

Millan was content to lean against the wall as the students argued among themselves. It seemed like the easiest way to fill the hour gap until he could leave for Nesinu with the other dons and Archdon Feranis. Letting his mind wander, the priest imagined riding into his hometown and finding Don Skully, mildly injured. He would run to his rescue and heal the old man's wounds. His daydream vanished as the class became unruly without his mediating. Millan reluctantly rejoined the conversation. "All right, let's calm down."

One squire pointed at his classmate. "Yeah, you would know. Your uncle is the overseer in Memorial City."

"Whoa! Whoa! Hey! Sit down," Millan commanded. "Heh, can't leave you guys alone at all, huh?"

"Targan started it. Said I was related to a Death God."

Targan defended his accusation. "Well, you *are* cousins with Founder Drevarius, aren't you?"

"I *told* you. He's a distant cousin. He's not even regarded as a member of our family."

"That's enough," Millan scolded. "Many people are related to Death Gods. Who cares? We're off topic. Where were we now?"

Benedoli helped him get back on track. "How Shinigami helped us stop the demons at the Assault."

"Right, thank you. That's enough about him, though. Let's discuss the demon lord. Who can tell me what happened there? How about you?" Millan motioned to a squire that hadn't spoken yet.

"There was a large earthquake that shook the city, and for the first time in history, a twisted gate appeared. It looked like an oversize fray pod, large enough to be seen from the city walls. The bloodseekers said the demon that emerged had the strongest aura they had ever felt."

"That's right. And bloodseekers are considered the best energy detectors in the kingdom."

"Even better than the Prima?" Benedoli asked.

Millan shrugged. "Well, maybe not all of them, but I'm pretty sure the champion bloodseekers are. They're the elite after all."

"My uncle's a Champion of the Light," Targan bragged.

"Oh, shut up, Targan," the squire said over the groans of the class. "He's just a guardian."

"Guardians are equally important!" he shot back.

Millan intervened. "Come on, everyone. This is Candelux, not the Paladin Order. There's no need to start a debate about which type of paladin is better than the other. Let them sort that out."

"But it's so obvious. Bloodseekers can hunt down demons and they're clearly the best physical fighters. All a guardian is good for is holding up a shield."

"Oh?" Targan said. "Is that why the guild master is a guardian?"

Millan held up his hands. "Angels help me. You guys really like to argue, don't you? But we're way off track here. This is a conversation about the Assault on Light's Haven. Now, I believe someone was going to tell me what happened after the demon lord came out of the twisted gate."

"The purge happened," one of the students answered. "It wiped out all the fray in the area, a bunch of lesser iymed, and even the Marksman."

"And were there any human casualties because of it?" Millan asked.

"No, the demon lord surfaced too far from the city."

"And who knows why the demon purged?"

The dark-haired girl proudly explained, "The demon lord is a class more powerful than the greater iymed, but its power comes at a price. The agony it's forced to suffer through is so unbearable that it's impossible for a demon lord to walk the Surface."

Millan contemplated Eriph's words from the night before. Maybe it wasn't impossible for a demon lord to exist on the Surface, but there was no point confusing the squires. "Correct. And ultimately, what was the fate of the demon lord?"

The same girl continued, "After Verago's forces

retreated, the priests and paladins went outside the city. When they found its unconscious body, the Prima cleansed it."

Millan was impressed at how well informed the Nolka squires were, and their participation made the class go smoothly. "I think it's important to realize the Devil's most powerful weapon was defeated in less than a day. Now, someone mentioned that the Marksman was killed by the purge. Can anyone tell me which greater iymed was cleansed inside Light's Haven during the attack?"

"The Zaidon."

Millan urged the student to continue. "Tell me about him. What happened?"

"For centuries, he was considered the right-hand demon to Verago. His proficiency was with dark spells and curses, able to heal demons like priests can heal humans. He used a cloaking spell to mask the energy of hundreds of fray and lesser iymed as they tunneled under the city walls. The sneak attack was meant to cause chaos within the city and allow the demons to open the gates. But thanks to Shinigami's warning, Candelux and the Paladin Order laid a trap. When they burst out of the ground, the Zaidon was restrained as the other demons were dispensed with. And then, he was cleansed by the Prima."

"So, the Zaidon was cleansed, and the Marksman was killed in the purge. That's two out of the five greater iymed. Who can tell me about the other three?"

Targan raised his hand.

"Name one, tell me about him or her, and what their contribution was during the Assault."

"The Brute. A fighter demon three times the size of any person. Her body is covered with plate armor, and she wields a massive morning star. During the Assault, she broke through the western gate with her brigade of demons. However, because the Zaidon had already been cleansed, the priests, paladins, and watchers were able to focus their efforts and keep her from advancing into the city. She later escaped during the retreat, and no one has seen her since."

"Very good." The Nesinu priest selected someone else. "You, give me another."

"The Shade. The deadliest assassin demon. He's known for his short stature and wears a wolf mask to cover his hideous face. His deeply serrated daggers are large enough to be classified as swords. His cloaking spell is a natural gift given to him by Verago. They say his targets are dead before they know he's even there. Only a Champion of the Light bloodseeker can sense him when he's cloaked, and even then, only at very short ranges. It's impossible to know how he made it into the city during the Assault, but the most likely explanation is that he slipped in when the Brute broke through the west gate. At one point, he was spotted in the castle, attempting to kill the king's two sons, but mysteriously retreated before doing so."

"Very good. That leaves only one more."

"She's widely accepted as the cruelest of the five. A master of deception and persuasion." Benedoli spoke softly, but her voice didn't waver. "She wears a long red dress. Her hair is black like coal and hangs gracefully around her neck. She's more beautiful than you could possibly imagine, and staring into her eyes puts you under her spell. She uses a long staff as her weapon, bladed on one end with a hook on the other. But, she's rarely known to use it because of her tail. During the Assault, she was seen in the royal gardens where she killed King Cato's only daughter."

Millan sympathized with the squire. He knew what she had endured. Gheron hadn't even come to class.

Benedoli whispered, "The Seductress."

****

"Don't worry, Sereyna. We'll save you!" The last fragment of his dream lingered.

Erynion awoke in the forest, the sun shining brightly through the leafless branches of the surrounding trees. His dream felt familiar, similar to the one from the previous night. Only this time, he was able to hang on to a small piece of it. As he sat up, he rubbed his neck, sore from lying on his back all night.

"Ah, kjjeva rujjnojj nire." The owner of the soothing voice was leaning against a tree.

Erynion recognized her from Nolka. "What happened?"

The demon in the red dress pushed off the trunk. "What's the last part you remember?"

"I remember…the light around me. It felt good. It took away the agony." Erynion noticed the bite marks on his forearm. The wound was completely healed, but the scars were apparent. He had a flashback to the moment when he sank his teeth into his own arm. His eyes drifted down to his wrist and then his hand. He checked its counterpart. His hands were human again.

"What the depths?" he said. "Why do I keep changing? What does it mean? My hands change, but my voice stays the same. What's going on?"

The female iymed licked her lips. "I can't help you there, love."

"Who are you?"

"You mean you've forgotten already?"

"I'm sorry."

"Don't let it worry your little head. I have a few names, but you may call me Sereyna because that's what I prefer."

Sereyna? Like from the dream?

As she moved toward him, her hips swayed prominently. "And is Erynion still your name or has that slipped your mind too?"

He rose to his feet. "I suppose. Some beggar called me that, so that's the name I adopted."

"The same Erynion from your memory?"

"My what?"

The demon covered her mouth as she giggled. "You talk in your sleep."

"My sleep? What does that have to do with my memory?"

"Oh, you haven't figured it out. I suppose you've only been here two nights. Don't feel bad. Do you remember any part of your dreams?"

"Very little. Just voices. But I feel like it's a repeat from the first night."

"Of course it's a repeat." She smiled sweetly. "Demons don't dream, at least not in the same sense as humans. Your dreams consist of memories from your past life when you were human."

"So, everything I dream is a memory?"

"You got it."

"Interesting. So, what *did* happen last night?" Erynion asked.

"Well, we left the city accompanied by that lovely priest. She was so helpful."

"The woman in the brown robe. I remember her. The watchers went to stop us at the gate, but she led us straight through. It gets hazy after that. The pain—"

A motionless body covered in brown caught his eye. He slipped by Sereyna and found the priest lying on her side. Her clothing was in good condition, aside from a bit of dirt. As he circled around the body, Erynion recoiled in disgust. Her hair was wiry and white, but it was her skin that was truly repulsive, clinging tightly to the bone as if she had been decaying for weeks. The plants around her were completely wilted and the surrounding trees had no leaves.

"Did I kill her?"

"No." Sereyna snuck up behind him and ran her hand along his shoulder. "She was dead long before we left the city."

Erynion gestured to the lifeless vegetation. "So, you did all this?"

"I suppose so. You helped, though."

"I did? I don't understand."

Sereyna stuck out her lower lip. "No, no, I suppose you wouldn't. You know about the agony, right? Unfortunately, you're too weak. Luckily, I got to you before those Candelux pigs could cleanse you."

According to what Erynion had been told to this point, the agony was evidence of his strength. "I'm weak?"

She massaged his arm. "Don't look so glum. It's not like you're fray. Those idiots can barely speak. I'm here to take care of you. Oh, I know! I lost one of my lieutenants last night. Tragic, really. You can take his place. What do you say?"

"I guess?" Erynion was unsure what other option he had. "You have lieutenants?"

"Well, that's what I call them. They're the lesser iymed who serve under me. Reaper performed admirably; but alas, he didn't escape the city."

"I'm sorry to hear that."

"Don't be. That was his purpose. Speaking of, what's yours?"

Erynion was taken aback by how apathetic she was about the loss of her lieutenant. "My purpose?"

"Sure." Sereyna's jaw dropped. "Did Verago send you all the way up here without one? No, wait! Don't tell me. You forgot, didn't you?"

"No. I have one. I'm supposed to kill the king."

"My, my, that would be quite a feat to complete on your own."

"So I've heard. That's why I was looking for the Brotherhood."

"You're much better off with me." Sereyna's hands moved down his chest and began to unbutton his torn shirt. He held his breath as she uncovered the unsightly scarring from his self-inflicted attacks. However, she didn't appear bothered and traced the healed wounds with her fingertips. With a crooked smile, she revealed a pristine

The Twisted Gate

fang among her teeth. "I will take great care of you."

CHAPTER 10

As the tower bells struck eight times, the squires—followed by Millan—filed out of the school. The dark-haired girl offered to escort their substitute teacher back to the rectory, but he politely declined. There were more pressing matters to attend to, and he couldn't have anyone slow him down. Millan left his students and rushed up the street. As he crossed the plaza, he didn't even give the fountain a second look. The streets were bustling just like the morning before, and he carefully weaved his way through the crowd. Sharply turning a corner, he collided with a woman.

Millan stooped and offered his hand. "I'm so sorry. Let me help you up."

The woman reached to accept the priest's help. Her sleeveless shirt left her well-tanned skin exposed, and her bicep bulged as she gripped Millan's hand. A blue bandana was tied across her forehead and partially covered her black hair. Appearing to be in her late thirties, the woman rose to her feet and dusted off her pants.

"Yeah, how about you watch where—" She immediately averted her eyes and bowed respectfully. "Don, I apologize."

"No, no, it was my fault. Please, don't bow. It makes me feel awkward."

She pushed a strand of hair behind her ear. "You deserve it, though. You helped keep our city safe last night. Thank you so much."

Millan lost himself in her hazel eyes. "Oh, well, of course. It's why I joined Candelux. To help people."

"It was very brave of you. May I ask your name?"

"Yes. Uh…Millan. My name is Millan."

The woman cocked her head. "Don Millan? I've heard of you. You're the priest from Nesinu, right?"

"Yes, that's right." He was curious as to how she came upon his name, but now was not the time. "Listen, I hate to be rude, but I'm in a terrible hurry."

"Oh. Leaving so soon?" She pouted playfully. "Where are you headed?"

"We're going back to Nesinu to see what's happened."

"Well, may the angels watch over you. It was nice to meet you, Don Millan."

As the woman turned to leave, the priest tapped her shoulder. "I'm sorry, but I didn't catch your name."

"Eleza, but don't tell anyone." She winked at him, and in a matter of moments, he lost sight of her in the crowd.

"Eleza," he said to himself. Millan resumed his course and was met by a group of priests in front of the rectory. He noticed that Eriph was still wearing the brown robe, but no scarf. The priests were all mounted atop marvelous-looking stallions with one spare to the side.

Feranis waved him over. "Ah, Don Millan, good morning. We've been expecting you. How was class?"

"Good morning, Your Grace. The class went well. Are we leaving for Nesinu now?"

"Indeed. Hop up on this fine horse, and we'll be on our way."

Millan lifted himself into the saddle. His father had taught him how to ride when he was younger.

Feranis rode to the front of the group and brought his

horse around to face the others. "Listen up, everyone! We're going to ride to Nesinu at a steady pace. We have plenty of time, but there's no need to waste it. There are three people missing, including Don Skully. As you all know, the Seductress graced us last night with her presence. We don't know where she or this Erynion demon have gone, but they left out of the north gate, which means it's possible they've returned to the twisted gate. We are to stay together and remain vigilant. It's unlikely the demons will attack us during the day, but we must be on guard nonetheless. Our mission is to investigate Nesinu, look for those who are missing, and destroy the twisted gate. Any questions before we go?"

When no one responded, Feranis instructed Don Niktosa to take the lead as the archdon rode to the back. Millan held the reins tightly, wishing to be close to Feranis so they could speak privately. They were barely out of the rectory courtyard when Millan leaned over. "Your Grace, may I ask you something?"

"Yes, what is it?"

He lowered his voice so no one else could hear. "It's about Don Eriph. Should we be bringing him on affairs that concern Candelux?"

"It would seem these affairs concern the entire kingdom." The archdon's tone was amicable despite his decision being challenged. "Between the Seductress, her minions, and a possible demon lord, it's important that we're at our best. Eriph was kind enough to agree to join our expedition. Just because he's no longer in the guild, doesn't mean he's lost his ability to fight demons. His skills will aid us in any type of predicament we encounter. Would you rather he not come with us?"

"It's not that. I was only thinking what the Prima might say."

"I won't tell if you don't. Plus, once we return to Nolka, Eriph is going to tell us about the Brotherhood."

"Is that allowed?" Millan's voice was no longer discreet.

"Accepting information from Alovajj?"

The archdon snorted. "Allowed? Is survival allowed? Many years ago when the matter first arose, I opposed the Death Gods. Their ideas, though potentially effective, were also very dangerous. Even now, I can't condone Eriph's decision to train with a founder. I would've excluded him as well. The Prima had no choice. Order must be maintained. However, to refuse useful information, that is a different matter entirely. For the first time since Deimor Outpost, we are receiving information from Alovajj that coincides with the appearance of this new demon. And his surfacing has brought one of the five greater iymed out of hiding. No, it would be foolish to refuse any information that might help us."

The party passed through the gates and left Nolka behind. Their goal was to reach Nesinu before noon. They didn't wish to tire the horses too much in case they needed to make a quick escape. As they neared what would have been the outskirts of the village, the woods ended abruptly. The road led directly into a large, empty field. The procession of priests stopped at the forest's edge. There was only scorched earth, black as soot. Not a single living thing existed inside the expanse. Not a single object could be seen. There was no trace of life or any type of structure. Where Nesinu once stood, there was only emptiness.

Millan flicked his reins, and his horse trotted into the clearing. "What is this? Did we pass it? Or perhaps it's a bit farther?"

The young priest didn't wish to accept it, but he knew the truth. The stories about the demon lord at the Assault detailed a field just like this after its purge.

Feranis rode out to meet him. "I'm sorry, Millan. I am so very sorry."

The Nesinu priest was unable to speak as he fought back the tears. He refused to make eye contact with the archdon. Millan gazed out across the black sand.

"We may still find him," Feranis said. "Hope isn't lost

yet."

Millan followed the archdon back to the other priests, where they each offered him condolences.

"All right, everyone," Feranis announced. "We're going to walk the perimeter of the field. Keep a watchful eye and an attentive ear for any survivors or demons. Don't forget, there's a twisted gate nearby that still needs to be destroyed."

The group stretched out into a straight line with minimal space between each horse. Feranis took the front position, and Millan brought up the rear. His heart was like an unbearable weight in his chest. He prayed that Feranis was right. That his mentor and friend had not suffered the same fate as Nesinu.

"I'm sorry, Don, about the loss of your village and home."

Millan found himself next to the recently excluded priest. "Oh, Don Eriph. Thank you."

"Please, it's just Eriph now."

"Oh, right, sorry." The Nesinu priest's thoughts drifted back to the previous night. Something didn't sit right with him. "Eriph, did you know Don Skully at all?"

"No more than any other priest, I would imagine."

Millan fiddled with his reins. "It just happened to be on my mind. Last night at the Scriptorum, Archdon Feranis said that Don Skully was no ordinary priest. Do you know what he meant by that?"

Eriph shrugged. "Well, Don Skully was pretty well known in Light's Haven. I mean, the Primus doesn't just pick any random priest to become his advisor?"

"What do you mean by that?"

"What do you think I mean? He was a powerful priest who served as an advisor to Primus Ayristark."

"Advisor to Primus Ayristark? No, that can't be right. He couldn't be an advisor to the Primus. Only archdons can be advisors, and Don Skully never completed his Ascension. Besides, Ayristark only had four advisors.

Kyara, Maxiteer, Omana, and Feranis." Millan extended a finger as he counted off each name and held up his hand when he finished.

"I don't know what to tell you other than you're mistaken. Primus Ayristark had five advisors, and Don Skully was the fifth."

"But that's not possible. Dons aren't allowed to become advisors."

The excluded priest pushed his mouth to one side. "I'm not sure how you don't know this, but he used to be an archdon."

"What? No, no, that…that can't be." Millan stuttered. "Why…why wouldn't he tell me?"

"I couldn't say."

"He told me he never went through Ascension because life within the guild becomes too political. He wanted a simple life. Why would he lie to me?"

"I don't know. Perhaps he was ashamed of the whole ordeal with the Death Gods."

This was too much for Millan to take in a short time. "Ordeal with the Death Gods? What? What happened?"

"Hard to say for sure. I was only a squire at the time, and most of the details are probably just hearsay. But what I do know is that after it was all said and done, Don Skully resigned his position as archdon and moved as far as he could from Light's Haven. If you want to know more, you should talk to Archdon Feranis. As advisors, they were close friends."

Millan's mind raced through the possibilities. Could it be true that his old mentor, at one time, was one of the highest-ranked officials in the guild? If so, why did he hide it from the young priest? And what was Skully's involvement with the Death Gods? The old man had barely mentioned the exiled group outside the context of a history lesson. There were no indications he was connected to them in any way. Millan sighed. He had all of these questions he wanted to ask Skully, but he probably would never get the chance.

Instead of dwelling on the unknown, Millan decided to change the subject. "So, how are you feeling today?"

"I'm well. Thank you for asking."

"You're not worried at all about your Exclusion?"

Eriph snickered under his breath. "I can't say I was all that surprised by the decision. It's not like they didn't warn me."

"Who?"

"Founder Brahawee and Archdon Feranis. I didn't see a reason to hide it, though. The Prima would've found out anyway at my Ascension."

"So, what will you do now?"

Eriph tilted his head, as if deep in thought. "Probably return to Alovajj. See if one of the founders will sponsor me."

"Sponsor you? To become a Death God?"

"Not just a Death God. Anyone can be a Death God. In fact, anyone who lives in Alovajj is treated like a member. They're allowed to live there as they please as long as they don't break the one rule."

"Only one rule?" Millan asked in disbelief. "What is it?"

"Don't be a—"

A noise came from the woods, and the entire procession came to a standstill.

"Do you see something?" Millan whispered.

The excluded priest put his finger to his lips. Without warning, a camouflaged deer sprang into view and bolted into the forest. Everyone laughed off the tense moment, and the search started again.

"What was I saying?" Eriph asked Millan. "Oh yes, anyone who lives in the city is considered a Death God, but most aren't involved in the hierarchy of the actual guild. They don't have a voice in the guild's decisions."

"And you want a voice."

"Wouldn't you? I want to be an officer and live in Moultia Palace, but to do that, one of the founders has to sponsor me."

The Nesinu priest scratched his head. "And they would let a member of Candelux into their ranks?"

"Where do you think Founders Brahawee and Mortis came from?"

"I guess, but they're founders, aren't they? They've been around since the beginning. How do they know you're not a spy?"

Eriph smirked. "And what good would a spy be for a guild that won't listen?"

"Don Millan!" Feranis called.

Millan dug his heels into the side of his horse and gave the reins a quick flick. He pulled his horse alongside the archdon's. "Yes, Your Grace?"

"I'm not sensing any dark energy in the vicinity. When I spoke with that young boy yesterday, he said there was a valley east of the village where he saw the twisted gate. Do you know what he's referring to?"

"I do."

"Good. I'd like for you to lead us straight to it."

"At once, Your Grace."

****

They are meant to serve you. Gather the demon army if you wish to complete your objective.

Erynion spun around. There was only the empty forest behind him. He searched high and low. Where was the voice coming from?

"Something the matter, love?" Sereyna asked.

"It's nothing."

"Nothing?"

"I thought I heard something, but I was wrong."

The demon in the red dress beckoned him over. "Come. I want to show you something. Look familiar?"

When he joined her, the pair stood at the top of an incline overlooking a valley. In the middle of the forest below them grew one massive tree. Its trunk consisted of vines twisted together and towered over the other trees. Sereyna led Erynion down the slope, and within a few minutes, dozens of demons surrounded them. Big and small, they mostly ignored the newcomers. As he neared the twisted tree, Erynion was captivated by the hole at its base. Something had violently torn its way out.

"You must excuse me. Wait here, please." As Sereyna departed through the group of fray, Erynion was mesmerized by her movements until she was obscured by the trees. His attention was drawn to the creatures that occupied the area around the tree. Some of the imps were chasing one another while the larger fray, annoyed by their antics, tried to swat at them. Where had all these demons come from? Why had they gathered here?

"Hey," someone said in a loud whisper.

Erynion scanned the ground.

"Up here."

Erynion cast his eyes upward and spotted a creature hanging upside down from a tree limb. Aside from the dirt stains, his clothing was vibrant with a checkered pattern of yellow and purple that reminded Erynion of a court jester. The funny hat that fit snugly on his crown had seen better days, clinging to its final jingle bell.

"What's your name?" asked the tree dweller.

"Erynion. Who are you?"

The demon on the branch made sure the coast was clear before swinging down to the ground. Erynion was surprised to find the iymed only came up to his ribs. Although short in stature, this demon's appearance was more human than the disfigured fray around them.

"Name's Flinch. I'm one of Sereyna's *lieutenants*," he mocked.

"A lieutenant, huh?"

The corner of his lip was pushed up in a half smile. "Sure, sure. We can't call ourselves *lesser* iymed. It's bad for our self-esteem."

"Oh?"

The small demon cackled. "Are you serious? Tell me you don't actually believe that."

Erynion stared blankly at the iymed.

Flinch stopped laughing. "Something wrong with you?"

"Smells human," said another voice. A bizarre-looking demon emerged from the crowd of fray. He was of average height, and his scalp was like a bare island surrounded by a ring of spiky black hair. He wore considerably less clothing than Flinch, and his arms and chest were covered by enough hair to be considered fur. But what stood out the most were his eyes, clamped shut and covered in gashes that had long since healed.

"Of course he smells human. He just came from the towns." Flinch pointed at the cloth wrapped around Erynion's head. "Hey, you two both got a bit of an eye problem."

"Go climb a tree, Flinch." As the second iymed moved toward Erynion, he kicked his foot in the direction of the jester demon. Flinch dodged the attack and scampered up to the branch above them. The bald demon looked up at the tree with his nonexistent eyes. "Not bad for being blind, huh?"

"It's a good thing you are, so you don't have to see how ridiculous you look," Flinch taunted.

"You think I look ridiculous? Sounds like you're losing your last bell. And what's a jester with no bells?"

The demon in the tree reached up and pinched the only remaining jingler, barely clinging to its thread. Flinch's face turned sour as the bell popped loose. He cradled it in his palm like a precious pearl. "You win this round."

"And who might you be?" the blind iymed questioned.

"Erynion. Are you another of Sereyna's lieutenants?"

"You could say that, sure. I'm Sonojj. Been in the towns, have we?"

"I was in Nolka just last night."

Sonojj sniffed the air. "Well, it certainly smells like it.

How'd you stay hidden for so long?"

"How do you mean?"

"You must've been there for at least a week."

"Let's see how good your hearing is in round two!" Flinch chucked his jingle bell at the blind iymed. The bell bounced off his bald skull and landed harmlessly on the ground.

"Would you excuse me for moment?" As Sonojj leapt toward the branch, his body drastically transformed into a jungle cat. Flinch scrambled, bounding from tree to tree, but the blind shape-shifting demon easily followed his trail. As Flinch attempted to escape, Sonojj tackled the jester and knocked him to the ground. The short demon, sporting a devious grin, removed his hat and muzzled the cat demon.

Flinch scurried out from under his attacker. Once he was a safe distance away, he grabbed his sides and laughed hysterically as his friend struggled to remove the jester hat with his paws. "Now who looks ridiculous? Don't you know that cats don't wear hats?"

"Enough!" The voice was deep and guttural.

Flinch tried to stifle his laughter. Sonojj returned to his humanoid form and tossed the jester hat aside.

Accompanied by Sereyna, an ogre-like demon pushed his way past the fray. His height was similar to Erynion's and his shoulders were broad. Every inch of him was covered in muscles that forced his clothing to tightly grip his body. His face was repulsive with a large pushed-in nose and pointy ears that appeared to be pulled back by invisible hooks. His beady eyes showed no sign of anything but distaste. "You two are nothing but buffoons. Dardan fools, if you ask me."

The ogre iymed squared off with Erynion. "Welcome," he said disingenuously.

"And who are you?"

"Your superior. That's who."

Sereyna squeezed the ogre's shoulder. "Now, now,

Maligus, there's no need to frighten our new recruit."

"As you wish." Maligus snarled at Erynion. "But you better follow orders. Sereyna runs a tight group here, and I make sure it stays that way. Reaper was a good soldier."

"Wait, Reaper's gone?" Flinch asked.

The ogre whirled around. "Silence, imp!"

Flinch stooped down to pick up his hat. When Maligus turned back to face Erynion, the jester stuck out his tongue.

"Speaking of soldiers," Sereyna said, "I hear you had a special visitor while I was gone."

Flinch dusted off his hat and restored it to his head. "That's right. Marksy came through."

Sereyna mused, "So, after all this time, Alejjir finally came back, did he?"

"Yes, ma'am. Only a lesser iymed, though."

"And he didn't wish to stay?"

"No, ma'am. When he heard about the purged land to the west and that you might be bringing back a demon lord, he said he wouldn't be caught anywhere near it. So, is this the demon lord?"

"Who? Erynion?" Sereyna snickered. "No, he's just like you all. That's why I've invited him to join us and take Reaper's place. Maligus also informed me that we received a message from the overseer in Nolka. Priests are on their way to seal this gate."

Sonojj turned his ear to the conversation. "Do we know how many?"

"More than I care to face at this point in time. We don't want to be around here when that archdon shows up. I may have taken something of his. We're going to head southeast and stay clear of Nolka. I believe the demon lord is headed to Alovajj, and so we will follow. Maligus, be a dear and rally the troops."

"As you wish." The ogre demon bowed and left to organize the fray.

Flinch hopped over to Erynion. "Don't worry about

him. Maligus is Sereyna's right hand. He likes to pretend that he's so important, but really, he's exactly like us. Just has some unresolved anger issues because his—" His voice trailed off as Sereyna sauntered toward Erynion.

"So, have you remembered anything more from your dream?" she asked.

"Should I have?"

"The twisted gate here is a connection between the Surface and the Depths. It represents a link to a time before the agony damaged your thoughts. Meditating here will increase your chances of regaining some of your memory, which is critical if you hope to control your power." Sereyna placed her hands on Erynion's waist. "This is a rare opportunity to learn about your past, but I urge you to not wait too long before following us. The priests are on their way to destroy the gate, and it would be a shame if those pigs got a hold of you."

"How long is too long?"

"Sonojj and Flinch will stay behind with you to stand guard. At the first sign of trouble, I want you all to run. Safe travels." She waved as she walked away. But before she was out of earshot, she peered over her shoulder. "Oh, and boys. You'll want to make sure you reach us before sundown."

"What does that mean?" Sonojj asked, but she ignored him.

The fray numbers that had filled the woods around the twisted gate slowly dwindled, leaving the three demons alone, sitting in a circle. Erynion closed his left eye and took cleansing breaths. He tried to clear his mind, but nothing was happening. "Why isn't this working?"

Sonojj lay back on the grass and propped his head with his hands. "You shouldn't be so impatient. Meditation gets easier the more you do it, but the first time is always a bit slow. It could take hours, but like Sereyna said, the gate should speed that up."

"And what exactly am I supposed to remember?"

"Who you are." Flinch chuckled. "Or rather, who you were when you were alive."

"Or anything about your past really," Sonojj added. "Your identity is crucial to understanding and controlling your power."

"You both know about your past lives?" Erynion asked.

Flinch offered his story first. "I was a jester in the royal court. But secretly, I was a thief in Anoctis. I had it all planned out. Even married the daughter of the guy in charge of the king's wealth. I was going to steal so much gold."

"What happened?"

"What do you think happened? I died."

"Oh. What about you, Sonojj?"

"I was a pan-mage in Summa Arcana. The whole philosophy appealed to me. You know, one with nature, and all that. I roamed the Umbral Valley to learn how to shape-shift into a jungle cat. It's a skill I was able to keep even after death."

Erynion paused. The mention of Summa Arcana, the mage guild, reminded him of something in his past, but he was unable to place it. The harder he tried to conjure up the reference, the more it slipped away. "Depths! I thought I had that one."

"One what?" Flinch asked.

"Memory. Something about Summa Arcana."

"You think you were a mage too?"

"I don't know. It came and went so fast."

"You can't force it," Sonojj said. "Next time you feel one, just relax and let it come to you."

"So, tell me. You both remember who you were. Are Flinch and Sonojj your real names?"

"No," the blind demon answered. "Demons learned early on to use pseudonyms. Your real name is your identity, the key to your soul, to your power."

"If a priest knows your human name, they can use it against you and quicken your cleansing," Flinch said.

"I see," Erynion muttered. He was unsure if Erynion was in fact his real name or not. The beggar had called him that, but he had also heard the name in his dream. Real or not, he had already given the name to the priests when they had asked the previous night.

There was a lull in the conversation until Flinch changed the subject. "I'd like to meet the demon who broke through here. Did you see the scorched field to the west?"

"Very funny, Flinch," the blind iymed said. "However, the smoldering smell was unmistakable. Definitely a purge. And, I'm pretty sure there used to be a town there."

"No joke. Verago definitely sent another demon lord, and it sounds like it's lasted longer than the last one."

"What happened to the last one?" Erynion asked.

Flinch hung his head. "Cleansed on its first day. Up, down, and out of town. Being a new demon, I don't suppose you were alive when the we attacked Light's Haven, were you?"

"Light's Haven?"

"Yeah, you know, the capital. Human or demon, everyone knows about the Assault on Light's Haven."

"The Assault on Light's Haven," Erynion repeated softly. A memory flitted about in the back of his head, and he listened to Sonojj's advice. He closed his eye and relaxed. As the images swirled around in his mind, the voices of Sonojj and Flinch became more distant.

The jester said something, but his voice was muffled.

Sonojj responded, but it was so quiet that Erynion couldn't make it out. And then, everything went black, and he was alone.

CHAPTER 11

The trumpets sounded in the great hall of Thoris Castle as Prima Mashira stood in the entrance to the throne room. It had been over two years since King Cato had fallen ill and handed over the crown to his son, Batar. From inside this castle, the monarchy had ruled over the kingdom for centuries. Mashira waited patiently as one of the royal watchers announced her arrival. "Your Highness, I present Her Luminescence, Prima Mashira of Candelux."

As she strolled down the purple carpet, her long blond hair swayed very little, tamed by the circlet she wore. She kept a keen eye on the king as he straightened on the throne. His smile extended from ear to ear, and his fingers twitched. Mashira was not as eager for this meeting to take place, but recent events had made it necessary. At the bottom of the stairs, she bowed respectfully.

King Batar reciprocated. "Please, come closer. To what do I owe the pleasure of this visit, Your Luminescence?"

Mashira ignored the request and stayed put. "Your Highness, I come with pressing news. May we speak in private?"

"Of course. Ready the side chamber!" he ordered the servants. Batar descended the stairs with his hands behind his back. He tried to suppress his smile, but he failed. "Shall we?"

Mashira nodded and followed him to an adjacent room. As they crossed the threshold, servants rushed out of the room, bowing deeply. When she heard the doors close behind them, the Prima folded her arms.

Batar stealthily approached her from behind and embraced her. "I count the days until you come and see me." He gave her a soft kiss on the neck. "It's like ever since I was crowned, you don't have time for me."

Mashira gracefully wriggled free. "It's complicated." Once there was some space between them, she faced Batar. "How's your father?"

"He's not well. The Pink Leaves send their healers daily to tend to him, but he doesn't seem to make any improvements."

"I'm sorry to hear that. I'm sure they're doing their best."

Batar eagerly returned to the original topic. "It's been over a month since I last saw you. And how long until next time? Don't you miss me at all?"

"Of course I do," Mashira said. The words felt forced, and she hoped Batar wouldn't notice. "But things are different now. You're no longer a prince. You have an obligation to keep this kingdom safe, as do I."

"I know that. But why should that keep us apart?"

"Please, Batar. I don't wish to revive this discussion right now," she pleaded. "There is a grave matter at hand."

Defeated, the king gazed out a window. "Fine. Tell me."

"Last night, Nolka was attacked by demons."

"I heard something of that nature. One of my guards was fetching the report when you arrived. Was it serious?"

"There were some casualties, but for the most part, the city is back to normal."

"Is that it?" His face was beaming. "You *do* miss me after all."

Mashira kept a stoic face, even though she knew he expected a smile. "This is serious. There's more. Your life is in danger."

"Is that so?" Batar sounded more curious than concerned.

"A twisted gate has appeared by Nesinu."

"A twisted gate?"

"Yes. And now there's a new demon loose in our kingdom, and apparently, his purpose is to kill you."

The king silently walked to the table and picked up a grape from the plate of fruit. Nonchalantly, he popped it in his mouth.

"It seems," she continued, "that Verago has not given up on claiming your life."

"So it seems. I can't say I'm surprised." After he swallowed, he picked up another grape. "Hmm, this is troubling, isn't it? So what is this thing? Iymed? Greater iymed?"

"Possibly. Probably. Maybe something more. There's a chance this thing could even be a demon lord."

The king furrowed his brow. "A demon lord? That's not possible, is it?"

Mashira knew he wanted confirmation that he was safe from the most powerful classification of demon. After all, they believed this demon rivaled the strength of the Devil himself. But how could she offer him comfort when she knew there was none to give?

Batar tossed the grape back on the platter. "Is it?"

"I'm sorry. I can't say for sure. We're looking into the matter. He came through a twisted gate, just like during the Assault. And since his descent to the Depths, Verago has successfully overcome many obstacles to create more powerful demons. So, is it possible? Sure, I suppose it could be."

"But I have this!" Batar yanked on the chain around his neck and lifted it out of his shirt. A large four-pointed star dangled at the end of it. The sunlight reflected off the crystalline object.

Mashira felt a warmth in her chest at the sight of the Talisman of Zavi. This was the only thing that could defeat Verago and stop the seemingly endless war. Typically worn by the reigning Prima or Primus, the artifact was a powerful conduit for casting blessings, but it also naturally protected its user from dark energy. Any demon who touched it would be cleansed instantly. Out of fear of the object, the Devil had stayed off the Surface for hundreds of years with only one exception.

"I still wear the Talisman," Batar said. "No demon can touch me. Even Verago would lose all his power, and he would never sacrifice himself. We already know that."

"That's true," the Prima conceded. "It's what saved you during Devil's Breach."

"So, there's nothing to worry about then." The king pinched the discarded grape and slipped it past his lips.

Mashira shook her head. "I wouldn't say that exactly. This demon entered Nolka undetected."

"What do you mean? Undetected?"

"I mean, he walked right past the watchers. Past a seeker. There was no indication he was anything but human. It wasn't until nightfall that they sensed him."

"And you think he'll come to Light's Haven and do the same? It's not as though anyone, demon or human, is simply permitted into this castle."

"No, but that's not the point."

He innocently challenged her. "Then what is the point?"

Mashira composed herself before lecturing the king. "The point is that you have to take this more seriously. Verago wants you dead. He stepped on the Surface for the first time in centuries just to kill you. He saw firsthand that you're wearing the Talisman, and yet, he's still sent this demon to kill you. There's more to this plan that we cannot see. Even the Seductress has come out of hiding to help him."

Batar shuddered. "The Seductress."

"Yes. Verago has lived for centuries, and he's no fool. He wouldn't have created and sent this demon to the Surface unless he thought it could fulfill its purpose. And now, one of the greater iymed is with him. This is the beginning of something terrible. Verago has been plotting since the Assault failed. We both know that. What we don't know is why you're so important to him. Why does he want you dead?"

"I keep telling you I have no idea!"

Mashira sensed his frustration. It couldn't be easy to be the only person on the Devil's kill list, even if he was wearing the Talisman of Zavi.

"So, this possible demon lord. Have you guys given him a name yet?" Batar asked.

"Not yet, no. He calls himself Erynion, though. We're not sure if that's a real name, but I'm having the scribes look into the records."

"Erynion?" The king tapped his lower lip. "Now why does that sound familiar?"

"I don't know. I've never heard the name before. Why? Have you?"

"I'm not sure. I could've sworn I've heard it before, I just have no idea where."

Mashira felt a glimmer of hope as she closed the gap between them. "Please, think. If we can make a connection to his human life, maybe we can uncover his identity. Is it someone in Light's Haven?"

Batar shook his head. "I'm sorry. Perhaps I was mistaken."

The Prima sighed. She was no closer to figuring out who this demon was or how he intended to fulfill his goal. "Well, whether or not you feel you're untouchable, I think it'd be wise to increase your guards and put them all on high alert. All the cities should be prepared for attacks. Also, the Seductress is not the only one who has reared her ugly head again. The Brotherhood is at it as well. They were involved in the attack on Nolka."

"What? I thought we had those traitors under control."

"We did. After a good portion of them followed Shinigami to Alovajj, we were able to infiltrate many of the city clans as they tried to replenish the ranks. And for a while, we felt like we had a good sense of what they were up to. However, over the last couple of years, everything has become extremely secretive. Even members within the same city often don't know what their comrades are doing. There's a level of isolation that makes it nearly impossible for us to get information."

"So, you're telling me the Brotherhood of Prevarra is a threat once again."

"A minor one, yes. Not to worry, though. We're going to cripple their operation as much as possible. I already spoke with the head of the Paladin Order. Anyone associated with the Brotherhood will be imprisoned on the spot."

"You already spoke with Champion Skarabin? Heh. Who's running this kingdom?" he asked sheepishly.

"I'm sorry, Batar, I've already given out the order. I should've let—"

"No, no, it's all right."

The monarchs were respected and recognized as the sole rulers of the kingdom. However, ever since its creation, the Candelux guild always had an unwritten control over the people. It was something the citizens accepted and would remain that way as long as the demon threat existed.

"Was there anything else?" Batar asked.

"That was it. Thank you for speaking with me."

"You know I always have time for you."

"Well, I have things to attend to." The Prima politely bowed as she backed away. "Please, be careful and stay safe."

"I will."

Mashira gripped the door handle and paused. Amid

controversy and against the advice of her advisors, she had allowed Batar—as a prince—to start courting her five years ago. But, everything changed the night of Devil's Breach. And despite Batar's best efforts, Mashira began to pull away from him. After King Cato fell ill and abdicated the crown to his son, the divide between the couple grew worse. And over the last year, their relationship barely limped along. As she opened the door, she considered uttering one more line, one of affection, but she decided against it. It would have been empty since her heart no longer belonged to him.

"May the angels watch over you, Your Highness."

CHAPTER 12

"Don't move!" Archdon Feranis ordered.

Millan and the rest of the Candelux posse had already dismounted. They left their horses nearby in order to venture closer to the unholy tree that served as a passageway from the Depths to the Surface. The group had come across three demons, two moved closer together and left the third sitting by itself.

"What do you suppose those two are talking about?" Don Niktosa asked.

Feranis turned his back on the creatures. "I'm not sure. Best tie them down before they bolt and leave their friend. You three, restrain the little guy with the jester hat. You three, deal with the hairy one."

Since he wasn't one of the six priests chosen, Millan watched the holy chains of light fly toward the two demons.

The jester hastily climbed a tree to dodge the attack, but the chains wrapped around the branches and pursued him. He acrobatically evaded the attacks until one blessing finally caught him by the ankle, slowing him down long enough for the other links to catch up. With their target captured, the three priests removed the slack on the chains, stretching the demon out in the treetop.

While the jester failed in his attempted escape, the furry demon dropped to all fours and took on the form of a large cat. Galloping away, he seemed to use the trees as a natural defense against the blessings and swiped at any spell that came close to capturing him. One set of restraints briefly caught him across the face, but after flailing about, the cat demon cut himself loose and fled deeper into the forest.

"Your Grace, the hairy one has escaped."

"Never mind him. Let's see what we have here."

"Zigip ujjnu adim tel!" the jester screamed. The energy pulsed around the bound parts of his body. "Lo ujjli klijja! Lo ujjli klijja!"

"You'll have your turn to speak, my friend, don't worry," Feranis retorted. The demon thrashed about in the web of holy energy and spewed insults, but the archdon ignored him. Feranis cautiously approached the third demon, who was still sitting peacefully.

Curiosity forced Millan to step forward, but a hand caught him.

"It's probably best if you wait here," Eriph said.

Millan opened his mouth but was unable to find the words to argue. The Nesinu priest nodded and stayed with the group.

****

It seemed very much like a dream. Deep within his mind, Erynion found himself behind a marble pillar. A young boy, barely a teenager, was crouched beside him. Erynion had the distinct feeling he wasn't much older than his companion. Before he could speak, another voice made an announcement. "Your Majesty, presenting High War-Mage Drevarius of Summa Arcana."

From behind the pillar, Erynion spotted one of the leaders of the mage guild, and the scenery flickered. The marble column transformed into the corner of a stone building, and he was transported outside.

A man raced past and nearly knocked him over. "The gates have been breached!"

Erynion stuck his head out from around the corner, and his eyes widened. It was chaos. Everyone was running every which way.

A watcher ran up and pushed him back behind the corner. "What are you two doing here? Where's Sereyna?"

Erynion identified her as a captain due to the decoration on her armor. "We left her at home."

"Thank the angels for that, but we still have to get you two out of here. Follow me and stay near the walls." She navigated the two boys through the streets as arrows sporadically struck the ground near them. Erynion felt the pounding in his chest. The fear of dying was a sensation he vividly remembered. They finally halted at a bridge, and on the opposite side were many watchers and priests apparently waiting for them.

"We're almost there. We just have to get across Vask Bridge." The watcher captain kept the boys beneath the roof of the nearby building. Screams came from the direction they had just come from. The watchers and priests were encouraging them to make a break for it. Arrows continuously rained down and then evaporated when they hit the ground.

"Captain!" Another watcher joined their small group. "They've breached the city gates!"

"Tell me something I don't know. We need to cross the bridge. I need your shield."

The watcher glanced down at Erynion and his companion. "Is that—"

"Yes," she said sharply. "We don't have time for this. Give me your shield."

Before he could obey, the watcher stumbled forward and groaned.

The captain caught him. "What happened? Are you

hit?"

"Back off!" Shoving his superior backward, he unsheathed his sword and charged at the captain.

She parried the attack and kept the two boys away from the deranged fighter. "Are you insane!? Get a hold of yourself!"

Erynion spotted a slender, black arrow shaft protruding from the back of the man. He attacked again, and the captain slammed him against the wall. His weapon clattered as it skipped across the ground. The two scuffled as she tried to remove his shield. With a jarring motion, she smashed the metal plate into his face, and he crumpled to the ground.

Erynion pointed to the bridge. "Look. The arrows. They've stopped."

"Now's our chance. You boys need to run as fast as you can," the captain instructed. "I'll be right behind you. Go! Now!"

Erynion snatched the hand of the other boy and sprinted into the open. He felt the tension in his arm as his companion struggled to keep up. They were about halfway across the bridge when the light on the ground faded, as if a cloud had passed in front of the sun.

"Angels help us," the captain said.

The sky was filled with thousands of arrows about to blanket the bridge. The watcher's shield was in no way big enough to protect them all from the impending doom. The captain slipped her arms through the straps of the shield so that it was positioned on her back and gathered the two youths close to her. She held them tightly with her back to the sky. Erynion found it difficult to breathe, and the other youth clung desperately to his arm. As he closed his eyes, he couldn't help but wonder if this was the end for him.

As Erynion braced for the impact, he heard the arrows land all around them. He opened one eye and then the other. He examined himself and the young boy before noticing a white scarf swaying beside him. A large woman in a black robe stood over them. Above her head, she held a circular shield which projected a dome of light and surrounded the small group. No arrows had penetrated her barrier.

"Let's go," the archdon said. Her dome faded, and all four completed the run across the bridge.

As they entered the shade cast by the gate on the other side, the scenery changed. Erynion couldn't see the faces, but he knew their guide wasn't the same. Instead of the watcher captain, there were four men covered in plate armor. Erynion figured that the two with large shields must have been guardians and the other two were likely bloodseekers, all from the Paladin Order.

"Iymed!"

"Where? Where is it?"

"There! Assassin! No wait, over there!"

"Shields up! Protect the boys!"

There was a commotion as the sound of colliding blades rang in Erynion's ears. He wasn't able to see much of the action because the two guardians blocked his view. As one rotated and deflected an attack, the paladin sent a small shadowy figure over their heads and against the wall. Despite the impact, the assailant was not fazed. Hunched over, he stood ready to strike again. In each hand, the fiend held a large serrated dagger. One was pristinely clean and gleamed in the light, while the other was lined with the blood of its first victim. Between the two guardians, Erynion made out the image of a wolf's head just as the two paladins stepped back in front of the youths. Behind him, one of the bloodseekers knelt beside the other.

"Oh depths! That's the fangling Shade, isn't it?" one of the guardians yelled. "We're so fangled. What the depths do we do?"

"Enough of that nonsense. Steel yourself. We protect the children," the gruff voice commanded. The guardian looked back at their fallen comrade. "How is he?"

"He's in bad shape, Diyel. He needs help now, or he

won't make it," the kneeling paladin stated. A large two-handed sword lay on the ground beside the speaker. The blade ended in two points like the tines of a fork.

"You know our orders," the guardian barked.

Erynion peered between the two massive shields. The demon was perfectly still like a statue. The blood from his dagger dripped steadily into a small puddle on the stone path. Suddenly, the assassin dashed away.

"Where the depths did he go?" the panicked guardian asked.

"What difference does it make? He left. Let's hurry before he decides to come back."

The kneeling bloodseeker cradled the head of his injured friend. "You two go on. I'm taking him to the Sanctuary."

"No," Diyel said. "You need to stay with us. The Pink Leaves have a station inside the castle walls. You can drop him off there."

The scenery once again shifted. The young boy was still with him, but the paladins were replaced by a group of other people. Erynion wanted desperately to ask his companion who he was and where they were, but his voice was silent. The doors to the large room burst open, and people started clamoring.

"It's over! The demons have all retreated!"

Some cheered and embraced while others streamed out into the open air. Outside, Erynion noted the paladins guarding the room. Everything began to fade to darkness. Erynion frantically searched for more clues, but he was only able to catch portions of statements from the faint voices around him.

"A demon lord surfaced…"

"…but he defected! The Brotherhood must be…"

"…heard the Marksman was caught…"

"…helped set the trap and killed hundreds of…"

"…hasn't been seen, and the Brute just retreated without…"

"...believe the Zaidon was cleansed, and I..."

"...attacked by the Seductress? What will..."

In the black void of his dream, Erynion's companion stood by him through the whole event. The boy moved his lips, but Erynion couldn't hear a single word. He strained to listen, but not even a mumble slipped past his ears. The boy receded into the darkness, leaving Erynion alone to reflect on his memories. He had seen so much but understood so little. What did it all mean?

A whisper broke the emptiness. "Awake, Erynion. Your time here has come to an end."

Erynion opened his eyes to see an unfamiliar man standing before him dressed in a long black robe and a white scarf.

"My name is Archdon Feranis. Please, don't be alarmed, and don't try to move. We have you adequately detained."

Brightly illuminated chains, just like the ones the priest had attacked Sereyna with the night before, covered his body. Erynion felt no discomfort, and so he remained still.

"You've caused quite a stir by coming to the Surface and telling people that you're here to kill the king," the archdon said. "That is your purpose, isn't it?"

Erynion's expression was flat. For the past day and a half, people asked him questions and offered little in return. He had no desire to engage in conversation, especially with a priest of Candelux.

"From what I understand, this is all quite new to you," Feranis said. "This is your first time on the Surface as a demon, correct?"

Erynion made no effort to speak.

"Well, I've been told that you can't remember your past life, so perhaps you weren't knowledgeable in demonology. Allow me to offer you this free lesson so we can move this along and make it easier for everyone. Demons cannot gain power during the day. That's why they hide or run. And since you and your friend here have been captured, there's no escape. The burning you feel is the holy energy of these chains attacking the dark energy that flows from your dark heart. It brings me no pleasure to see anyone or anything suffer. So here's my suggestion. Tell us what we want to know, and I'll make the pain stop. Understand?"

Erynion glanced up at Flinch, who struggled against the restraints to no avail. "What pain?"

"Are you saying that you don't feel anything?"

"What could you possibly know of pain?"

"I suspect that wound on your face must have hurt pretty badly."

The demon scoffed. "It was a relief."

"From the agony?"

Erynion grumbled.

"It's strange," Feranis said. "Everything I've heard tells me you're exceptionally strong, but what I sense from you is so much weaker. I feel the dark energy within you, but it's more in line with someone who's alive, not a demon. It's nothing close to what it should be. Why would the Seductress come out of hiding for you?"

The demon was tired of the questions he couldn't answer.

The archdon inspected the scars that peeked out from the cloth wrapped around Erynion's head. "I wonder what did that to your face."

"Is that another question?"

"If you wish to answer it. Although I'm more curious as to how much damage was inflicted. Let's take a gander, shall we?"

****

Millan watched intently as Archdon Feranis interrogated the large demon. The dons kept their distance but were still close enough to hear the conversation. Feranis motioned to the priests who had Erynion restrained, and they pulled the demon so that his body straightened up. Millan slipped to the other side of Eriph, so he could get a better look.

Using the star on the end of his staff, Feranis pushed up the cloth wrapped around the demon's head. "Just as I hoped. The Devil's Eye. How fortunate."

Millan leaned over to Eriph. "The Devil's Eye? I've never seen one."

"I saw some while I was in Alovajj. They're quite impressive."

"I'm going to get a closer look."

Surprisingly, Eriph didn't try to stop him this time. Millan took a couple of steps forward when a whistling sound pierced the air. An object skimmed past him, and the priest next to him dropped to his knees.

Millan squatted. "Are you all right?"

The fallen don gritted his teeth. There was another whistle, and one of the priests restraining the jester demon stumbled backward, allowing his blessing to dissipate. A slender black arrow was lodged in his shoulder.

"We're under attack!" someone cried out.

Millan stayed low to the ground. Thinking the priest beside him must have sustained a similar injury, he tried to find the wound. However, it became increasingly difficult as his patient fought him off more and more aggressively. Millan finally located the shaft of the black arrow in the leg of the priest, but he was thrown backward.

"Get off me!" Despite the projectile in his thigh, the fallen priest sprang up with no difficulty.

Millan scrambled to his feet. "I'm sorry, I just—"

"Yeah, you're going to be." The Nolka priest made a fist and advanced toward him.

Eriph intervened and shoved the deranged priest backward. "What are you doing? Get a hold of yourself!"

"Don't fangling touch me!" The Nolka priest swung wildly and missed. A third arrow whistled into the group. A fight broke out as two dons tackled each other. One by one, the holy chains fell away from the captives. Millan focused his energy in preparation to cast his own restraint blessing.

Eriph patted Millan on the shoulder. "Hey, forget about them. We need to deal with this. Keep them away from me." Eriph slid his shield from his back. After a quick incantation, he lifted the shield over his head, and a dome of light encompassed the group. Millan kept a watchful eye as the uninjured priests subdued the wounded. Archdon Feranis crossed into the safety of Eriph's spell and immediately cast holy energy on one of the arrows. The black shaft disintegrated, and the afflicted priest stopped fighting his comrades.

With Feranis healing the injured, Millan directed his attention toward the demons again. The jester iymed soared through the air. With daggers in hand, the beast slashed through Erynion's remaining chains. As the giant demon rose to his feet, Millan caught a glimpse of the Devil's Eye, shimmering with vibrant oranges and reds. The jester iymed tugged on Erynion's arm until the pair finally ran into the forest.

The Nesinu priest pursed his lips. "Your Grace, the demons are escaping."

The archdon gave no response as he healed the leg of the injured priest.

"Your Grace, should we pursue?"

"No." Feranis calmly shuffled over to the next priest being held by his companions. "No, we stay here and make sure everyone is healed. And then, we destroy the gate. Let them go for now. There will be other chances."

CHAPTER 13

This is no simple task, and you need not go it alone.

The voice was faint, but the words were clear to Erynion. Flinch and Sonojj, however, didn't appear to hear a thing. Where was the voice coming from? Erynion didn't wish to alarm his new friends, so he said nothing. It had been over an hour since their narrow escape from the priests.

"Can you smell them?" Flinch nervously checked behind them as he rubbed his wrists, coated with dark, dry blood.

The shape-shifting demon growled. "For the last time, look at my face. I may not have eyes, but you do, so use them for once."

Although Sonojj had reassumed his humanoid form, the chain-linked scar across his nose was still quite visible. "Besides, they're not going to follow us. Destroying the twisted gate will be more important to them."

The three demons walked in silence until they came upon a stream running through the forest. Sonojj bent down and splashed water on his face. Flinch removed his checkered shirt and flung it on a nearby rock. He waded into the creek and began to clean himself. Erynion remained on the bank and reviewed the condition of his clothing. His pants were still stained with the blood from the first night he arrived, however he chose not to wash.

Erynion plopped down next to Flinch's shirt. He gently pressed the eye hidden behind the cloth. He thought back to his encounter with the priests. After his restraints had fallen away, Erynion had briefly observed the group. Everyone glowed with a yellow light, but the archdon in the black robe outshined the others by far. Erynion had been particularly captivated by the sight of the holy dome. It was exactly like the spell from his meditation, the one that had saved his life during the Assault.

Erynion pushed the cloth up so his right eye was exposed. Sonojj was enveloped in black energy with a tinge of green.

Flinch retrieved his shirt from the rock. "So, that archdon was right. Make sure you keep that eye hidden from the priests."

Flinch's aura was like Sonojj's, except it was only black.

"Why's that?" Erynion asked.

"Ask Sonojj. He knows firsthand."

The blind demon cocked his head. "Ask me what?"

Flinch struck his temples to get the water out of his ears. "Erynion has an exposed Devil's Eye."

"Best to take it out then."

"I don't see why I should," Erynion shot back. "It shows me some sort of energy when I look with it."

"The auras." Sonojj joined them by the rock. "That eye lets you see a being's energy."

"Any being?"

"Sure. Humans, demons, even animals. The color tells you what power they wield. Priests use light energy and have a yellowish glow. War-mages are usually red or blue depending if they mastered fire or water. Pan-mages are green, lighter if they're healers, and darker if they're shape-shifters. The stronger the power, the more intense their aura."

Erynion found it ironic that it was the blind demon who explained the function of the Devil's Eye. "How do you know all this?"

"I used to have two myself. They were great for fighting. I could figure out who was my biggest threat. But in the end, I had to tear them out."

Erynion studied the scratches on the demon's face. "Why? What was the problem?"

Sonojj shook his whole body like a wet dog. "You've heard the phrase 'the eyes are the windows to the soul,' right? Well, that's especially true for the Devil's Eye. With the right skill, a priest can stare into it and uncover your identity."

"And if they know my name, that would quicken my cleansing."

"Yes, but not just cleansing. If a priest invokes your real name in *any* blessing, it becomes many times stronger."

"What if it's the wrong name?"

"Then it's the opposite effect," Sonojj said. "Granted, not any priest can just look into your eye. They must be trained for it, or they could get lost in your mind. It's safe to assume all archdons are capable of this, like the one leading those priests. That's why all iymed have human eyes that cover their real ones. How did you lose yours?"

Erynion slid the cloth back into place. "I think I tore it out to numb the agony."

The two lesser iymed were silent.

Erynion unbuttoned his shirt. "I also wounded my chest, but that healed up very fast. Why hasn't my eye healed?"

Sonojj bobbed his head. "The eye is different. It's more complex. It's the only part of us that can't regenerate. The human eye can never grow back. And if you tear out the Devil's Eye, you're left with nothing."

There was a long pause before Flinch changed the subject. "So, I guess we should keep moving. Sereyna said to meet up with the group before nightfall."

Sonojj took a seat on the ground. "Don't worry, we'll make it. We just have to wait here for a bit."

"Why?"

"Because, we just do. Trust me."

Flinch's fingers drummed along his thigh. "Aw, come on. You know I'm terrified the priests are going to follow us. Why don't you just be a pal and tell us what we're waiting for?"

"Fine. Did you happen to see what freed you?"

Flinch pondered the question. "Honestly, no. I felt the chains loosen, got free, cut Erynion loose, and then we bolted like a bat out of the depths."

"I heard some whistling noises," Erynion said. "I think I saw an arrow nearly hit that archdon."

The jester perked up. "An arrow? Marksy came back?"

"There's that name again. Who's Marksy?"

"His name is Alejjir," the blind demon explained. "Before the Assault on Light's Haven, he was one of the five greater iymed. The humans call him the Marksman."

"And you call him Marksy?" Erynion asked.

Flinch smiled. "It's an old joke that goes way back. I followed him for centuries before he died. So, he came back to help us, huh?"

Sonojj nodded. "I was a ways off from the gate when I paused to catch my breath. I was figuring out how I'd be able to return and save you both. I suppose I was lucky he was still in area. Apparently, he heard me running through the forest. So, I convinced him to help me, and he said he'd join us after. We agreed to meet up here at the stream."

"Wait a minute. I thought he was afraid of the demon lord."

"I told him Sereyna hadn't found the demon lord because it's headed for Alovajj. But when she does find it, he said he won't be caught anywhere nearby."

"Hmm, speaking of not being caught, Erynion, I had to yank on your arm a few times to get you running. What happened back there?"

"That barrier spell. I saw it in my vision."

"Oh, right," the jester said. "The vision that almost got us all cleansed."

Sonojj cut in. "That hardly matters now. Tell us what you saw in your vision."

Erynion turned his gaze from the iymed pair to the flowing stream. He found the motion of the water calming, and it allowed him to better recollect what he saw. "It was the day of the Assault. I was with someone. He was young, a teenager maybe, but barely. This watcher captain was trying to get us to safety while arrows rained down from the sky. An archdon ended up saving us with that same barrier spell, a dome of light. It started to get hazy after that, but when it was clear again, we were attacked by an assassin. It was the Shade."

"Draeko?" Flinch leaned in. "You saw him in your memory?"

"Draeko? Is that the Shade's name?"

"Well, that's his alias. Who knows his real name?"

"Well, then yes, that's what the paladins said."

"Paladins?" Sonojj asked. "What happened to the watcher?"

"I don't know. Time was skipping around."

Flinch jumped back in. "*Psh*, who cares about the watcher? Tell us more about Draeko."

"I'm not sure what else there is to say. He was quite short. He wielded a massive dagger in each hand. He was gone as quickly as he came."

"Did you see his face?"

"No, I didn't. He was wearing a wolf mask."

Flinch punched his own hand. "Depths! No one ever sees his face."

"Is that important?"

The blind demon waved dismissively at Flinch. "Ignore him. What happened next?"

"After that, my vision skipped again. People were

celebrating the demons' retreat. They talked about the Brotherhood. I think the Marksman was mentioned. Everything was so fragmented, though. It didn't really make a lot of sense to me."

"So, you were alive during the Assault on Light's Haven," Flinch said.

"I suppose so. It's not much in the way of figuring out my identity, but I guess it's a start."

"Ah, the Assault on Light's Haven." Sonojj rested on his elbows. "It seems like just yesterday, and yet so much has changed."

"Yeah, you had eyes back then," Flinch remarked.

The shape-shifting demon ignored the comment. "Shinigami betrayed Verago. The Brotherhood fell to pieces. Umaro Lijjo was cleansed. Draeko hasn't been seen since. Sarjjore disappeared soon after."

Not wishing to interrupt, Erynion simply listened, unfamiliar with some of the names.

"Marksy died in the purge," Flinch added. "Ever since then, it's been dangerous on the Surface. Demons killed during the Assault weren't given the energy to return. Rumor has it that Verago became so obsessed with creating another demon lord he hasn't made any more fray or iymed since the Assault."

"A rumor that appears to be true now," Sonojj said.

"I wouldn't say that's entirely true." The new voice was suave with a hint of arrogance. Dressed in a beige trench coat with a quiver slung across his back, a stranger emerged from the woods. On his head, he wore a wide-brimmed hat that matched his ensemble.

"Marksy!" Flinch dashed over to greet the iymed.

The newly arrived demon grinned. "Depths, Flinch, now you know I hate that name."

"Oh, sorry. I guess I'd forgotten that after *sixteen years*." The jester playfully slapped the demon's ribs with the back of his hand. "Hey! Where've you been all this time?"

"Hilarious. I see you haven't lost your sense of humor."

After patting Flinch on the shoulder, the new demon tipped his hat toward Erynion. "Hi there. The humans call me the Marksman, but around my friends, I go by Alejjir, despite what Flinch might have told you. Nice to meet you."

The iymed produced his claw to shake hands, a gesture Erynion had not yet experienced with the demons. He brought up his human hand and shook the demon's claw. "I'm Erynion."

"So, where we headed, Sonojj?" Alejjir asked.

The blind demon hopped to his feet. "We're following the stream toward Lake Ivorus until we catch up to Sereyna and the others. We better get moving if she wants us there before nightfall."

As Sonojj and Flinch led the way, Erynion and Alejjir walked side by side behind the jester and shape-shifter. They had barely left their resting spot, when Erynion noticed Alejjir scrutinizing him. "Something wrong?"

"Of course not." The Marksman gave a crooked smile. "So, Erynion, you came through the twisted gate?"

"That's right. The night before last."

"They tell you about the demon lord?"

"I've heard him mentioned, but other than that, not really."

"Let me give you some advice. When they find it, stay away. That demon is a ball of energy aching to go off."

"What do you mean?"

"He's talking about the purge," Flinch interrupted.

Alejjir explained, "During the failed attack sixteen years ago, the demon lord who came to the Surface couldn't control its power. As a result, a massive attack was released right in the middle of the demon army. The purge manifested in a physical form. If it was just dark energy, like the Corruption spell, we would've been fine. But this? This destroyed everything."

"And how do you know a demon lord has come back again?" Erynion was curious about the purge.

Flinch chimed in, "The oasis in the black desert."

Alejjir shot him a look, and the jester fell silent.

"The oasis in the black desert?"

"The aftermath of the demon lord's purge," the Marksman said. "A wasteland of black soil with no sign of life or anything. And in the middle of it all, a tiny patch of earth, untouched by the purge, where the beast stood."

Erynion reflected on the words. This was exactly what he witnessed when he woke up after the first night.

Alejjir raised his eyebrow. "Something wrong there, friend?"

"Nope."

"I know. It can be terrifying. I was caught in it sixteen years ago, reducing me to the lesser iymed who stands before you now. Whatever came out of that gate first is by far the most powerful and most dangerous creature on the Surface."

CHAPTER 14

The sky was losing light and dinnertime was fast approaching. The city of Nolka rested uneasily thanks to the excitement of the previous night. Despite no indication of a demon threat, many citizens remained inside once dusk arrived. Even around the rectory, there was little activity. Don Millan reported to the office of the archdon. The old priest was using his elbow to prop up his head while Eriph was reclining against the wall with his arms crossed.

Millan approached the desk. "Your Grace, is something the matter?"

"Nothing serious. I'm only concerned about the demons who got away."

"I have to ask. What were those arrows? It was like a scorcher was attacking us with some unholy spell."

The scorchers were a guild of elite archers with limited abilities in enchantment. They could temporarily imbue their arrows with fire, ice, and holy energy, depending on what specialty they chose.

"A scorcher? Maybe when he was alive," Eriph said.

"You don't think—" Millan was afraid to complete the thought.

"Why not? He was never cleansed. He just died. It was only a matter of time before he came back."

Feranis nodded. "There's no doubt about it. Our group was attacked with arrows of deceit. I don't know of any other demon with such an ability, or with such audacity to attack priests in the daylight. During the Assault, he rained down thousands of those arrows on Light's Haven. It's definitely the Marksman."

Millan struggled with the idea that after over a decade of peace, two of the greater iymed had reappeared. "First the Seductress, and now the Marksman?"

"I know. Now throw a possible demon lord on top of that. Verago is definitely up to something. The strange part is the Marksman doesn't seem to be a greater iymed. Thank the angels for that, otherwise we may not have been so lucky. But, we accomplished our goal. We saw what happened to Nesinu, and we destroyed the gate. Were the horses returned to the stables?"

"I believe Don Niktosa took care of that, Your Grace."

Feranis stroked his chin. "Good. Good. Let's discuss what we must, and then we can all grab some dinner. After everything that's happened, I think we could all use a good meal, followed by some rest. When we returned to Nolka, I sent my report to the Council. About a half an hour ago, I received a letter from Light's Haven. The first portion was regarding your Exclusion, Eriph. By tomorrow, it'll be public knowledge that you are no longer in the Candelux guild."

"Whatever will I do now?" Eriph reeked of sarcasm.

"Yes, well, I'm sure you've got an idea. The Prima has also sent out instructions for all cities and villages to be on high alert. Anyone associated with the Brotherhood is to be detained. We could really use the information you brought from Alovajj. Also, major cities will have strict entrance policies as bloodseekers will be used to determine any demon threats."

"What about Erynion? The seeker couldn't sense he

was a demon," Millan pointed out.

"Each report includes a description of what the demon looks like. Tall with long white hair and a nasty scar across his face. He'll be hard to miss, especially with the Devil's Eye exposed."

"So, will they be sending a bloodseeker to Nolka?"

"A few actually, not that you should worry about Nolka," the archdon said. "The last portion of the letter is for you, Don Millan. You are to report to the Sanctuary for reassignment."

"Reassignment?"

"Yes, and there's something else. During the evacuation, you brought all the horses from your stables, including Don Skully's. In his absence, his possessions will be handed over to Candelux in Light's Haven. You are to take his horse with you and drop it off at the Sanctuary. It's all explained right here. Give this letter to Kona Magara at the stables, and she'll have the horse prepared for you."

Millan grasped the folded paper. He hadn't considered the possibility of Nesinu or Don Skully being gone for good. "I have to go to Light's Haven?"

"Does this surprise you? Until there's evidence to the contrary, Don Skully, may the angels guide him, is assumed to be dead. And with Nesinu destroyed, you have no home to go back to."

Millan broke eye contact with Feranis.

Eriph clicked his tongue. "I doubt he needs to be reminded."

"And you," Feranis addressed the excluded priest. "I've been given explicit instructions not to include you in any Candelux affairs from here on out."

"Is that in reaction to today?"

"No, it's just something that Prima Mashira added. I actually left you out of today's official report."

Eriph placed his hand on his chest. "Awfully nice of you."

"Don't mention it. She probably assumed you tagged along, but seriously, don't mention it. And seeing as how the announcement of your Exclusion isn't official until tomorrow, I would be grateful if you shared the information concerning the Brotherhood. That is, if you're still willing."

With his ties to Candelux broken, Eriph was free from any obligation to help the priests. The suspense mounted until he pushed off from the wall and produced a piece of paper from his pocket. "I took the liberty of writing down the names of some of the higher-ranked members."

"How did you get these names?" Millan asked.

Eriph let the list float down to the archdon's desk. "When the Brotherhood fractured after the Assault, many of those who followed Shinigami stayed in touch with those that didn't. Friends. Family. Some of the information also comes from captured iymed."

"Let's see here." Feranis's index finger glided down the paper. Millan strained his neck to take a peek.

"Some places even have the overseer listed, indicated by the O next to the name," Eriph stated. "As far as we know, there's still no Grand Overseer."

"So, this one at the top. Overseer of Nolka would be Eleza."

"Correct."

"Eleza?" Millan's mind conjured up the lovely face, dark hair, and blue bandana.

Feranis glanced up from the paper. "Yes, do you know her?"

"No," Millan answered abruptly. Eriph and Feranis both stared at him silently. Not wanting to be associated with a leader of their greatest living enemies, the young priest determined he may have been overzealous in his response. He felt the heat in his face and stuttered. "I...I mean, no. No, I don't know her, but I...I think I ran into her on the street this morning. I mean, I ran into someone, and I think her name was Eleza."

Feranis bit his lower lip. "Hmm, seems odd. You just happened to run into the overseer?"

"Well, I didn't know she was the overseer," Millan nearly shouted in his defense.

"Did she ask anything of you?"

"Um, no. She simply thanked me for keeping the city safe. What? That's it. I swear."

"Can you at least describe her then?" the archdon asked.

"Sure, I suppose. She was shorter than me."

"That narrows it down, doesn't it? What else?"

"She had black hair. Uh, a white shirt with no sleeves. Her skin was a darkish, lightish color."

Eriph smirked. "'A darkish, lightish color'?"

"Well, yeah. It wasn't really dark, and it wasn't really light."

"What about her eyes?"

"They were nice."

Feranis groaned. "Color?"

"Oh. Brownish? Maybe with some green? Or was it yellow?"

Eriph snorted as he stifled his laughter.

The archdon rubbed his forehead, making the creases more pronounced. "That's fine. We'll find her."

Millan frowned. Her picture was in his head, but the details weren't so clear. He slumped down in the chair.

Feranis resumed his search of the list. "Millan."

"Yes, Your Grace?" The Nesinu priest finally cast out the image of Eleza.

"What was the name of your watcher captain again? The one that's missing?"

"Captain Pirok."

Feranis rotated the paper and slid it to the other side of the desk.

Millan checked the name the archdon was pointing to. "No, it can't be. But that section is for members in Nolka, not Nesinu. There must be another Pirok."

The Twisted Gate

"How long ago did he arrive in Nesinu?" Eriph asked.

"I don't know. It was after my Acceptance. Around two years ago?"

"Well, this is a cumulative list over the past ten years. Names are added, but rarely removed. Some of the people on this list might even be dead," Eriph said. "It's possible his name was discovered while he still lived in Nolka."

"It's certainly a possibility." Feranis shrugged. "But it's not like I learn the names of all the watchers."

Millan clenched his fists as he relived the night of the evacuation. "He stayed behind on purpose."

"I'm sorry, Millan." Eriph patted the priest on the shoulder.

The archdon pulled back the paper. "Yes, the treachery of the Brotherhood affects us all. That's why they'll be imprisoned. I cannot thank you enough for this list, Eriph."

"You're welcome. I only wish the Prima would look at it as well."

"Perhaps, in time."

As Feranis and Eriph continued to review the list, Millan spaced out. His heart ached as he came to terms with Pirok's treason. The whole village had trusted this man with their safety. Millan had no doubt now that Pirok had betrayed Don Skully. Nesinu's head watcher probably even helped the demon lord destroy the only home he had ever known. The priest's gaze swept across the floor and over to the corner that housed the archdon's staff with the star on top. It wasn't the ornate weapon that caught his eye, but rather the wooden handle beside it.

"What's this?" Millan inspected the long piece of oak with a broken blade protruding from one end.

"What? That? Just a souvenir from last night," Feranis said. "I don't believe Reaper will be needing it. I was going to get it reforged."

The second piece of the scythe blade lay on the ground beside its counterpart, and Millan studied it. "It's not dark anymore. You disenchanted it?"

"That's right. What do you know of enchantments?"

"Don Skully taught me about how Archdon Bamby was the first enchanter, how to sense the aura of an enchanted object, disenchant it, and even enchant it again with holy energy. I wasn't very good, though."

"I get the feeling Don Skully taught you more than he should have. Dons aren't supposed to be instructed on such blessings. It's best they stay focused and master the basics of fighting and cleansing demons before trying to learn a specialty like enchantment."

"Oh, I...I'm, uh—I'm sorry," Millan stammered. "I...I didn't know."

"Don't let it worry you. Although, perhaps you should refrain from telling others."

"What's your ratio?" Eriph asked.

Millan had never heard the term before. "My ratio?"

"You know, for enchanting. Time to cast compared to time to last?"

The archdon clarified. "He means, how long do your enchantments remain relative to the time you spend casting the blessing."

"Oh." Millan thought for a moment. "Not very long. Probably like three times longer than my cast?"

"Better than one, but that's really low." Eriph nodded at Feranis. "How about you, old man?"

Feranis glared at the former don. "I haven't kept track for years now. Last time I checked, it was just over five hundred."

"Whoa!" Millan blurted out. "Five hundred?"

"Years and years of practice. Many bloodseekers and guardians have come to me requesting my services."

"That's amazing." Millan was still stunned.

Feranis took a deep breath. "Well, it's been a long day. I think we can call an end to our meeting here. I don't know about you two, but I'm famished. Eriph, will you stay on in Nolka? As my guest, of course."

"Thank you, but no. I'll join you for dinner, but tomorrow I ride for Royal Oak. And then after that, on to Alovajj."

"Very well." The archdon shoved his chair back.

Millan spoke up. "I'm sorry, Your Grace. I don't mean to keep us from dinner, but may I speak with you alone?"

Feranis slowly lowered himself back into his seat.

Eriph winked at the old man. "I'll save you a spot at the head table. Don Millan, it was a pleasure meeting you."

"And you as well."

The excluded priest hoisted the shield over his shoulder and left the office.

Feranis cleared his throat. "Now, Millan, what is it you wish to discuss with me?"

"I was talking with Eriph during the expedition, and the subject came up concerning Don Skully."

"Ah, I see."

"I've never been outside Nesinu except for my Acceptance. Don Skully never told me about his life before coming to my town. I didn't know he was an archdon. I didn't know he was an advisor. Eriph suggested I speak with you to find the truth about what happened. What was his involvement with the Death Gods? Why was he demoted from his rank as an archdon?"

Feranis placed both of his elbows on the table and interlaced his fingers. "I knew Skully very well. Ayristark too. During our time together, the three of us understood one another, saw eye to eye. We became very good friends during the twenty years that Ayristark was the Primus. As you know, when Mashira took over the role, Ayristark was chosen as her first advisor, as is the custom. I suppose it all started on the day of the Assault when Shinigami showed up in the castle. But the real issues didn't arise until a few months afterward when they had formed their group. Back then, they weren't called the Death Gods. They were Sect Eighty-Eight. They started small. Shinigami was their leader, and much of his support came from High War-

Mage Drevarius. He was one of the two leaders of Summa Arcana at that time.

"Sect Eighty-Eight had many ideas and suggestions for defeating Verago. As you may know, some of the things they proposed were dangerous to the people in many regards. As they publicized their plans, the issue first went to King Cato. Kings and queens have always had it within their power to disband any sect or guild, particularly one that is seen as a threat to the kingdom. Many of us were scared and wanted to see Sect Eighty-Eight go the way of the Royal Throne."

"The Royal Throne?"

"You've never—" Feranis shook his head. "It doesn't matter. It's just an expression. We wanted to see the sect gone, dissolved. As expected, because their questionable methods would be used against Verago and the demons, King Cato passed the judgement onto the newly appointed Prima Mashira. The matter was meant to be private, discussed between only the Prima and her five advisors. However, Ayristark found himself caught between the two sides, seeing merit in both arguments. Unable to come to a decision, he went outside the Council and discussed the affairs with Skully and myself. It would figure such a sensitive issue would be the one time we completely disagreed. I had no doubt Sect Eighty-Eight should be disbanded. There were too many risks and too many chances for loss of innocent life. Skully was on the opposite end. He thought they should be praised for their ideas. Our disagreement didn't help Ayristark, but eventually, I was able to sway him to my side. Even the promise of stopping Verago doesn't justify putting innocent lives in danger. As it turns out, three other advisors agreed with me as well."

"And the last one?"

"Advisor Mortis. He not only stood in favor of Sect Eighty-Eight, but he became one of the founding members, along with Shinigami and Drevarius. He believed their sect was the answer we needed to put an end to Verago once and for all. Skully agreed, and he thought the people of the kingdom would support them if only they knew. I pleaded with him to let the Council handle the issue, but he and Mortis took it upon themselves to inform the citizens. Chaos broke out as people took sides. Light's Haven was divided. With little time to consult with her advisors, Mashira decided she had to act swiftly before word spread to the other cities. Backed by King Cato, she gave them all a choice. Disband or be exiled. And so, the members of Sect Eighty-Eight, including Advisor Mortis, chose exile. During her speech, the Prima famously referred to them as gods of death, a title they have since graciously accepted."

Millan felt light-headed. "This is a lot to process. So, Don Skully never joined them?"

"Not that I'm aware of."

"And he was demoted from archdon because he supported them?"

"No. Mashira didn't take any action against supporters if they left well enough alone. The Death Gods moved to Alovajj, and many chose to follow. Skully resigned his position willingly and took up residence in Nesinu, wanting to be as far from Light's Haven as possible. He felt betrayed, but honestly, so did I. Although, despite all that had happened, I still considered him a close friend. I requested this post in Nolka so I could be close by, in case my friend should need my help. But, he never wrote or said a single word to me for the past fifteen years. Stubborn."

"I see," Millan said quietly. "Thank you for telling me."

"You're welcome. Now if there's nothing else, we should go grab some dinner before all the food is gone. And don't forget to speak with Kona at the stables."

"Of course. I'll head there after dinner."

CHAPTER 15

There was still about an hour before sundown as the four demons followed the stream. For most of the trip, Flinch and Alejjir recounted the time they had spent together before the failed assault.

"Yeah, and so with most of the greater iymed either killed, cleansed, or just missing, I eventually joined up with Sereyna," Flinch explained. "That's when I met Sonojj and Reaper. Poor Reaper."

Sonojj tilted his head. "Hmm, sounds like we're here."

Erynion noticed the crowd of fray along the shore. Some of the imps were splashing about in the water.

"I wonder what we're doing here," Flinch muttered.

"And where's here?" Alejjir asked.

Flinch tapped his lips. "Well, this river leads to Lake Ivorus. But, we rounded the bend only a few hours ago. There's no way we're anywhere near there. I'd guess we're close to Malarekita."

"Malarekita? I thought we were going to Alovajj," Erynion said.

"Well, technically, it's on the way. There's no way we'd reach the lake before dusk, but I don't know why we're stopping so close to a town."

"You're here. Good!" Maligus emerged from the group of fray. "Well, well, if it isn't Alejjir. I'll be damned."

The Marksman tipped his hat. "Aren't we all, though?"

Maligus narrowed his eyes. "Clever. Thought you'd run off to hide from the scary demon lord."

"I don't think we've ever met," Alejjir said. "You must be Maligus. You're just as pleasant as Flinch and Sonojj described."

"Some of us have to maintain order," the ogre demon grumbled. "We can't all hide in the back like cowards."

"Indeed."

As the two demons bickered, Erynion marveled at Alejjir's calm in the face of insults, and it was Maligus who grew more agitated.

The ogre caught his stare. "What are you looking at?"

Erynion was quiet. He didn't fear the overly aggressive demon, but he was unsure how to respond. Maligus snarled and produced a large machete that matched his size.

"That's enough, Maligus," came the soothing voice of their leader.

Both Erynion and the ogre refused to break eye contact. Maligus menacingly lifted the machete. But even as he felt the demon's blade rest against his neck, Erynion didn't look away. He didn't fear death.

"Are you listening? Put it away, dear." Sereyna delicately squeezed the ogre's shoulder. As he lowered the weapon to his side, the machete vanished into thin air.

"Damn puppet." Maligus stormed off into the crowd of fray.

Sereyna rolled her eyes and smiled sweetly at Erynion. "Forget him. He's threatened by greatness."

"Me? I'm just one of them."

"Even among lesser iymed, there are varying degrees of power. This is why it's important you learn to control yours. Come, the sun will be down soon, and we have a lot to cover. The rest of you, play nice with Maligus. Oh, and welcome back to the Surface, Alejjir."

"Thank you. Sereyna, is it now?"

"Yes, it will do you good to remember it," she shot back with a wink. "Will you stay on as one of my officers?"

"I suppose I don't see the harm in it. Yet."

As the three lieutenants joined the camp, Sereyna journeyed into the woods. Trailing behind her, Erynion admired her features, from the long black hair down to the small of her back. Wrapped around her waist was a strange belt that appeared to be woven out of a thin rope. He was so captivated by her figure he didn't notice she had slowed her pace and was observing him over her shoulder.

"Like what you see?" she asked.

Erynion looked away.

Before long, the pair arrived on a hilltop overlooking a small village, and Sereyna found rest on the trunk of a fallen tree.

Erynion watched as the lanterns in the town lit up to compensate for the setting sun. "Why did you bring me here?"

"Patience, my love. You, my sweet Erynion, have two problems you must resolve sooner than later. The most important is your identity. Were you able to remember anything at the gate?"

"Some. I remembered that I was alive during the Assault. I remembered arrows raining down. I remembered hearing your name. I think I was a teenager at the time. And I was with another boy who was about my age."

"Interesting. But no name?"

"No. What's the other problem I have to resolve?"

"Isn't it obvious? The agony, of course."

"How? Where does it come from?"

Sereyna crossed her legs and adjusted her dress. "It comes from you. From your own strength. Let me give you an example. Imagine your body is a leather pouch. Your energy is like water. When the sun dies each day, the pouch begins to fill with water. The stronger you are, the bigger your pouch and the faster it fills. When you use your energy, like for fighting or healing, it's like pouring out some of the water. The stronger the attack, the more water is lost. Make sense so far?"

Erynion nodded.

"Good. If you don't use your energy, then naturally your pouch fills with water. But just because it's full, doesn't mean the water stops. For demons like the fray, the rate of energy they receive is so slow and weak that they feel nothing when their pouch is full. They don't experience the agony at all. But as an iymed, the pressure is stronger, stretching your pouch, forcing it to expand. That stretching is the pain you feel. As a demon gets stronger, the agony only gets worse. Until finally, it's unbearable, and your pouch breaks, releasing all that water."

Erynion folded his arms across his chest. "That release of energy. That's the purge."

"That's right. It manifests in different forms depending on the demon."

"I see. The first night I was here, I felt the agony from the moment I emerged. When I scratched my chest and my face, it went away for a bit."

"You wounded yourself, and your energy healed you," Sereyna explained.

"And later on, I was urged to kill a priest in the town. When I attacked him, there was a flash. Spikes of light were sticking out of my chest. There was a searing pain, but again, the agony subsided. Was I using my energy to counter the attack?"

"Something like that. Light and dark naturally negate each other. His attack drained some of your energy."

Erynion paced back and forth. "But the agony always returned."

"It's a never-ending struggle."

"The next time it hit me, I tried to fight it, but I…well, I don't really remember what happened."

Sereyna patted the log, inviting him to sit beside her. "Fatigue. Your body released its energy, and you passed out. The same thing happens to any demon that purges."

Erynion sat down, keeping some distance. "When I awoke the next morning, I found myself in the middle of a huge black field. Alejjir called it the oasis in the black desert. He said the demon lord caused that. Does that mean I—?"

"No, no, no. I know what you're thinking. Don't worry, you're not the demon lord that everyone's talking about. I could see how you would think so, waking up in the middle of the demon lord's purge, but that's just not true. Trust me. If you were the demon lord, do you really think you could just walk into Nolka without being detected? I had to use the Brotherhood and sacrifice one of my lieutenants just to get in, and you think you're stronger than me?"

Erynion could tell her question wasn't serious but still felt the need to explain. "No, it's not that, it's just—"

Sereyna giggled. "It's fine. Look. The reason you've felt so much pain is because you have practically no control over your energy. Flinch, Sonojj, Reaper, Maligus. None of them experience the agony anymore."

"You're stronger than all of them. What about you?"

"It's rare. Nothing quite like the first time, though."

"So, I just need to use my energy, and the agony won't bother me?" Erynion asked.

"That's where your first problem comes into play. Your identity is the key to unlocking everything. Without it, you have very limited access to your power, and your pouch will always fill faster than you can empty it. There's no easy way to tell you this, but you need a lot of help. And I'm willing to offer you my assistance because you could become my strongest lieutenant. I can't simply let you go without your identity. You would just end up hurting yourself."

"So, what do I have to do?"

The Twisted Gate

"Patience, love." Sereyna stood and offered him her hand. "You're in good hands. The two of us are going to take a walk. I'll keep your energy in check, so don't worry about that."

Erynion cautiously placed his hand in hers, and she helped him up. The last rays of sunlight dwindled, and the stars made their debut for the night. Erynion winced as the energy flowed into him. It was the same discomfort from the previous nights.

Sereyna rubbed his back. "How are you doing?"

"I can feel it there. It's small now, but it'll just get worse. Should I try to do something?"

"No, just relax."

Her voice calmed him as he closed his eye and followed her instructions. Something crawled up his leg like a snake, but Erynion remained still. The sensation passed his waist and slipped under his shirt. It was soft to the touch and tenderly caressed his back. He took a quick breath as he felt a prick in the back of his neck, but then the pain was gone, including any hint of the agony.

"Excellent. Open your eyes," she commanded.

Erynion obeyed and looked out over the valley.

"How do you feel?"

A faint smile appeared on his lips. "At peace. Like I feel during the day."

"Good. Now, let's take a walk."

Erynion descended the slope after Sereyna. "You never told me why you brought me here."

"Giving you a little test. Don't worry, everything will be fine," she reassured him. Her voice was even sweeter than usual and put him completely at ease. "Now, if I remember correctly, Malarekita has an outpost of—"

Erynion's eye was drawn skyward as a single arrow, engulfed in fire, soared though the night air. The projectile landed a few feet in front of the pair.

"…scorchers. Come, let's check out this town."

As Erynion crossed the field, Sereyna slid behind him

and placed her hand on his right shoulder. He glanced behind and caught her cloudy-blue eyes in the flicker of the arrow's flame. They were breathtaking.

"Who goes there?" a distant voice called out from the watchtower.

Sereyna brought her lips close to his ear. Her breath wafted over his neck. "Ignore them, my dear."

Three more arrows, lit with fire, blazed across the sky and struck the ground before them.

"Warning shots," she said, but Erynion already knew that.

"I say, who goes there?" the voice hollered again. "Identify yourselves or the next arrows will not be aimed at the ground."

"Stay strong. This is the first part of your test. Trust me." She kissed his back through the clothing.

The bell at the top of the watchtower clanged unevenly as arrows flew from the tower. Some hit the ground, while others struck the demon. Erynion recoiled slightly at the impact of each projectile, and part of his clothing caught fire. With a few pats of his claw, he extinguished the flames. His claw. His hand was no longer human, but that fact didn't faze him as he lowered it back to his side. The physical pain from the wounds paled in comparison to the last couple of nights. The bell continued to ring, but the arrows eventually stopped.

At the edge of the town, Sereyna rejoined his side. "How are you feeling?"

Erynion tore out the arrows, grunting as each one was liberated. "Invincible."

"Congratulations. You passed the first test."

"Was that all?"

"Not quite. That was only the start, but you're doing wonderfully so far. Let's see who comes out to greet us."

A group of people confronted the two demons as they entered the town. The rest of the village appeared deserted. Erynion studied their clothing and weapons.

Four wore brown robes and black scarves, similar to the priests he had already encountered. Beside the priests stood fighters with weapons drawn, including a few archers with nocked arrows, glowing with a yellow aura.

One of the priests stepped forward. "Come no farther, demons. We only wish to protect our homes. Leave now, and we will not be forced to cleanse you."

"Cleanse us?" Sereyna pretended to be oblivious. "We're not demons."

Erynion noticed she was intently focused on the group of humans. Her pupils dilated and her irises subtly pulsed with energy.

"Depths! Don't look at her eyes!" one of the priests instructed. Each member of the group used his or her arm to break eye contact.

"We're just a happy couple out for an evening stroll," Sereyna insisted.

"A couple that speaks Kisejjad? Right. We have a seeker. We know how strong you are, Seductress. You won't entrance us, so please just leave. What could you gain by attacking our humble village?"

"A few less priests on the Surface, for one."

A strange sensation washed over Erynion. The fear of the humans was palpable, and it made him uncomfortable. Sereyna was clearly stronger and enjoyed listening to them beg for their lives and the safety of their village.

"May we leave?" Erynion asked her quietly.

Sereyna gaped at him. "Leave?"

"Please."

"But we just got here."

Erynion furrowed his brow. "Something doesn't feel right. I think we should go."

As she crossed her arms, her face shifted from sweet and innocent to irritated and angry. "Go? I brought you to this insignificant village so you could have a little fun. Explore your power. No one here can harm you. Not while I'm here. Don't you want to learn? Don't you want my help?"

Erynion pitied the priests, huddled together. He felt out of place. He wished them no harm. Erynion caught Sereyna concentrating on something behind him. He followed her line of sight to the watchtower. An archer aimed at the intruders with her bowstring pulled back to full tension. Erynion was about to shield Sereyna when she stopped him. The scorcher removed the arrow from the string and placed it back in the quiver. Then, she dropped her bow, positioned her hands on the railing of the watchtower, and vaulted over it. When she struck the ground, she lay motionless.

"Nobody move unless you'd like to join her," the villager warned.

Erynion couldn't tear his eyes away from the scorcher's body. Sereyna gently held his chin and brought his eyes back to her. "See? Fun."

"What do you want from us?" one of the priests asked.

Sereyna faced the humans. "I want—" She shuddered.

"Are you all right?" Erynion asked.

"I want—" Her body convulsed, and she dropped to her knees. Her breathing became erratic.

Erynion stooped beside her. "Sereyna, what's going on?"

"Oh my, that's incredible." The demon moaned as she ran her hand down her face and chest. She started panting, and a black mist seeped from her mouth and drifted to the ground. The mysterious cloud emerged from her sleeves. The streams of gas flowed together, growing thicker and surrounding the demonic pair.

The humans backed away as the black cloud crept toward them. "It's Corruption! Get inside! We need to get marked defense up as soon as possible!"

The villagers scattered from the thoroughfare. As the cloud enveloped the demons, Erynion lost sight of the buildings. A chill traveled up his spine, and he stumbled forward onto one knee. It was difficult to breathe, but it wasn't the agony this time. It was exhaustion. He searched the cloud for Sereyna but failed to find her in the mist. Even the stars above him had disappeared. His head grew lighter, so he put his hand down on the ground to support himself. The world spun around him, and he struggled to maintain his balance. And in the end, Erynion collapsed.

CHAPTER 16

The dining hall was nearly empty. Leaning on his elbow, Millan pushed the food around his plate with his fork. He sat alone at his table, having just said good-bye to Tyro, who would join the squire classes in Nolka. Millan put down the utensil and left the bench. As he headed toward the rectory's exit, he opened the folded letter from his pocket and began to read it.

"Don Millan."

Millan looked up from the paper.

Eriph excused himself from a conversation and approached the Nesinu priest. "I heard you spoke to Archdon Feranis about Don Skully."

"That's right. I did."

"Good. I'm glad to hear it."

Millan glanced down and crinkled the paper in his hand.

"Well, I guess I better get back to my room at the inn. Long ride tomorrow. Good night." The excluded priest reached for the door latch.

Millan suddenly had an idea. "Eriph, may I ask you something?"

"Sure. You need to head to the stables, right?"

The young priest laughed nervously. "Yes, but that's not what I was going to ask you."

"Well, walk with me then. I'll show you anyway, and along the way, you can ask me whatever you like."

"Thank you."

The two descended the steps of the Candelux rectory. Everything was so quiet outside it reminded Millan of how peaceful Nesinu was at night. He looked up at the stars and imagined he was home.

Eriph finally broke the silence. "So, what did you want to ask me?"

Millan bit his lip. "I was wondering if you would be bothered by a traveling companion."

"No bother, but we'd have to part ways before Inssen. After all, I'm not going to Light's Haven."

"No, of course not. I was actually thinking about going with you to Royal Oak."

"Really? Defying the Prima's orders?"

Millan kicked a small stone out of his path. "Well, I wasn't told I had to be in Light's Haven right away, so I figured I'd make a small detour. I've never been to Royal Oak. I've heard the tree is magnificent."

"That's true, it is. Are you sure you want to come with me?"

"I'm sure." Ever since he found out about Don Skully's connection to the Death Gods, Millan had become curious about the exiled group. And, Eriph was his best link.

"Well, Royal Oak is about a day's ride from here at a decent pace, so we need to leave early. Eight strikes should do it. Don't get any ideas about following me to Alovajj, though."

Millan smiled. "Of course. Thank you."

After walking for a few minutes in silence, the angel fountain came into view. Eriph pointed down one of the side streets. "That road will lead you to the stables. I suggest you speak with the stable master before she goes to bed, so your horse is ready in the morning."

"Understood. Thank you again."

"No problem. I'll meet you tomorrow morning in front of the stables."

"Eight strikes," Millan repeated before parting ways with the excluded priest.

"Hey, Millan," Eriph called after him. "When you spoke to Feranis, did you get the answers you were looking for?"

"I suppose."

"Disappointed?"

The Nesinu priest reflected on his conversation with the archdon. "A bit."

"Just remember whose perspective you heard. Others saw Archdon Skully as a strong soul, standing up for his beliefs. He was a good man and a powerful priest, no matter what his rank was in the end or what grudges some may still hold against him."

"Well, he was the reason I became a priest." Millan was starting to feel better.

"Then remember how he inspired you. Good night."

"Good night, and see you in the morning." Millan's mind drifted as he headed toward the stables. He recalled that night of his youth, peering out the window into the main thoroughfare of Nesinu. He was only nine at the time. Don Skully had arrived in town the year before. The bald old man had always frightened Millan; however, his opinion of the priest had changed drastically on that one fateful night.

At the stables, Millan made his way to the small house next door. He stood before the plain door and wondered if anyone would help him at this hour. His father had worked in the Nesinu stables, a small building that housed about a half-dozen horses. Owners were free to take their animals in and out as they pleased, but the workers were usually gone before dinnertime and didn't return until dawn. The young priest struck the door three times. The lock slid out of place, and a large muscular woman filled the space between the door and its frame.

"Can I 'elp you?"

"Hi, my name is Don Millan. I'm from Nesinu. I'm looking for Kona Magara."

"Eyo, that's me," she answered with little emotion.

"Well, then I'm supposed to give this to you." The priest handed her the letter.

Kona Magara barely moved her lips as she perused the letter. "This 'ere then appears to be an edict from Prima Mashira. 'In acc'rdance with the Candelux guild charter,' blah blah blah."

The young priest gripped his wrist behind his back while she finished the note. He listened carefully as her accent was difficult to follow at times.

Kona grunted. "So, I'm to 'and over the 'orse of Don Skully to Don Millan, which is apparently you, right?"

"That's correct."

"And y're going to ride 'im to Light's 'aven and turn over the reins to that there stable master at the Sanctuary?"

The priest hesitated as he considered his detour to Royal Oak. "Uh, yes, exactly."

"Looks real enough to me. Even that fangling geezer, Feranis, signed it. When do you plan on leaving this 'ere city then?"

"Tomorrow morning at eight strikes."

"Oof, very well. Let me grab my shoes. Y're lucky, you know. We lost our night-shifter about a week ago, but one of them there townspeople from Nesinu came by yesterday looking f'r work. You probably know 'im. What the depths was 'is name? Dilly? Danny?"

Millan wasn't familiar with the name. Kona Magara slipped into her shoes and escorted him toward the stables. The building was broken into multiple sections and was clearly larger than what Millan was accustomed to. The Nolka stable master pointed at one end. "Y'r people added there a small group of 'orses to our count when you came in two nights ago. We put them all in that c'rner over there. You 'ead on over, and I'll track down my worker."

Millan treaded lightly down the aisles. The barnlike structure was mostly quiet as the horses slept. The young priest had learned how to ride and care for the beasts when he was younger, but his family was never wealthy enough to purchase their own. And ever since he could remember, Don Skully had always ridden the same animal with a dark-and-tan brindle pattern covering most of the body and white hair around the hooves. As he reached the area, Millan spotted the animal he had been sent to retrieve. The horse moved to the gate to greet him.

"Hey there, Orfius." Millan patted the beast on the head. The horse moved forward, giving the priest access to its neck. He lovingly stroked the animal as it nudged its head into his chest. Millan looked up as Kona rounded the corner.

"Eyo. Found 'im," she said. "It wasn't Danny. It was Damion."

As the stable hand stepped into the light of the lantern, the young priest locked his eyes on the horse.

"Sorry about that there, Damion," Kona said.

"Think nothing of it."

"Anyway, I assume we can skip the introductions 'ere seeing as 'ow you two must know each other already. I spent most of my life in Kotsky out there to the west. I know what it's like to be from a small town. There wasn't a soul that lived there that you didn't know. That there the 'orse? Don Skully's?"

"Orfius. Yes, this horse belonged to Don Skully." Millan slowly made eye contact with Damion. The stable hand was pushing fifty years old, and the lantern showed off the shiny silvers that dominated the black hairs.

The stable master handed the letter to her employee. "This then is f'r you. The 'orse is the property of Candelux now. Prima's 'rdered that Don Millan take this 'ere 'orse to Light's 'aven. The young man aims to leave at eight strikes, so you make sure 'rfius 'ere is ready to go bef're then."

"Understood," Damion said.

"Excellent. Is there anything else then that you require, Don Millan?"

"No, thank you for your help."

Kona extended her hand to the priest. "Then, allow me to show you the way out of these 'ere stables."

Millan was about to step away from the beast but froze when Damion spoke. "Please, let him stay for a moment. I need to speak with him."

The stable master glanced sideways, first at Damion, then at Millan. "That there then is y'r business. Don Millan, our business is concluded. If you wish to stay with Damion, then that there is y'r choice, but I'm 'eading back to the 'ouse."

The young priest didn't budge, and soon Kona Magara departed. The two men stood in silence as Orfius nuzzled up to Millan's hand.

"You're leaving then?" Damion finally asked.

The priest indicated the letter in the man's hand. "Orders from the Prima. You can see for yourself."

"Were you going to say anything to us at all?"

Millan felt guilty because he knew deep down what the truth was. But rather than admit it, he asked his own question. "Since when do you care?"

Damion closed the distance between them. "Since when do I care? Millan, I am your father. No matter what disagreements we've had, I will always care."

"You have a funny way of showing it then."

The words slipped out. Anxiety seized him as he prepared for the scolding, but it never came.

Damion sadly shook his head. "What has that guild done to you?"

"Done to me?" Millan knew the path this conversation was taking, but he couldn't stop himself. "I've been given the opportunity to help people. To really help people."

"I've tried to warn you. Candelux doesn't help anyone. It puts their lives in danger."

"How can you say that?" the priest asked timidly. "What about the evacuation of the town? If it wasn't for Don Skully—" Millan cut himself off. Damion had never concealed the fact that he despised his son's mentor.

"What? If it wasn't for Don Skully, then what? Our home wouldn't have been completely wiped off the map? Or do you think he actually saved us? Let me tell you something about Don Skully."

"Please, Dad, not this again."

"Nesinu stood for fifteen years without incident before that man arrived. And then within the year, we get attacked by demons."

Millan rolled his eyes. "There's no conspiracy. Why can't you just accept that it was a coincidence? Why can't you just be thankful like the other villagers?"

"Oh! Thankful? Is that what you want? My gratitude? And where's your gratitude? Your mother and I gave up everything for you to give you a life away from all this nonsense. And now, because of that man, we have to start all over again. Why is it so hard for you to see? All we've ever wanted was for you to be happy, maybe find a nice girl, settle down, and have children of your own. It pains me knowing that my only son is in that fangling guild run by that Dardan fool of a Prima."

"She's not a fool." Millan lashed out. "Besides, I'm happy here. What would you have me do? Work in the stables my whole life?"

Damion scowled. "Don't you take that tone with me, son. I shovel horseshit for a living. I hear condescension every day. I don't have to hear it from you too. I've worked in the stables since before you were born. Your mother has been scrubbing the floors of other people's homes since before she can even remember. Everything we've done was to give you a better life. And then, you go and join Candelux. It's like a slap in the face. That guild represents everything that's wrong with this kingdom. There's been nothing but suffering since the moment it was formed. They've been whispering into the ear of every king and queen for the last four hundred years, and yet the demon threat is worse than ever. You see how they live. You've seen the Sanctuary in all its glory. They expect us all to bend over backward for them. They're paid by the king using the taxes we give to the crown. Why? Because they're the self-proclaimed saviors of humanity. You can't put a price on that, can you? They're as bad as the nobility, looking down on us common folk. And look at you. You're just like the rest of them now. What gives you the right?"

Millan sank back into his passive demeanor. "That's not true."

"Oh? Don't you think it's the slightest bit odd? You always have years of minor demon activity, and then, just when folks start to think things are safe and Candelux isn't needed anymore, *BAM!* A horde of demons attack, and the priests ride in to save the day. I think the Prima and Verago are working together."

"That's ridiculous." Millan fought back halfheartedly, not because he doubted the Prima, but because he was never able to truly stand up to his father.

"Is it? Tell me, Millan. What happens to Candelux when Verago's defeated?" The priest had no response, and so Damion answered himself. "I'll tell you what happens. It becomes useless and falls apart. The Prima, whose power in the kingdom is said to rival or even exceed that of the king, would be completely powerless. You think if there was real opportunity to kill Verago, she would really take it and give up all that power? No way. I've told you countless times before, and I'll tell you again. Candelux is corrupt, and I'm ashamed that my son is now involved with them."

Deep down, Millan knew he'd made the right choice by joining the guild of priests, but he'd never found the right words to convince his father. Their relationship had gotten progressively worse during his tenure as a squire, but after his Acceptance, Millan was kicked out of the house by his father.

The priest cast his eyes to the ground. "I don't want to fight about this anymore."

"Fine. But make sure you tell your mother you're leaving. I'll make sure the horse is ready by morning."

"Thank you." Millan hesitated before walking past Damion and quickly saying good-bye. "May the angels watch over you."

CHAPTER 17

The next morning, Don Millan prepared his things. As the tower bells began their count to eight, he rushed toward the stables to fetch Orfius. He was feeling apprehensive due to the encounter with his father, but when an unknown stable hand brought out Don Skully's horse, the young priest breathed a sigh of relief. As Millan attached his small sack of belongings to the saddle, he heard hoofbeats behind him.

"Good morning, Don Millan."

"Oh, good morning, Eriph. Please, no title is necessary."

"If you insist. Are you still sure about going to Royal Oak? We can ride together for a couple of hours before the road splits toward Light's Haven."

"I'm sure."

"Well then, hop on up and let's get going." Eriph pulled the reins, directing his horse away from the priest. Millan grabbed the saddle and hoisted himself into the seat. Orfius leapt into action and trotted to catch up to Eriph's steed. As they passed through the city's southern gate, the two riders nodded to the watchers on duty and left Nolka behind. The city shrank in the distance, and before long, it was out of sight.

Eriph cleared his throat. "So, Millan, I have to ask. Why did you wish to come along with me? I know you haven't seen much of the kingdom, but coming to Royal Oak doubles your travel time."

"Well, I did it for the company. I feel like I can learn a lot from you, even if it's just a day."

"What exactly are you expecting to learn?"

"I, uh, I'm not sure," Millan said with some hesitation. "It's just, well, if I may speak candidly?"

"By all means. There's no need for formality with me."

"Your decision to train in Alovajj. You were specifically told not to go, and yet you went anyway. Why?"

Eriph chuckled. "Doesn't seem to make sense, does it?"

"Not really, no."

"Have you ever had the feeling that something just didn't seem right? That you weren't privy to the whole truth?"

"What truth?"

Eriph made a sweeping motion with his arm. "About the world. The way it all works. Humans, demons. Haven't you ever felt that dizziness when you first realized something wasn't necessarily the way you've been taught?"

"Actually, yes. I felt it when you said Don Skully was an advisor, and again last night when Archdon Feranis spoke on the subject. It's like the world I knew was a lie."

"That's what I felt about the Death Gods. There's no one left to defend them here, and so what you hear about them is what the Council wants you to hear. They want you to believe these people are sinister and dangerous."

"So they lie?" Millan asked.

"Not exactly. Everything they say has truth to it, but it's distorted. There are other facts that get omitted to avoid dissension."

"Like what?"

Eriph pushed his mouth to one side. "Well, take the Wall of Light, for example. You've heard of it?"

"No, Don Skully never really talked about the Death Gods or their ideas."

"Well, I won't get into the details, but it's basically a way to keep a city's walls enchanted with holy light all the time. The Council didn't think it would work. They thought it was too dangerous, that people would die. Well, the Death Gods created it in Alovajj, and guess what. It works. And, no one's been hurt by it. In fact, it keeps the city safe. Much safer than even Light's Haven."

Millan was taken aback. "Really?"

"Absolutely. It's been working for a few years now. You see? The Council would never tell people that. It would look like they'd made a mistake by exiling the group. You know, I personally believe if Candelux had supported Sect Eighty-Eight and worked together with them, we wouldn't be facing a demon lord intent on killing the king. In fact, I think this war would be over."

Eriph had barely revealed anything, but already the young priest was having doubts about the Prima's decision to exile the Death Gods. He was starting to question what he'd been taught.

"I think I'd like to visit Alovajj one day," Millan said. "With permission, of course."

"Of course."

"Heh, listen to me. I'm off on a trip to see one new city, and I already want to see another. And a forbidden one at that."

Eriph smiled. "Well, I think you're going to enjoy Royal Oak. It's ripe with history, not about Candelux, but the kingdom in general."

"Really? I didn't learn much about kingdom history when I was younger.

"Why not? Doesn't Nesinu have a school for the children?"

Millan looked away sheepishly. "Yes, it does, but my father insisted on teaching me himself. I'm not sure why."

"So you don't even know about Thoris?"

"*Pfft*. Come on. Everyone knows about Thoris."

Eriph held up his hand. "Fair enough. Well, how about you tell me what you learned about him, and I'll try to fill in the gaps."

"Uh, not much. He controlled the territory around Light's Haven about seven hundred years ago. And he was the one who united the four clans."

"Then you know the leaders of those clans?"

"Thoris, Shabinne, Kasaverr, and Deimor. They're the ancestors of all royalty and nobility."

Eriph motioned for him to continue. "What else do you know?"

"Hmm, I know about Verago and Prevarra, and how they're descendants of Thoris."

"Now you're jumping ahead a few centuries. What about how Thoris united the clans? The legend of the royal oak?"

"I didn't realize that there was one. I thought it was just a big tree."

Eriph snickered. "Just a big tree, huh?"

"Mm-hmm. So, what's this legend?"

"Well, the story goes that when Thoris met with the other three clan leaders about uniting under a single banner, he gave them one month to consider his proposal. Deimor and Kasaverr returned to their respective capitals to confer with their clans. Shabinne, however, stayed behind. The next day, having recognized how great and just Thoris was, Shabinne entered the house of Thoris and bent his knee. Then and there, he agreed to join the kingdom and became the first to serve under the new king. In recognition of his allegiance, Thoris traveled with him back to his capital, which was well known for the spring that feeds Lake Ivorus. The water from the spring comes from deep below the Surface and is still believed to have magical properties. During his visit, Thoris likened their new relationship to that of a tree, constantly growing and expanding. And then, he tossed a single acorn into the spring. The tree that grew from that acorn became known as the royal oak, for which the city was renamed. It still stands today, massive as ever."

Millan was intrigued by the story and wondered what other segments of history were left out of his lessons as a kid. "And what about the other clans? They obviously joined too."

"True, eventually. At first, they didn't like the idea of being under someone else's control, but with Shabinne's support and a promise of equality, they finally relented and joined the new kingdom."

"Wait. Promise of equality with a king? My father always said as long as the monarchy and nobility existed, equality would never be possible."

Eriph rocked his head from side to side. "I suppose that's true to some degree, but Thoris was talking about equality between him and the other three clan leaders and their families, who all became high nobility. Their power was almost unchanged as they were allowed to preside over their respective cities and territories. Shabinne, Kasaverr, and Deimor became the first members of The Royal Throne."

"The Royal Throne? What is that? When I spoke with Archdon Feranis, he said that people wanted Scct Eighty-Eight to go the way of the Royal Throne."

"It's just an expression. When something goes the way of the Royal Throne, it ceases to exist. I suppose growing up in Nesinu, you were never really exposed to nobility. It's a sore spot for them."

"So, what is it? Some sect?" Millan asked.

"Not a sect. A guild. And not just any guild. The Royal Throne was the first guild to ever be created, and it was done so by King Thoris himself. Members of high nobility were invited to join and act as advisors to the king. It went on for centuries."

"So, what happened?"

"Well, after the demons appeared and Candelux was

formed, the monarchy began to turn to the priests more and more for council. The nobles grew restless since they were being ignored. The king at that time, King Vask, feared that the kingdom would fall apart if there was a revolt against the crown. He saw the guild as a meeting place for the nobles to plot their rebellion, and so he had it disbanded indefinitely."

Millan brought his eyebrows together. "Wouldn't that just make them angrier?"

"Absolutely. But in the end, he calmed them by allowing Corriani, who was in line to be the next duchess of Royal Oak, to marry his son."

The Nesinu priest recalled this part from his homeschooling. At some point in history, each of the three noble families married into the monarchy. "You're talking about the unification of the bloodlines."

"Yes, or at least the start of it."

"Hmm, wait a minute. Wasn't it also during the reign of King Vask that Verago stole the Amulet of Yezda?"

"Yes, that's right. I'm curious. What exactly did Don Skully tell you about the Amulet?"

Millan thought back to his lessons. "Well, he said its origin is unknown, but it's responsible for the emergence of demons. It was discovered a few hundred years ago near the city of Alovajj. Candelux created the Talisman of Zavi to merge it with the Amulet and negate the dark energy flowing from it. Later, when Verago betrayed humanity, he stole the Amulet and used it to become the Devil. Right?"

"More or less. So, all Don Skully told you was the Amulet's origin is unknown? That's it?"

"Yeah. Why? Do you know where it came from? Do the Death Gods know?"

Eriph shrugged. "I couldn't say. I'm not a Death God. Yet."

"But you know something?"

"There are always stories. The tricky part is figuring out which one is the truth."

Millan was starving for information. "Like what?"

"Hmm, let me see. I heard one theory as a squire that the darkness of all evil deeds and intentions from around the kingdom materialized into an unholy relic."

"And you think that's possible?"

Eriph's face was serious for a moment before his smile broke through. "I think it's a ridiculous idea."

"So, out of all the stories you've heard, what do you think is the real origin?"

Eriph lightly pulled the reins to stop his horse, and Millan did the same. Despite the pair being obviously alone on the road, the excluded priest craned his neck to check the area. "What I'm about to tell you, you can't repeat to anyone. Understand?"

The tone concerned Millan. "No. Why not?"

"Let's just say you'd be hard-pressed to find anyone in the kingdom who'd believe you. If you go around talking about it, people might think you're crazy."

"But, you're still willing to tell me?"

"I wouldn't have thought so a couple of days ago, but I sense now that you don't follow blindly. You have an open mind, much like I do."

"So, is this theory crazier than the first one?" Millan asked.

"Perhaps, but I'll let you be the judge of that. It involves another race of humans. A shadow race."

A lone cricket chirped in the forest. The whole reason Millan wanted to ride with Eriph to Royal Oak was because he represented a fountain of knowledge to the young priest. Millan had a lot of respect for him. Eriph had followed his instinct to do what he believed to be right, even in the face of Exclusion. Even Archdon Feranis had sought information from the former don. Up until this point, Millan wanted to absorb everything Eriph was willing to divulge, but this last statement crossed a line for the Nesinu priest.

"You're messing with me again." Millan hoped this was

the case.

"Not this time. Feeling dizzy yet?"

"Look, I'm trying to keep an open mind, but a shadow race? What the depths is that?"

"Well, you know how war-mages use elemental energy to conjure fire or water spells? And how priests use light energy in our blessings? Well, these people are masters of dark energy. Instead of dons, they're all zaidons."

Millan had an unsettling feeling in his stomach. "Zaidons? Like the greater iymed? I thought only demons could manipulate dark energy."

"Humans are quite capable."

"So, these masters of dark energy. Where did they come from? And where are they now?"

"South of the kingdom, beyond the Yaggi Mountains."

"The *uncrossable* Yaggi Mountains?"

Eriph had a smug look on his face. "So they say."

"Then how would anyone know they exist?"

"There are…books."

Millan narrowed his eyes. "What books?"

"Books in Alovajj. Books that were unintentionally protected by demons for centuries."

"And you've read them?"

"Well…" Eriph scrunched his face. "Not exactly. Only the Death Gods are allowed access to the library in the palace. But, I look forward to reading them when I get there."

"Hmm, well, what else do these books supposedly say? Do they explain where the Amulet's name came from? I mean, was Yezda a place or a person?"

"No clue. I never heard much detail on the artifact's name, but I bet someone from that other race would know."

"Right." Millan straddled the line between belief and doubt. "I see what you mean now about how people might think you're crazy."

"The things you see and hear in Alovajj will change

your life." The excluded priest flicked his wrists, and his steed began to walk again.

The Nesinu priest softly kicked his horse to catch up. "Let's say everything you've said is the truth. A shadow race of people, who are masters of dark energy, created the Amulet of Yezda and somehow crossed the uncrossable mountains. Then what? They just left the Amulet here?"

"I don't know. I don't know exactly how the Amulet ended up in our kingdom or why, but I do believe it was created by those people."

"Why?"

"Think about it. Something like the Amulet doesn't just appear out of nowhere. It had to be created by someone. Someone very powerful. Just look at what was involved in making the Talisman of Zavi. Now, you have two artifacts of opposite energy, but equal strength. It only stands to reason that the effort to make either one would be the same."

"The early priests spent years creating the Talisman," Millan noted.

"All masters of light energy with the help of an angel. You know the Talisman couldn't have been created without the help of Verago, right?"

Millan reflected on the story of Verago, once the savior of humanity, now its greatest enemy. "Yes, I know. And now, he wants nothing more than to see it destroyed. Ironic, isn't it?"

"I suppose so."

The two spent the next few hours discussing more of the kingdom's past mixed in with personal history until they came upon a fork in the path with posted signs.

Eriph moved his horse to the middle path. "Well, this is it. Last chance."

Millan silently read each of the five pieces of wood from top to bottom. The top two arrows pointed to the right path and read "Light's Haven" and "Inssen." The middle sign indicated that the path straight ahead would lead them to "Royal Oak." The fourth pointed back the way they came, and the fifth directed them down a narrow road that ended at "Malarekita."

The excluded priest rested on the front of his saddle. "Well?"

The young priest had convinced himself he would go to Royal Oak no matter what, but he knew there was always the option to change his mind. Millan tightly gripped the reins and took a deep breath. "Royal Oak it is."

"Excellent. We should probably pick up the pace, though."

Millan agreed, and the two urged their horses into a faster gait.

****

"You fools! You cannot hope to defeat me!"
"You've already lost, Erynion!"

The dream faded as a nearby voice intervened. "Hey, are you all right?"

A wave of water splashed on Erynion and forced him awake. The demon moaned and opened his eye to find the jester iymed crouching beside him. "Flinch, what happened? Where are we?"

"Lake Ivorus. Did you know you talk in your sleep? And that you speak the language of the land when you dream?"

"I do? What does that mean?"

"Probably nothing. I wouldn't worry about it. Happens to some demons. Something or other related to the subconscious state. Sonojj could elaborate. But, I just thought it was odd that the Erynion in your dream doesn't speak Kisejjad." Flinch cocked his head. "Anyway, what happened last night?"

Erynion was silent, stuck on the jester's previous comment. Why did the Erynion in his dream not speak like a demon?

Flinch waved his hand in front of Erynion's face. "Hey, you there? Last night? Where'd you go? Did you pass out from the agony again?"

Erynion cradled his head in his hands. "I don't remember. How did I get here?"

"Well, Sereyna brought you back all unconscious. I mean, down and out, lost the bout. And, she wouldn't tell us anything."

Erynion studied the placement of the sun in the sky. "I've been asleep for some time then? It looks like midday."

"Yeah, Sereyna wanted to be at the lake so we can organize an attack on Royal Oak tonight. And when you didn't wake up after last night, one of the greater fray carried you."

"Ah, Erynion. Pleased to hear you're awake and well." Sonojj joined the two demons. "Flinch told me you came back less than conscious."

"He told me the same. How's the nose?"

The shape-shifting demon traced the scar with his fingers. "It's healing. I'm starting to get my sense of smell back. Where did you and Sereyna run off to last night?"

"I'm not sure. I vaguely recall a small town. I assume it was Malarekita."

"Most likely. So, what happened? The agony?"

Erynion sat up. "It didn't feel like it, but I'm not sure. My memory's failing me."

"You know, that's becoming a common theme with you," Flinch blurted out, giving him a light jab in the shoulder.

"Best to not force it," Sonojj said. "Try to relax. You remember leaving the camp with Sereyna?"

"Yes."

"And then what happened?"

Erynion closed his eye and breathed in through his nose. His exhale was drawn out and controlled. "We were on a hill overlooking a town. We were talking about filling pouches with water. Energy and the agony. We approached the town. There were arrows and fire. Arrows on fire. I'm pretty sure I was hit multiple times."

"You were wounded?"

"Yes—no. No, I was hit, but I wasn't hurt. I pulled the arrows out."

Flinch tittered. "I suppose that explains the burn marks on your shirt."

Sonojj spoke over the jester. "Keep going. You're doing great."

"We were met in the town by some priests. They were begging us to leave. Things start to get unclear after that. The last thing I remember is a black cloud surrounding us."

"A black cloud? From Sereyna?"

Erynion slowly opened his eye. "Actually, yes, now that you mention it. It was flowing out of her mouth."

Flinch gasped. "Corruption. Why would she use that on a nothing town?"

Sonojj tilted his head and his ear twitched.

When the blind demon remained silent, Erynion said, "Fine, I give up. What's Corruption?"

"We must find Sereyna." The iymed shifted into his cat form and raced toward the demon camp. Flinch motioned with his head that they should follow.

As they gave chase, Erynion repeated, "So, what's Corruption?"

"It's a very powerful spell. Most notably, it's Sereyna's purge."

"I thought the purge was a safety measure to escape the agony."

"It can be. But that's for demons like you who can't control their powers. When you learn to master your energy, your purge becomes your most powerful attack. Hers is Corruption, a cloud of dark energy that decays all it touches."

"Is it harmful to demons?"

The Twisted Gate

"Nope. We're made of dark energy. It only harms living things."

When the two caught up to Sonojj, he was back in humanoid form, alongside Sereyna, Maligus, and Alejjir. The Marksman had already summoned his weapon, a large, intricately carved bow. The ornamental offshoots that grew off the handle were small twisting vines that reminded Erynion of the gate he had come through.

"What's going on?" Erynion asked before he was immediately hushed by Maligus.

Sereyna leaned over. "Sonojj hears a rider coming from the east."

The blind demon lifted his hand and pointed. Through the trees, a horse and its rider galloped along the dirt path.

"Probably coming from Malarekita to warn Royal Oak. Wouldn't want that to happen. Alejjir, be a dear and put an arrow through his heart."

The Marksman pulled the bowstring back to full tension and aimed his weapon. The tip of the arrow drifted as it followed the traveler's path. The rider's brown robe was flapping wildly in the wind. Alejjir finally let the arrow fly. The projectile whizzed past the horse, and the rider pushed the beast to run faster. Without a second attempt, Alejjir walked away from the group.

Maligus growled. "Shall we pursue?"

"No point," Sereyna said. "There's no way to catch him now."

"But he'll warn the officials at Royal Oak," the ogre demon cautioned.

"I suppose it'll just be more of a challenge then. You know how much I like a challenge. Wait here, please."

****

The Seductress left the group behind and made her way out of the camp to where the Marksman stood alone. Removing his hat, Alejjir ran his hand through his hair, pausing to scratch his head momentarily. With his back still to her, he restored the wide-brimmed hat to his head.

"Any particular reason you disobeyed me?" she asked in her typical dulcet tone.

"What do you mean?" Alejjir responded. "Hundred yards out, between trees, flying by on a horse. No one could hit that mark in one try."

Sereyna scoffed. "Come now. How long have we known each other? Who do you think you're fooling?"

"I'm not trying to fool anyone. I guess I'm just a little rusty."

"You may have returned as a lesser iymed, but I'm sure you could've made that shot with your eyes shut."

The Marksman glanced over his shoulder. "You're sure, huh? Beware of what you think you know, or your overconfidence will be your undoing."

Sereyna circled him like a shark. "Are you threatening me?"

"Of course not. Just a warning from one old friend to another."

"Speaking of warnings, that priest is going to warn Royal Oak."

"Why should that matter? Why are you even attacking Royal Oak?"

"Why not? It happens to be on our way to Alovajj."

"Right, Alovajj," Alejjir said. "Where the demon lord is, huh?"

Sereyna caught the sarcasm. "Of course. You think I would lie?"

The Marksman grabbed her by the arm. "You don't know what you're dealing with, Ezmi—"

"*Don't* call me that!" she interrupted sharply, tearing her arm from his grasp. "And I know exactly what I'm dealing with. A source of unbridled power that I will soon control."

"I doubt Verago will be pleased."

"Verago?" Her upper lip curled in contempt before

returning to the sly smile. "You know, as well as I, that coward won't show his face on the Surface as long as the Talisman exists. So, if I decide to take control of his new creation, what can he do about it?"

"How is that even possible? Your puppet trick doesn't work on demons."

"You're right, but this is different somehow. I wish I knew why. I only discovered it by accident on the first night. He was just seconds away from laying waste to the forest and everything nearby, which included me. In desperation, I gave my tail a try. The way I figure it, he had no control over his power, and so when his energy was looking to escape, instead of purging, it willingly flowed to me."

"And what happens when he learns to control it?"

"Well, he won't have the chance. He remembers so little from his dreams, he'll never discover his identity in time. It'll only take another prick or two, and then he'll be mine forever."

Alejjir shook his head. "This is a mistake."

"Don't be sad, my dear. You should be happy. Once I have control of him, there will be no risk of a purge. With time, I'll even be able to restore you to your former glory." The Seductress moved in closer and caressed the side of his face with the back of her hand. "Just think of it. You with your bow. Me with my pet. We'd be unstoppable."

"I'm leaving. Despite what you think, the demon lord is dangerous. And I certainly won't be a part of your little rebellion."

As he walked away, the Seductress followed and tried to persuade him. "Think about what you're doing. I'm giving you the chance to be great again. To be my right hand."

"Maligus seems to fit nicely in that role."

Sereyna caught him by the wrist. "Maligus is a brute, an ogre, an oaf. He's not nearly noble enough to ascend any higher. It's you I want."

"Is that so?"

"Please," she begged sensually as she brought her lips up to his. Pulling back from the kiss, the Seductress grinned innocently and stroked his arm. With the demon lord and the Marksman by her side, she really would be unstoppable.

"How many have stared into those eyes and given their lives without a second thought?" he asked.

The question caught her off guard. "Alejjir."

"Good-bye, Sereyna."

CHAPTER 18

Millan's experienced a rush of excitement as the walls of Royal Oak came into view. They reminded him of Light's Haven. The horses trotted up to the main gate where he and Eriph were greeted by three guards dressed in armor.

"Name and business in Royal Oak?" one watcher asked firmly.

Millan's travel companion took the lead. "Eriph, former don of Candelux. Perhaps you've heard of me in recent news. This here is Don Millan. He was good enough to keep me safe on the road today."

"Eriph, yes, I've heard the name," the watcher grumbled. "What about you? Don Millan, was it?

The young priest straightened up. "Yes, that's right."

"Does your friend speak the truth?"

"Every word," Millan promptly answered.

"Nothing to add?"

"Nope."

Cities rarely closed their gates, even at night, but with the Prima's new orders, this would be the norm until the demon lord was defeated. The watcher looked to the man in the middle who was dressed in more elaborate armor.

Although Millan had never learned the armor differences between the two types of paladins, he found it safe to assume that this was one of the bloodseekers.

"They're clear," the paladin said softly.

"Please, follow us in," directed the first watcher.

The two travelers entered through the gate after the guards. Once the horses had passed through, the door was sealed again.

"Some lockdown you have here," Eriph said casually. "Is it really necessary to close the main gate during the day?"

"Prima's orders. We're taking every precaution against the new threat. I suggest you go and speak with the head archdon. I'm sure he'll be interested in your arrival."

"Perhaps. Are we in danger here?"

The guard snorted. "Inside the walls?"

"Then why's the gate closed? Are we expecting an attack while the sun is up?"

"As I said, Prima's orders," the soldier snapped back. "You should speak with Head Archdon Scarit."

With a friendly smile, Eriph bid farewell to the guards at the gate. Millan was still taking in the city around the entrance when he realized his companion had left him behind. The Nesinu priest jogged after Eriph to catch up. "Shall we head to the rectory?"

"Eventually. Let's put the horses in the stables, and then I'll show you around. I'm sure whatever they fear will happen won't occur until after sunset."

After leaving their horses in the care of the stable hands, the duo walked to the center of the second-largest city in the kingdom. In the distance, Millan could already make out the silhouette of the massive oak tree, backlit by the setting sun. He gaped in amazement as the tree grew larger. He had never seen such a presence in nature. They crossed the square and entered the shadow of the tree. The retaining wall that held back the spring water was at chest level.

"Magnificent, isn't it?" Eriph leaned his back against the wall.

Millan watched as the water flowed around the base of the massive trunk and toward the aqueduct, which carried the water out of the city. "It's hard to imagine there was ever a time when demons didn't threaten the kingdom, and yet this tree stood before any iymed or fray ever existed."

"It's a symbol of our resilience. No matter what happens, it stands tall and proud. For seven hundred years, it's kept watch over these people, and it'll likely do so for another seven hundred."

Millan's eyes climbed the branches to the countless leaves. "I'm glad I came. This alone was worth the detour."

"Uh-oh. Here comes trouble."

A man donning a brown scarf hurried toward them. As the middle-aged squire reached the retaining wall of the spring, he gave a quick bow to the pair. "Don Millan and Eriph, I presume?"

"Yes, how did you know?" Millan asked.

"I was told to look for two men, both dressed as priests—"

"But I'm not dressed as a priest," Eriph interjected. "See, no scarf."

"One of which would be carrying a shield." The squire motioned to the metal plate that Eriph was hauling on his back. "Not exactly discreet."

"What makes you think I was trying to be discreet?"

"My apologies. I didn't mean to imply that you were. Simply put, your shield made it easy to spot you."

"Is there something we can help you with?" Millan asked.

"Yes, Head Archdon Scarit has requested to speak with you. There's talk about a demon attack tonight, and he'd like to enlist your help."

"I suppose we could lend a hand," the Nesinu priest answered.

Eriph raised his eyebrows. *"We?"*

"Yes. What? You won't help?"

"When the Seductress or Erynion crosses the border into Alovajj, then it'll become my concern."

Millan was stunned by his response. "But...but you're here now. If the demons strike, you won't fight by our side?"

"No scarf, remember? I'm not a don anymore. I've been excluded. It means I'm no longer bound by Candelux's code. Why should I risk my life?"

"Candelux's code, no, but what about your own?"

Eriph sighed. "Fine, let's see what the old man has to say. But I'm not making any promises."

The corner of Millan's mouth pushed up as he took pride in his powers of persuasion. The squire led the two men through the streets, and the young priest marveled at the size of the city. Royal Oak was larger than Nolka in every way. Even the rectory was bigger, but it still paled in comparison to the Sanctuary in Light's Haven. The group made their way through the halls until they arrived at a large office where an elderly man sat with a woman standing beside him. Both were dressed in black robes with white scarves.

As the door shut, the old man invited them to approach his desk. "Eriph, I was sorry to hear about your Exclusion. How unfortunate. And Don Millan, my condolences to you for Don Skully and your home."

"Thank you, Your Grace," the Nesinu priest said.

Age had taken a toll on his voice, and the old man struggled to speak louder. "Welcome to Royal Oak. I am Archdon Scarit, the head archdon here. You may already know my associate, Archdon Omana."

"Nice to see you again," Eriph said.

"Archdon Omana? As in, former advisor to Primus Ayristark?" Millan asked incredulously.

"That's correct," Scarit said. "I want to thank you both for coming to see me. For some time now, I have felt unrest in the darkness. My suspicions have been confirmed by recent events: the twisted gate, the demon lord, the reappearance of the Seductress, and the attacks on Nesinu, Nolka, and now Malarekita."

"What?!" Millan exclaimed. "Malarekita was attacked?"

"Yes." The head archdon coughed. "Perhaps you're wondering why we've locked down the city while the sun is up?"

"Well, to be honest, the thought had crossed my mind," Eriph said.

"Earlier today, Don Diche from Malarekita arrived at the city gates. His horse nearly died from exhaustion. It seems the Seductress, along with a brute matching the description of our new demon threat, Erynion, walked into the village last night—amid a rain of arrows—and proceeded to release her Corruption spell."

Millan was taken aback. "What? Another purge?"

"I'm afraid so. The priests of Malarekita prepared for the worst and kept the protection blessings up through the night to ensure the safety of the villagers. When morning came, they realized the demons were long gone and the spell had dissipated. Thankfully, there were no casualties. With no Scriptorum, Head Don Galyval sent Don Diche to come here and warn us."

"And you believe the Seductress is coming here next? Why?"

"Nesinu, Nolka, Malarekita. Don Diche also reported a demonic presence by Lake Ivorus. If they follow the same general direction, Royal Oak would be the next in line. We're not sure what their goal was at Malarekita. It may have been some sort of a warning, a demonstration of power, or maybe just a scare tactic. Whatever the case, we're not taking any chances. I suspect there will be some activity tonight, and I would be grateful if you two joined our ranks in case of an attack, especially since you've both seen this new evil."

"Of course, Your Grace, I would be honored to help in any way I can," Millan stated.

Eriph was slower with his response. "I'm no longer a member of Candelux."

"Yes, I'm well aware of that, but your help would be appreciated nonetheless."

"I'm sorry. My service to Candelux is over and not by my choice. Tomorrow when the sun rises, I will continue to Alovajj. If the demons advance on the city tonight, I will leave them in your capable hands."

"Eriph," Millan muttered.

"I understand," the old man said. "Though I'm sorry to hear it. You're free to leave. If you change your mind, you know where to come."

"Of course."

Archdon Scarit lifted his hands. "May the angels watch over you and guide you on your travels."

"Thank you. May the angels give you all strength in the battles to come." Eriph extended his hand to Millan. "It was a pleasure riding with you, Don Millan. Feel free to visit if you happen to be in my neck of the woods."

Disappointed at the choice his new friend had made, the Nesinu priest reluctantly shook hands. Fighting back the urge to scold him, Millan managed to say, "May the angels watch over you and keep you safe."

Eriph departed, and Millan turned his attention to the head archdon.

"Thank you for your support, Don Millan," Scarit said. "Though we have many priests and squires in our city, an extra hand is always welcome. A squire will show you to the guest quarters. Please prepare yourself for the inevitable battle tonight."

****

You are my weapon and you answer only to me, the voice called out.

Erynion brought his hand to his head.

"Something the matter?" Flinch asked.

Erynion gazed across the peaceful lake. "I'm not sure the meditation is working."

"Patience isn't your best quality," Sonojj quipped. "What are you focusing on?"

"Focusing? I thought I was supposed to clear my mind and let the memories come back naturally."

"Doing so opens your mind to any memory. Yes, you want to be free of distractions, but you should have a goal in mind and focus on that."

"And what goal would that be?"

"Your identity," Sonojj said matter-of-factly.

Flinch smiled. "The aim of the game is to claim your name."

"How am I supposed to focus on something I don't know?"

"Then focus on something you do know," the blind demon suggested. "The name, Erynion, came from somewhere in your past, right?"

"I suppose. I thought it was just a random name given to me by a beggar, but it's clearly in my memory as well."

"So, find out who Erynion was."

Erynion rubbed the back of his neck. "And how do you know that will help with my identity?"

"I don't. But aside from the Assault, it's the only link you have to your memories. Explore it."

The large demon closed his eye once again. Air rushed through his nostrils and into his lungs. His chest grew to accommodate the breath. His shoulders relaxed as he slowly exhaled. He kept his mind clear, save for a single word: Erynion. Scenes flashed in his head. The different pieces of his recurring dream lasted longer and longer with each appearance. The ambient noise of the forest faded away. A young girl screamed for help. Another child reassured her. A third voice called out in the recesses of his mind.

"You fools! You cannot hope to defeat me!"

"You've already lost, Erynion!"

He remained calm as the dream took shape. The surroundings were dark and shadowed, but he could see a figure not far from him. A young boy, no older than ten, was gripping a wooden sword. His face was unclear, but Erynion felt a sense of familiarity. He shared a strong friendship with this child. Behind the boy, Erynion spotted a silhouette of a man holding onto a little girl.

"Come on, get up," his young friend urged. "Go around back and sneak up behind him."

Erynion examined himself and discovered he was barely a teenager. He, too, was armed with a wooden sword. Erynion stayed low and walked through the emptiness that was his dream. Maniacal laughter filled the void, and the figures began fading into shadows.

"Don't worry, Sereyna. We'll save you," the young boy said reassuringly.

Erynion felt his grip on the past weakening, but he refused to let it go. He forced the memory onward and attacked the large shadow who had taken the girl hostage.

"You are brave indeed," the shadow taunted. "But now you must cross blades with the mighty Erynion!"

The name echoed in his mind. Everything else dissipated, and Erynion stood alone in the abyss. "Come back, you coward! Come back and face me!" Nothing remained of his dream but the name.

"Erynion. Erynion," Flinch said softly while nudging the large figure.

The demon opened his eye. "Damn it all to the depths. Why did you wake me? I nearly had it."

"Had what?" Sereyna asked.

Erynion was startled by her presence. "Uh. My memory. My dream."

"You were meditating?"

"Yes, to figure out my identity."

"Hmm." Sereyna bit her lower lip. "I'm afraid I have to ask you stop that for the time being."

"Stop? But you said my identity was the key. You said

you would help me."

"It is, and I will. But for now, we need to focus on the preparations for tonight. I can't have you in some trance while we're trying to take the city. Come, I wish to discuss our plan of attack."

Sereyna trudged up the shore and back toward the congregation of demons.

Flinch came alongside Erynion. "I'm sorry for waking you."

"It's fine. I just thought I'd have more time."

"More time? It's been almost an hour. Did you remember anything more this time?"

"Sort of. It's becoming clearer, but I still don't know who anyone is. Or who I am."

Sonojj offered some consolation. "I understand it can be frustrating, but progress is a good sign."

"You know what the strange part is? All demons use pseudonyms, right?" Erynion asked.

"Sure."

"In the memory, I could swear the young boy is yelling to a girl named Sereyna. Could it be a coincidence that she shares the name with…?" Erynion jerked his head in the direction of the Seductress.

"Maybe you should ask Sereyna how she came to choose her name," Flinch suggested. "I've heard that she's been called other things before, right, Sonojj?"

The blind demon nodded. "When I first joined, she called herself Mantira. But ever since the Assault on Light's Haven, she's demanded to be called by only one name. And, that's Sereyna."

Erynion had a sinking feeling in his chest he couldn't explain. Something urged him to exercise caution around his benevolent leader. There was more to the name "Sereyna" than he knew. And if he wanted to find the connection, if any, between the girl in his dream and this demon, he would have to do so quickly. Erynion replayed the dream in his mind. "Flinch, you were right."

"Of course I was." The jester grinned for a moment before turning serious. "Right about what?"

"About Erynion. The one in my dream. Or my memory. Whatever. He doesn't speak Kisejjad."

"Well, maybe he's not really a demon.".

"Yeah, I don't think he is. Erynion was the name of my enemy in the dream. I was just a boy trying to slay him with a wooden sword."

Sonojj mused, "A man pretending to be a demon and fighting with children? Sounds like a game to me."

CHAPTER 19

Millan was shown to his quarters to rest from his journey. Placing his small travel bag on the bed, he slowly opened it. A multitude of emotions tugged at his heart. He feared the new terror, worried about the upcoming battle, was disappointed at Eriph's decision, and despite being surrounded by hundreds of Candelux members, he was alone. However, as he unpacked his bag, an overwhelming sorrow replaced all those emotions. He carefully reached into the cloth sack and took hold of the final object resting at the bottom. As he pulled it out, he sat on the bed and stared at the item in the palm of his hand. It was a gift on his day of Acceptance from his teacher, but it represented so much more. It was the reason Millan had decided to join Candelux. The young priest closed his eyes and recalled that fateful night from his youth.

"Millan! Millan! Where are you?"

Nine-year-old Millan had spotted his mother frantically searching for him along the streets of Nesinu. He had ignored her calls as he played with his friends.

"Aren't you going to be in trouble?" his friend asked.

"I'll just pretend I didn't hear her. It's not like the sun is—hey!"

"There you are. Didn't you hear me calling you? How dare you ignore me!" she scolded as she twisted his arm and pulled him away from his friends.

"Come on, Mom, the sun isn't even below the tree line."

"I don't care where the sun is. When I call you, you come. Understood, young man?"

"Yes, Mom." Millan's tone was sullen, upset his mother had embarrassed him in front of his friends. Other parents were now combing the streets for their children, which Millan found strange. His mother took him straight home. They resided in a two-story building near the stables, but Millan and his parents only lived on the top floor. Inside the small home, Millan sat in his little room and tapped the back of his head against the wall. He had been sent to bed right after supper even though he insisted he wasn't tired. A commotion in the other room made him pause. He strained to listen but could only hear the muffled voices of his parents arguing. Tiptoeing to the door, he gently placed his ear to it.

"But why trust him?" his father said.

"Why not? He would know, wouldn't he?"

"Yes, but you know what they say about him, about his involvement with that sect."

"Well, what choice do we have?" his mother asked. "Would you rather our boy wander the streets and be attacked by a demon?"

"It's not that. What if this isn't a random attack?"

"What are you suggesting? That he called them? Is that even possible?"

"Why not? It's just like Candelux to stir up trouble. Nice quiet town that hasn't needed a priest to date, but now they need to justify their presence."

"I don't know, Damion. Seems a bit farfetched to me."

"Farfetched? It's been the same for centuries!"

"Lower your voice. You'll wake Millan."

Millan identified this as the perfect opportunity to feign

that he'd been woken up. Opening his door, he rubbed his eyes and innocently mumbled, "What's going on?"

His father remained by the window as his mother tended to him. "Go back to bed, dear. It's nothing."

"But I can't sleep. I'm not tired. Can I stay up for just a little?"

He could tell from the look on her face that she wasn't going to fight him. Proud of his tactics, young Millan happily took his spot next to his father. He poked his head over the windowsill and scanned the main street. Night had fallen, and lanterns cast the only light on the streets. The house was quiet as a distant and unnatural roar swept through the town. Millan's heart did a backflip. The single bell in the watcher's tower chimed in a way the boy had never heard before. Millan turned away from the window and wrapped his arms around his father's leg.

"Angels help us," Damion said.

His mother tried to usher Millan away. "Let's go to your room, dear. You'll be safe there."

Any other nine-year-old boy would've taken the opportunity to flee from the scene, but Millan's paralyzing fear was gradually overcome by curiosity. After all, if his parents would be safe here, so would he.

"I want to see." He knew about the demons and why he wasn't allowed outside after sunset. He knew the fiends had even tried to conquer Light's Haven a couple years earlier but had failed thanks to the might of Candelux. And it was only last year when the new priest had arrived in Nesinu. Millan didn't know much about the old man in the brown robe. His father had ordered him to stay clear of Don Skully, and he dutifully obeyed.

His mother grasped his hand. "Millan, this is not something for little boys to see. You'll get nightmares."

"I don't care." He yanked his hand away. "I want to see."

"No, come with me."

"No!" The boy stomped his foot. "I don't want to go to

my room."

"Let him watch," Damion interrupted.

Millan's mother glared at her husband and crossed her arms in front of her chest. "Fine, but you'll deal with the consequences. When he can't sleep, you'll be the one to comfort him."

"Fine," he answered flatly. And then under his breath, barely loud enough for Millan to hear, he said, "Assuming we survive tonight."

A lump formed in Millan's throat. Maybe he should go to bed. But no, he had already fought to make it this far. The young boy moved back to the sill. A small group waited at the edge of town. They appeared human only in shape, but their features were all wrong. The leader, Millan assumed, towered over the streetlamps. His nose was elongated like a muzzle, which pushed his eyes more to the sides. Around him stood six child-size beings. A couple had funny ears and one stood on all fours. Millan sensed there was something wrong with them. An evil festered inside them. He felt uneasy as this was his first sight of demons.

"Here comes our savior now," Damion said. Millan knew he was being sarcastic. His father never had anything nice to say about priests.

Don Skully was the lone human on the street as he confronted the demons. He stopped a stone's throw from Millan's home, and the demons had halted on the other side, giving Millan the ideal view for the upcoming fight. The young boy noticed the priest playing with an object in his right hand but couldn't make out what it was.

"Leave this town, demon," Skully said. "What you seek is not here. I don't want to risk the lives of these villagers, so I give you this chance to withdraw."

The demon leader uttered gibberish in the demonic tongue that little Millan couldn't yet understand.

"You're mistaken. Leave now or face Verago in the Depths."

The large iymed snarled and the six fray demons charged toward their foe.

Most of the initial battle was a blur to Millan. Lights flashed as the little demons seemed to melt away. As they advanced toward Skully, the fray did their best to dodge his attacks, but the streaks of light always found their marks. Before long, only the giant remained. A darkness gathered around his claw as he pulled a massive weapon from seemingly nowhere. It was an enormous scimitar that was almost as tall as the demon himself. Millan squinted as the light from the lanterns danced off the blade.

"Your friends are gone. Go back to wherever you came from and never return."

The demon responded and brandished his weapon.

Don Skully sent a pulse of light at the fiend, but he didn't budge. The blessing landed, leaving an imprint seared in the demon's chest. The iymed snickered and walked menacingly toward the priest.

Within striking range, the demon readied his blade, but a chain of light burst forth from the ground and caught his wrist. As he struggled to break free, more blessings emerged and pulled the beast to his knees. Don Skully strolled up to him and held out his hand.

"What's going on?" Millan asked.

His mother inched toward the window and craned her neck. "He's cleansing the demon, so he can't return to the Surface and harm us."

Millan smiled and quietly clapped his hands. The restrained iymed bellowed and struggled against the chains, but Don Skully remained unfazed and resumed his ritual. The demons were dealt with, and no one was hurt. Everything was going to be all right.

Millan looked up at his father. "He kept us safe, didn't he?"

Damion stared stoically at the priest. He barely moved his lips. "So it would seem."

The young boy turned back to witness the cleansing,

and his smile vanished. The large demon's yell reverberated off the buildings as he broke free of the holy shackles. The beast spun around and swung the scimitar to take the head of the priest. Millan cringed at the thought of their only defense falling prey to this monster. As the blade sliced through the air, light shot forth from the object in Skully's hand, creating a blade that danced like fire. The demon's weapon struck the light with such force that it knocked the priest backward a few yards and onto his back.

Skully returned to his feet with a lack of urgency. As the beast marched toward him, a yellow glow consumed the old man. The iymed whirled around once again and slashed at him. The holy aura around Skully intensified until it burst into form. Two wings of light exploded brilliantly from his shoulders, and his blade became like an untamable flame. The wings flitted up and then back down as the demon brought his scimitar in for the kill. Don Skully was whisked into the air and out of harm's way. The iymed raised his head toward the night sky to locate his adversary. Skully's blade of light blazed, and as the priest descended, his weapon tore effortlessly through the demon's body.

Millan clearly remembered the silence of the night when the battle had finished. No trace of demon could be found as the remains melted to the Depths. The wings of light had flickered and fell away like dust. The blade that had been summoned from the object in Skully's hand had vanished as well. There was no applause and no cheering. After taking one last look around, Don Skully had made his way back to the newly built rectory.

A sharp knock came at the door as Millan clutched the replica of the Talisman of Zavi. It was just like the one at the end of Feranis's staff, a conduit imbued with the power of holy light, manifested by the user. It was the gift that Millan received from Skully at his Acceptance and the last remaining object that reminded him of his mentor.

"Who is it?"

"Squire Aler. Head Archdon Scarit has called an assembly to discuss the battle ahead. I was sent to retrieve you."

Millan slid the star-shaped object into his pocket, opened the door, and followed the squire out.

****

A slithering whisper slipped into his mind. *The preparations have been made.*

Alone by the lake, Erynion rubbed his temples.

"How are you feeling?" a voice asked from behind.

Erynion glimpsed over his shoulder. "Fine."

"You haven't been meditating again, have you?" Sereyna stepped in front of him.

"No. It's just this voice I keep hearing."

"What kind of voice? Another memory?"

"I don't know. This isn't like the dreams I've been having. This voice is different. It seems to be giving me instructions."

"Instructions? To do what?"

Erynion shrugged. "Kill the king. Find the Brotherhood."

"You never mentioned it before."

"I've been trying to figure out the source. I guess it didn't seem worth mentioning."

"I see." Sereyna urged him to get up. "Come. It's time to go. Where are your friends?"

He remained seated. "What?"

"Flinch? Sonojj? Where are they?"

Erynion surveyed the area. "No idea. I thought they were in the camp with you."

"Interesting." Sereyna clasped her hands together. "Well, no matter. We don't need them anyway. We'll crush Royal Oak together."

"Why?"

"*Why?* Why not? Humans are the enemy. Royal Oak happens to be the second-largest city in the kingdom. It would give me such joy to cut down that ridiculous tree and burn the city to the ground. Wouldn't that make you happy?"

Erynion felt ill at the thought of mindless killing. "Not particularly. All I know is my purpose."

"Which you need me to help you with, correct? I'm helping you, and you're helping me as my soldier."

"If Royal Oak is so easy to destroy, why have you waited this long to do it?"

Sereyna hesitated. "It…uh…what do you mean?"

"According to Sonojj, you've been around for quite some time. Humans have always been there. The tree has always been there. Why the sudden interest in attacking the city now? What's changed?"

"There's a first time for everything. I never attacked Malarekita before either."

Erynion groaned. "Why don't you stop pretending? I know what I am, and you know as well."

Sereyna gasped. "Your identity?"

"No, not *who* I am. *What* I am. I know there's no demon lord in Alovajj because he's right here, sitting on this shoreline."

"You're sure of that?"

"Very. I suspected I was something terrible when I awoke that first morning and the town was gone. The same thing would've happened in Nolka if you hadn't shown up. Tell me I'm wrong."

Sereyna slid her hands down the back of her legs, fixing her dress as she sat beside Erynion. "You're not wrong. It's also possible that in your weakened state—caused by the agony—the archdon there could've cleansed you. I couldn't take that chance."

"You used one of your lieutenants as a distraction, a sacrifice."

"Reaper? Yes. And I would've given up the other three

as well if it meant getting you out of the hands of those priests."

"So, you admit it. I'm the demon lord everyone's been talking about."

Sereyna pursed her lips and took his hand into hers. "Yes. It's true."

"Why did you lie to me?"

"Very simple, really. I thought if you believed you're weaker than you actually are, then your mind would only try to tap into a small amount of your energy. I was trying to save you from the agony, so you could explore your identity."

Erynion was drawn to the moon's reflection in the lake, shining brilliantly in the wake of the dwindling rays of sunlight. "I have to admit that when you said I wasn't the demon lord, I wanted to believe it. But when the others told me about the purge at the Assault, I knew. Were you ever planning on telling me the truth?"

"Of course, love. I know you're no Dardan fool. If the others told you about the last demon lord and the purge at the Assault, then you must also realize how terrified they all are at the prospect of another one."

"That's the real reason why Alejjir left, isn't it? He knew what I was."

"Yes, I'm afraid so. And imagine if the others discovered that you're the demon lord. After the last one, we'd have no army."

Erynion eyed her suspiciously. "We?"

"Yes, we."

"I thought I was just your soldier."

"Aww, my sweet Erynion." Sereyna laid her head on his shoulder and squeezed his hand. "Did you take offense to that? You may have a massive power festering inside you, but it means very little if it can't be controlled, just like Maligus."

The demon lord pulled his hand away from hers. "Maligus? What does he have to do with this?"

"Poor demon. He has so much power within him, but he has no access to it. He could be the strongest lesser iymed on the Surface, maybe even a greater iymed. Not as strong as me, mind you."

"How is it possible that he harbors so much power?"

"He absorbed the energy of his brother."

"Absorbed? He killed his own brother? Who would do such a thing?"

Sereyna shook her head. "No, no, no. That's not how it works. Only Verago can move energy from one demon to another. Maligus and Rojjiro were unique. Verago linked them as part of an experiment that exploited their familial bond. They became the first of their kind, known as kindred demons. Fighting side by side made them more powerful. It was a loophole to the agony problem Verago was facing with stronger demons."

"They both served under you?"

"That's right. Pledged their undying loyalty. But a couple of years after the Assault failed, Rojjiro wandered off. No one seems to know why for sure. We found out later he had attempted to raid some small village up in the northeast of the kingdom, probably somewhere close to where you popped out."

"He died in the raid?"

"Yes," Sereyna said softly.

"So, how does that affect Maligus?"

"Aside from his terrible temper now? The strength that kindred demons receive when fighting together is only one advantage. There is a more powerful outcome from their connection. When one of the demons falls in battle, his energy is transferred to the other. The rush of power is intended to give the surviving demon a temporary burst of strength to overcome the odds and avenge his sibling. Unfortunately, Maligus was nowhere near Rojjiro when he died. He had no idea what was happening. The darkness invaded his body, and Maligus was infused with the power of his brother."

"Then why isn't he any stronger?"

Sereyna placed her hands on her knees. "The effect is supposed to be temporary. Gaining so much energy would undoubtedly drive any demon to madness from the agony. That's why the intent is that it's used in battle. But, we weren't. And so, I did the only thing I could think of. I created a barrier to separate Rojjiro's energy from Maligus."

"Wait a minute." Erynion shot to his feet. "You can do that?"

"I can do a lot."

"Why don't you just do that with me?"

"It's not the same. Rojjiro's energy was foreign to his brother. Because Maligus feared the agony, his body inherently tried to reject the influx of power. This is what allowed me to create the barrier successfully, and that is what remains locked inside him to this day." Sereyna patted the ground. "Sit back down."

Erynion obliged. "And he can never access it?"

"He can. If he chose to, he could dissolve the walls that I put in place, but he never will."

"Why do you say that?"

Sereyna's fingers danced on her knees. "He came to me after the whole incident, asking for my help. He wanted to control his new power. I tried to help him, of course. My expertise allowed me to slowly peel back the spell. But no matter how cautious I was, the power was too great for him."

"You mean the agony."

Sereyna nodded. "He panicked. He inadvertently punctured the barrier and his brother's energy mixed with his. Maligus nearly went insane. It took some time, but I fixed his mistake and locked away the energy once again. But the damage was already done. Maligus didn't speak for a month after that. When he finally did, his first words to me were, 'Never again.'"

In search of the ogre demon, Erynion stared at the

demon camp. "So, he's afraid."

"Indeed. But I wouldn't mention this to him. The whole incident can make him unstable." She softly caressed his face. "And just as I tried to help him, I'm also trying to help you, but you must listen to me. Don't let fear manipulate you, and I promise that you'll gain control over your power. I know that will allow you to rise above me, but until then, you must fight under me. So, yes, the mighty demon lord is my soldier. Is my command so terrible that you cannot endure it?"

The demon lord considered her words. "I'll follow you if you answer me this."

"What's on your mind?"

"Why did you choose the name Sereyna?"

"Why do you ask?"

"That's irrelevant. Will you answer the question?"

Sereyna seemed to ignore him as she smoothed out the creases in her dress, but she eventually relented. "It's simple really. It's the same reason I chose any of my pseudonyms. I adored the name, so I made it my own."

"Where did you hear it?"

"I don't know. It was years ago. What does it matter?"

Erynion growled. "It matters to me!"

The Seductress put her hand on her chest and leaned back. Though she remained seated, she put some distance between herself and Erynion. Her eyes were as open as they could be. "Very well. If you must know, Sereyna was the name of my sister. I always liked her name better than my own. She didn't live past the age of nine, though. I, of course, was still not allowed to change my name even after she died. But, when I became a demon, it was the perfect pseudonym for me."

"I was told you went by other names before you chose Sereyna."

"Other names? Of course. I couldn't use my sister's name in the beginning. There were still people alive who would have connected me to her. It was no secret I wanted her name, but that was many years ago. No one would remember that now, and so I'm free to use it. Satisfied?"

Something about her story was off, but Erynion couldn't pinpoint it. He studied her face for any hint of deception. Could there be a connection between the girl in his dreams and this demon's sister? The humans called her the Seductress after all, well versed in telling people what they wanted to hear.

"For now," he grumbled.

CHAPTER 20

Millan was admiring the large oak tree when the watchtower bells began to ring. The noise didn't startle him since a demon attack in some form was expected tonight. He had received instructions from Head Archdon Scarit to find Archdon Omana at the north gates of the city and join her group. Few demons were capable of scaling walls, and so their point of attack was always the main gate. And although Royal Oak had never been breached by demons, the issue of this demon lord had put everyone on high alert. With the sun departing from the sky, Millan looked to the north, but remained still. Deep down, it still bothered him that Eriph chose not to fight. The inn where the excluded priest was staying was close to the city center, so Millan decided to ask him once again. By the time he left the plaza, the streets were nearly empty. The markings on the doors glowed as the Blessing of Marked Defense was cast within the rectory.

At the inn, the Nesinu priest was surprised by the amount of noise coming from it. It was almost as if everyone from the street had funneled directly into this establishment. And despite the possibility of an attack, the patrons seemed to drink and socialize like nothing was wrong. No one paid him any attention as he stepped inside and made his way to the opposite end of the room.

Sitting behind a desk just outside the bar area, a silver-haired woman greeted Millan. "Welcome to the Golden Branch. Would you like a room?"

"Hi, and no, thank you. I'm looking for someone. He said he'd be staying here tonight."

"Oh? What's the name then?"

"Eriph."

The woman ran her finger down the ledger. "I see. I'm sorry to say, but that gentleman specifically requested not to be disturbed."

"I understand, but the matter is quite urgent. Candelux business. I promise I'll only take a few moments of his time."

"Urgent, you say? Well, I wouldn't want to interfere with Candelux business. Take these stairs to the second floor. At the top, take a right, and he'll be the third door on the left."

"Thank you very much."

Millan followed her directions and soon found himself in a staring contest with a door. How would Eriph react to his presence? He forced his hand into a fist and gave the wood three sharp knocks.

"Who is it?"

Millan parted his lips, but his throat closed.

"Who is it?" The voice was louder.

The young priest tried to speak his name but failed.

"Got a demon tongue? For the sake of the angels, who is it?" Eriph flung open the door. "Shouldn't you be defending the gates?"

"May I come in?"

"I heard the bells. You shouldn't be here."

"It'll only be a minute. May I come in?"

Eriph opened the door wider and gestured for the Nesinu priest to enter.

Millan hastily accepted the invitation. "I wanted to

come see you one last time. To ask for your help."

"Uh-huh. I figured as much. That's why I told that woman I didn't want to be disturbed."

"Look, I know you're a bit sore because of how the guild has treated you, but there's a lot of panic right now. No one knows what this demon lord is capable of. To be honest, the only time I've felt safe since Don Skully died was when you were there. Who knows what would have happened at the twisted gate if you hadn't been there to shield the group?"

Eriph held up his hand. "Please, stop. Just stop. I can appreciate the fact that you haven't been outside Nesinu much. And perhaps you don't understand the power that each archdon holds, because it's far greater than what I possess. Royal Oak is in very good hands. A dozen archdons and hundreds of priests. Believe me when I say the city is safe. If I truly thought there was a chance that human life could be lost tonight, I would be out there as well."

"But what of Erynion?"

"The demon lord? I don't know, Millan. Erynion stood—no—knelt before a handful of priests and was helpless. The Marksman was the threat in the forest. And before you mention Nolka, Don Yatiga was killed by the Seductress. Erynion is just a distraction."

Millan bit his thumbnail. "You don't really believe that. You came from Alovajj to warn us about him. You sacrificed your place in Candelux to deliver your message. What about Nesinu?"

"Again, I'm sorry for your loss. Your mentor, your home. For hundreds of years, Verago has threatened to create a demon lord that would lead his armies to victory. A creature so fierce and powerful it would lay waste to cities. That claim became reality at the Assault but ended the same day. I came to warn you because we thought this one might be different, but Erynion clearly doesn't have control over his energy or his mind."

"So, what if he purges tonight?"

Eriph gazed out the window. "The ground is glowing, which means Scarit and his group are casting the Blessing of Sacred Ground. You're going to be late."

Millan remained, defying what he knew he was supposed to be doing. "What if he purges tonight?"

"Then my involvement will have no consequence. You must understand that my participation is not going to sway the results of the fight."

"You don't know that for sure."

"You're right. But what I do know is that you will be expected to help. The longer you stay here, the more trouble you're going to be in. You agreed to help, and so that's what you should be doing. You'd best be off, lest you end up like me."

Millan couldn't understand why someone would be so unwilling to lend a hand to protect innocent people. But there was nothing left to say. "I suppose this is good-bye again."

The excluded priest crossed the room and opened the door. "Take care of yourself, Millan. You're young and you have a good heart. I feel our paths will cross again."

"In Alovajj perhaps."

"Perhaps. May the angels watch over you."

"And you as well." Millan rushed down the stairs and was inundated by the social ambience of the bar. He was in awe at how unconcerned they all were about the potential threat. Before he crossed the bar, the innkeeper grabbed his arm.

"Oh, Don, please, I need your help."

"You do? What is it?"

The innkeeper pointed toward one of the windows. "Some of the patrons think they spotted a demon outside."

"A demon? Inside the city?"

"That's what they said. Would you mind speaking to them?"

"I suppose I could."

The innkeeper guided him through the room to a table where a small group of men huddled around the window. "Hey, fellas, I found a priest."

"Hello, gentlemen, my name is Don Millan. I'm told you all saw a demon?"

One of the men laughed. "You actually brought a priest?"

"Yeah, there's nothing out there," another explained. "Lem just had too much to drink."

"That's not true! I've only had two pints!" the man yelled in defense. "And Quill saw it, too, didn't you?"

"I mean, I saw something. I don't know if it was a demon, though. It was kind of short."

"Well, I saw it all, and it had claws!" Lem held up his curled fingers. "And it was carrying an anvil!" He dropped his arms and pretended to hold a large invisible object. His back was hunched over from the incredible weight, and he shimmied away from the table, dragging his back foot along the floor. "He was walking like this."

The rest of the group erupted in laughter.

His friend slapped him on the shoulder. "How ridiculous. How could you even tell if it had claws from this far away?"

Lem released the invisible object and straightened his back. "I just did. The claws were huge."

As the argument waged on, Millan knew it was leading nowhere. Whether the demon existed or not, the young priest decided to put the issue to rest. "All right, listen. Now, the city's in lockdown, so I don't know how there could possibly be a demon inside the walls. And even if there was, the Blessing of Sacred Ground is in effect."

"But I saw it running along the glowing ground." Lem pleaded his case to the group. "It was short, just like Quill said, and it was wearing some funny clothes. The blessing didn't seem to bother him at all. Did I mention he was carrying a fangling anvil?"

"Then perhaps it wasn't a demon after all," one of his

friends suggested. "Maybe it was just a short blacksmith or his kid."

Lem gasped. "Or maybe it's that demon lord everyone's been talking about."

"Demon lord? Really? How far are you going to take this?" one of his friends asked.

"I'm serious. Didn't you hear about it? All of Nesinu is living in Nolka now. Birka's cousin's in the guard there."

Millan interrupted. "Trust me. What you described is no demon lord. Look, I'll go out and see what I can find. Can you point out where you saw it?"

"Sure thing," Lem said. "He was over by the corner of the tailor shop, and he was running up that side street, like toward the oak."

"Thank you. Everyone please remain calm and indoors. May the angels watch over you."

The patrons thanked him, and Millan weaved his way through the tables to the front door of the Golden Branch. Back on the empty streets, the Nesinu priest scoped the area. He would've been more at ease if Eriph had come along with him. Following Lem's directions, he took the side street that would lead him back toward the massive tree. It was only a small detour, and once he found no demon, he could head toward the north gate and join Omana's group. It was like Eriph said. Royal Oak was home to a dozen archdons, a hundred priests, and even more squires. Nothing was going to get into the city. And why would a demon need an anvil? That part of the story made Millan question Lem's testimony the most.

The Nesinu priest rounded the corner toward the oak when he spotted two figures sitting on the retaining wall around the tree. Millan immediately retreated behind the corner and peered out. He recognized one from the tattered clothing and jester hat. This was the iymed they had caught in the tree near Nesinu. The impish demon was soaking wet. The other one was his companion who had escaped. Millan searched the square, but there was no sign of an anvil. There was also no one else in sight. Everyone was either indoors or at their post like they were supposed to be. Millan felt more alone than ever until he slipped his hand into his pocket. His fingers grazed the gift he had received from Don Skully. A rush of confidence overpowered his fear. Pulling out the star, he gripped it firmly in his hand. Hiding it behind his back, he walked out into the open to confront the two iymed.

****

"Whoo! That was kind of fun." Flinch swam to the retaining wall.

Sonojj sat on the wall as his friend climbed out of the spring. "Fun?"

Flinch struck the side of his head repeatedly to dislodge the water. "Yeah. Just that last part."

"I have to say I'm surprised. I didn't think it'd be this easy."

"Ha! You call that easy?"

"Seriously, though," the blind demon said. "I never thought we'd just walk right in with no opposition."

Flinch plopped down beside his friend. "Well, swam, but I know what you mean. Not a soul in sight. We're all alone."

Sonojj's ears twitched, and he sniffed the air. "Not for long, it would seem."

The jester glimpsed in the direction Sonojj had pointed his nose. A young man in brown robes with a black scarf slinked out from behind the corner of a building. Flinch sneered. "A priest. I see your sense of smell is returning."

The young man took small steps toward them, and his voice wavered slightly. "What are you two doing here? How did you get into the city?"

Flinch patted his friend on the shoulder and used him for support to stand. The jester iymed circled the tree toward the priest. "Did they stop teaching manners in

The Twisted Gate

Candelux? No introductions? Just straight to accusations?"

"My name is Don Millan. Now, what are you two doing here?"

"You don't actually expect us to answer that," Sonojj retorted in Kisejjad.

"We're going to find out one way or another. The others are coming."

"He's lying," Sonojj said softly.

The jester grinned as he pulled forth his daggers. "We know you're alone, pig. What stops us from killing you right now?"

The priest was rooted in place.

"Probably not the best timing," the blind demon called to his friend. "We should leave."

"And let him rat us out?" Flinch spun around. "There's no one here. We can do it lickety-split. A little slice and dice. Plus, I want some payback for those priests who strung me up in that tree."

"Fine." Sonojj relented and splashed into the spring.

"You may be iymed, but you're weakened by the sacred ground," Millan warned. His shaky voice gradually became steady. "If you feel like you can kill me, then have at it. Otherwise, I'll cleanse one of you and restrain the other for information."

Flinch chuckled. "A man with a plan named Dardan. We'll happily grant your death wish."

The jester slid off the wall as his companion emerged from the spring in his cat form. Both dripping wet, they slowly advanced on the priest. Millan's breathing became uneven. Flinch sensed his panic, and it delighted him. The two demons split up and circled the priest in order to flank him. Millan eye's darted back and forth between his two enemies.

As the two iymed converged on the priest, a yellow aura enveloped Millan, and a radiant light burst forth. Flinch stopped abruptly and tried to shield his eyes. Through a half-opened eye, he barely made out the form of his demon friend, leaping through the air toward the priest. Millan sidestepped Sonojj's attack, and another surge of energy forced Flinch to close his eyes momentarily. When the jester iymed recovered his sight, he was horrified to find Sonojj motionless in a crumpled heap on the ground. His front paws were severed from his body, and the dark blood from the wounds flowed freely into the dirt.

Flinch bolted to his unconscious friend and knelt beside him. The jester clenched his teeth. Wings of light adorned Millan's back and lit up the area. By his side, he wielded a sword with a blade that danced like yellow fire. But then, the light from both the wings and the weapon flickered and disappeared into the night. Millan dropped to his knees and panted.

Flinch bared his fangs. "You're dead!"

The demon's muscles tingled as he charged the defenseless priest. Retribution for his friend would be swift. No games. No jokes. Just his dagger slicing through Millan's throat. Flinch came within inches of striking his target when a sudden wave of light knocked him back toward the massive oak tree. The iymed tumbled, but gracefully recovered from the blow. Scooping up his daggers, he prepared to face his new attacker.

Close to Millan stood a man with blond hair. He wore a brown robe with no scarf. In his right hand, he held up a shield, ready to defend the priest on all fours.

Flinch snarled. "Another priest?"

The man ignored the question and nudged Millan with his leg. "Hey, are you hurt? Can you fight?"

Millan's lips moved, but his words were inaudible. A moment later, the young priest fainted.

The newcomer stepped in front of the fallen priest. "I don't know how you made it into the city, but you should run while you still have the chance."

"I'm not leaving my friend." The jester called to the blind demon, "Sonojj, get up!"

"You're wasting your time." The man lowered the shield.

"Demons aren't weak like humans. We can endure such injuries with no problem."

"I'm well aware, but that attack was not like a normal blade. Look at this priest. He poured everything into that one strike. Your friend there was exposed to an incredible amount of holy energy. And the Blessing of Sacred Ground certainly isn't helping him."

"I'm not leaving," the demon repeated.

"I'll make this very simple for you. You're in the middle of a major city, standing on sacred ground. It won't be long before the paladins sense you. If you stay, I'll restrain you until they arrive. Then, you and your friend both get cleansed. Personally, I'd rather tend to my friend here, but I can only do that if you're gone. So, what's it going to be?"

Flinch squeezed the handles of his weapons until his arms shook. He took one step back. The newcomer's shield indicated he favored defense. There was nothing the short iymed could do. Sonojj hadn't moved a muscle since his injury. Taking another step back, Flinch gritted his teeth. "Forgive me."

CHAPTER 21

Sereyna led the demon army from Lake Ivorus toward Royal Oak. Her loyal lieutenant, Maligus, marched on her left side. His machete drawn in anticipation of the upcoming fight. Erynion was on the opposite side, lost in his thoughts. Between the dreams, his meditation, and the help of his new friends, he struggled to piece together the fragments of his past.

"What's on your mind, love?" the Seductress asked.

Erynion lied. "I was just wondering where Flinch and Sonojj ran off to."

"Hmm. I was wondering that as well."

Maligus growled. "Who cares about those vermin? They'd only get in my way."

Sereyna swooned. "My ruthless killer longs for battle."

"It's been too long since we've had a decent attack."

"Just a little longer. You'll get your chance."

The large iymed swung at a branch and severed it cleanly from the trunk. This was the first time Erynion had ever seen him smile. It was disturbing.

In the distance, bells started clanging. Sereyna clasped her hands. "How nice. They're announcing our arrival. You think the nobles will come to meet us?"

The Twisted Gate

"Who cares about nobles?" Maligus asked rhetorically. "Give me the priests and paladins."

"Well, you're in luck then. There's sure to be plenty waiting for us."

"Good!"

Erynion made no effort to join the conversation. It was bizarre, but the thought of attacking the city bothered him to no end.

Sereyna nudged him with her elbow. "Maligus is ready to kill. How about you?"

"There's only one person I need to kill. You know that."

"Yes, and we've been over this before. Batar will be next. Why aren't you more excited?"

"Why should I be? I have no desire to attack this city or its people."

Sereyna slipped her arm under his. "Well, you should. Attacking this city is the next step to controlling your power. And if we can take down Royal Oak, just the three of us with our army of fray, then this war will be as good as over. Nothing will be able to stop us. And you, my sweet Erynion, can go to Light's Haven and kill the king."

"How can you be so confident?"

"Because you're what makes this all possible. You're unstoppable. This is what I want you to realize tonight."

Erynion looked at her from the corner of his eye. "Like last night?"

"Malarekita was a test. Tiny town. No danger to us. I needed to see what you were capable of. This is the real thing, though. A true challenge. And like I explained earlier, just stay with me, and everything will come up black."

Maligus's grin widened. "I'm going to chop them all into pieces."

By the time they reached the edge of the forest, all evidence of the sun was gone. The demons took their place behind the trees, scouting the wall across the small clearing. A lone arrow streaked across the sky and landed a few feet away from where Erynion knelt. Holy energy illuminated the projectile. The Seductress slid her hand up his back and tenderly kissed his neck.

"I can feel it," the demon lord said.

"Mm, I'm sure you can."

"The agony, I mean. I can feel—" There was a sharp prick, and he bit down before exhaling in relief. A dark mist soon surrounded them.

"This is it," Sereyna whispered.

The black fog seeped out of the forest. As it passed the enchanted arrow, the projectile lost its glow. Moments later, more arrows were fired from the walls of Royal Oak, but each was swallowed by the cloud. Erynion heard clamoring in the distance as the Corruption spell spread to the north gate.

"Let's not keep our guests waiting." Sereyna helped the demon lord to his feet, and together they exited the forest under the cloud's cover. Maligus roared and, along with the fray army, advanced on the city's gates.

"Help!" a girl shrieked.

Erynion paused and strained to see through the cloud.

"What is it, love?" the Seductress asked.

"I heard…never mind."

But as they continued, the cry came again. *"Help!"*

Erynion stumbled, but Sereyna caught him. As she lifted him back up, he took another step before falling to his knees.

"What are you doing?" Her voice had lost its sweet tone. "Get up!"

"I don't—"

"Help me, please!" The shout was closer than ever. The fog grew so thick Erynion could no longer see the Seductress. He strained to listen to her voice but there was nothing. All the noise from the charging demons faded away. When the mist dissipated, he was on his knees, alone in complete darkness. He found the silence and solitude

unsettling until a figure materialized in the void.

"You fools!" In one hand, the man carried a large axe made entirely of wood, and in the other, he held a little girl. "You cannot hope to defeat me!"

A young boy appeared. "You've already lost, Erynion!"

The demon lord's thoughts were jumbled. He'd lost? How? But then, he realized the boy was shouting at the man holding the girl hostage. Of course. He was back inside his dream. There was a flash and the darkness was instantly replaced by a large courtyard with stone paths running between small trees and bushes.

Erynion glanced down and discovered he was once again in the body of a young teenager holding a wooden sword. Kneeling behind a shrub, he peeked out and surveyed the scene. He was in the royal gardens of Thoris Castle. The man and the little girl stood in the middle of the courtyard where two stone paths intersected. The young boy, his friend, was hiding behind a tree with his back pressed against the trunk.

"Come on, get up," the boy said. "Go around back and sneak up behind him."

Erynion tightly gripped the handle of his sword. Staying low, he scampered from bush to bush. The sun shined brilliantly overhead, but the cool breeze kept the sweat off his brow. Once he was in position, he gingerly parted the branches to spy on his target.

The man with the wooden axe laughed maniacally as he held his prisoner close. "Once I have Princess Sereyna in the Depths, my plan will be complete."

Despite the threat, Erynion felt no fear. Sonojj was right. The girl was in no real danger. This was only a game. The villain, a demon who didn't speak Kisejjad, was only a man.

"Don't worry, Sereyna. We'll save you," the younger boy said.

With the villain's attention diverted, Erynion rushed out from his hiding spot. He swung the wooden sword and struck the man on the arm.

"*Arg!*" The man released the girl, and his arm appeared to go limp.

The other boy dashed out from behind the tree, grabbed Sereyna by the hand, and escorted her to safety.

The villain squared off with Erynion—the teenager—and hoisted the wooden axe over his head. "You are brave indeed. But now you must cross blades with the mighty Erynion!"

The demon lord shook his head. Hearing someone else use his name was quite strange. When he met Dulo, the beggar in Nolka, he thought the name was random. How odd that it was connected to his true identity.

With a tame roar, the man slowly swung the axe, and Erynion easily blocked the attack. The villain exaggerated his movements as he went in for another strike.

The little boy and girl cheered on the demon lord. "Get him…!"

His name. Erynion gasped. His focus was pulled to the two children. *His name.* They were saying his real name, but it wasn't clear.

"Don't take your eyes off me!" The man lifted his axe overhead and brought it straight down. Erynion dodged the blow and deflected the villain's weapon to the ground. Lunging forward, he made his move.

The man snatched Erynion's sword and placed it under his armpit. "No! It can't be!" He stumbled backward and then slumped over.

"Cleanse him!" the little boy shouted.

"Yeah! Cleanse him! Cleanse him!" Sereyna repeated.

"Too late! I am vanquished." The villain pointed menacingly at Erynion. "But I shall return when your attention is elsewhere. Mark my words. I will…return." The man lay back and stuck his tongue out.

The two children joined Erynion, and the little boy exclaimed, "We did it! Another victory for humanity! Way to go…!"

There it was again, but his name was still garbled. Erynion managed to mutter. "Thanks."

The man sat up and allowed the wooden sword to clatter onto the stone pavers. "Yes, well done. And nice diversion, Batar."

"Thanks," the little boy replied.

Erynion felt the blood rush to his head. *Batar?* This little boy, his friend, was Batar?

The little girl ran up and hugged him tightly. "Thank you for killing the monster and saving me…"

It was just jargon. He strained his ear to find some pattern or some hint as to his name, but it was no use. The dream was beginning to collapse. The distant scenery distorted, and the man who had played the villain vanished first. The young boy, Batar, was next to go as the distortion moved in from all sides and cast a long shadow on the surroundings.

Erynion looked down at the young girl, Sereyna. He had to figure out his name before he woke up. He opened his mouth, but there were no words. Like sand blown away by the wind, she disappeared, and Erynion was once again alone in the void. Everywhere he looked was pitch-black.

"Wake up already!" The voice pulled the demon lord from his dream. As he opened his eyes, Erynion felt a firm object strike the side of his face. He quickly brought his arm up in defense.

"Glad you could join us in our defeat!" Maligus buried his machete into the trunk of a tree. "Fangling useless!"

"Calm yourself, Maligus. You of all demons should know the difficulties of containing your power." Sereyna wiggled the ogre's blade free and returned it to its owner. "Give us a moment."

Maligus snatched the machete and stormed off.

"What happened?" Erynion asked.

The Seductress delicately lowered herself to the ground. "I was hoping you could tell me. I thought we had an understanding."

The demon lord furrowed his brow. "What do you mean?"

"You were supposed to help me while I help you learn your identity. We were halfway to the gates when you closed yourself off."

"I don't understand." Erynion sensed the frustration in her voice, but she maintained her soft tone.

"Your energy. Last night, I used it to poison that little town. You gave it to me freely. I was expecting the same tonight. But just as we were getting started, you cut me off. What caused you to stumble?"

"I heard a voice."

"A voice? You mean the one that gives you instructions."

"No, not that one. This one was from a little girl. The girl from my dream."

Sereyna squinted. "You're saying that when you collapsed, you fell back into your dream?"

"Yes. What does that tell you?"

"That your mind is pushing hard for you to remember who you are." She repeatedly pinched at her dress. "Did you…recover…your identity?"

"No, but I know I'm getting closer. The dream becomes clearer every time."

Sereyna gave a half smile. "That's good news, but you picked the worst possible moment to have it. By the time I realized the Corruption spell was forming from my own energy, it was too late. I had already lost much of my power. There's no way we could've faced Candelux without your help, so I called for a retreat."

"You had me carried back?"

"Of course. You're too important. I had to concentrate on protecting you, and so most of the Corruption spell dissipated, leaving the scorchers the freedom to barrage us with arrows. We made it back unscathed, but many of the fray did not. The whole event was an utter failure."

Truthfully, Erynion cared little for the results of the

battle. He was more preoccupied with his dream. He had just experienced it more clearly than ever before.

"Erynion" was just a name made up by a man pretending to be a demon. A game for children. And while the demon lord clung to this name, his true identity still remained elusive. The young boy, his companion, was none other than Batar. Did that boy really grow up to be king? Had Erynion really been sent to kill his friend? The demon lord eyed the Seductress as he thought about the little girl. Who was Sereyna and why was this demon using her name? It couldn't be a coincidence, could it?

The greater iymed caught his stare. "Something on your mind?"

"Should we be worried about a counterattack?"

"Unlikely. Candelux isn't exactly known for going demon hunting at night. And despite what happened, they're probably still scared of you."

"So, what now? Do we attack again later tonight?"

"*Pfft*, I don't think so. I told you I had to concentrate on protecting you. That used the rest of my energy."

"Protecting me how?"

Sereyna nodded at him. "How's your head?"

"It's fine. Why do you— The agony. Where is it?"

"Gone. At least for another hour or so. Before you completely shut me out, I created a barrier around as much of your energy as I could."

"A barrier? Like you did to Maligus?"

"Sort of, yes."

Erynion narrowed his eyes. "Last night, you told me that you weren't able to do that to me."

The Seductress covered her mouth as she yawned. "Similar spell, but different conditions. I'd love to explain it to you in detail, but I have other things on my mind."

"Such as?"

"Such as, what do we do in an hour when the spell wears off? It's only temporary." Sereyna got up and wiped the dirt from her red dress. "If you'll excuse me, I'm going to consult with Maligus on the matter. You just wait here."

As she went to leave, the nearby bushes rustled, and the jester iymed emerged, breathless.

"Flinch! Where have you been?" Sereyna asked.

The jester huffed and puffed. "We have to go back! They got him!"

"Got whom?"

"Sonojj. He's caught in Royal Oak! We have to go save him!"

"Impossible. Now, how about you tell me why you two ran off?"

The jester tightened his lips and breathed heavily through his nostrils.

Sereyna's hips swayed as she neared the short demon. She lifted his chin and locked eyes with him. "I know it wasn't my orders you were following, so out with it. Or would you prefer we leave Sonojj to rot in that city?"

"No, ma'am."

"Then?"

Flinch scowled. "Last night, while you two were off doing devil knows what, a pod came up. A messenger from Verago. We were given eight gate seeds and instructions to plant them in Royal Oak. We knew your attack tonight would be a perfect distraction, and so Sonojj and I snuck in through the river once the bells started to ring."

Erynion tried to piece the story together. "The river?"

"Yeah, the river that flows to Lake Ivorus. It's fed by the spring that rises from the middle of Royal Oak. There's an old grate in the aqueduct that hasn't been changed in ages."

Sereyna put her hands on her hips. "Fine. So, you slipped into the city using the river. What happened next?"

"Once we completed our mission, we were about to leave, but there was a stray priest. Sonojj said we should take the opportunity to go, but it was just one priest, and I wanted revenge for yesterday. We went to kill him, but it all went to the depths. I don't know how it happened, but before I knew it, Sonojj was seriously injured. He lost his front paws. He couldn't move. Another priest showed up, and I had no choice but to leave him behind. We have to go back."

The Seductress turned her back on the jester. "As I said, it's impossible. There are more pressing matters we must deal with. You two stay here and get some rest."

"But what about Sonojj?" her lieutenant demanded.

"Forget him. For all we know, he'll be cleansed tonight."

CHAPTER 22

"You doing all right, Flinch?" Erynion asked.

High up in the tree, the jester iymed rested against the trunk. "I keep replaying it over and over in my head."

"What happened in the city?"

"I don't know. I was blinded. It doesn't make any sense. But it was all my fault. I convinced Sonojj to stay. He and Reaper were my best friends, and now they're both gone."

"You've known them since the Assault on Light's Haven, right?"

Flinch allowed his foot to hang down and sway forward and back. "Pretty much. After Marksy and most of our battalion died in the purge, there was only a handful of iymed left. They all wanted to take control of whatever remained of our squad and be the new leader, but I didn't want any of that. I'm not a leader. While they were fighting one another and splitting up the fray, I wandered around for a few months. Reaper found me while he was on a scouting mission. I was surprised to hear Sereyna was recruiting. She always kept her army really small. Trust issues, I think. And as an assassin, I was more interested in joining Draeko."

"That's the Shade, right?"

"Right. But with Draeko in the wind, I decided it was best to join Sereyna. Safety in numbers. Iymed came and went, but Reaper, Sonojj, and I were always together. And believe it or not, Maligus wasn't so bad either. Don't get me wrong. He was no basket of fun back then, but it wasn't until his brother wandered off and died that he became a huge jerk."

"You mean Rojjiro. Yeah, I heard about that."

Flinch sighed. "First, Reaper. And now, Sonojj. Can't help but think there's something I could've done."

"I'm sorry, Flinch. What do you think will happen to him?"

"I don't know. Sereyna might be right. They may just cleanse him. But he lost his hands…his paws during the fight. He's not much of a threat, so they may try to interrogate him first." The jester hung his hat on a twig and ran his hands through his hair. "Ugh, it's Alovajj all over again."

"What do you mean?"

"Eh, you don't want to hear about that. Long story."

Erynion looked around. "I don't think we're going anywhere anytime soon. I'm all ears."

At first, the jester didn't speak. The demon lord assumed the conversation was dead, but then Flinch broke the silence. "Not long after I joined up with Sereyna, we found ourselves in the southern part of the kingdom, not too far from Alovajj. There's a place down there called the Den."

"I think I've heard of it. It's a hideout for demons, isn't it?"

"It's much more than that. It's a tunnel, a permanent opening between the Depths and the Surface. It's the only way demons can come to the Surface without a twisted gate or a pod. The Den has always been a gathering place for demons. No humans have gone near it in centuries. Anyway, there was a rumor that Draeko went missing around Alovajj, and Verago had ordered Sereyna and Sarjjore to investigate."

"Sarjjore?" Erynion had heard the name before in an earlier conversation. "He went missing, too, right?"

Flinch smirked. "She, actually. And yes, she went missing not long after this whole thing."

"So, who is she?"

"The humans call her the Brute. She's one of the five greaters. Huge demon with a battalion to match. No one knows where she is, and so the majority of her army occupies the Den. I remember she had these six lieutenants, just massive. The Ash brothers, we used to call them. But, I digress.

"So, there we are, relaxing at the Den, when we get orders to go investigate Alovajj. Now, there's a group of humans called the Death Gods who had just cleared all the demons out of the city and reclaimed it for themselves. Rumor has it that Draeko was sent to deal with some of their founders but was never heard from again. His soul never returned to the Depths, so the assumption was that he was captured, locked away in the dungeon beneath the palace."

"So, what happened?"

Flinch sat up and let both legs hang off the branch. "Back then, the Death Gods didn't have the numbers to defend the whole city. There were only a few dozen of them. Moultia Palace was where the nobles lived when the city was still alive centuries ago. A nice fortified position. That's where the Death Gods stayed. So, Reaper, Sonojj, and I sneak into Alovajj and look for a way into the palace unnoticed. This archdon on patrol spots me somehow, and I get restrained. She seems to be alone, and so Sonojj dives at her. But this other guy comes out of nowhere, pins Sonojj to the ground, and puts a blade to his neck."

The jester pulled out his dagger and took hold of an invisible adversary. He brought the weapon close to his empty fist. "He's about to slice him right through, but the priest calls for him to stop. So, he stops."

"Just like that?"

"Just like that. He's just frozen. I'm still in the chains. He's no farther from me than you are right now. I know deep down this guy could've killed us both. I'm talking serious high-level Anoctis assassin. And he's just crouched over Sonojj, steel resting against his neck. This guy is ready to execute Sonojj at a moment's notice, and I'm…I'm next if that's what this priest wants."

Erynion shook his head. "And this story doesn't somehow end with you both in the Depths?"

"I'll never forget the next part." The jester gazed out into the dark forest. "The assassin looked up at me. He wore this creepy white mask with an expressionless face, but it was his eyes that terrified me the most. His dead, soulless eyes."

Flinch shuddered. "Next thing I know, Reaper jumped in and cut my chains. The whole commotion caused more priests to come out, and so we ran for it, leaving Sonojj behind. A couple of days later, we went back to the city and found him outside the walls. His eyes were gone. He'd torn them out."

Erynion pressed his Devil's Eye through the cloth.

Flinch stood up on the branch, held out his dagger, and fixated on the blade. "I have to go back and save him, no matter the cost. He already lost his eyes because of me, and now his paws. I don't know what I'd do if he were cleansed. I need to help him."

The demon lord cleared his throat. "I'm sure you're a talented assassin, but I doubt the Shade himself could accomplish what you're planning to do."

"But you and me together. You have the power."

"What are you talking about?"

Flinch snickered. "You don't have to pretend with me. I know what you are. Sonojj overheard Marksy talking to Sereyna about it. You're the demon lord, aren't you?"

Erynion quietly nodded.

"So, will you help me? Will you help me rescue our friend?"

"Believe me. If I could help, I would, but I don't have any control over my power. Not to mention, Sereyna put up a barrier to prevent me from purging. But even that won't last much longer. I'm sorry, but there's nothing I can do."

"Hmm, I guess it's up to me then."

Before the demon lord could wish him luck, Flinch leapt away and vanished into the night.

Left alone with his thoughts, Erynion wondered what Sereyna was planning, and more importantly, if he could trust her. She had been around for many years, and Erynion knew he was alive sixteen years ago during the Assault. There was no way the Sereyna from his dream was also the sister of the Seductress.

"Erynion." The Seductress emerged from the trees with a solemn look. Maligus was close behind with his blade drawn.

"What's going on here?"

"I have a plan."

"And that?" The demon lord motioned to the iymed's weapon. "Is that part of it?"

"Only as a last resort. If I fail and the agony takes you, Maligus will relieve your suffering."

"And what if I don't want him to?"

Sereyna pressed her lips together. "I suppose you two can sort that out if it comes to it. In the meantime, we should get started. The barrier will fall soon."

"So, what's the plan?" Erynion kept a close eye on her as she knelt before him.

"Simple. You go back into your dream and discover who you are. Once you know your identity, you should gain control of your energy, at least enough to let me back in."

He didn't believe her. "So, you're going to wait until I fall asleep?"

Erynion straightened up as something pricked his neck. "Just relax," she said.

His eyelids grew heavy, but he fought to keep them open.

"I'm trying to help you. You need to relax."

The struggle was futile and the dream swept in. The surroundings were identical to earlier. In the castle courtyard, the man with the wooden axe held the young girl prisoner while Batar huddled behind a tree. Kneeling behind a bush, Erynion was back in the body of a young teenager.

"Come on, get up," Batar called to him. "Go around back and sneak up behind him."

Erynion nodded. Maybe the Seductress was right after all. If he could replay this memory to completion, perhaps he'd learn his name this time. He shuffled from bush to bush until he arrived at the same hiding spot as before. Next step, defeat the villain. He parted the shrubs but quickly retreated when the Seductress materialized on the stone path.

"I don't believe it!" she exclaimed. Though her appearance was the same—black hair, red dress—her voice was human. "Thoris Castle? It's been years since I've been in Light's Haven."

The man with the wooden axe released his hostage. "Who are you? You don't belong here."

As she sashayed toward him, the Seductress slowly produced a long staff with a hook on one side and a glaive on the other. "Oh, don't mind me. I'm just here to take what's mine."

From his hiding position, Erynion quietly observed as the demon sliced through the man. As the blade ripped through the flesh, there was no blood. The body simply evaporated into the air, leaving nothing between the woman and the little girl.

"Well now," the Seductress said. "This is certainly a surprise, Sereyna."

The little girl took a step back. "Who are you? What are you doing here?"

"Seizing my opportunity. I'm here to kill your brother and take control of his body."

"You can't do this. You have to leave. You've done enough harm."

"Oh, that's so sweet. But, I can do this because I've done it before hundreds of times. I even did it to you."

The child gasped. "You killed me?"

"And took over your body. It actually happened in these gardens."

Something clicked in Erynion's mind as he watched the scene unfold. Pieces of his past came flooding in. Sereyna was *his* sister. The Seductress had killed her during the Assault on Light's Haven. She knew who he was since the start. His head felt as if it were hanging over a fire. He placed his hand on his forehead and closed his eyes. What was happening?

"You're an evil woman!" the little girl hollered. "You lied!"

Erynion winced in pain but managed to pry open his eyes.

With a devilish grin, the Seductress grabbed the front of the girl's dress. "I've waited centuries for an opportunity to finally take back what's mine. What do you know? You're not even alive. You're just a shadow from the past in the head of a misguided fool."

Kneeling behind the bush, Erynion clenched his fists. Blood flowed from his palms, as strands of white hair fell in front of his eyes and his heart thumped wildly in his chest.

Princess Sereyna grasped the wrist of her attacker and struggled to break free. "Let me go!"

The Seductress lifted her into the air so the two were at eye level. "This has been fun, reminiscing and all. But time is short, and your brother won't kill himself. If it's any consolation, he'll be joining you soon."

The Twisted Gate

The girl kicked and screamed. "No! No! Let me go! He's going to kill you, *you fangling*—!"

The tip of the glaive pierced the little girl's throat. For a moment, she choked, but then her body transformed into sand, and she was scattered into the wind.

"Mm, déjà vu. Good memories." As the Seductress smoothed out her red dress, she glimpsed at the tree where Batar was hidden.

Young Batar peeked out before promptly retreating from sight.

"Erynion, is that you?" she asked, facing the tree. "I have to admit, this dream of yours seems like such a nice memory. I almost hate to taint it."

The demon lord rose to his feet and discovered he had reassumed his demon form. He glared at the back of the Seductress as she strolled down the stone path toward Batar.

Does she really believe I'm the young boy? Erynion wondered.

"You know, it's funny," she said. "That first night I met you, I was terrified. I knew what happened at the Assault. I didn't want to end up like Alejjir, sent back to the Depths and reduced to the strength of a fray. Verago promised it would be different this time. But when I saw you clawing at your body, I knew the agony was too great for you. In desperation, I used my talents to try to tame it."

Her tail unwound from around her waist, and the needle point at the end hung in the air by her shoulder. With her index finger, she played with the sharp end of the tail. "But the energy was so overwhelming, it was the first time in a long time that I purged uncontrollably. I realized then and there, for whatever reason, I could harness your power. I'm still not sure why exactly. Verago made certain I couldn't enslave other demons. Perhaps you had so little control that your body let me in willingly. Anything to stop your agony."

Erynion quietly followed the Seductress as she stalked her prey. Her deception infuriated him, but he restrained himself to listen to her confession.

She extended her arm and leaned against Batar's tree. "Whatever the case, I figured out that piercing your neck each time brought me one step closer to gaining control over you. But then, you had to ruin it. I suppose I should've expected as much, but I didn't think your body would start building a defense against me so quickly. You would've shut me out completely if I hadn't acted when I did. This barrier I created not only stops your agony, but it's also my foot in the door to your mind."

As she circled the tree, her fingers surfed across the bark. When she reached the opposite side, Batar fled from his cover. The Seductress lunged forward and hooked his leg with her staff, and the boy tumbled to the ground. She laughed derisively. "Look at you. The mighty demon lord. Stuck in this memory as a weak, helpless child. Once I kill you in here, I'll have control of your mind and body. You'll have no choice but to follow my every command."

Batar slowly crawled backward as the demon in the red dress drew closer.

Erynion leaned against the tree trunk and watched as she advanced on the young boy. Though anger consumed him, he felt a sliver of delight at her mistake.

"Oh, Erynion, my dear," the Seductress said. "I'm going to enjoy leading you around, conquering the Surface, having my revenge. Thank you."

The child mumbled inaudibly.

"What's that? Last words? Come now, dear, speak up."

"I'm not...I'm not Erynion," Batar said.

"Well, of course you're not. You're just helpless Prince—"

"I'm Batar."

"You're...what?"

Erynion pushed off the tree and loomed behind the Seductress. He cast a large shadow over her and onto Batar's face. The demon lord placed his claw on her shoulder, and she cautiously faced him.

He curled his lip. "I am Erynion!"

The eyes of the Seductress widened to their fullest. She launched her glaive forward, stabbing the demon lord in the gut. Unfazed by the injury, he secured a tight grip around her throat.

"I knew you were full of lies," he managed to get past his teeth. As the Seductress struggled to pry his claw from her neck, she opened her mouth.

"No!" His arm trembled as he exerted as much force as possible on her throat. "You will not speak! Your last words were probably the most truth you've uttered in your whole existence, and I will not let you foul it with your deceitful tongue. No, I like you better this way."

****

Flinch spied on the scene from the treetop. Sereyna had pierced Erynion's neck with her tail, while Maligus monitored the situation. The jester iymed desperately wished to infiltrate Royal Oak and rescue Sonojj, but as he was about to leave the camp, he overheard the Seductress's plan for Erynion. He had to decide which friend he could realistically help: Sonojj, trapped in a walled city guarded by watchers, priests, and paladins, or Erynion.

Flinch dropped from his branch. "Hey there."

Maligus stepped between the jester and Sereyna. "What are you doing here, imp?"

"I was wondering the same thing about you two."

"This doesn't concern you." The ogre threatened Flinch with his machete.

"Whatever you two are doing to him *does* concern me. Because of this, Verago sent us to plant those seeds in the city, which caused Sonojj to get caught."

"It's too bad you both weren't caught. Now be on your way, or you'll be seeing Verago sooner than you think."

Flinch slowly produced both of his daggers. "Speaking of Verago, when he comes to the Surface, do you really think Sereyna can protect you? He's not keen on being betrayed, or haven't you heard?"

"Ha! That coward would never show his face on the Surface while the Talisman still exists."

"You're getting awfully good at repeating the thoughts of your master. I mean, I know you can't help the ugly, but don't you get tired of being so stupid?"

The ogre gave the jester a death stare that could only mean one thing. "Now *that* was stupid."

"Oh?" Flinch feigned ignorance. "Well, you would be the expert."

"Why she kept you three idiots around, I'll never know. She's the only reason I didn't cut you down all these years. But now, you pose a danger in a moment of great significance."

"Hmm, I suppose you're right. I guess you'll just have to deal with me."

A toothy grin spread across the ogre's face. "Nothing would give me greater pleasure."

With a swing of the massive machete, the duel was underway. Flinch used his size and speed to dodge the heavy strikes of the ogre demon. Darting back and forth, the jester waited for his opportunities, but every opening was closed. There was no way he could get close enough to even leave a mark. Maligus was surprisingly agile for a demon his size. After a few minutes of fighting with little to show for it, Flinch stepped back to catch his breath.

"You're pathetic," Maligus taunted. "You're just a pathetic assassin. I'm a warrior. You really think you can beat me?"

Flinch dropped to one knee. "Reaper's gone. Sonojj's gone. If you kill Erynion, there's nothing left for me here."

The ogre sauntered toward the jester. "Just remember that you asked for this. You can walk back to the Depths, or I can send you the fast way."

When Maligus was within range again, Flinch grabbed a handful of dirt and flung it into the face of his adversary.

The Twisted Gate

The ogre demon grimaced as the dagger cut through his leg. The second strike was blocked, and a counterattack forced Flinch to retreat once again.

The jester iymed smirked. "Looks like you might see your brother before I do."

"What did you say?"

"Your dead brother. You know, the one that was killed by a don, the lowest class of the Candelux order. Now that was pathetic."

"Shut your mouth!"

"I remember when you got his energy. How you cried when you found out your brother was dead. Or was it because you were too weak to handle the agony? I can't remember now. Which was it?"

The roar from the brutish iymed momentarily paralyzed Flinch. As Maligus bore down on him, the jester narrowly dodged the first attack which sliced through his hat. However, he managed to evade subsequent strikes with ease as the large demon's swings became more erratic. Flinch cut his opponent at each opportunity, but the injuries seemed to only fuel the ogre's rage. After dodging another blow, the jester iymed was knocked off balance by an unexpected left hook, followed by a powerful kick to the chest. Flinch tumbled through the dirt before scrambling to his feet. He brought up his blades to block the mortal strike from his opponent, but the attack came down with full strength. The daggers gave way, deflecting the machete into his right shoulder and cleanly severing his arm.

Flinch wailed as he grabbed the wound and scampered backward. Maligus's smile returned wide as ever. The ogre kicked the severed limb into the nearby brush. "Satisfied? This is what you wanted, isn't it?"

As the jester applied pressure to his injury, he tried to speak but then decided against it.

"What's the matter? Did I get your tongue too?" Maligus inched toward him, and Flinch crept back to maintain the distance. "Originally, I was just going to kill you, but now I have a better idea. I'm going to cut off all your limbs and leave you at the gates of Royal Oak. Then you'll be with your Dardan friends forever with the—"

The sound of choking interrupted him, and they both looked over to discover Erynion with a firm grasp around the neck of the Seductress. The demon lord bared his teeth, and his arm quivered. Maligus shifted toward Sereyna.

Flinch knew exactly what the ogre was thinking. "If you turn your back on me, I'll bury my dagger so deep in your skull, it'll be the only thing on your mind for eternity."

Maligus's knuckles turned white as he squeezed the handle of his machete.

Erynion gave his hand a quick shake, and Sereyna's body went limp. The demon lord's face was contorted by rage. His nose and eyebrows were scrunched together. With his claw still clutching her throat, he growled menacingly at the lifeless Seductress. As her body began to disintegrate into black dust, the ogre howled and stormed off into the night.

"Yeah! You better run, coward!" Flinch shouted into the darkness. The jester lingered for a moment to make sure Maligus wasn't coming back before he put his dagger away. Sereyna melted and her dark energy was absorbed into the ground. Her tail was the last piece to go. The tip slipped out of Erynion's neck and burrowed into the ground like a snake.

Flinch made his way toward Erynion. "Hey, what the depths happened?"

The demon lord inspected his claws. "I don't know. She invaded my mind. She awoke something within me."

"Like what?"

"It wasn't—Flinch! Your arm!"

"Oh, this? I came to stop them, and Maligus may have gotten a piece of me."

"You came to protect me? Thank you. Does it hurt?"

"A little. Not as bad as it did at first. Fortunately, Verago designed us to only really feel the initial pain. Agony excluded, of course. I'm just talking physical pain. Right now, it's just somewhat of an annoyance, like a reminder I've been hurt."

"Well, we may have a problem. The barrier I told you about earlier is gone. I fear the agony will force another purge tonight."

Flinch was silent for a moment before he perked up and made his way to the brush. "Wait a minute. I have an idea. You just need to use your energy, right?"

"That's what I've been told."

"And you probably have tons of spells sitting up in that mind of yours, but you can't remember them."

"What makes you think that?" Erynion asked.

"You don't think Verago would send you to the Surface with an empty head, do you? The last demon lord was trained by Umaro Lijjo, so it would only make sense that he taught you as well."

"Who?"

The jester kicked at the bushes. "You know, the Zaidon."

"The Zaidon? That was from my memory of the Assault."

"Makes sense. He was there. He was another of the five greaters before he got himself cleansed at the Assault. But, he's been around as long as the Devil. Lots of knowledge. I mean, without him, Verago would've been years behind in creating his army. Few centuries back, before I joined up with Alejjir, I got to see Umaro Lijjo in action. Incredible stuff. Anyway, the reason I mention him is because he was a master of unholy energy, *including*, I might add, healing of demons. Aha!" Flinch located his missing limb and scooped it up. The jester demon hobbled over and handed Erynion the severed arm.

The demon lord hesitated before accepting and studying it. "So, you think I can heal you?"

"I certainly hope so. A purge would just make my injury worse." Flinch forced a smile. "And we really have nothing to lose. You need to use energy, and I need to get my arm back on. This would take weeks, months for me to regenerate. What do you say?"

"I'll try, but I've never cast a spell even as a human, or at least I don't think I have."

"I might be able to help with that. A crash course in spells, if you will. No matter how physically focused an iymed is, we all learn at least one spell. It's the summoning spell for our weapons. What we're taught is that it's all about visualization. You have to see yourself pulling the weapon from the other side." Flinch brought his fist across, revealing first the handle and then the blade, inch by inch, until it reached its point.

"Seems simple enough. How do I know what my weapon looks like?"

Flinch reversed the direction of his hand and sent the blade back to the Depths. "Just like your identity, it's locked in your memories. But as for healing, you understand how that works, right? This arm belongs here." The jester patted his right shoulder.

Erynion stared at him blankly.

The jester took his arm back from the demon lord and held it in place. "Just hold your hands over it. Imagine your energy flowing into my shoulder and connecting my arm back to my body."

"Nothing to lose, right? I'll see what I can do."

"Well, not so much 'see' as your eye should probably be closed, but—" Flinch sensed Erynion wasn't amused. "Yup, I'll stop talking."

The demon lord shut his left eye and held his hands out as directed. Flinch kept his arm in position and quietly hoped this would work. He wasn't certain if he'd be able to outrun Erynion's purge. Black smoke wafted from the hands of the demon lord. The cloud gradually became more dense and enveloped Flinch's torso. The energy swirled around him, and as it rose higher, he lost sight of Erynion. Even the stars overhead were soon obscured by the dark cloud.

The jester dared not move lest he disrupt the healing process, not that there was anything to see anyway. He couldn't even feel if his arm was being reattached. As time slipped by, his thoughts drifted back to Sonojj. Flinch knew that returning to help Erynion was the right choice, but now that was over. It was time to save his friend. Of course, he would need both arms. The quiet hours that followed allowed him to imagine all the possible rescue scenarios. He had been to Royal Oak when he was a human, but that was centuries ago. Would he be able to navigate the city now and complete his mission? What if Sereyna was right and they had already cleansed Sonojj?

The short iymed squinted as the haze began to evaporate. The trees and bushes were dead, and Erynion lowered himself to his knees.

"I don't believe it." Erynion lay down on the ground.

As the mist cleared, Flinch moved his shoulder up and down. "Hmm, well, it's certainly attached."

The jester demon grabbed his right wrist and flung it to the side. The arm swung back and forth like a pendulum.

Erynion mumbled a few indiscernible words, but he was already asleep.

"Well," Flinch said with a crooked smile, "at least I won't lose it now."

CHAPTER 23

Millan gasped as he jolted awake. With the help of the morning light, he inspected his body for injuries but was unable to find any. The young priest flopped back on the pillow and chuckled. The angels had surely been watching over him. With a sigh of relief, he dragged himself out of bed and threw on his robe. When he attempted to open the door, he failed. Millan anxiously rattled the handle, but it refused to budge. He pounded on the door and called for help. Someone must've locked him in by accident. Seconds became minutes before he gave up. The priest plopped down on the mattress and wondered how this could have happened.

The blessing had taken a lot of energy out of him. Millan slipped his hand into his pocket to search for Skully's gift. When he felt nothing, he let his fingers slide along the crease. Still nothing. He frantically checked his other pocket, but the result was the same. He scoured the small room for the object until he heard someone at the door.

The young priest stared at the lock as the key turned, and then the handle. When the door opened, Millan hastily knelt as a woman dressed in a pristine white robe and a long red scarf entered the room. His lips parted, but the words wouldn't leave his mouth.

"Don Millan, please rise."

The Nesinu priest obeyed. Behind the Prima stood a paladin dressed in golden plate armor with a sun imprinted on her breastplate. The helmet matched her ornate armor and covered much of her face. Millan couldn't help but think she seemed too thin and frail to be such a decorated fighter.

"You may leave us," Mashira said to the paladin.

"Yes, Your Luminescence."

When the door closed, Millan asked, "Is she a Champion of the Light?"

"Yes. Lady Sundancer is a champion bloodseeker. I've asked her to accompany me as my bodyguard."

"Sundancer? That sounds like—"

"Para Paya. Yes, she was once a part of that community."

Most of what Millan knew about these people came from his parents. The Para Paya were free-spirited individuals who lived on the west coast of the kingdom. They were considered outcasts, though never formally exiled like the Death Gods. The Para Paya followed no official laws, and their code of ethics were astonishingly simple. Don't harm another soul.

Millan pressed on with the issue at hand. "When I awoke, I was locked in here. Am I in trouble?"

Mashira was quiet, and the silence worried the young priest. His thoughts immediately turned to Exclusion. Perhaps he could contact Eriph and be accepted into the Death Gods.

The Prima interrupted his panicked train of thought. "These past few days have been chaotic, to say the least. And you always seem to be at the center of it all. Is there something I should know?"

"I'm not sure what you're referring to."

"Millan, there have been four attacks in four nights and

you've been at three of them. Is there some connection between you and this new demon?"

"I...I don't understand," he stammered. "Are you saying that I'm causing all of this? The demon lord is following me?"

Mashira waved off the notion. "No, no. We're just trying to figure out what's been happening. You were there at Nolka. Last we heard, this demon's objective was to kill the king. And yet, instead of marching to Light's Haven, he moved south to Malarekita and now Royal Oak. Is there anything we should know?"

"I'm sorry. I've just been following orders. I don't know any more about Erynion than you do."

"Following orders? If I'm not mistaken, your orders were to go to Light's Haven." She grabbed a nearby chair and sat in front of him. "Please, sit down. Tell me. What compelled you to come here?"

Despite the feeling that he was about to be punished, Millan felt calm in her presence. He lowered himself onto the bed. "Forgive me. I had every intention to travel to Light's Haven today. I had never seen Royal Oak. Eriph was traveling through and recommended it."

"Eriph. I see. We're all disappointed by the decision Eriph made, but that was his choice, and he's already left for Alovajj. He's gone. A critical decision lies before you today, and I want you to realize this, since I personally have come to speak with you. Do you know how often I reprimand dons?"

"Not often?"

"Never. But given the situation, and the loss of Don Skully, I thought it crucial I speak with you directly. Understand?"

Millan nodded quietly.

Mashira fished around in her pocket and pulled out the star. "Do you know what this is?"

"It's the conduit Don Skully gave me at my Acceptance."

"Not exactly. An ordinary conduit can be any object used to facilitate any blessing. This is no ordinary conduit. Do you know where it came from?"

"No."

Mashira flipped the trinket over in her hands. "During his tenure, Primus Ayristark gave each of his five advisors a gift, enchanted conduits that allow the user to augment a specific blessing of their choice. It's very powerful in the right hands. Is there a particular reason Don Skully passed this on to you?"

"I was always fascinated with it. The night I decided I wanted to become a priest, I saw Don Skully use it to kill a large iymed. I remember being terrified. The demon was huge. I thought, 'how could this old man stop it?' But he did, and it was awe-inspiring. Even after he saved the town, the adults still gossiped about him. My father forbade me from studying with him, but that didn't stop me. When I turned sixteen, I went to Don Skully. I told him about that night and how I hadn't stopped thinking about becoming a priest since that moment."

"You wanted to train specifically with him?"

"I suppose it sounds strange. No one else would stay with him. I had friends who left Nesinu to train in other cities or towns, but it was different for me. I wanted to be taught by him. My mother blamed my father for letting me watch Don Skully fight the demon that night. He used the Ultimate Blessing."

"The Ultimate Blessing?" Mashira asked.

"Yes. Don Skully said it's the most powerful spell a priest can wield. The caster creates wings of light and a blade blazing with holy energy."

"Ah. The one you performed last night?"

"That's right. He only started teaching it to me a couple of months ago. It was more taxing than I expected."

The Prima pinched the bridge of her nose. "I'm not sure where to begin. Do you realize how close you came to death last night?"

Millan jerked back. "What?"

"That blessing has a rather controversial past. Originally, it was called the Blessing of Verago, because he was the one who first performed it as an angel. However, after his betrayal of humanity, it was renamed to the Blessing of the Fallen Angel. Don Skully was correct. It is the most powerful spell ever conceived for priests. But, this is because it draws on the life energy of the caster to the point where misuse or inexperience could lead to death. For this reason, we've always restricted those allowed to train in it and use it. The priest must be at least the rank of an archdon, and permission must be granted from the standing Prima or Primus."

The background of the blessing interested Millan, but this last part caught his attention. "Archdon? Permission?"

"Yes, I'm afraid Don Skully was teaching you a blessing that you're not supposed to be casting."

"I..." Millan's jaw trembled. "I didn't know."

"I know. But promise me that you won't cast it again without proper training."

"Yes, Your Luminescence. I promise."

Prima smiled. "You know, you actually remind me a lot of myself."

"Really?"

"Yes, I was always very ambitious, ever since I was a squire. I suppose it runs in the family. When my brother became an archdon, he received permission from Primus Ayristark to learn the Blessing of the Fallen Angel as part of his specialization training."

"You're talking about Founder Mortis?"

Mashira bit her lip. "That's him. Mortis learned the Blessing of the Fallen Angel from Archdon Omana, well Advisor Omana at the time. After his Ascension, I begged him to teach me that blessing. Despite his eventual departure from the guild, he abided by our laws. I was persistent, though. Every chance I had, I asked him to teach me."

"And did he?"

"Nope. No matter what I said or did, he never relented. Finally, he told me a story about a young girl who joined the Whisper guild. Don Skully taught you about them, correct?"

"Yes, Your Luminescence."

"Good. So, many years ago, there was a young lady who lost her mother. And one day, on the outside of town, she spotted her mother's soul as a wanderer. Distraught that her mother was still trapped on the Surface, the girl decided to help her transcend, and so she joined the Whisper guild. Now, I don't know how much you learned about whisperers, but they had to learn to control their mind, thoughts, and emotions before trying to commune with a wanderer. Without proper training, a spirit can invade the mind and cause serious damage, whether they intend to or not. These were the warnings she received from her mentor when she joined the guild. But seeing her mother linger about, anchored to the Surface for some unknown reason, tore at the girl's heart. All she wanted was to help her mother leave this world in peace.

"One day, she felt she was ready. Her teacher cautioned her once again, but she ignored the advice. And so, she went to the edge of the forest and used her underdeveloped skills to call on her mother's spirit. The call attracted other wanderers as well. When her mother approached her, the girl opened her mind and began to understand why her spirit was still bound. But the other wanderers refused to stand idly by. A whisperer was in their presence, and this was their chance to finally leave the Surface. They interfered with the ritual and demanded help from her. Wishing for her mother to transcend first, the girl cast the others aside. And when they retaliated, there was nothing she could do to stop them. She was too weak, too inexperienced to hold them back, and the spirits overwhelmed her mind."

Millan shifted to the edge of the bed. "What happened

to her?"

"They say she went insane. The villagers heard the screams, and by the time they got to the area, she was gone. Haunted by all those spirits, the young girl roamed the forest until she died. And since she was unable to help her mother, she died with regret and became a wanderer too."

"I understand."

"I'm glad to hear it. Yours is a unique situation, Millan. I knew there would be a time when I would need to intervene. I'm sure you know of Don Skully's affiliation with the Death Gods. He was as close to being a member as you could be without officially joining. Despite all of that, he had served the guild his entire life, including the twenty years as an advisor. And so, as long as he adhered to our stipulations, I agreed to let him take on a student."

"Stipulations?"

"Yes, the Death Gods would stay out of your training, except in a strictly historical sense. You were to be trained as a priest of Candelux and nothing beyond that. I see now he took some liberties with our agreement, but I cannot in good conscience hold you accountable for his decisions. This star is a conduit specifically designed to help in the casting of the Blessing of the Fallen Angel. It takes some of the stress off the caster. Using it last night is probably the only reason why you're alive today. But, that doesn't mean it's safe for you to cast. I'm going to return it to you because of its sentimental value, but remember your promise to me."

"Yes, Your Luminescence."

Mashira held the trinket in front of him. "I advise you don't carry it into battle. The temptation to use it may be too great. I must emphasize how dangerous this blessing is to the untrained caster."

The Nesinu priest cradled the star in his hand. "I understand. Really, I do."

"I'm glad to hear it. Now, there's a second matter we

need to discuss. Thanks to you, we were able to capture one of the iymed last night, but we still don't know what they were doing inside the walls. Is there anything you can tell me? Anything they said before you were attacked?"

"No. I just saw them by the tree. That's all."

"I see. Well, I'll leave you to get ready. The demon lord is out there, and we're going after him while it's still light out."

"Yes, Your Luminescence."

The Prima left Millan alone with his thoughts. He gripped the star, and his fist trembled. When the conversation started, the young priest assumed he would be excluded next. Why had Don Skully taught him what he wasn't supposed to know? Why had he kept so many secrets? Millan thought of Eriph and how he followed his heart. He cared little for the disapproval of the advisors, and journeyed to Alovajj to train with a founder. The young priest recalled Eriph's words the night before they left Nolka. *He was a good man and a powerful priest. Remember how he inspired you.*

****

Sonojj awoke from his slumber in complete darkness. The sun was up. He felt its warmth, though not much of it. He breathed in deeply through his nose. Humans. Everywhere. He must've been captured. The stubs at the end of his arms touched, and he shuddered. The smell and the voice of the priest were clear in his mind. *My name is Don Millan. Now, what are you two doing here?*

Sonojj remembered the pain. How did this happen? How was that priest capable of wielding such power? Dons were supposed to be easy, especially when it was two against one. The pan-mage demon sighed as he put his back to the cold stone wall. His mind was blank after the attack. He must've lost consciousness. He took another sniff.

"Looks like things came up black for Flinch," he thought.

His ears perked up. Muffled voices were coming from above him, but he couldn't quite make out the words. There were too many conversations mixing together, and it was too difficult to focus on any of them. He needed to rest. He laid what remained of his arms on his thighs. It would take too much energy to regenerate his hands, and who knew what the priests had planned. They wouldn't be able to unlock his secrets with his eyes missing, but inflicting pain would be another issue. He had no choice but to wait.

The hinges on the prison door squeaked, and footsteps clamored in his ears. His nose was greeted by a mix of scents. Sonojj estimated four or five people, definitely human, most likely priests. The fabric of their robes had a particularly pleasant wool smell. Another squeal came from metal rubbing against metal, but this time it was much closer. The gate to his cell must've been opened, but the demon made no attempt to escape.

"Good, he's awake. Restrain him."

Sonojj readied himself for the sting of the holy chains. Two pairs of feet shuffled as someone took their position on either side of him. The burning sensation spiraled up his arm and around his torso. The Blessing of Divine Restraint was a spell Sonojj was all too familiar with. The iymed tensed at the initial pain as his energy was slowly pulled from his body. After a few moments, he was able to cope.

"Now, what were you and your friend doing in the city last night?" The voice was female, but deeper than expected. Her tone was stern, yet uninterested and monotonous. She spoke in a hurried manner, as if she were annoyed.

Sonojj saw no reason to answer her questions.

"No eyes. No hands. I see ears. No tongue?" the interrogator asked.

"Go to the depths," Sonojj said softly in Kisejjad.

"Heh, typical. Look, let's just get this over with. Tell us what we want to know, and I'll return you to your master. If not..." She left her statement open-ended.

"If not what? You'll torture me? I've been through this before. Do your worst."

"No, we don't torture souls. But I promise you'll be locked up for a very long time. It won't be a pleasant stay either."

Sonojj snarled. "If you keep me on the Surface, I swear to you, I'll be free by tonight. I will hunt you down and send you to the Depths myself."

The demon strained his ear to listen to her breathing. It was calm. Her tone was unchanged as well. "Mm-hmm. A bold statement given your present situation. You don't even know what I look like."

"But I know what you smell like."

The interrogator stepped forward, and her aroma grew stronger. Her robe was clean. The wool was laced with a hint of roasted walnuts, which told Sonojj that her clothing was dyed black. The smell of sweat was minimal, but what he caught was sweet with a slight musty odor, which he attributed to aging. She must have been inches from his face because as she spoke, he knew she had eaten eggs for breakfast. "Take a deep breath."

He knew exactly where she was. Sonojj shape-shifted, which loosened his restraints. He opened his mouth wide and inhaled deeply. Delighted by the smells, the demon lunged at his captor. As his fangs reached for her throat, he felt a searing pain in his shoulder. His jaw snapped shut but caught nothing except air. He lurched forward again for another bite, but the chains were pulled tight. Sonojj stumbled backward and collided with the wall.

"Archdon Omana, are you hurt?"

"Yes, I'm fine," she snapped. "I thought you two were holding him!"

"Apologies, Your Grace, we didn't realize he was a

shape-shifter."

Wincing from the pain, Sonojj snorted as he slid down the wall until he was sitting. His muzzle receded and his ears dropped to the side of his head, returning him to a humanoid form. What a stupid thing to do. Certainly not worth the pain. But how could he pass up an opportunity to rip out the throat of an archdon? The stench of perspiration on her neck was prominent now.

"Damn pan-mage demon." Her tone had definitely changed from indifference to anger. Sonojj wouldn't have been surprised if she changed her mind about the torture. "Don't think we'll send you back to the Depths so easily. We'll get the information we want from you. We're done here for now."

"Until next time, Archdon Omana," he muttered.

Her scent drifted away. "Release him. Let him lick his fresh wounds."

The holy restraints disappeared, and Sonojj slumped forward. The metal gate to his cell clanged shut. A dozen footsteps moved away. The squeaky hinges of the prison entrance echoed in the prisoner's ears, followed by the door slamming shut. Left alone, the demon rolled onto his back. He still heard their voices on the other side of the prison door. Despite his desire to rest, Sonojj did his best to focus on their conversation.

"Anything?" a new voice asked.

The tone of his interrogator was calm once again. "Nothing yet."

"You think he'll talk?"

"Have you seen him? There's no way he can heal while we're holding him. He's a mess. No demon in their right mind would stay here if given the choice. Give it time."

Another voice cut in, much younger. "Your Luminescence!"

"Yes, what is it?"

"This letter was left for you at the Golden Branch."

"For me? Give it here."

The Twisted Gate

"What does it say?" asked Omana.

"It's from Eriph. He received news from Alovajj before he left."

"And what do the gods of death have to say?"

"The Den is empty."

A grin crept across Sonojj's face.

CHAPTER 24

Inside the rectory of Royal Oak, the Prima entered the office of Head Archdon Scarit. Behind her followed Lady Sundancer and two of her advisors, Razza Merona and Deidok. The Prima took her seat across the desk from Head Archdon Scarit. Her advisors took the only other chairs in the room, leaving Lady Sundancer and Archdon Omana to stand.

Mashira cleared her throat. "Thank you all for gathering here. Before we run off and hunt down these demons, I'd like to discuss something. First, whatever happened last night regarding Don Millan does not leave this room. When this is finished and we return to Light's Haven, he will accompany us. Any questions?"

When no one spoke up, she continued, "Good. It's no surprise that the demon we captured has been uncooperative. I asked Don Millan if there was anything he could tell me, but he didn't know what they were doing last night."

"I don't suppose they were just here to sightsee," Advisor Deidok said.

Mashira ignored the comment. "It's unsettling. Why would demons sneak into a heavily armed city? They had to have had some objective."

"Maybe Don Millan interrupted them before they could carry out their mission," Scarit offered.

"It's possible. But what could be so important that they would take that kind of risk?"

"Do we really expect this iymed to divulge anything to us? I think we should do as we've always done and cleanse him," Advisor Razza Merona suggested.

"I have to disagree," the Prima said. "There's a very clear danger out there, and we know next to nothing about it. This demon knows. We just need to give it more time. Right, Archdon Omana?"

"Right. If we're in a hurry, though, perhaps we could be a bit more persuasive in our—"

"No! Absolutely not. He may be corrupted, but he's still a human soul. We can't allow ourselves to go down that path. We have to think of something else."

Scarit cocked his head. "I'm a little confused. Do you believe Royal Oak is in danger?"

Mashira contemplated the question. Her reign as Prima had begun with such a stressful event, the Assault on Light's Haven. And three years ago, Verago tried to kill Batar during Devil's Breach. But aside from that, the rest of her time leading the guild had been a breeze with little to no demon activity. And now, there was a deep pit in her stomach, something she was unaccustomed to. "Normally, I would say no. But in light of Verago's new demon lord, who has successfully remained on the Surface for four nights, I'm not sure what our enemy is up to. The reappearance of the Seductress after years of nothing. Attacks every night. Towns being destroyed or poisoned. There's something looming on the horizon, and it doesn't bode well for us if we cannot uncover their plot."

Deidok grunted. "It seems the only part we know is that this demon lord, Erynion, has been ordered to kill King Batar."

"And we don't even know if that's a real threat. There

are so many questions. If you only want to kill one person, why not just send an assassin? And then there's the fact that the king wears the Talisman of Zavi as protection. Batar stood face-to-face with Verago at Devil's Breach and was untouched because of the Talisman. What can Erynion possibly do?"

Omana stepped in. "No one wants to say it, but perhaps the time has come to extend a sign of peace to our exiled brethren to the south. They always seem to have more information than us."

The Prima rubbed her neck. "You may recall we tried that after Devil's Breach. It didn't exactly end the way we would've liked."

"Perhaps we could take a more diplomatic approach this time."

The comment stung. Mashira's first instinct was to lash out at the archdon, but there was some truth to her statement. There was a lot of bad blood between Candelux and the Death Gods because of what happened after Devil's Breach. It could have been handled better. The Prima let the comment slide; however, Advisor Razza Merona seemed to decide otherwise.

The advisor spun around. "Are you blaming Her Luminescence for—"

Mashira placed her hand on Razza's shoulder. "It's quite all right. I'm sure that's not what Archdon Omana meant to say."

Omana bowed slightly. "I meant no disrespect. I was simply agreeing that there are many questions, and we should get some answers. The Death Gods are one possible solution. There's an advantage to their methods of interrogation."

Mashira adamantly shook her head. "No! No! Interrogation and torture are not the same. I won't condone their methods. Right now, we have no reason to believe we need their help or that they could even help if we needed it."

"I agree," Razza added emphatically. "By looking to the Death Gods for help, we will lose the faith of our citizens. It will appear as though casting them out was a mistake."

Deidok stroked his chin. "Hmm. Yes, but the decision to cast them out was because they would endanger the lives of the citizens. Is it possible that we are endangering lives now by not consulting with the Death Gods?"

Silence filled the room, and Mashira felt all eyes on her. "Your point is noted, but maybe we're getting ahead of ourselves. This whole situation stemmed from the appearance of Erynion. We know he's out there somewhere. Let's hunt down this demon and resolve this ourselves right now. Head Archdon, how long do you think it would take to assemble a hunting party?"

Scarit interlaced his fingers and rested his hands on the desk. "Oh, I'd say an hour or two. If you want the paladins to join us, I can speak with Sir Illian."

"Very well. And yes, please, paladins and watchers. We should be ready to leave by noon."

"At once, Your Luminescence."

Over the next couple of hours, the priests, paladins, and watchers organized outside of the rectory. Excitement was in the air at the prospect of a demon hunt. The Prima walked through the open doors, followed by her entourage. The individual conversations created a loud murmur as the distant clock rang out twelve times. Mashira looked out over the crowd and nodded in approval. She had left Light's Haven at daybreak, riding furiously toward Royal Oak to take control of the situation. It was time to finally put an end to this disruption. She would return Erynion to the Depths herself if she had to. She brought up her hands and quieted the crowd.

"There is an evil that Verago, the traitor to humanity, has released upon our kingdom. It has already claimed Nesinu and, with the help of the Seductress, infected Malarekita. Their attempt on Royal Oak last night was a failure, and they are now in retreat, hiding until the night falls once more. Well, we will not give them that chance! It's time for us to hunt these vermin down. We will move swiftly through the forest, striking at any evil foolish enough to rear its head. Erynion and the Seductress will be cleansed!"

A cheer went up as the crowd dispersed into their teams. Mashira had ordered Head Archdon Scarit and Advisor Deidok to remain behind as a precaution.

Don Millan emerged from the front of the crowd and knelt before the Prima. "Your Luminescence, I was not told what group I belong to."

"Archdon Omana, to which group is Don Millan assigned?"

Omana scanned the list. "It appears Don Millan was overlooked during the creation of the list."

"You're with me then," Mashira said.

Millan's eyes lit up. "As you wish."

****

I have given you all you need to defeat your brother. There was the voice again. Who was speaking to him? Erynion opened his eyes and found himself in the royal gardens. He was young again. The man who played the villain was lying on the ground. Cheering, Batar and Sereyna ran to Erynion. The game had just concluded. His dream seemed to be the same, except everyone's clothes were different.

The man stood and brushed the dirt from his shirt. He scooped up Erynion's wooden sword and handed it back to him. "Keep this safe. Who knows when you'll need it again?"

Sereyna, the little girl, stomped her foot. "Do you really have to leave us, Sir Bix?"

"I'm afraid so. I've been given a great honor, chosen as a Champion of the Light, like my brother. I have a sacred duty and must always be vigilant."

The Twisted Gate

"What's vigilant mean?" Batar asked.

"Watchful. I must always be ready to serve the people where I'm needed. I will help to keep the kingdom safe. But you three. You are the future of our kingdom. One day your father will pass his legacy on to you, A…"

It was his name again, but why couldn't he make it out? Erynion waved at the paladin. "Hey! What's my real name?"

Sir Bix ignored the question and strolled over to the other young boy. He tousled the youth's hair. "Be good, Batar. Your role as prince will be no less important than your brother's as king."

Erynion's eyes widened. "Wait. Batar's my brother?"

The young Batar grinned at Erynion, whose mind was going a mile a minute. Of course. Sereyna was his sister. It only made sense that Batar was his brother. How had he not made the connection before?

The paladin moved on to the little girl. "And you, Princess Sereyna, you will be a symbol of beauty for the kingdom. The most fair and virtuous princess the people have ever seen."

Sereyna giggled, but her smile quickly faded. She opened her arms to hug the paladin. "I'm going to miss you, Sir Bix."

Bix knelt and embraced her.

"Yeah," Batar said as he joined the hug.

Erynion stood back and studied the scene. There was something familiar about the paladin—kneeling—that he hadn't noticed before. He had seen Bix somewhere else.

"Maybe when I'm back in the city, Erynion will arise once more." Bix curled his fingers into claws.

The little girl beamed with joy. "Promise?"

Batar hopped back and assumed a defensive pose. "We'll be ready for you, right, A…?"

His name again. Erynion earnestly played the spectator, not wanting to miss anything critical.

"Look at him. He's terrified of the thought," the

paladin joked. "You could always get help from the Sanctuary."

The Sanctuary? That voice. He had definitely heard Sir Bix somewhere else besides this dream. But where? The demon lord stepped back as the image of a body appeared on the ground beside Bix. It was another paladin, bloody and wounded. Neither Bix nor the children acknowledged its presence.

He needs help now, or he won't make it. The body flickered and then vanished.

"Am I losing my mind?" Erynion thought.

Sir Bix bade the children farewell and departed. At the edge of the courtyard, he picked up the large two-handed sword that had been resting against the stone wall. The weapon was split halfway up the blade and formed two tips, instead of one. With the base of the blade wrapped in leather, the paladin slung the sword over his shoulder and faded away.

Batar tugged on his sleeve. "Come on. Get up!"

"Yeah, get up!" Sereyna added.

Creases formed on Erynion's forehead. "What are you talking about? I'm already standing."

The children ignored his statement. "Get up! Get up!"

The intense heat from the sun beat down on Erynion. He struggled to open his eye, but the rays of light restricted him to only squint.

"Get up!" Flinch pulled on his arm.

"What's going on?" the demon lord asked, only half awake.

"We have to get going. It's well into the day, and the hunting party is leaving Royal Oak."

Erynion positioned his hand to block out the sun. "Hunting party? What are you talking about?"

Flinch quit yanking on the demon lord's arm but kept a firm grip on his wrist. "Long story short, there's a large group of priests and soldiers on their way here, searching for demons to cleanse. And unless you want to be included in that group, we need to go *now!*"

Flinch arched his back and pulled with all his might using his one good arm. Slowly, he helped Erynion rise to his feet. The jester iymed took a few steps before he realized his companion wasn't following. "Come on. Let's go!"

The demon lord scouted the immediate area. All the plants and trees were dead and barren. "Where are we going?"

"Not far. Lake Ivorus."

"Back to the lake?" Erynion still felt disoriented.

"Yes. Water has the ability to mask our energy, like our auras."

"Our auras?"

The jester glared at him. "Are you serious right now? Did you hit your head when you fell asleep? Yes, our auras. You know, the stuff you can see with your Devil's Eye. We need to get going."

Erynion dawdled toward the iymed but halted after a couple of steps. "But how can they find us? Humans don't have Devil's Eyes."

"Archdons can sense us, but it's the bloodseekers we need to really worry about. They can track us down to an exact location. The stronger your aura, the easier you are to trace."

"But water hides us from all of them?"

"Exactly. Look, can we have this lesson later when we're not being hunted?"

Erynion lifted the cloth covering his Devil's Eye. A yellow glow in the direction of Royal Oak reminded him of his encounters with the priests so far. There were definitely a lot of them out there. The demon lord slid the cloth back into place. "Fair enough. Lead the way."

****

Moving through the forest like a massive wave, the

search party marched toward the lake. Each band of fighters was led by a bloodseeker, with Lady Sundancer leading the group with Prima Mashira and Don Millan. Mashira kept her eyes peeled for any movement. There was a snap, and Sundancer handed a skinny branch from a bush to Mashira.

The Prima studied it. The leaves were brown and shriveled, and the wood was covered in black spots. "Corruption?"

The bloodseeker nodded. "Recently. Less than a day. There's still some residual here."

Mashira allowed the branch to slip from her fingers. "Let's find the center. Maybe we can pick up a trail from there."

"Agreed. It appears to get worse in this direction."

The group followed Sundancer deeper into the forest, and the foliage became progressively worse. Advisor Razza Merona knelt to study the flowers. "The petals and leaves are completely gone. We must be getting close."

Mashira swept the dead leaves with her foot. "This has to be either the Seductress or Erynion. Lady Sundancer, do you see anything resembling a demon?"

The bloodseeker's head twitched to the side.

"What is it? Do you see them?"

Sundancer sidestepped over to a petrified tree and knelt by the exposed roots. She ran her fingers through the dirt. "A demon died here. A powerful one. The ground is still stained with darkness."

"Finally, some good news," Razza Merona said. "Is it the same energy as the Corruption spell?"

The bloodseeker scooped up the dirt and held it beside the dead tree. "No. Different."

"That means at least one of them is still out there." Mashira surveyed the area. "And if we can't sense them, they've either fled beyond our reach or taken a dip in the lake. Either way, there won't be much we can do."

"Should we return to Royal Oak then?" her advisor

asked.

The small group of priests, paladins, and watchers huddled around the Prima.

"We have a lot of light left. Let's continue to the lake and search the area. If we get some confirmation that they're hiding there, maybe we can set a trap."

****

Erynion did his best to keep up with Flinch's pace as the jester scampered through the forest. "What do you mean we have to stay below the surface the whole time? How do I hold my breath for that long?"

The jester threw up two fingers. "Lesson two. Air isn't as crucial to demons as it is to humans."

"What the depths does that mean?"

"It means we can stay under the water for quite a long time. That's how Sonojj and I snuck into the city last night."

"Really?"

"Yup. It's simple. You know, once you get past the drowning sensation."

With the lake barely visible through the trees, the demon lord slowed to a walk. "What?"

Flinch put his hands on his hips. "Don't worry. You'll be fine. It's just a natural reaction. A holdover from when you were human. Once you're under the water, you'll see, no problems."

As the two demons passed the tree line and descended toward the shore, Erynion gazed out over the large body of water. A feeling of isolation overcame him. He was used to being in a large group, but now it was just him and Flinch. With the Seductress returned to the Depths and Maligus having run off, the demon lord wondered about the fray that had previously constituted their army.

Flinch wasted no time and waded knee-deep into the water. "What's wrong now?"

The demon lord watched the ripples come into the shore and rebound back into the lake. "Why am I running?"

"Uh, that's easy. Because if you're captured, then they'll cleanse you, and you'll be stuck in the Depths forever."

"As opposed to staying here? When night falls, the agony will show me no mercy."

Flinch scratched the back of his head. "Yeah, that's a tough one. I don't know how that feels for a demon lord, but we've all gone through it to some extent. Once you discover your identity and your abilities, the agony will be a thing of the past."

The demon lord unbuttoned his shirt to reveal the scarring on his torso. "Every night since I've been here, the Seductress has stolen my strength to keep me safe from the agony. The first night, she wasn't there, and this is what I did to myself."

Flinch slapped the water. "She wasn't helping you! She was trying to control you. And you forgot about last night. You avoided the agony by healing me."

"So? Are you going to cut your arm off every night?"

"I don't know. Maybe. You're missing the point. There are ways around it. Don't you see you're free to fulfill your purpose?"

"My purpose? Yeah, well, here's the thing about my purpose. My dreams have been clear. My order is to kill the king. To kill Batar. To kill my brother. Why would I want to kill my own brother?"

"I don't know the answer to that, but I'm sure there's a reason. We can sort this out later. We don't have much time before the priests come through those trees and capture us. Come on and get in the water."

"What's the point? I should let them take me."

"Fine," the jester said. "Lesson three. You've been given free will. Any demon stronger than fray has it."

"So?"

"So? Only a small percentage of wanderers are even

capable of becoming something more powerful than fray. And for those of us who are, we have to willingly give our allegiance to Verago."

The demon lord's eyes narrowed. "What exactly are you saying?"

"For whatever reason," Flinch said as he pointed at Erynion, "you agreed to kill your brother."

****

The trees thinned out as Prima Mashira and her group arrived at Lake Ivorus. The still water glistened in the afternoon sun and calmed her. What a beautiful sight. It was a shame she couldn't just sit down to enjoy it. Groups of the hunting party exited the woods and congregated on the shore.

Don Millan came up beside Mashira. "It's huge."

"There could be thousands of demons underwater and we'd never know."

"Then how do we find out?"

"Keep an eye on the surface of the lake. Demons can hold their breath for a long time, but not forever. We should get some boats out there too. I believe there's a dock on the south—" The Prima stopped abruptly as she caught sight of a priest sprinting toward them.

As he reached the group, he dropped his hands to his knees and gasped for air. "Your Luminescence…we've found…someone…on the shore."

"Demon?"

"We think so." The priest panted. "We think it's him."

"Erynion?"

"That's right. Archdon Westan has instructed that no one is to go near him until you arrive."

"Take us right away."

CHAPTER 25

The sun crept across the sky and beat down on the shore of Lake Ivorus as the Prima trudged along the mix of coarse sand and small stones. The heat of the sun baked her blond hair while the sunlight reflected brightly off Sundancer's armor. Ahead of her, several priests and paladins were gathered around something.

"Right up here, Your Luminescence," said the priest leading the way.

The crowd parted for the Prima's group until only a lonely figure near the water remained. No one dared to move in any closer. From a safe distance, Mashira observed his back as he sat quietly on a large rock. His shirt, soaked, appeared to be a thin fabric, like a nightgown. His hair, drenched, was silvery white and extended down past his neck.

An archdon with a black goatee bowed to Mashira. "Your Luminescence."

The Prima returned the gesture. "Archdon Vikard."

"We just found him sitting here. He hasn't moved or spoken. Since there was no immediate threat, Archdon Westan and I thought it would be best to wait for you."

Mashira focused on the figure on the rock. "Do you

think he's surrendering himself?"

"Maybe. Why would he do that, though?"

"Good question. Well, I suppose we should ask and find out."

"Would you like us to restrain him?" the archdon asked.

"Not yet. I don't want to startle him. Surround him, but keep your distance. And be at the ready."

"Yes, Your Luminescence." Archdon Vikard rejoined his group.

The Prima took a deep breath. Accompanied by Lady Sundancer on one side and Advisor Razza Merona on the other, Mashira inched toward the possible demon lord. The other priests fanned out to form an arc around them. Sundancer subtly removed the two sickles secured across her back.

"That aura." Mashira was baffled by what she saw. "There's darkness there, but nothing that would indicate a powerful demon."

"He appears human, but his energy reminds me of a zaidon," Razza stated.

"Yes, you're exactly right. This is what I felt around Mortis the last time I saw him. But if this is Erynion, the demon lord, why can't we sense his full energy?"

"Maybe he's like the Shade."

Mashira continued her approach. "Perhaps. Instead of being invisible, his aura makes him appear human. No wonder the watchers at Nolka let him through."

Sundancer blocked the Prima with her arm. "If you wish to move closer, I must insist he's restrained."

Mashira abided by the bloodseeker's suggestion and paused well out of reach. There was no way for her to know if her enemy was armed. "Hello there."

The shape on the rock didn't budge.

"You're him, aren't you?" the Prima asked. "Erynion? The demon lord?"

He turned his head so Mashira could see his face. She

noted the cloth wrapped around his head. Scars peeked out from the linen above and below the eye. Archdon Feranis had told her about the Devil's Eye that lay beneath. If only she could get a glimpse, perhaps she could learn his identity and cleanse him.

As the Prima took another step forward, Sundancer cut off her path once again. "With all due respect, Your Luminescence, it's not safe. I must insist on restraints."

The figure finally spoke in demon tongue. "I'm no threat to you. At least, not until nightfall."

The bloodseeker glanced over her shoulder. "You'll excuse me if I don't entirely trust you."

Mashira politely pushed Sundancer's arm aside. "I'll be fine. Trust *me*."

Razza Merona joined the two women. "I wasn't aware that paladins were taught Kisejjad."

"They're not," the bloodseeker said under her breath. "Para Paya are."

Mashira addressed the demon again. "So you're Erynion then? You're the demon lord that's been terrorizing our land?"

"I am," he said. "And who are you?"

"I am Prima Mashira, leader of Candelux. We've come to stop you."

The demon lord smiled sadly. "Good. I'm glad to hear it."

"You want to be killed?"

"I want to be free of the agony."

"You've survived for four nights. The last demon lord didn't make it past four hours. And now you want to surrender?" the Prima asked.

"Survived? Barely. The first night I destroyed a town. And the last few nights, the Seductress was stealing my power."

"The Seductress? And where is she now?"

"Dead." The demon lord sneered. "I killed her. She promised to help me with the pain, but she was full of lies."

"What do you expect from a demon called the Seductress?"

"I suppose. So, do we have an agreement? You'll kill me?"

"You're the biggest threat to the kingdom since the Assault," Mashira said. "I won't pass up an opportunity to send you back to the Depths."

"Excellent. Excellent." The demon lord turned the rest of his body to face her. "Make it quick."

"I'm afraid we can't simply kill you outright."

"What?"

"If we kill you right now, yes, you'll lose your strength and return to the Depths. That's for certain. But, nothing prevents Verago from empowering your soul and sending you back here again. He's been searching for centuries for someone capable of becoming a demon lord, and you've proven that your soul is quite capable."

Erynion tilted his head. "What are you saying? You won't kill me?"

"Not in the same sense, I suspect, that you killed the Seductress. You see, she can still return to the Surface. I'm afraid the only way to keep the kingdom safe is to cleanse you."

The demon lord rose from the rock. "No, that was not the agreement."

Mashira instinctively retreated as Sundancer hopped in front of her. The bloodseeker raised her weapons in preparation for a fight, however, the demon made no attempt to attack. The Candelux leader marveled at the size of the beast. She had heard descriptions of his height, but it wasn't until he stood that she felt threatened by his presence.

After the initial panic subsided, the Prima stepped out from behind Sundancer. "What were you expecting? You said you wanted to be free of the agony. I told you I would do that. You're telling me you've changed your mind?"

"No, I want to be free of this curse, but I know about cleansing. There would be nothing worse than being banished to the Depths for eternity."

"I'm sorry, but it's the only way to ensure the safety of the kingdom." Mashira shouted to the arc of priests, "Restrain him!"

Light flooded the shoreline as blessed chains of energy filled the air around the demon. As the blessings were pulled tight, Erynion sat down on the large rock.

The Prima eyed the demon lord. "Does this hurt you at all?"

"I feel nothing."

Even a greater iymed would've reacted to the pain of all these chains, but Erynion showed no sign of it. Mashira closed the gap between them. "A friend tells me you're hiding the Devil's Eye under that cloth."

"Do whatever you like."

His expression was so blank, so empty. She had never encountered a demon who was so calm or apathetic when faced with their own cleansing. Her hand twitched as she reached out and lifted the cloth covering Erynion's right eye. The Devil's Eye glowed and pulsed with oranges and reds. The catlike iris pulled open the pupil and created a gaping black hole.

"Advisor Razza." The Prima waved her over. "I'm not sure what I'm going to find. But once I'm in, I won't have any sense of time. I'll need you to alert me if it's taking too long, if the sun is dropping."

"I understand."

Mashira placed the tips of her fingers on the demon's temples and gazed into the Devil's Eye. The periphery of her vision steadily faded until darkness enveloped her. The hunting party, the lake, Erynion. It all vanished. A flurry of sounds and pictures surrounded her. She kept a sharp eye out for any evidence that would lead to discovering the demon's true identity, but so much of it was fragmented. Blurred images and garbled words discouraged her as she was unable to make any sense from them.

"Who were you? Who was Erynion?" she shouted.

More shapes and voices of memories flitted by her, and the experience became increasingly disorienting. Finally, a little girl screamed in the distance. "Help me! Erynion has me!"

Mashira remained wary as the girl begged for assistance. "Where are you?"

"I'm over here!"

The Prima tried to follow the sound of the voice, but there was no one around her.

"Here! Here!" the girl yelled.

Mashira whirled around to find a small child. The face was unclear, but the dress she wore had a regal flair. "Little girl, who are you?"

"Don't you recognize me?" she asked, dumbfounded. "I'm only the most beautiful princess in the whole kingdom."

"So young, and it's been so long. Is that you, Princess Sereyna?"

The face unscrambled, and the little girl grinned from ear to ear. "Of course it is!"

"What is Sereyna doing in here?" Mashira asked herself. She nearly jumped as a hand landed on her shoulder.

An image of Razza Merona with her eyes closed materialized behind her. "Your Luminescence, can you hear me?"

"Yes, what is it?"

"I apologize for the interruption, but you've been in this trance for over an hour. The sun is not far from the treetops. We need to leave soon if we're to make it back to the city before nightfall."

The Prima groaned. "I understand. Pull me free when we can't wait any longer."

The advisor transformed into sand and scattered into the sudden wind. Mashira returned her focus to the demon lord's mind, but panicked when the little girl was nowhere to be found. "Sereyna! Sereyna! Where did you go?"

The little girl suddenly reappeared. "Here I am!"

"Good. Sereyna, please listen. I need you to help me. Where are we?"

The little girl shrugged. "Wow, you're really pretty."

The Prima bent over and gently grasped the hand of the princess. "Dear child, I don't have much time. Whose mind are we in?"

"I can't tell you that."

"Why not?"

"Because I can't. Ask me something I know."

Mashira straightened up. "But you said Erynion had you. You don't know who he is?"

"Oh, Erynion? Yeah, I know who Erynion is."

Her eyes lit up at the child's response, but Mashira felt her body being pulled out of the darkness. She struggled to get one last answer. "Who's Erynion?"

"Sir Bix!" the child responded cheerfully.

The lights and sounds of her world flooded her senses. As she left the trance, the Prima dropped to one knee.

Sundancer caught her and helped her back to her feet. "Are you all right?"

"Yes." Mashira held her head. "Yes, I'll be fine."

"We must return to the city now or we'll be vulnerable out here in the darkness," Razza cautioned.

The Prima nodded her head. "Give the order for me, please. Have Archdon Westan's group keep the restraints on the demon. We'll take the road."

"Wait. You mean to bring the demon lord back to Royal Oak?" Sundancer asked.

Mashira sensed the hesitation in her voice. "Yes, but there's nothing to worry about. I know who he is. I need some time to recover and clear my head, but the cleansing is happening tonight. So, we must bring him back to do the ritual."

As Advisor Razza Merona relayed the Prima's orders to the crowd, Mashira closed her eyes and replayed the

Devil's Eye experience in her head. There was no doubt in her mind she had heard the correct name. Sir Bix was a well-known member of the Paladin Order, specifically a bloodseeker. He had been bestowed the title of Champion of the Light the year before the Assault on Light's Haven, only to throw it away when he became one of the nine founders of the Death Gods. But prior to his move to Alovajj, Mashira had briefly met him a few times. Though the two of them were not close, both she and Bix came from noble families with close ties to the monarchy. It would make perfect sense that he would know Princess Sereyna.

****

The priests, paladins, and watchers dispersed and walked north to the road leading back to the city. Those reporting to Archdon Westan readied the demon lord for transport and followed the others. Out of the corner of his eye, Millan observed Archdon Omana approaching Mashira, Sundancer, and Razza Merona. Even though the hunt was over, the young priest still considered himself part of the Prima's group, and so he inconspicuously tagged along behind the archdon.

"How are you feeling?" Archdon Omana asked Mashira.

"I'll be fine, thank you. It was just harder than I thought it'd be, especially without the Talisman."

"*And* he's a demon lord. Even if we can't sense his energy, it's still there. Speaking of which, are you sure this is the correct course of action?"

"I understand the reservation, but we have the chance to cleanse him. We can't do it before nightfall, so we can't stay out here. We have to protect ourselves. Once we're in the city walls, we can do the ritual and be done with all of this. I know his identity. Erynion is Sir Bix."

Millan tried to recall where he had heard the name

before.

"The Champion of the Light?" Sundancer asked.

"The Death God founder?" Razza Merona added immediately after.

"The same," the Prima said. "I saw Princess Sereyna in his mind, which makes sense because his father was good friends with King Cato. Bix and his brother were always close to the royal family."

"So, that means Sir Bix is dead," Razza concluded.

"I suppose. Not that we would've heard anything from Alovajj."

"It's interesting. Sir Bix definitely wasn't that tall," Sundancer pointed out.

"Demons come in all shapes and sizes, regardless of their appearance while alive," the Prima reminded her. "Plus, I don't think it could've been any clearer. I just asked Sereyna who Erynion was, and she told me it was Bix. It was really incredible in there."

Archdon Omana interjected. "Your Luminescence, I must insist we reconsider this course of action. I can understand your wish to cleanse the demon. I wish the same. But bringing him into the city could be extremely dangerous."

"Your concern is noted. I've evaluated the risk, and I believe with a hundred priests at our disposal to keep him restrained, as well as the Blessing of Sacred Ground, the demon lord poses very little risk to the civilians of Royal Oak. If we leave him out here, there's no telling how many may die."

"Prima, I must protest. Think of Nesinu."

Millan assumed the mention of his hometown gave him the right to speak up. "Yes, please, Your Luminescence. I was there. I saw what he did!"

"That's hardly valid." Mashira directed her response at Omana only. "A single priest stood against him there."

Millan persisted. "But if he's a demon lord, how do you know if a thousand priests can stand against him?"

The Twisted Gate

Mashira glared at the young man.

Although he wanted to press the issue, Millan knew he'd spoken out of turn. The Prima had been kind not only to let him free this morning, but to also let him join her hunting group. This by no means gave him the right to challenge her. Millan slowed his steps and straggled behind the high-ranking group of priests.

A hand patted him on the shoulder. "You don't want to be up there anyway. Trust me." A fellow don walked beside Millan. The priest was older and had a scruffy complexion. He extended his hand in greeting. "Don Tuarsh."

The Nesinu priest shook his hand. "Don Millan. I hope they know what they're doing, bringing a demon lord into the city."

"It's only one demon, friend. He doesn't stand a chance against hundreds of us. Not even Verago himself could."

"But what if the demons try to attack again tonight? Some of us would have to protect the city."

Tuarsh chuckled. "An attack? I wouldn't worry about that. After the failure last night, I think it's safe to say we're in the clear for a while. Besides, the watchers, the scorchers, and the paladins could keep them at bay. You know, no demon has ever set foot inside the walls of Royal Oak."

"What about the two from last night?"

"Hmm, yeah, I forgot about them. I heard the Brotherhood took down the grate to let them sneak up the river and into the city."

"Really?" Millan noticed another priest come up on the other side of him. She was more pleasing to look at than the first, although, her robes left a lot to the imagination.

"*Psh*, the Brotherhood? They couldn't find the end of the spring's river even if they were washed out by the current. I heard the grate just rusted and no one thought to replace it. It's been missing from that hole in the wall for years. I'm sure it's been fixed now, though."

"Don't underestimate the Brotherhood, Hess," Tuarsh cautioned the female priest. "They're still out there."

"Conspiracies," she shot back. "They're as dead as the Royal Throne."

Millan adjusted his pace once again to move away from the two priests. They didn't seem to notice his absence at all as they continued to argue.

"Don't mind those two." The archdon with the black goatee came alongside him.

"Oh?"

"Brother and sister. Always arguing."

Millan gave a halfhearted smile. "I see. Your Grace, may I ask you a question?"

"Fire away."

"What do you think about the Prima's decision to bring the demon lord back to the city?"

"I don't think it merits discussion."

"Why do you say that?"

"Well, it's not our place to question the Prima. There's a reason why she has advisors. The best we can do is put faith in her decisions, trust that she'll keep us safe, and carry out our duties."

The answer bothered Millan. He was looking for confirmation that this was the wrong course of action, and this archdon refused to give it. "So, then I'm expected to hold my tongue if I think something's wrong?"

"Do you know something more than the Prima?" the archdon politely challenged.

"I'm not sure I understand."

"Is there any information you have that the Prima does not? Are you hiding anything from her?"

Millan was taken aback. "What?! No, of course not."

"Then with no additional knowledge, what makes you think you know better than her?"

Millan opened his mouth, but closed it soon after. His eyes fell to the archdon's swaying white scarf. "Nothing, Your Grace."

"My apologies. It was not my intention to browbeat you into following blindly or to feel guilty about a difference in opinion. I was merely trying to get you to see the situation from another perspective."

"I understand."

The archdon held out his hand. "Archdon Vikard."

The Nesinu priest shook his hand. "Don Millan."

"Yes, I know who you are. I've heard what you've been through. I was sorry to hear about Don Skully. He was a great man."

Millan perked up. "Did you know him?"

"Not personally, no. But my father knew him quite well and spoke very highly of him."

"Even though he openly supported the Death Gods against the wishes of the Prima?"

"We were all saddened by his defiance, but one such act doesn't erase years of service to the guild. He spoke up because he thought it was the right thing to do, just like you did. So, let me ask you this. What makes you think her decision is wrong?"

Millan crossed his arms in front of his chest. "I don't know."

"Come now. I'd like to hear your side. There must be something. I know you didn't challenge our leader without a reason."

"Archdon Omana spoke first."

Vikard stroked his goatee. "Hmm, yes, a well-respected archdon and former advisor. I think that's acceptable. And perhaps that gave you the confidence to speak, but that still doesn't explain why you think she's wrong."

"I don't know." It was all the Nesinu priest could manage to say as he struggled to stay silent.

"Don't worry. You can tell me," the archdon coaxed.

Millan looked ahead, past the siblings and past Mashira, to the shackled demon lord. The band of priests holding him was breaking from the shore of Lake Ivorus and entering the forest. His mind was racing until it focused on a single image, the wasteland where Nesinu once stood. "It's just a feeling, a very bad feeling. I saw what kind of destruction he's capable of. There was nothing left. Just...just nothing. And now we're going to parade him into the city, past our walls, and I'm supposed to just accept that? We don't know anything about his power."

Vikard placed his hands behind his back. "Interesting, but I have to disagree. We know he can't be stronger than Verago. And if Verago could defeat a dozen archdons and a hundred dons all at once, I don't think the Surface would belong to us anymore. Besides, last time the Devil showed his face, he turned tail and ran like a coward."

"You're talking about Devil's Breach."

"A tragic night, but we learned how weak and scared the Devil truly is. We also learned how the twisted gates are created."

"The gate seeds," Millan said.

"That's right. And thanks to the Blessing of Sacred Ground, that tactic can't be used against us again."

"Did they ever figure out who planted them?"

"Rumors mostly. Some think it was a demon years before, during the Assault. I've heard others suggest the Brotherhood had their hand in it. I'm sure those two up there"—the archdon motioned to the squabbling siblings—"know the truth."

"Were you in Light's Haven when it happened?" Millan asked.

"Devil's Breach? No. I haven't been back to Light's Haven in years. What about you?"

"No, but my Acceptance took place a month after it happened. The people there were constantly talking about it. How the whole ground shook. How the gate scarred the royal gardens. I was told the only reason King Batar survived was because he was wearing the Talisman of Zavi."

"Yes, I heard the same. It really shows you how powerful the Talisman is. One touch could cleanse any demon, including Verago."

Millan clicked his tongue. "It's unfortunate there couldn't have been a second artifact to protect his brother."

"Indeed. King Cato has been through the depths and back. Losing two of his children? That's something no father should have to endure."

CHAPTER 26

As the procession rounded a curve in the road, the gates of Royal Oak came into view. Millan noted the sun's position as it sank below the treetops before peering over his shoulder.

"Something the matter?" Archdon Vikard asked.

Millan's head snapped around. "No, sorry." His fingers danced furtively on his thighs. The truth was that even with the archdon at his side, the Nesinu priest felt exposed.

"I can tell you there are no demons behind us."

"I know. That's what's bothering me."

"Oh?"

The young priest leaned in close to the archdon. "Where are all the fray from last night? Shouldn't they be attacking us to save the demon lord?"

"Hard to say. Maybe the army was following the Seductress and not Erynion. Fray can be unpredictable once they lose their leader."

"What about the iymed that got away last night?"

"One iymed, in the daytime, against all these priests and soldiers? He's probably hiding deep in the forest, terrified out of his mind."

The Twisted Gate

Millan envisioned the jester iymed brandishing his daggers by the massive oak tree. As he recalled the brief battle, his heart swelled with pride before it sank within his chest. Eriph had let the demon go to keep Millan alive. Not to mention, though he didn't realize it at the time, the young priest had broken the rules of his guild. He thought back even further to that night in Nolka when Archdon Feranis found out about his ability to do enchantment. What else had Don Skully taught him that he wasn't supposed to know? What would he do next that was against the rules?

"See," Vikard said. "Safe inside the walls."

Millan ended his period of reflection as they crossed the threshold into the city. There was a loud metallic knock as the gates collided against their frame.

"Archdon Vikard!" the Prima called out.

Mashira was off to the side, accompanied by Lady Sundancer. A man stood with them who Millan didn't recognize. As Vikard responded to the Prima, Millan instinctively followed. But halfway there, he halted, embarrassed by the earlier exchange. The Nesinu priest tried to seem inconspicuous as he remained close enough to hear their conversation.

Vikard joined the small huddle. "Yes, Your Luminescence?"

"After some consideration, I've decided it's best if we evacuate all civilians to the southern half of the city."

"If you deem it necessary, of course."

"I do. I don't want to leave anything to chance. But we don't have much time. When you reach the rectory, I need you to send all squires to the watcher headquarters to help with the evacuation."

"Understood."

Millan waited patiently as he heard the footsteps behind him. As Vikard passed by, the young priest hopped beside the archdon and matched his gait. Millan was tempted to look back, but he feared making eye contact with the

Prima. "So, who was that man with Prima Mashira?"

Vikard glimpsed over his shoulder. "Who? That guy? I don't know his name, but he's the lead watcher on duty. Why do you ask?"

"No reason. Just curious."

When the pair reached the rectory, the courtyard was filled with hundreds of priests and squires. In the middle of the crowd, twelve dons had their Blessings of Divine Restraint cast on the demon lord. Erynion was still as a statue, and Archdon Omana had taken her position beside him.

Vikard cupped his hands around his mouth. "By order of Her Luminescence, Prima Mashira, all squires are to report to the watcher headquarters immediately! I repeat, all squires please report to the watcher headquarters immediately!"

Then, he bypassed the crowd and ascended the steps of the rectory. Without a second thought, Millan did the same. The archdon grabbed the door handle. "Where are you going?"

"In-in-inside," Millan stammered. "Inside the rectory."

"Why? Don't you want to watch the cleansing?"

"Of course. I, uh, just thought I'd speak with our other prisoner, the one we caught last night. We still don't know why he and his friend were in the city."

"Uh-huh."

"Thought I would ask him a few questions," Millan continued. "You know, try to get some answers."

"It's fine, I understand." As he entered the rectory, Vikard left the door open, and Millan followed.

****

Erynion stood in the courtyard with his eyes fixated on the ground. He cared little about the people who had gathered to help with his execution. With only the moon and stars to fill the sky, he felt the power inside him trying to grow, but the shackles kept him in check. The light energy burned his skin, but the pain was hardly noticeable. He was being spared from the agony, and so he was at peace.

"So, Bix, are you ready?"

Erynion looked up to see the brilliant aura of the Prima. "Bix? Why are you calling me Bix?"

"Because that's you, isn't it? That's your original identity."

The demon lord pictured the kneeling paladin from his dream. "You're mistaken."

"We'll see about that. Archdon Omana, I want nothing to go wrong. Please restrain him as well."

The former advisor stepped in front of the shackled demon lord. She closed her eyes and extended her hands toward the prisoner. Thanks to the exposed Devil's Eye, Erynion observed the light from Omana's aura intensify and flow toward her arms. When the archdon spoke, her voice was deeper than he expected from a woman.

"May the angels grant me strength so that I may shackle this demon to the Surface for as long as I am able. I invoke the Blessing of Unbreakable Binding!" Omana curled her fingers like eagle talons as light burst forth from the ground. Bands of energy clasped Erynion's wrists. The chains were far thicker than the blessings of the other priests. Four more emerged from the dirt, reached for the beast's neck, and created a large collar.

Gritting her teeth, Omana closed her fists, as if she were gripping the restraints, and pulled her arms to her side. Any slack in the blessing recoiled back into the ground and fiercely jerked Erynion to one knee.

The demon lord growled loudly. In addition to the other restraints, the archdon's blessing caused more than a little discomfort, but the pain still paled in comparison to the agony. Erynion was more annoyed at the ferocity with which he had been forced to his knee. The unbreakable binding on his neck made it impossible to look away from his executioner. He resented the priests for their decision to cleanse him, but all in all, it made no difference. Why care anymore? Verago had chosen him to be the most powerful demon, but what was the point if he had no control over it? He couldn't even remember his own name. His dreams seemed to be taunting him. The answers were so close but never within reach. And then, there was his purpose. Why would he agree to kill King Batar, who also happened to be his brother? Perhaps he was just another failed experiment like the first demon lord. And after five miserable nights on the Surface, he was about to share the same fate.

****

The hinges on the jail entrance squeaked as Millan pushed it open. He had barely taken a step across the threshold, when a hand blocked his path.

"Hold it right there. Who are you?" A priest stood in his way. Millan nearly jumped as a second priest came up from behind him.

"I'm Don Millan. I'm from Nesinu."

"Nesinu? Yeah, I've heard about you. You're the reason we have this one," said one guard.

"Yeah, and the reason we're stuck in here on guard duty," the other added.

Millan raised an eyebrow. "I'm sorry?"

"Never mind her. She's just upset we can't watch the cleansing ritual. So, what brings you down here?"

"I'd like to speak with the prisoner, if I may."

The guard moved aside. "If that's what you want, be our guest. But just so you know, the fiend hasn't said a word all day, at least not since Archdon Omana finished with him."

Millan shuffled his feet across the stone floor as he slipped by the two guards. The enchantment on the cell bars illuminated some of the prison, but left the walls

The Twisted Gate

mostly in the shadows. The Nesinu priest barely made out the outline of the demon.

"Hello there," Millan said.

The iymed sat against the wall in silence.

"My name is Don Millan. What's yours?" The young priest glanced over at the guards. Engaged in their own conversation, they weren't paying him any attention. Millan sighed. What was he doing? He had never interrogated a demon before. This was a waste of time. He should be outside helping to cleanse the demon lord. Millan turned to leave.

"Og tanod tjjev," the demon said softly.

Millan came back to the bars. "You have a name?"

"Sonojj."

"My name is—"

"I heard you the first time," the demon interrupted. "And when you introduced yourself to the other priests. And when you caught us by the oak last night."

"You remember me then?"

Sonojj snorted. "Your voice, your stench. I knew it was you from the moment you stepped in here."

"So, what were you and your friend doing by the tree?"

"Why do you ask?"

"Because I need to know. You infiltrated the city and made it all the way to the center. If it wasn't for me, you probably would've escaped."

Sonojj held up his forearms. "I would applaud your achievement, but—"

The Nesinu priest was unamused by the display. "Why were you in the city? Nothing is out of place. No one was attacked besides me. Why were you there?"

"No reason."

"No. You knew the risks would be high. There's no way you would've waltzed into the city without some plan, some objective, some purpose."

Sonojj moaned. "That may have been true, but it doesn't matter now. You stopped us. Quest failed."

"You're lying."

"Maybe. What does it matter?"

Millan gripped the enchanted bars. "If you truly failed, then what's the harm in telling us your plan? What would you have gained if I hadn't interrupted you?"

"My freedom. My hands."

The Nesinu priest pushed away from the bars. "You're just wasting my time. Why did you call me back if you're not willing to talk?"

"Did it ever occur to you that maybe I want to talk about something else?"

"Like what?"

"I hear a lot of commotion outside. When you came in, one of the guards mentioned a cleansing ritual. Tell me who you've captured."

"You're in no position to make demands," Millan said.

Sonojj carefully slid up the wall. He staggered toward the cell door, taking his time with each step. The Nesinu priest winced at the sight of the demon standing in the light of the bars. The previous night, he had only seen the cat form up close. Sonojj's humanoid form was grotesque with unsightly scars that crisscrossed his face. Tufts of hair circled his head, but left the top a bald island.

"Let's make a deal, shall we?" Sonojj proposed.

"What type of deal?"

"An exchange of information. Tell me what I want to know, and then I'll tell you what you want to know."

The priest contemplated the terms. Revealing any details about the day's events to the prisoner didn't appear to have any foreseeable consequence. "How can I trust that you'll hold up your end of the deal?"

"Did you want to shake on it?" The demon outstretched his arm.

"Ask your questions and be quick about it. Then you'll answer mine."

"Agreed. Who did you capture and bring back to the city?"

"The demon lord, Erynion."

"Only him?" Sonojj asked.

"Yes."

"And you're sure it's him?"

Millan paused. He had never considered the possibility of a decoy. "You tell me. Tall with long white hair. Four scars that run down the right side of his face. He'd pass as human if it weren't for the Devil's Eye."

The demon grunted. "I told him to tear it out. Have you discovered his identity?"

"Yes, the Prima knows. The cleansing will be completed tonight."

"Even so, I doubt there'll be enough time."

"Enough time for what?"

Sonojj appeared to ignore his question. "But that's why you brought him back into the city, isn't it? How fortunate."

"Fortunate?" Millan was having a difficult time following the ramblings of the iymed.

A smile crept across the demon's face. "Of course. They'll come to rescue him, and that means I'll be rescued as well."

"Is that so?"

The smile receded. "But you're pulling my tail now, aren't you? This is a trick to get me to talk."

Millan threw his hands into the air. "What trick? You wanted to make a deal. I've told you what you want to know, and now it's time for you to hold up your end of the bargain."

"I don't believe it."

"I don't care what you believe. The facts are that Erynion, your demon lord, is at this very moment restrained outside this building. Prima Mashira will soon begin the ritual to cleanse him. And when the sun rises in the morning, this nightmare will be over."

Drawn by Millan's outburst, the prison guards gradually made their way to the prisoner's cell.

"I've been in the company of liars for a long time," Sonojj said. "I'd bet you haven't told a single lie your entire life."

"I was not raised to be deceptive like demons," Millan calmly answered.

"Indeed. So, it's all true then."

"Of course it's true. Why would you be happy about that?"

Sonojj's laugh was barely audible. "You really fangled this up."

"Me?" Millan said, as the two priest guards joined him.

"All of you. Candelux. Humans. Dardan fools, the lot of you. I suppose it's not entirely your fault. A bit of bad luck. There's no way you could've known."

One of the guards nudged Millan. "What's he going on about?"

"Our deal," the demon explained. "I'm holding up my end of it."

Millan jumped at the opportunity. "What were you and your friend doing last night?"

"We were planting gate seeds in the middle of your city."

"He's lying," one of the guards blurted out. "The Blessing of Sacred Ground was active last night for the Seductress's attack. The seeds would've been detected, if not completely destroyed."

Millan considered the guard's statement before forming his next question. "Are you saying that when I found you two by the royal oak, you had already planted the seeds?"

"That's correct."

"Ridiculous," the other guard said dismissively. "He's a demon. He lies."

"For what reason?" Millan asked.

"It's obvious," the first guard chimed in. "He wants us distracted, searching the royal oak for gate seeds, so the demon lord can escape."

"Not that demons need a reason to lie," the second

The Twisted Gate

guard said. "It's in their nature."

"Exactly. Come on. Go enjoy the cleansing. Leave him be. He only has a few more hours left on the Surface anyway."

"Sounds like your friends have me all figured out. What about you?" the demon asked.

Millan didn't budge. A pit sat inside his stomach. He ran the conversation again through his mind. Everything the demon had said made sense to a point. If Erynion was captured, Verago would want to free him, but he'd need an army to do that. The only way that could happen would be using a twisted gate, and it would already have to be within the walls. The prisoner was clearly pleased at the prospect of being rescued, but there was still the missing piece.

"How is it possible?" Millan asked.

The iymed feigned innocence. "Why, whatever do you mean?"

"How is it possible we weren't able to detect them?"

"Water has an interesting effect on energy, doesn't it? Masking auras, dampening blessings."

"You'd still have to bury the seeds in the Surface," the guard blurted out. "And like I said before, the sacred ground would've destroyed them."

Sonojj turned his ear in the guard's direction. "And what if they weren't planted in the Surface?"

"What? Under the water? The riverbed is part of the Surface and is equally protected. Are we done here?"

"I don't know. Are we? The spring goes down quite deep, doesn't it? A little too close to the Depths, perhaps?"

The guards were silent as Millan grasped at the final piece of the puzzle. It was true the Blessing of Sacred Ground was only effective for a small distance below the ground. To cover an area the size of Royal Oak, it would take an unimaginable amount of energy to extend the spell so deep. "You planted the seeds at the bottom of the spring."

"That's right," the demon said.

The other guard scoffed. "Impossible. The current of the spring is too strong to swim down, even for a demon."

"And it would take a lot of holy energy to extend the blessing down that far," the first guard said. "I told you he's just trying to distract us. To have the Prima use her energy elsewhere, so they can save the demon lord."

Millan pushed aside the reasoning of the guards. "How did you get to the bottom of the spring?"

Sonojj stretched his arms and yawned. "You know, I believe I've held up my end of the deal, and then some. What you do with the information is your decision, not that any action can save you at this point."

The iymed walked back into the shadows and gingerly lowered himself to the floor. Millan wanted to believe the guards. It would put him at considerable ease to know the shape-shifting demon was lying all along. But the final missing detail of the story pestered him. The Nesinu priest grasped the prison bars. "How did you get to the bottom of the spring?"

The demon silently rested his head against the wall.

One of the guards patted Millan on the shoulder. "Let it go. It was all a lie."

"Yeah," the other guard said as they escorted the young priest back to the entrance. "You really should ignore him. Never trust a demon."

"Go enjoy the cleansing. And the celebration afterward."

"Ha, yeah, I'll definitely be there later."

"Me too. I could use a drink."

The Nesinu priest stopped in his tracks. "The anvil."

Millan suddenly realized Lem, the bar patron from the night before, was the key. His ridiculous claim and reenactment of a demon hobbling through the city made sense of everything. The final piece of the puzzle fell into place.

"What did you say?" one of the guards asked.

Millan's eyes widened. "Angels help us. It's all true.

They used the anvil!"

"What anvil? What are you talking about?"

"Last night—one of the bar patrons—out of my way!" Millan shoved his fellow priest aside. He flung open the prison entrance and raced up the stairs. Sprinting through the empty rooms of the rectory, he hurdled over pieces of furniture, barely clearing them. Adrenaline coursed through his body, pushing him to move faster and faster. He nearly slammed into the front door, pressing the handle just in time to open it.

Back outside, most of the guild had the demon lord surrounded. As Millan entered the courtyard, the ground trembled lightly. The young priest stumbled but quickly regained his balance. He pushed his way through the crowd. "Let me through! I need to speak to the Prima! Let me through!"

Brown robe or black robe made little difference to him. He shoved them aside all the same. There was only one color he sought, and he caught glimpses of it through the crowd. When he reached the inner edge of the circle, the ground shook violently, and Millan tumbled forward at the feet of his leader.

Mashira bent to help him up. "Don Millan?"

The priest locked eyes with her. "There's a twisted gate in the royal oak!"

CHAPTER 27

For hundreds of years, the royal oak towered majestically over the city named after it. It had seen kings rise and fall, the throne change lineage. It was already a symbol of the city when Verago betrayed humanity, using the Amulet of Yezda to become the creator and master of all demons. Residents and visitors alike would come and stare in awe at the glory of this powerful tree. Each ring within the trunk held a crucial memory, and tonight would've marked the greatest of all, the cleansing of a demon lord. But the next time the sun illuminated the city, those memories would all be gone.

The night had started out peculiar enough. Citizens flocked to one side of the city, keeping a safe distance from the rectory. There was some excitement as rumors spread regarding the precautionary measure. But other than that, there was no sign of distress in the air, not even a small breeze to shake the leaves on its splendid branches. The center of the city, where the tree had grown for centuries, was quiet and empty. Deep beneath the ground, a rumbling disturbed the peaceful night, followed by a small quake. Though it had no effect on the royal oak, the tremor would have caused some alarm had there been anyone in the main square. As the shaking grew more severe, dark vines emerged from beneath the tree, burrowing their way into the massive trunk.

They started out small, rising in a spiral fashion, but grew thicker and thicker as they made their way to the crown of the royal oak. The bark on the symbolic tree cracked and splintered as the vines expanded the trunk outward. Large branches snapped, and while some fell outside the retaining wall, others plunged into the spring and were taken downstream. Fighting to maintain its structure, the tree groaned, but it was helpless to stop the attack. As the vines emerged from the crown, the mighty oak fractured into three pieces and collapsed. Centuries of growth and prosperity had been destroyed in a matter of minutes. In its place now stood the dark and ominous twisted gate.

At the rectory, the priests fought to keep their balance. Some of those restraining the demon lord had released their blessings, however, Omana's binding never wavered. When the earth ceased trembling, there was a moment of serenity before chaos broke loose. In the distance, the watchtower bells rang out across the city.

Prima Mashira barked out commands at those around her. "Get those restraints back up! You! Get inside and tell them to get the ground glowing! Archdon Vikard, take some priests and get the Blessing of Marked Defense up around the city. Focus mainly on the areas around the center. Archdon Westan, you and your group stay here and protect these priests. Archdon Omana, whatever happens, keep him bound. Angels help us if he gets free in the city. Everyone else, get to the royal oak!"

Millan felt the excitement and terror mix within his mind as the majority of the crowd headed south away from the rectory. The small battle he'd fought at Nolka was invigorating, but this would be different, much larger. Interestingly, though, it was not the thought of hordes of demons bursting from a twisted gate that made his heart throb with worry, but rather the one demon they were leaving behind. A couple of minutes into the run, the ground began to glow. Millan occasionally checked over his shoulder to see if the Prima was still close by. Although he had walked through Royal Oak the previous day, he hadn't realized just how large the city was until this moment. As the massive twisted gate came into view, his hometown popped into his head. It was going to be a lot harder to destroy this one. A loud roar emanated from the vines, not from the voice of a single beast, but the cumulative rage of demons as they poured out of the gate. Millan wanted desperately to pick up the pace, but he knew he needed to save his energy for the battle.

The Nesinu priest noticed the Candelux symbol light up on the buildings that lined the street, indicating the Blessing of Marked Defense was activated. He was close to joining the fight. The light beneath his feet intensified as the Blessing of Sacred Ground was brought to full ritual. Its warmth had a calming effect on the young priest, but he suspected the fray demons would find it a far more painful experience. Millan finally made it to the large area, which held the once symbolic royal oak at its core. The paladins and watchers had already engaged the enemy.

An archdon called out instructions, "Forget the cleanse! Chain them for the soldiers!"

Two major rifts in the twisted gate had allowed the first wave of demons to flood into the city. Based on their size and behavior, Millan deduced that these were mostly fray demons. The creatures did their best to avoid the enchanted ground and vaulted toward the humans. By the time the priests joined the fight, the soldiers had the twisted vines mostly surrounded. Millan and other dons began casting the chains of light. The Nesinu priest roped a funny-looking demon with shredded ears, and the closest paladin put a sword through its chest. The vines of the unholy tree ruptured as a third hole tore open. The demons flowed freely from the new exit and scampered along the unprotected path. Some of the fiends skipped along the dirt, burning their feet, while others managed to move unscathed, using the fragmented remains of the oak tree to stay off the ground. Millan circled around the gate with a group of fighters toward the new opening, but some of the demons were already out of their reach.

"Don't chase! Stay with the gate!" someone shouted.

Millan cursed under his breath. It seemed a group of fray would soon be loose in the city, but then a hail of arrows descended on the demons. The scorchers had joined the fight just in time. The impaled demons shrieked as they were pinned to the Surface and seared by the blessing. Those that weren't struck retreated toward the twisted gate into the waiting blades of the paladins and watchers. Things were looking up for the humans.

Millan's head swiveled back to the unholy tree as a second wave of demons bellowed in unison. The openings in the twisted gate expanded as what appeared to be greater fray and lesser iymed emerged from the tree. It was easy for Millan to spot the difference. The greater fray, large brutish demons, charged into battle, swinging wildly and trying to inflict as much damage as possible with little regard for themselves. The lesser iymed, on the other hand, surveyed the battleground and strategically engaged their foes.

Millan squared off against an iymed with a small mohawk. The creature wore an open vest, and a metal chain of dark energy snaked up his arm. His size reminded the young priest of the jester demon he'd fought the night before.

"Blessing of Divine Restraint." Millan thrust his hands forward, and the chains of light flew at the demon. The iymed copied the gesture, and his unholy links hurtled at the priest. The enchanted metal intertwined midair, and each side heaved to pull the other off balance. Amid the tug-of-war, Millan glanced at the unholy tree. As the demons continuously emerged from the gate, their numbers rose at an alarming rate.

"Forget the chains! Spike what you can!"

Instructions were flying in from different directions. Millan wasn't even sure who was giving them. He made a throwing motion with his free hand. "Blessing of the Lumenail!"

The spike of light struck the demon with the mohawk in the shoulder, and Millan jerked back the chains as hard as he could. The iymed stumbled forward and flung himself at the young priest. The collision knocked Millan onto his back, and his spells vanished. He scurried to his feet to guard himself against the next attack, but the iymed with the unholy chains had already scampered off.

Millan continued to cast his lumenails at any enemy within range. As he spun around to spike a fray streaking past him, the young priest spotted Prima Mashira. The gleaming white robe and red scarf stood out like a beacon in the battle. And like moths to an open flame, fray and iymed alike seemed to be drawn to the powerful priestess. Those that didn't suffer at the hands of her blessings met their demise at the end of Lady Sundancer's sickles. The Prima and the bloodseeker moved seamlessly between enemies, disposing of the creatures left and right. Millan gaped in awe at the two women, distracting him from the present danger. The young priest felt a sharp pain on his cheeks as a fray landed on his shoulders and grabbed his head. Almost immediately, the demon was knocked off, but not before leaving claw marks on one side of Millan's face. The Nesinu priest grimaced, pressing his palm to his cheek. He pulled back his hand to find light streaks of blood.

A watcher swung his blade and separated the demon's head from his body. "Are you all right, Don?"

Millan gave a quick nod. "Just a scratch."

The two rejoined the fight with fervor, but moments later a third cry forced all eyes to the gate. More fray poured out, but the more terrifying sight was six ogre-like

The Twisted Gate

iymed, each standing nearly ten feet tall, climbing out of the tree. The massive beasts with muscle upon muscle surrounded the twisted gate on all sides. Each of the six ogres took hold of the retaining wall and ripped a gaping hole in it. The spring water, which was already brimming, gushed onto the battlefield.

"No," Millan said quietly to himself. "Not the sacred ground."

The young priest watched helplessly as the wave washed over the enchanted dirt. The water absorbed the light energy and dampened the blessing's effect. The demons rushed to the safety of the pool and splashed about. The humans were slowly losing their advantage. The sting from his wound reminded Millan to stay focused. In the short reprieve from fighting, he brought his hand to his face. A small amount of light energy pulsed from his palm and closed the wound.

****

Mashira remained calm as the demons swarmed around her and Sundancer. It had been years since she had engaged in any battle with demons, but the Assault on Light's Haven was much worse than this. She had the utmost confidence in the bloodseeker to keep her safe. Mashira kept an eye on the six ogres that had just destroyed the spring's retaining wall as they appeared to be searching for something. When one of the large demons pointed in her direction, all six cried out and abandoned the gate.

"Protect the Prima!" Sundancer shouted at the top of her lungs.

The massive beasts charged toward Mashira and the bloodseeker. Restraints flew from the nearby priests, coupled by scorchers' arrows. Four of the ogres were caught, slowly pulling their captors with them. But as the massive demons dug their heels into the muddy ground, they were unable to keep their footing. The middle two ogres, on the other hand, passed the gauntlet untouched by any blessing. The Prima steeled herself as she witnessed the soldiers in the demons' path easily knocked aside.

Before Mashira could say anything, Sundancer bolted toward the two demons. As the bloodseeker neared the ogres, the leading iymed swung his fist at her. She brought the sickle over her head, and the blade punctured the beast's arm. The momentum of the attack forced Sundancer to swing up like a pendulum, cutting even deeper before being flung into the air above the demon. The powerful iymed stumbled and clutched his wound. Mashira watched as he desperately searched for his assailant before he looked up at the night sky. The bloodseeker hurtled toward her foe and buried her blades into the base of his skull, forcing the beast to crumple to the ground.

As Sundancer pulled her weapons from the decaying demon, Mashira kept track of the dark energy. It seeped from the slain foe but refused to sink into the dirt. The wisps of darkness spread out and divided itself among the remaining five demons.

The Prima sighed. "Kindreds? Seriously?"

Empowered by the energy of his fallen brother, the second ogre demon was nearly upon her. The beast bellowed, lifted his fist high in the air, and struck at the Candelux leader with all his might. Mashira extended her arms outward, and a small dome of light encapsulated her. The demon's fist struck the holy barrier with a loud *thud*. His flesh sizzled and the ogre recoiled, grasping his badly burned hand. Before the beast had a chance to fill his lungs, his head slid off his shoulders. Sundancer landed beside the decapitated corpse.

Mashira scowled as her dome of light faded away. "I really wish you hadn't done that. Look. They're kindred demons."

The dark energy from the second slain beast traveled to

the four remaining ogre demons. A group of fray and iymed attacked the priests casting the holy chains, and the kindred demons began to break free of their restraints.

"We need to get this under control before it gets—"

A bone-chilling wolf howl came from the twisted gate. The Prima shuddered as a second howl, even louder than the first, followed closely behind. What else could Verago possibly have hidden in the Depths?

****

The ground lightly trembled as two massive demonic wolves broke loose from the unholy tree. Millan gazed in disbelief while the demons cheered. The newly arrived beasts shook their bizarre fur as if dogs fresh from the water. With his shoulder measuring twice the height of any man, the larger wolf was pitch-black with a thick dark cloud seeping from his fur. The smoke made it difficult to pinpoint his body, but his vibrant red eyes showed clearly through the haze. His companion was more slender and slightly smaller, and her glowing fur lit up the immediate area. Like hot embers on a dying fire, her body pulsed with shades of ebony and crimson. Steam wafted up from the water beneath her as she eyed the enemy with her beady black eyes.

"Restraints!"

Along with other priests, Millan thrust his hands forward to capture the newcomers, but the chains were slashed through by the demonic wolves. The fiery beast leapt in Millan's direction and growled menacingly. The Nesinu priest quivered as his fellow priests retreated. He had to summon every ounce of strength and willpower just to move his feet and take up rank behind the paladins and watchers. The black wolf sat back on his haunches and howled to the night sky. The dark essence, which had initially oozed from his fur and evaporated like a wisp into the night, spread like a heavy smoke outward from the beast. Millan watched in horror as the dark energy consumed those closest to the wolves.

"Get back! Stay away from the Corruption!" The priests did their best to contain the attack. Millan retreated, and as he encountered other fighters, he repeated the instructions.

"Fire!"

Arrows flew through the air. Millan felt a glimmer of hope, but it rapidly faded as most of the projectiles deflected off the thick fur of the wolves. The few that found their mark seemed to only anger the monsters. Corruption completely encompassed the giant beasts.

Many fray and iymed flocked to the protection of the wolves while the rest worked to free the four ogre demons near the Prima. Millan looked back and forth between the two problems. The four ogres wouldn't stay restrained for much longer, but who knew what the wolves were capable of? The situation was spiraling out of control.

"Contain the beasts together! Blessing of the Holy Prism!"

Millan raised his arms with his palms facing the Corruption. A wall of light shimmered into existence as the priests unified their efforts into one spell to keep the dark cloud from spreading. An unnatural silence fell on the battlefield. What were the demons planning inside the prism? Millan knew the spell was only meant to contain the smoke. If the priests wished to trap their prey, they would need a lot more help. The quiet was interrupted by shouting from the other side of the city center. Millan spotted Mashira and Sundancer racing toward the four iymed that had finally broken free of their restraints. He wanted very badly to join her, but his feet remained planted. His role in containing the Corruption was equally important.

"Here they come!"

"Wait until they break through!"

Millan's hands shook in anticipation. The paladins and watchers raised their weapons, and the scorchers loaded their bows. Greater fray smashed through the holy wall, and the inhabitants spilled out along with the cursed cloud. The arrows were loosed, and the battle was underway again. Millan let his part of the holy prism vanish as he prepared to fight, but all he could do was gawk as the wolves emerged from the Corruption and soared over the fighters.

"They're heading toward the rectory!"

The Nesinu priest didn't waste a second as he began sprinting back toward the courtyard. Back toward Erynion. He had no idea what he was going to do when he got there, but every fiber of his being told him to get to the demon lord as quickly as possible. As Millan gave chase, he thought back to his lessons with Don Skully. Never was there mention of monstrous demon wolves. What the depths were these things?

CHAPTER 28

Erynion had knelt while the ground trembled and the priests scattered like terrified mice. The Devil's Eye had shown him their fear, their energy recklessly flitting about like a flickering flame. And though their initial panic had subsided, terror still appeared to grip most of the priests who remained in the courtyard. The demon lord wondered what had caused the quake, but made no attempt to free himself. Wrapped in divine restraints, he found the burning sensation quite pleasant. He had no desire to experience the agony anytime soon.

The rectory courtyard was quiet. Even the priests who had stayed behind to guard Omana and the other restrainers didn't socialize. The demon lord smirked. Just minutes ago, he faced execution, but now, with the fear of the priests so palpable, it seemed as if he were the only one at ease.

"What's so funny?" Omana asked.

His smile faded.

"What's the matter? Shy?"

Erynion wasn't in the mood to talk.

Her eye twitched. "It must be something. Tell me. What is it you find so amusing?"

"Everything. All of this. This cleansing ritual. Whatever's happening right now inside your city. All of this just for me. Why?"

"You annihilated an entire village. With your help, the Seductress infected another with Corruption."

"That must be terrifying to you since I don't even know my identity yet."

"You don't?"

"I don't."

Omana clenched her jaw. "Depths. That would mean you're not Sir Bix."

"What makes you say that?"

"If you don't know who you are, then there's no way the Prima could extract your identity using the Devil's Eye. You're not him, are you?"

"Afraid not."

"Then who the depths are you?"

"I wish I knew." The demon lord scanned Omana up and down. The dreams had given him many clues about who he was. He merely lacked a name. Erynion had no doubt this archdon, and probably anyone else in the vicinity, knew exactly who was the brother of King Batar and Princess Screyna. He yearned to learn the name. It was the key to his power. But in captivity, it could also be the key to his destruction. "Not that I'd tell you if I did."

"You know, for a demon wrapped completely in blessings, you don't appear to be in pain at all."

"Pain is relative."

"What does that mean?" Omana asked.

"Let's just say, given the alternative, I rather enjoy the feel of the chains."

"Is that so?" The archdon addressed one of the priests restraining the demon lord. "Don Shatha, drop your chains and spike his heart."

"Uh, y-yes, Your Grace."

Erynion sensed the fear festering within the priest. Don Shatha's breathing became more pronounced as he inched closer. His trembling hands pushed back the sleeves of his brown robe.

"Have no fear," the demon lord said reassuringly. "I won't attack. Nothing you do can harm me anyway."

The priest hesitated, his anxiety evident by his twitching fingers.

"Get on with it!" Omana urged.

Shatha's light energy churned chaotically within him. The priest lifted his hand, and his aura intensified in his arm.

"We have him. He's not going anywhere. Do it!"

"Blessing of the Lumenail." Shatha's voice was shaky as the energy seeped from his palm. A glowing spike hovered above his hand, and the priest thrust the blessing into the demon's chest. Shatha closed his eyes and turned his head.

Erynion was surprised to find the spell did very little. He felt it penetrate his skin, but after that—nothing. With the spike of light sticking out of his chest, he addressed the archdon. "What was the purpose of this?"

"Hit him again!" Omana commanded.

Shatha pulled back his arm, and the blessing followed. The spell had lost much of its strength, but soon it lit up once more. Shatha forced the spike back through Erynion's heart.

Nothing.

"You don't feel that at all?" Omana asked.

The demon lord raised his eyebrows. "What exactly should I be feeling?"

"That's not possible. It's going right through you. How do you not feel that?"

"Perhaps, you should give it a try."

****

"Come on!" Vikard waved to the priests under his command. Finished with their task of casting the Blessing of Marked Defense on the city, the archdon moved on to

The Twisted Gate

his next order. "Let's head back to the rectory."

"Your Grace, don't you think our skills would be of better use at the twisted gate?" Don Tuarsh asked.

Don Hessestra came up behind her brother and slapped him on the back of the shoulder. "Because I'm sure His Grace hadn't considered that already."

Vikard stroked his goatee. They were approximately halfway between the rectory and the center of the city. Archdon Westan's priests were the only ones assigned to protect Omana and those restraining the demon lord. "It's fine, Hess. The gate's here because of the demon lord. Where do you think the demons are going to run if they get out of the center?"

"But Archdon Westan—" Tuarsh bit his tongue as the archdon tilted his head. "Could probably use our help."

Hess snickered. "Nice recovery."

"Everyone, back to the courtyard!" Vikard called out. Despite the distant rumbling behind them, he was sure he'd made the right call. There were six other archdons and nearly a hundred priests taking care of the twisted gate, not to mention the Prima and all the watchers, paladins, and scorchers. Westan was an experienced archdon, but there was no reason for him to guard the demon lord alone. After all, wasn't Erynion the greatest threat in the city?

The rectory came into view and there was no sign of demon activity. Archdon Omana and the other priests still had the demon lord restrained.

"Archdon Vikard." Westan sat on a wooden crate with his back against the rectory wall.

"Archdon Westan, everything quiet here?"

"So far."

For as long as Vikard knew him, Westan was never a man of many words. There were archdon meetings where he wouldn't speak the entire time. Kindhearted and humble, he was well liked and well respected. If Head Archdon Scarit decided to step down, Omana and Westan would be the two likely candidates to take his spot.

"I wonder how it's going. Must be one depths of a battle," Vikard said.

"Mm-hmm."

Everything was so serene by the rectory that Vikard began to second-guess his decision. "Maybe I should take my squad and head up there."

"Up to you."

"So, no demons have even come close to the rectory yet? No activity at all?"

"All quiet here." Westan gestured toward the demon lord with his head. "Except for Omana. Seems like she's struck up a conversation with the prisoner."

"Heh, pleasant, I'm sure." Vikard sprang to his feet when he spotted a priest attacking the demon lord. The archdon raced across the courtyard. "What are you doing?! Get away from him!"

Don Shatha stepped back as Vikard arrived at the scene. Westan was right behind, along with a handful of priests.

"Relax." Omana made no effort to hide the annoyance in her voice. "They were my orders."

"Are you trying to make him angry?" Vikard asked in disbelief.

"Everything's fine. As you can see the prisoner hasn't budged. We're doing our part. Did you do yours?"

"If you're referring to the marked defense, then yes."

"And why are you here?"

"I thought our help would be needed."

"You're mistaken," Omana said sharply. "Perhaps you should join the fight at the oak."

Vikard had been an archdon for the last ten years and had always found Omana to be somewhat crass. When she returned home to Royal Oak after Mashira's Illumination ceremony, many thought Head Archdon Scarit would give Omana the opportunity to take his role. After all, it was customary for a head archdon to offer the title to a former advisor. And while some believed this slight was the source of her rough demeanor, Vikard knew Omana had always been this way. He'd heard the stories from his father, who had also served as one of Primus Ayristark's advisors.

"Perhaps you're right," Vikard acknowledged.

A loud howl echoed between the buildings. The priests murmured to one another.

"What the depths was that?"

"Sounded like a wolf."

"A wolf?"

"In the city?"

"What else?"

A second howl pierced the air.

Vikard's eyes darted between Westan and Omana. "You don't think they were right, do you?"

"I didn't before. We never had any evidence," Omana answered. "It was only just a story."

"The *Denhauli*?" Westan asked.

Vikard nodded. "If they're real, it makes sense Verago would send them to free his demon lord. And if the stories are true, I doubt they'll be contained at the oak."

"I guess we may need your help after all," Omana relented.

Westan stepped back. "Vikard and I will keep them away from the demon lord."

The two archdons positioned the priests around the courtyard, focusing mainly on the entrance. There was a half wall with an opening in the middle, separating the courtyard from the rest of the street. As Vikard took up his post opposite Westan, another howl swept through the area.

"Whatever it is," Westan said calmly, "they're coming."

Vikard imagined what the monsters might look like. Four years ago, before the relationship between Candelux and the Death Gods went from bad to worse, there was a rumor circulating among the higher priest ranks. Reports from Alovajj talked about two massive demon wolves that served as guardians to Verago. Since they had never left the Depths, there wasn't much detail about them, only that they were unique among demons and incredibly strong. Due to the questionable interrogation methods of the Death Gods, determining the accuracy of information coming out of Alovajj was always a challenge. And so, since no one had ever seen these wolves, there was understandable skepticism. After the incident at Deimor Outpost, the story faded away. But as Vikard waited for their forms to be revealed, he no longer believed the Denhauli, Verago's wolf guardians, were a myth.

His heart hurled against his chest. His feet felt the vibrations as something large galloped toward them. There was an audible gasp from the other priests as a giant black wolf leapt from behind the corner and squared off with the group. Almost as tall as the buildings beside him, the beast bared his fangs. His companion, an equally massive red wolf, emerged next and paced menacingly back and forth.

"Fangle me," Vikard said softly. "I suppose cleansing is out of the question."

"I suppose," Westan replied.

"Don't let them near the demon lord," Vikard instructed the priests behind him. "Take them down as fast as possible. Chains, spikes, whatever you can throw at them."

"Aim for their hearts if you can," Westan added.

Without warning, the black wolf bolted down the street. Vikard's hands glowed as the shadowy demon barreled down on the humans. The giant animal pivoted and bounded onto a nearby roof, exposing the fiery wolf behind him.

"Hit the red one!" Vikard shouted.

The demon spun her vibrant red body, and her tail sent a wave of fire, embers, and ash toward her opponents. Vikard took cover behind the wall. The screams of his

fellow priests filled his ears.
"I'm blind! I'm blind!"
"I'm on fire! Put me out!"
"It burns!"

Vikard hastily patted out the small flame on his own robe before attending to the priest who lost his eyesight. The shadowy wolf flew from the rooftops and into the rectory courtyard. The red wolf dashed past the injured priests to join her partner. Westan led the attack as chains and spikes of light flew at the demon wolves. Meanwhile, Vikard hurried between the priests who had been badly burned. Healing was his specialization, and so his priority was to get the injured priests back into the fight.

****

In the courtyard, the two demon wolves snarled while Omana's group kept Erynion bound. Those uninjured under Vikard's and Westan's commands did their best to keep the wolves away from the demon lord.

"Ha! I told you they were real!" Don Tuarsh called to his sister.

"Really? You want to gloat now?" Don Hessestra shot back.

Omana cursed Vikard for assigning these bickering siblings to protect her. "Will you two Dardan idiots just shut up and kill those things?"

"Yes, Your Grace!" they said in unison.

Vikard moved between downed priests while Westan rallied those still fighting. Omana knew it wasn't going to be enough. Her group had to help hold off these wolves in time for the rest of the fighters to arrive. She looked down at Erynion. His head hung low and his body was limp. Was he unconscious? There was no time to debate with herself whether this was a trick. "I have the demon lord! Drop your restraints and help kill those wolves!"

All at once, the holy chains disintegrated, save the

unbreakable binding. As the priests under her command joined the battle, Omana studied her prisoner. When did he fall asleep? And how could he fall asleep with the light burning him?

A battle cry filled the air as the priests and soldiers from the oak sprinted down the street to engage the Denhauli. Corruption surged from the black demon, creating a small haven for the wolves. As the red wolf pointed her muzzle skyward, her fur shifted to bright orange before turning nearly white. With an ear-piercing howl, a ring of fire flew out in all directions. Omana wailed as the blaze licked her robes, but her blessing stayed strong. Don Hessestra and Don Tuarsh extinguished the small flames that had latched to Omana's clothing.

"Are you all right, Your Grace?" Hess asked.

The archdon fought back the pain. "I'm fine. I'm fine."

A second battle cry came from the rooftops where dozens of iymed and hundreds of fray brandished their weapons. The paladins and watchers provided a row of protection in front of their robe-wearing allies. The demons roared again as they descended on their foes.

"Ogari vojjirol gadrof!"

"Lome dalik!"

Light and steel flashed across the courtyard as the humans tried to thin the numbers of the demon army. The enemy countered with Corruption, fire, and blades of their own. But on the outskirts of the fight, Omana determined the true goal should be killing Erynion as soon as possible. She recalled how he'd been unaffected by Don Shatha's lumenail. If Erynion was to be killed, it had to be with a real blade.

Omana scoured the area for a paladin. "Sir Illian! Sir Illian!"

Sir Illian was a Champion of the Light guardian and leader of the Paladin Order in Royal Oak. Illian effortlessly finished off his quarry before rushing to the archdon. A demon crossed into his path, and without hesitation, he sent the imp sideways with his shield.

"Your Grace?" Illian said.

"I need you to kill the demon lord this instant!"

The paladin hesitated.

"There's no time," the archdon insisted. "Hurry, before it's too late!"

Illian handed his shield to Don Hess and raised his arm to deliver the mortal blow. However, the blade didn't fall. The paladin's hand was caught in the jaws of the massive black wolf. Illian shrieked as the beast jerked his head and sent the guardian sailing through the air. The monstrous wolf towered over Erynion and locked eyes with Omana.

"Angels, help us," she whispered.

The black beast lowered his head and prepared to strike. Tuarsh and Hess stepped in front of Omana, but the wolf batted them aside. Blessings of Lumenail embedded into his fur, but he kept his gaze fixed. As the beast launched himself forward, Omana dropped her Blessing of Unbreakable Binding and dove out of the way. She hastened to her feet and cursed herself. Although Erynion appeared unconscious, the demon lord was no longer restrained. The black wolf's lip curled and his jaws parted. He shifted his body into a striking position. Omana opened her hands to reveal the two small Talisman replicas chained to her palms. She began to glow as ripples of light moved down her arms.

"May the power of the angels flow through me. Grant me the strength to fortify my soul and summon the light to strike down my foes. I invoke the Blessing of the Fallen Angel!"

CHAPTER 29

The Denhauli.

He'd heard that word before, but where? The demon lord winced as his mind felt an incredible pressure. When the two giant wolves appeared, an image flashed through his mind. His eyes grew heavy, and he felt the dream pulling him in. Although the next memory might reveal his identity, Erynion didn't wish to lose consciousness amid the conflict. Not here. Not now. But his fight was futile. He carefully sat on his feet and allowed his head to fall at the same time as his eyelids.

When he was able to see again, he expected to be in the royal gardens, playing as a young teenager with his brother and sister. But what he saw was nothing of the sort. From his height, Erynion determined he was an adult in this memory. He stood in the center of a large room, dimly lit by torches. The walls and floor, though cut out of the earth, appeared smooth and well crafted. Before him was a figure on a throne, shrouded by the shadows. On either side of the throne rested a giant wolf, the red one nearly as large as the black one.

The silhouette spoke. "Welcome, Altheus."

Instantly, everything was clear in his mind. No blurred

image, no misunderstanding. He knew where he was, when he was, who he was. The voice of the figure was the same voice that gave him instructions during his time on the Surface. The same voice that told him his purpose was to kill his brother, King Batar.

And the name. After all the torture and misery of the last few days, Erynion finally remembered his real name, his identity: Prince Altheus, son of King Cato. Three years ago, he was captured alive by Verago and brought to the Depths. This was the memory he was witnessing.

"What's going on? What do you want with me?" Altheus asked.

"Truthfully, it's not you I wanted, but your brother."

"Batar? Why?"

Verago rose and made his way to the massive red wolf. His fingers combed her fur. "Your brother is not as innocent as you believe. You have been betrayed."

"Oh? And I'm supposed to believe that? You're the traitor to all humankind."

"A harsh title, to be sure," Verago said calmly as he descended the stairs. "But unjust and all propaganda. I was humanity's greatest hero once. They even put my name on a big wall. But, that's a story overshadowed by the lies of a deceitful king, just as your story will become twisted by your brother."

As the Devil stepped into the light of the torches, Altheus cringed. Even in the royal gardens, moments before capturing the prince, Verago had stayed in the shadows. Altheus expected a deformed monster, but his fear subsided as Verago's appearance was ordinary. He was of average height with modest features. His hair a mix of brown and blond, and his eyes the color of chestnuts. His shirt was made of cloth with tightly interwoven laces across the front, keeping his chest hidden. His baggy pants were made from old leather.

"May I show you something?" Verago asked politely.

"Um, I suppose." Altheus was thrown off guard by the

hospitality. They moved to an adjacent room, and Verago presented a large painting on the wall. The canvas depicted an angel, amid a plethora of demons, wielding a large axe in one hand with light radiating from the other.

"That looks like you," Altheus commented.

"That's because it is me, once upon a time. The kingdom was in serious danger. The demon army was growing stronger from the Amulet. The wanderers had absorbed power without focus and had created an army of fray, thousands of them. Alova had already fallen. Memorial City was their next target."

"I know this story."

"Do you?" Verago challenged.

"You led the charge into battle on the Plains of Deimor. You were killed. But before the fight, the Candelux priests tethered your soul to King Prevarra so you could return from the beyond in case you died."

"In case I died?" The Devil snorted. "The plan *was* for me to die."

"The plan? You went in knowing you would die?"

"Yes, can you imagine that? It was a willing sacrifice, though. It had to be. If I had any regrets about it, I wouldn't have transcended."

The captured prince stared at the painting. "And you never would've gained your power."

"Yes, but that's not what happened. I did transcend. And the power I returned with as an angel turned the tide of the war. The kingdom was saved. We retook Alova and the demons fled down here, into the Depths."

"Then why did you betray us? Why did you steal the Amulet of Yezda and rebuild the demon army?"

Verago sighed. "It didn't jump straight to that. There were many events that led to what happened. There was one other sacrifice I made that no one speaks of in your history lessons."

"Oh?"

"The soul binding cost me eternal rest. Once I crossed

back to the Surface, I'd be trapped here. The tether that pulled me back would prevent me and the person to whom I was connected from transcending. One soul would always act as an anchor for the other."

"Then how'd you transcend to begin with?"

"The initial ritual between me and my brother was just a connection, like an open road between two cities," Verago explained. "It simply exists, but there's no substance, no energy. An empty path. When I died, the bond was filled with energy and that's what created the tether that brought me back. Once it's made, it cannot be unmade."

"So where's King Prevarra now?" Altheus asked.

"My brother is no doubt an angel on the other side. Though the soul bond can never be destroyed, it can be transferred to other souls of similar energy. In order to prevent Prevarra from suffering, his side of the link was passed on to his daughter, Thira, when she became queen. And again, to her son, Vask, when he took the throne."

"King Vask? It was during his reign that you stole the Amulet."

Verago's nostrils flared. "I had no choice. Except for a handful of faithful supporters, humanity had turned its back on me. Under the reigns of my brother and niece, there was progress. I worked tirelessly with Candelux to produce an artifact that could counter the Amulet."

Altheus's eyes lit up. "The Talisman of Zavi."

"Yes. It was the only way to stop the demons for good. But things took a turn for the worse when Vask became king. He was always such a petty and spoiled boy. Despite my efforts to counsel him, he saw me only as a tool to be ordered about. I was like a slave to him, and the kingdom was just a playground for him to rule over. Due to the constant demon threat, Candelux grew rapidly, and soon Primus Zavi became one of the main advisors to the king. Vask became sick of the nobility, and his thoughts were poisoned with talks of conspiracy and rebellion. I advised caution. We were so close to stopping the demons. A war among ourselves would've put all that at risk and thrown the kingdom into chaos. But, he didn't listen. He recklessly dissolved the Royal Throne. The three noble families became restless as their influence outside of their respective cities was all but gone."

"But, there was no war. Vask prevented conflict by allowing Corriani to marry his son."

Verago grabbed his wrist behind his back. "That's true. The joining of the Shabinne and Thoris lineage put an end to the unrest, but that came more than a decade later. In the meantime, the nobles built their armies in secret, waiting for their opportunity to strike the capital. But who would dare attack a king with an angel by his side?"

"Yes, that would seem foolish."

"It was around that same time that Zavi and I finally completed the Talisman. We discovered the artifact was so powerful, there was a way it could help me to transcend once again. If Vask allowed it, his side of the soul bond would be transferred to the Talisman. And when the Amulet of Yezda and the Talisman of Zavi were brought together, they would destroy each. In one single action, my soul would be free, and the demons would lose all of their power. Vask agreed to the transfer, but once it was complete, he hid the Talisman away."

Altheus was unfamiliar with this story. "That's not what happened. With the help of the priests, Vask combined the Talisman and the Amulet. Their powers negated each other. The kingdom was at peace until you broke the artifacts apart and took the Amulet for yourself."

Verago laughed. "Yes, that's the lie he told everyone. It's the same lie that sits in all the history books. But, the Talisman and the Amulet never met. You see, the noble families were dying to overthrow Vask. He promised me if I stayed by his side and protected him, he'd give me the Talisman to complete my mission. He just needed to calm the nobles first. But he lied about that too. For five years, I protected him. I was essentially trapped in that castle. In my absence from the battlefield, the demon numbers started to grow again. I finally realized Vask would never cease being selfish, caring only for his own life, his own power. He had no intention of saving the kingdom."

There was no proof that the Devil's account was any more accurate than the history books, but Altheus was intrigued by the tale. "How can you expect me to believe anything you're saying? Everyone I know believes King Vask was a hero, and you lashed out at him and stole the Amulet."

"I suppose that's to be expected. Perhaps I'll explain what really happened when you're ready to hear it. But no doubt, you know of the Brotherhood of Prevarra. They know the truth, and they're my only human support. Before Vask destroyed all trace of my legacy, the Brotherhood salvaged this one image of me. It took me years to get it just right, but I've recreated myself as closely as possible. Come."

Verago lead the prince back into the throne room. The fires on the walls had grown considerably, and no part of the room fell in the shadows. Verago ascended the stairs and sat on his throne. "Altheus, there's no easy way to tell you this, but you have been betrayed, much like I was."

"Again with this? My own brother wouldn't betray me."

"Of course, I don't expect you to believe me at face value. You can decide for yourself. Growing up, you were always better than Batar, weren't you? More athletic, more charming, more intelligent, some might even suggest more handsome. I've heard the whispers from the souls. But then, something changed. Seven years ago, he unexpectedly beat you in one-on-one combat. The women began to swoon over him as they overlooked you. Your father even began to consult with him on official matters. It's no wonder that the all-powerful Prima Mashira allowed him to court her."

The prince scoffed. "Is that the extent of your proof?

People grow up and get stronger. Beating me made him more confident, and everyone knows women love a man with confidence. Plus, I was engaged to marry Nila, which took me out of the picture. And as for my father, he was probably just waiting for Batar to come of age before consulting with him."

"Yes, yes, naturally. But, you don't really believe that. Whether you realize it, your suspicion has always been apparent. Admit it. The change was so drastic and in such a short period. You went from dominating him physically to never being able to beat him again in a fair fight. Even during your engagement, women ignored Batar and fawned over you, but then they suddenly took interest in him. And not long after that, your father began to favor Batar as an advisor and possibly his successor."

The words cut him to his core. For over twenty-five years, he'd been the favored son. Batar never came close. And then one day, everything was different. Once Altheus noticed things beginning to change, he became jealous of his younger brother, but he never took it out on Batar. Ashamed, Altheus buried his jealousy deep inside, but somehow Verago saw right through to it.

"It's true," the prince said in a hushed voice. "I love my brother, but he was a Dardan fool. And then, out of nowhere, he's the pride and joy of the kingdom."

Verago stroked his chin in an exaggerated manner. "Hmm. It's almost as if he received some help, perhaps during one of his trips."

"Batar didn't travel much outside of Light's Haven. But now that you mention it, this all started after he went to Memorial City. He told me he received a letter from a champion bloodseeker and was going to spend a month there, training. I thought it odd he had to travel at all when the paladins in Light's Haven were already teaching him. When he came back, though, he was completely different."

"Your brother never met with any Champion of the Light in Memorial City. The letter was a fake, sent by the

Brotherhood, to lure him out of Light's Haven."

"A fake?"

"That's right," Verago said. "The Brotherhood set up a tent outside the city where the Para Paya gather. A lot of desperate people seeking help go there when they have nowhere else to turn."

"What kind of help?"

"Fortune-telling, energy reading, and whatnot. Once Batar showed up, Agalia did the rest. You probably know her better as the Seductress."

"Her again?" The prince groaned. "She's a plague to my family. She killed my little sister."

"Yes, I know. You may not believe me, but I'm truly sorry for that. I would've never given such an order. Unfortunately, she's a product from a time before my rise to power among the demons, and so I have little control over her."

"What did she do to my brother?"

"Honestly, nothing. She merely offered him an opportunity on my behalf."

Altheus narrowed his eyes. "What opportunity?"

"Batar was given the chance to rule the Surface. First, Agalia gave him a seed which—"

"A seed?" Altheus interrupted. "What do you mean? What seed?"

"Your anger is misplaced. There was no deception. I'm merely explaining the events that took place. May I?"

The prince folded his arms across his chest and nodded.

"Thank you. As I was saying, Agalia gave him a seed. This is my method of storing spells, so they can be brought to the Surface. This particular seed gave your brother wonderful abilities. It made him smarter, stronger, and more appealing. His life was enhanced in every way."

"And the price?" Altheus tapped his foot, afraid he already knew the answer.

A crooked smile appeared on Verago's face. "Free. As a

man who once lived in the shadow of his older brother, I understood his plight. But the effects were temporary. After one month, he would return to his old self."

"But the effects didn't wear off. He's been this way for years now."

"Before Batar left the tent, Agalia presented him with a gift, a small box containing nine more seeds. But none of these spells were the same as what he'd first received. If he wished to make his new qualities a permanent fixture in his life, he had to complete her instructions before the month's time was up. First, he had to plant the eight gate seeds within the walls of the castle in Light's Haven. And second, he had to ingest the binding seed and willingly link his soul to mine."

"Soul binding," Altheus said with disgust. "I knew it. You tricked him, or he was seduced."

"Consider the following. Even if he were seduced at the time of the exchange, the effect would've worn off long before he returned to Light's Haven. And the binding seed simply doesn't work through deception or coercion. Both parties involved in the link must understand exactly what is happening and accept the result. Batar knew exactly what he was doing."

The prince bit down so hard, his teeth ached. "Lies. And more lies. Batar would never consort with the likes of you or the Brotherhood. You're wasting your breath."

"The truth can be hard to accept. I don't blame you for your reaction, but I think you underestimate the power of jealousy. You had the strength to bury yours, but you only felt it for a short time. Tell me, Altheus, do you know what it's like to live in someone's shadow your entire life? To be a prince with so much expected of you, but you're never quite as good as your older brother?"

Altheus had no response. He had never considered that Batar had to endure such a struggle.

"Well, I do." Verago grasped the arms of his throne and strolled toward the prince. "It can breed desperation.

Prevarra excelled at everything. I was certainly no fool, but I was always compared to my brother. It made it impossible to live up to anyone's standards, including my mother. In the end, my greatest contribution to this kingdom came with my own death. Now that is a level of desperation you could never truly understand."

There was a long pause as Altheus stood face-to-face with the Devil. What if he was right? What if everything that had just happened was because of some arrangement Batar had made with Verago? The prince took a deep breath. "I'm not saying I believe you, but assuming you're telling me the truth, why am I here?"

"Years of planning were thrown to the wayside when your brother went back on our deal. Seven years of bliss at my expense, and he thought he could take advantage of me. He was in the royal gardens tonight to destroy the gate seeds he'd planted. So rather than let him ruin everything, I activated the gate to claim my prize."

"But he was wearing the Talisman."

The Devil sneered. "Yes. Apparently, having won favor with the Prima using the gift I gave him, your brother convinced her to let him wear the Talisman, making him invulnerable to my attacks."

"So…you took me instead."

"Something like that. I captured you because I thought he'd give himself up to save your life. When he refused, I realized that he meant for you to take his place. He must've lured you to the gardens."

"What? He didn't lure me."

"Didn't he, though?"

"No." Altheus's response lacked resolve.

"Don't forget your brother is very clever. Or *was* very clever, I should say. I know it's difficult for you to trust me because of what you've learned, but believe me when I say your brother is the one I want. He's the one who made the agreement with me, and he needs to accept his fate."

"Why is he so important to you?"

"How is that relevant?" Verago shot back. "The point is that he's sacrificed you in his place. Even I can see how wrong that is. And to be honest, I want what was promised to me. The unfortunate part is that there's only one way I see that happening."

"And what way is that?"

"You must become my demon lord and kill your brother. It's the only way I can take what's mine."

Altheus stepped back. "You're going to kill me?"

"If I was just going to kill you, do you think I would've spent all that time explaining what your brother did? If you died right now, your soul would transcend. I can sense how little burden you carry."

"Then what?"

"Well, I need you to stay on the Surface."

"You want me to willingly stay? You can't really believe I'd do such a thing. You want me to doom my soul for your benefit?"

"Doom your soul?" Verago feigned offense. "I hardly see it that way. But I'll tell you what. Despite what my descendants teach up there, I'm a fair man. You have another choice."

"Oh? And what might that be?"

"I can let you go."

Altheus rolled his eyes. "You would just let me go?"

"Of course. I can't force you to do anything. But before you decide, do you know why the priests have never tried to invade the Depths?"

"I can't say that I do."

The Devil took an exaggerated breath through his nose. "The air down here is so saturated with dark energy that no human can enter here unprotected by holy light. If they did, they'd instantly go insane."

"Then how is it that I stand here with no issue?"

"I've cleared the immediate area of dark energy. However, if you refuse to help me, I'll have no reason to keep it that way. Now, as you make your decision, bear in mind that it's Batar's fault you're here in the first place. If your brother cared for you, if he had any sense of dignity, he wouldn't have cast you aside as his replacement."

Altheus pinched the bridge of his nose. "So, let me get this straight. The two choices you're giving me are either I return to the Surface as a demon lord and kill my own brother, or I stay here in the Depths and go crazy for eternity?"

"Essentially, yes. Again, he's supposed to be here, not you. I'm just trying to make things right."

"Make things right," Altheus repeated as he weighed his options. How could his brother have been so foolish to not consider the consequences of his actions? Why did it always fall on Altheus to save his brother? His contempt for Batar grew, but in the end, the prince spoke his heart. "Nonetheless, he's still my brother. Whatever mistakes he's made, I will not throw my life away just to get revenge."

"Interesting, but it seems to me that the only choice where you throw your life away is the one where you don't get revenge."

Altheus pitied the Devil. "Have you been down here for so long you don't know what life is anymore? Do you really consider dying and becoming your demon lord to be a reasonable alternative?"

"Dying? Who said anything about dying?"

"You did. Earlier. Didn't you?"

"Actually, it was you that mentioned it."

"But people have to die before they can become demons. Everyone knows that."

"Not necessarily. There is another way." Verago gestured to the two demon wolves behind him. "I give you the Denhauli, two of the most powerful demons I've ever created. Ordinary wolves that never died."

"This is a trick."

The Devil chuckled lightly. "Altheus, I've been nothing but straightforward since you've arrived down here. I'm a strategist, not a deceiver. I learn as much as possible, and then I take the actions I deem best for achieving my goals. For example, I know you have a wife and daughter. Taking my offer is the only way you can be with them again."

"But it's not possible."

"Yes, it is. It just takes a lot of time and energy. And, there will be some drawbacks."

Altheus shifted uneasily. "Drawbacks? Such as?"

"You'll have no home. You're not going to die, your body will still be human, and so the Depths will infect your mind. But your soul will be infused with so much dark energy, you'll become the most powerful demon on the Surface. Which means, you'll suffer the agony while you're up there. During the day, you'll appear human, but your tongue will still be warped. Also during the day, holy energy may have little or no effect on you. But at night, when the demon inside you takes over, the light will burn you. The more you're physically wounded, the more the dark energy will heal you and pull you further away from your humanity."

"What happens if I die?"

"A fair question. Again, I'm no deceiver. When a demon dies, its energy returns to me. Your soul will be intertwined with dark energy. If you die, your soul will be dragged back to the Depths. However, if you succeed in your purpose, then I'll remove all of the dark energy from you properly. You'll return to being alive, human. It'll be as if you had never come to the Depths."

Altheus rubbed his lower lip. "This is a lot to consider."

"I agree. I'll give you three days to make up your mind. In the meantime, you'll stay here as my guest. Anything you need, let me know. Allow me to show you where you'll be staying."

Verago motioned for the prince to follow him out of the chamber. As they reached the threshold, Altheus glimpsed at the inscription over the door.

"Demons are humans. They are the forgotten."

As someone who was alive, it was easier to view

demons as something else, something nonhuman. It made it easier to despise them and make them the enemy. But deep down, the inscription was right. Every demon was a human soul. Dark energy or not, he would still be the same person. Altheus halted. "I'd like to request a favor."

The dream blurred as the demon lord was thrown forward in time. It was as if they never left the Devil's throne room. When the image became clear, Altheus stared at the claws that had replaced his hands. He tugged at a strand of long white hair that hung before his eyes. This body felt like his, but at the same time it wasn't. There was something dark within him.

"Master Verago, I present to you your new demon lord." The voice was from a ghostly figure that manifested as an old man with a crooked nose.

"Thank you. Great work. Welcome back, Altheus. May I introduce you to Umaro Lijjo. Or as you may have heard the humans call him, the Zaidon. Although he's merely a wanderer now, his ability to pass on his knowledge of dark energy to others has proven him invaluable in your transformation process."

Altheus pressed his temples. "Nibti zag nolua?"

"Three years. How do you feel?" Verago asked.

"Stronger, but confused," he said in Kisejjad. "What am I speaking? How am I understanding? I don't feel like myself."

"That's normal. Everything has gone according to plan. As I told you before, your tongue would be twisted by the process. The disorientation is caused by the dark energy, which I need to activate the gate. It'll wear off once you leave the Depths, which is why we must hurry. Are you ready to return to the Surface?"

"Yes."

"The gate seeds have already taken root. I've given you all you need to defeat your brother. Know that your father has fallen ill, and in your absence, Batar has taken your place on the throne as the new king."

"I understand," the demon lord said quietly.

"Before I send you back, listen closely and remember my words. A lot of planning has gone into this, and the preparations have been made. Whatever happens up there, remember that until you fulfill your objective, you are my weapon and you answer only to me. This is no simple task, and you need not go it alone. I have a vast army on the Surface, some roaming free, some in captivity. They are meant to serve you. Gather the demon army if you wish to complete your objective. There are many like you, but none are your equal.

"Be wary of the Candelux priests. They are your greatest enemy, especially the Prima. Truthfully, humans in general cannot be trusted except for the Brotherhood of Prevarra. Their numbers have dwindled greatly since the Assault, but if you need help, seek out the Brotherhood. They have always been loyal to me. And remember, when Batar is dead, justice will be done, and you will get your life back. It's time now. Go and fulfill your purpose. Kill King Batar."

Altheus was escorted by Verago and Umaro Lijjo to the opening in the roots that had burrowed to the Depths. The demon lord held his head as he stood in the designated spot. Verago waved his hand, and the roots twisted together. The ground beneath Altheus shot up and forced him to his knees. The disorientation was beginning to wear off just as Verago had promised. And after a single moment of clarity, his mind was assaulted by the agony.

Altheus dug the heels of his palms into his eyes and wailed. Snippets of his life raced through his mind. Voices slithered into his ear as the memories jumbled together into a nearly nonsensical burst of thought. Now that he was trying to awake from the dream, he was suffering the consequences of unlocking his identity. Parts of his mind that had originally been closed off were now opened wide like floodgates and revealed everything in a matter of moments. For a few seconds, he stood in the royal courtyard with Sir Bix.

"One day your father will pass his legacy on to you, Altheus."

The scene switched to some workshop where the prince discovered his brother working on something. The boy seemed younger, perhaps only seven or eight. Batar must have heard his footsteps because the boy frantically hid his work from Altheus.

"Don't look! It's a surprise!"

The prince was viciously thrown into the midst of the Assault. As each new memory forced its way into his mind, the pain worsened. He recognized the scenes from his previous meditation a few days earlier. The paladins were ushering him and his brother through the outdoor walkways of the castle. Bix was there when the Shade attacked. And then, they all vanished.

Alone in the darkness, the demon lord gasped for air, trying to recover from the mental anguish. But, he wasn't allowed any reprieve. A final series of images streaked through. Images of spells, dark clouds bringing panic and fear, tall spikes rising from the ground, wanderers being turned into demons, humans falling under the caster's control, a large blade with mangled steel. It was too much. It was just too much, too fast. He regretted everything. Why had he agreed to kill his brother? Why had he listened to the traitor of all humanity? The agony peaked, and just before Altheus was pulled from his dream, before the demon lord Erynion would awaken to his true identity, a single voice called to him in the darkness.

"Your brother is not so innocent. You have been betrayed."

CHAPTER 30

At the center of Royal Oak, Mashira, Sundancer, and a few dozen humans formed a ring around the four remaining kindred demons. The rest of the demon army had abandoned them once the two giant wolves bolted for the rectory. But that didn't make the situation any better. If these iymed weren't dealt with properly, the city might suffer at the hands of one very angry and seriously powerful entity.

The flooding made it difficult to summon the Blessing of Restraints from the ground, and so the priests tried to lasso the beasts by hand. The effort was uncoordinated, and as the brutes flailed about, they sent the brown robes flying.

"How are we supposed to kill them at the same time?" Sundancer asked

"Just make sure the other soldiers are ready to strike."

As the bloodseeker circled the group to pass on the message, Mashira extended her hands toward the four demons. "Priests, give me whatever you can!"

The warmth of energy surged into her body. As she mouthed the incantation, her fingers curled like claws and light surrounded her hands. The tiny lake that had drowned out the sacred ground glowed beneath the demons. Four chains broke the surface and attacked their prey. The thick collars of light seized the beasts' throats. Mashira closed her fists and brought them down to her side. The four restraints became taut and recoiled into the ground, forcefully pulling the iymed down.

As the brutes crashed into the puddle with a mighty splash, the paladins and watchers charged in. As each demon was slain, the dark energy escaped from the body in search of a new host. Mashira watched anxiously as each of her unbreakable bindings lost its captive to the black cloud. The energy swirled around them before finally sinking into the water and returning to the Depths.

Panting, the Prima used her knees for support. "Good work, but this is far from over. Get to the rectory!"

The fighters obeyed, leaving Mashira with Lady Sundancer.

The bloodseeker patted her on the back. "Summoning four unbreakable bindings through water. That's pretty impressive."

The Prima cracked a smile. "Well, I had some help."

"Still."

Mashira straightened up. "Let's go. We have to finish this."

The Prima jogged at a decent pace, hoping to regain some of her energy. She could only imagine what was happening at the Royal Oak rectory. With any luck, someone had already killed Erynion. But something told her that wasn't the case. She silently prayed they wouldn't be too late. Angels help them if Erynion broke free from his shackles. And though the Denhauli were not the most dangerous threat to the city, they could easily be regarded as a close second.

Mashira briefly recalled her meeting with Mortis years ago. When he told her about the wolves, she had been dismissive. For centuries, rumors circulated about the Devil's attempts to create demons from living creatures.

But there was never any evidence. There was no reason to believe he'd finally succeeded.

The Prima thought about her brother. The rift between the kingdom and Alovajj, between the Death Gods and Candelux, between Mashira and Mortis, came down to one major event. The decimation at Deimor Outpost would be forever engrained in her mind, along with a single word: unforgivable.

Her anger was replaced with concern as the rectory came into view. The battle raged on as priests, paladins, watchers, and scorchers fought fiercely with their demon foe. Mashira spotted Omana, light blades ablaze, squaring off with the black wolf. A group of priests tried to subdue the red wolf with little progress. But perhaps the most disturbing sight was Erynion, untouched and unrestrained, kneeling in the middle of it all.

"Sundancer," Mashira said.

"I know."

"He needs to be killed."

"I know," the bloodseeker repeated.

"Be swift, strike quickly. This may be our only chance."

In a flash, Sundancer was gone.

Mashira hurried to a group of scorchers who were firing arrows at the demons scampering along the rooftops. "Scorchers, I need your attention! I need everyone to aim for the demon lord right now. Draw your arrows, and I'll enchant them."

The archers loaded their bows and targeted Erynion.

Mashira cast her blessing. "May the angels make your arrows straight and your aim exact."

The projectiles glowed brightly, and the twang of bows resounded as the enchanted arrows lit up the sky.

****

There it was. Something he hadn't truly felt since the first couple of nights. It consumed him like a raging

The Twisted Gate

current and felt as if daggers were being driven into his skull. Erynion woke from his dream with a scream for the ages. His eyes opened, and the world was set afire with different colors. He saw who was with him and who was against him, light and dark, demon and human, weak and strong. The incoming arrows were prominent in his vision, and he raised his arm defensively. He wanted them to be diverted away, but he had no power over the objects. The enchanted metal pierced his skin, and the light energy seared him from the inside. It was painful, and it felt good.

The agony's temporary recession allowed Erynion to notice the warrior charging toward him. As demons tried to block her path, she either dodged their attacks or effortlessly cut them down. Nothing slowed her advance. As she came into range, the blade of her sickle reached for his throat. The demon lord stood and struck her with a strong backhand. The fighter tumbled to the ground and her helmet landed even farther away.

Erynion analyzed the arrows stuck in his scarred flesh. Their auras were negated by his own energy. A spell came to mind, emerging from his clouded memories. With his arm outstretched, the demon lord manifested his energy, spiraling around his hand. As its size increased, the dark spell pulled in the light from the fighters closest to him. Another hail of arrows descended upon him, but he made no attempt to dodge the attack. Moments before the arrows made impact, a streak of red crossed his line of sight as the red demon wolf landed beside him. The fiery beast shook wildly to dislodge the projectiles before jumping back into the fight.

Erynion gazed at the brightest aura, the woman who wanted to cleanse him. The void gained more strength, and the surrounding light auras began to dim. He heard the Prima shouting.

"Group up and fortify yourselves! Don't let him steal your energy!"

Matt Glicksman

****

Lady Sundancer lifted herself to one knee, wiped the side of her face, and surveyed the battlefield. As the Prima barked orders, most of the holy fighters retreated in preparation for a unified effort. The demons mirrored that effort by gathering behind the red wolf, positioning themselves between Mashira and Erynion. Sundancer caught a glimmer of light from the corner of her eye. On the other side of the courtyard, Archdon Omana stood alone, fighting the black wolf. Her wings of light were brilliant, but they seemed to offer her no advantage as the wolf matched her in speed. The two were locked in a stalemate.

Sundancer rose to her feet. Her strawberry blond hair, once braided in loops and hidden beneath her helmet, hung haphazardly over her eyes. She brushed the stray hair behind her ears. Erynion was unprotected with one hand dedicated to a ball of dark energy. The bloodseeker searched the ground for her weapons but only found one of her sickles. Stooping, she took a firm hold of it. "Be swift, strike quickly."

Sundancer sprang forward. Prima Mashira, Archdon Omana, the priests, paladins, watchers, demons, and even the Denhauli faded away. Her vision tunneled, and only Erynion remained. With each stride, she soared across the ground. As she neared her target, a stray fray blocked her path. Without a second thought, she placed her hand on its head and hurdled the imp. Once she was within range, the bloodseeker went in for the kill. Her sickle *whooshed* as it sliced through the air, but it stopped inches from the demon's neck. Erynion had caught her hand.

As Sundancer struggled to free her blade, the demon lord released his ball of dark energy, and it sank into the Surface. The void burrowed into the dirt, and the glow from the Blessing of Sacred Ground vanished. The bloodseeker felt a sudden chill as Erynion pulled her closer and placed his hand on her forehead. Sundancer was paralyzed as he siphoned her energy from her body. Weak, she collapsed to her knees, and her weapon dropped to the ground. Tired, her heartbeat slowed to a crawl as she fought for air. Helpless, she had no choice but to lose herself in the eyes of the demon lord. The edges of her vision grew darker, and his face was all that was left.

A bright light forced her to close her eyes, and the bloodseeker felt the connection break. She fell forward onto all fours while she regained control of her body and steadied her breathing. As she fought to push back her eyelids, Sundancer spotted two severed fingers on the ground beside her. Dark energy wafted up from them. Archdon Omana positioned herself in front of the bloodseeker with arms outstretched. The light from her wings made it difficult for Sundancer to make out much more than the glistening fangs of the black wolf.

****

"Group up and fortify yourselves! Don't let him steal your energy!"

Millan spun around as he recognized the Prima's voice. With the constant fighting, he hadn't noticed her arrival. He and the other holy warriors gathered around the Prima while the demons took their place behind the giant red wolf. Millan was pleased to find himself close to Mashira, but he wouldn't be there for long.

"Don Millan," the Prima said. "Go inside the rectory and get everyone out of the basement. We need them out here."

Without hesitation, he ran for the rectory door. Out of the corner of his eye, he saw the red wolf shift her body sideways. The beast flicked her tail at the young priest, and a wave of embers filled the air. It was too large and too fast to escape. Millan crouched and covered his head. His body tensed in anticipation of the pain, but something spared him. He peered over his arms to find a guardian with a raised shield standing over him.

"By the angels, thank you!" Millan exclaimed.

"Anytime."

The young priest frowned. The front of the rectory had caught fire. It was unfortunate the Summa Arcana group in Royal Oak had followed Founder Drevarius to Alovajj all those years ago. Some ice war-mages would've been extremely helpful in this battle.

"Allow me." The paladin used his shield as a ram and charged through the door.

Millan rushed inside. "Can you help me with something else?"

"Of course."

Millan led the guardian down the stairs, to the prison door. "There are two priests guarding a demon in here. Tell them the rectory's on fire, and the Prima needs them in the courtyard."

The paladin nodded, and Millan hurried down the corridor. In the far room, the priests, including Advisors Razza Merona and Deidok, were casting the Blessing of Sacred Ground. As the Nesinu priest burst in, he found all of them quietly meditating. One by one, they raised their heads.

"Her Luminescence, Prima Mashira, has directed me to bring you all out of the rectory," Millan said. "The building's on fire, and we need you in the courtyard right now."

Most of the priests in the circle were slow to rise, however, Advisor Razza Merona jumped to her feet and sprinted out the door. Advisor Deidok and Head Archdon Scarit were the last members to leave. Millan followed the two old priests down the hall, but paused at the dungeon. He poked his head inside to find the jail completely empty. The paladin had done his job and evacuated the priests, but the demon prisoner, Sonojj, was also missing.

The young priest backed out of the room and bounded

up the stairs. The fire was spreading rapidly, and smoke was filling the main floor. Millan lifted the neck of his robe to cover his mouth as he navigated to the entrance. Through squinting eyes, he saw the open doorway and the smoke escaping though it. When he exited the rectory, he coughed and wheezed. Looking up, Millan was shocked to find everyone retreating out of the courtyard. Prima Mashira, with the help of Advisor Razza, Archdon Westan, and Archdon Vikard, held up part of a holy prism spell to keep the demons from attacking, however, neither the wolves nor the iymed made any attempt to do so.

"Move! Move!" Mashira shouted. "Don't stop!"

Millan searched for Erynion amid the demons, but was unsuccessful. The young priest ran to his leader. "Your Luminescence! What happened? What's going on?"

"It's the purge. You need to get out of here. Go with the rest of them."

The words terrified Millan. Royal Oak was about to suffer greatly if they did nothing. "We have to stop it! We can kill him!"

"Millan, it's over. The spell has already begun. You need to retreat right now. We can't stop it with the demons interfering, especially the wolves. Get to the city center and use the Blessing of Holy Prism to create a wall with everyone else. We need to protect the rest of the city."

Archdon Omana walked up with Lady Sundancer, who had her arm around the archdon for support.

"Are you hurt?" Mashira asked.

"I'll make it," the bloodseeker said weakly, as she gently pushed Omana aside.

Millan examined Sundancer. What had happened to her? Her face and arms were white like the Prima's robe. Her hair was disheveled and had changed from reddish blond to a solid shade of burgundy.

"Your Luminescence, we must go. Even the demons are beginning to flee toward the north wall." Vikard spoke the truth.

Except for the Denhauli and a few iymed, all the enemies were withdrawing. As the demon crowd thinned, Millan observed a translucent sphere of dark energy with a figure inside.

"We're done here! Retreat and join the others!" Mashira dropped her hands, and the wall of light faded. Razza Merona led the way out of the courtyard as Vikard and Mashira supported Sundancer. Millan wanted to follow, but something kept him rooted.

Archdon Omana cast the Blessing of the Fallen Angel once more and advanced on the two wolves.

Archdon Westan chased after her. "Omana, it's too late."

Millan shuffled his feet toward the two archdons. He made sure to stay behind them as the Denhauli snarled at the remaining priests.

"No, it's not," Omana said. "The wolves won't allow themselves to die to the purge."

"What?! You don't know that. How could you possibly know that?"

"They're too strong. They have too much to lose. And when they retreat, he'll be all alone."

"But so will you." Westan extended his arms. "Look around. The Prima's gone. There's no Talisman. We have to leave right now."

"I'm going to end this."

"Fine." As he turned, Westan nearly ran into Millan. "What the depths are you still doing here? Didn't you hear the Prima?"

"I agree with Archdon Omana. We have to stop him. We can't let him destroy Royal Oak like he did Nesinu!"

The archdon shook his head and hurried out of the courtyard.

Millan took his place beside Omana. "What do we do now?"

"We hold position. Once the wolves leave to avoid the purge, we strike with everything we've got. Understand?"

"Yes, Your Grace." This was it. He was putting his life on the line to prevent a complete disaster. But what if Westan was right? What if the wolves never left?

The black wolf howled, and a wave of Corruption flowed from his fur. The black cloud rolled across the ground toward the two priests and obstructed their view of the demons. Omana slashed at the Corruption with her blades of light and created a clear path. When Millan followed her through, he discovered the wolves were running away.

"He's alone and vulnerable! Now's our chance!" Archdon Omana charged toward Erynion, encased in his black shell. She repeatedly struck at the enclosure with her holy weapons, but every time she sliced through, the tear was immediately healed.

Millan did his best to help with spikes of light, but none of his spells penetrated the barrier. His blessings fizzled and disappeared.

Omana bellowed like a wild animal and stabbed the demon lord's shield of energy. The wings of light on her back shimmered, but even Millan knew the attempt was fruitless. The archdon tried to maintain the blessing, but her weapons flickered as the dark energy negated her power.

There was nothing left to try. Millan seized Omana's arm. "Your Grace, come on! Let's go!"

The archdon's blessing faded, but as they began to cross the courtyard, a chain wrapped around Millan's ankle.

"Leaving so soon?" The iymed with the mohawk taunted him from the rooftops. Millan recognized him from their short battle by the twisted gate. The demon yanked the unholy metal links, and Millan crashed to the ground.

"You're a Dardan fool! You'll die too!" With a flash of light, Archdon Omana cut the young priest free.

"You're the fool!" The demon cackled as he coiled up

his weapon. "I'm already dead!"

As Millan picked himself up, the iymed threw his chains again. Omana slid in front of the attack, but a large object from nowhere knocked her to the dirt. The demonic chains wrapped around the waist of the young priest.

"You're staying here!" the iymed cried out.

The young priest gripped his end and fought to pull the iymed off the roof. Omana screamed, and Millan's jaw dropped at the sight of a black jungle cat sinking its teeth into the archdon's forearm. The animal had no eyes and no front paws. This beast was the escaped prisoner, Sonojj. Omana summoned her light blade and buried it into the demon's chest, forcing the jungle cat off her.

The archdon grimaced. "You."

Sonojj reassumed his humanoid form. "I told you I'd hunt you down."

A loud *boom* brought everyone's attention to Erynion as the dark dome protecting him flew out in all directions. Millan protected his eyes from the gust of wind, but as it died down, he found the demon lord with his claws buried in the dirt. He sensed this was the end. The purge was imminent. Images of the aftermath at Nesinu raced through his mind—the emptiness, the black, scorched earth. The priests who searched for Don Skully had crossed the expanse in the hope of finding something, anything, but there was no sign of life. Nothing. Not one single thing except for a few patches of grass in the middle of it.

Millan's eyes widened. "Your Grace! Get to the demon lord!"

"You're too late!" the iymed with the mohawk screamed.

The young priest fired a holy spike at the demon on the roof. When the iymed shifted his weight to dodge the attack, Millan heaved on the dark chain with all his strength. The beast lost his balance and plummeted from the roof. With an abundance of slack, Millan bolted toward Erynion. His legs pumped furiously, and he felt weightless, as if hovering across the ground at an incredible speed. He dove at the feet of the demon lord, and when he looked back to find Archdon Omana, there was nothing but twisted metal.

CHAPTER 31

As Mashira, Sundancer, and Vikard entered the plaza where the twisted gate stood, the Prima was comforted by the sight of all the fighters on the far side. Passing the unholy tree, she glanced back at the empty road. What had happened to Westan, Omana, and Millan? A glimmer of hope sparked in her mind as Mashira considered the possibility that they were able to stop the purge. A sudden *boom* in the distance snuffed out that thought. Her party arrived at the line of priests just as a gust of wind blew past.

Mashira cupped her hands around her mouth. "Holy prism! Let's get it up!"

As she took her place near the middle of the group, the Prima heard her orders being passed down the line. She lifted her arms with her palms facing north. A wall of light gleamed as the distant tremors began.

"Do you really think this can stop his purge?" Sundancer whispered.

"It should. The farther away we are, the weaker it'll be."

There was a collective gasp from the fighters as the demon lord's purge materialized in the distance. Spikes shot up from the ground near the rectory and rose higher than the city walls. They burst through in random directions, chaotically colliding with one another. They were like incredibly long needles crisscrossing to form a dense mesh of mangled metal. The spikes drew closer as the spell radiated out from its source.

The battlefield was strewn with the bodies of priests, paladins, and watchers who had fallen during the fight. Sadness struck the Prima as she realized the purge would wipe out the dead bodies, not allowing the friends and families of the fallen to properly mourn their losses. And with no remains, anyone missing after tonight would be considered lost in combat.

"Look! There's someone out there!"

"It's Archdon Westan. He's not going to make it."

The answer was depressing, but true. The purge was nearing the plaza and swiftly gaining on the priest.

Mashira dropped her hands. "No. No, we're not losing anyone else tonight."

"Your Luminescence, no," Sundancer said. "I can't—"

The Prima wasn't sticking around to hear the rest. She crossed the holy barrier and raced toward the doomed archdon. The margin for error was razor thin, but she believed she could reach him. The purge entered the square, and the rising needles moved at an incredible pace toward the opposite side. As she closed the gap to Archdon Westan, Mashira concentrated on the blessing she needed to cast. The events of the night had taxed her energy, and any misstep now would cost her her life. The purge was nearly upon them as they met near the twisted gate.

"Westan, bubble, now!" Mashira shouted.

Both priests extended their arms to the sides and created a hemisphere of holy light. The energy poured freely from her body. This was not the time to ration her power. As the spikes assaulted their tiny haven, Razza Merona and Sundancer slipped into the bubble. Advisor Razza joined in supporting the spell, while the bloodseeker was poised to attack any intrusion.

The ground trembled as the purge passed around them. The Prima adjusted her footing to keep her balance. The dome vibrated and loud *thuds* reverberated within as the needles sought to break through. A couple of stray spikes succeeded as the purge weakened the barrier. One narrowly missed Sundancer, while another caught Razza Merona in the side. The advisor pressed her hands over the wound as she dropped to the ground. The blood trickled over Razza's fingers, and Mashira resisted the urge to help. The holy spell had to remain intact until the quaking ended.

The tremors lessened and finally ceased. Mashira scurried over to heal her advisor. Westan joined her side, and the holy bubble dissipated.

"I'm all right." Razza insisted. "It's just a scratch."

"Nonsense," the Prima shot back. "Stay still."

"Yes, this is more than a scratch," Westan said. "This will help with the pain, but you'll need to get proper healing once we're out of here."

Sundancer said something, but Mashira wasn't listening. As she finished the healing spell, the Prima stood and faced the bloodseeker. "What?"

"Well, we're trapped. What do we do now? Wait?"

Mashira inspected the metal spikes. "No. No, we can't wait. The second part will start any moment."

"The second part?"

"Yeah," Westan answered. "We might be fangled."

"Not helping," the Prima muttered, despite the truth behind Westan's comment.

"What second part?" the bloodseeker repeated.

The sound of thunder rolled in the distance, and Mashira recalled the purge during the Assault on Light's Haven. From the safety of the city walls, she had watched as a dense jungle of metal surrounded the demon lord. There was little hope for anything caught within it. But it was what followed that was truly devastating. A cleansing fire, which must have burned hotter than the sun, had devoured everything in its path.

Mashira wrung her hands together. "Think. Think. We need to get out now. The flame travels faster than the spikes."

"The flame?" Sundancer twirled her weapon in her hand. "I guess this is pretty useless then."

"That's it!" The Prima needed something holy and sharp to cut through the metal jungle. A blessing by itself would require too much energy, but using a blade as a conduit for her spell might be the perfect solution.

"Quickly, give me your sickle!" Mashira snatched the weapon before the bloodseeker had a chance to respond. "Westan, whatever you have left, give it to me!"

The archdon held his hands over Mashira as she focused her energy into Sundancer's blade. The wave of fire grew louder. As soon as the sickle glimmered a soft yellow, Mashira swung the blade ferociously at the mesh of needles. A wave of light sliced through the spikes with each swing of the blade. When she finished, several severed pieces of metal fell to the ground and revealed a narrow escape tunnel.

The Prima returned the sickle to the bloodseeker and placed Razza Merona's arm over her shoulder. "Let's go!"

Sundancer led the way down the thin corridor and cut down any stray pieces that interfered with their escape. Mashira held on to Razza to be sure she kept up, while Westan brought up the rear. Past her bodyguard, the Prima noticed the priests at the end of the tunnel.

"Run! Come on! You can do it! Hurry!"

The rumble of the cleansing flame bore down on them and drowned out the words of encouragement. Mashira mustered whatever strength she had left as she dragged Razza along. The fatigue was overwhelming and her body was past its limit, but Mashira pressed on. This was life or death.

Sundancer exited the tunnel and stepped to the side.

Mashira and Razza were nearly out when a powerful shove from behind sent them tumbling out of the metal jungle. The Prima collapsed on the ground. The fatigue overcame her, and she made no attempt to open her eyes. This moment of rest was well earned. They had made it to safety.

But, the moment was short-lived. Her eyes shot open as people yelled, "Put him out! Put him out!"

Mashira lifted herself to her knees. Archdon Westan was motionless and facedown in the dirt. His robe was ablaze, and several priests patted his back to extinguish the fire. Archdon Vikard rushed in with glowing hands.

Razza Merona groaned as she sat beside the Prima. Her bloodied hand covered her partially healed wound.

A priest scurried toward them. "Your Luminescence, I can heal her."

"It's nothing, really," Razza insisted.

"Go with him," Mashira demanded.

The advisor complied, and the priest healer helped her up. Mashira observed the final moments of the demon lord's spell. The wall of fire, which incinerated half of the city, receded from the barrier of light. Thank the angels they had evacuated the area for the cleansing ritual. The flames danced about, climbing over one another before evaporating into thin air. The prism blessing that spanned the plaza faded away. And when the last embers were snuffed out, there was nothing left but scorched earth and the terrifying memory of it all.

In the darkness, sporadic camps of fire illuminated small areas, but they quickly died out, leaving only smoke. Mashira thought back to earlier when they had found the demon lord on the shores of Lake Ivorus. If only she had killed him then and there, this might have all been avoided. But now, where the majestic tree once stood, there was only emptiness. If one good thing had come from the purge, it was that the twisted gate had been destroyed as well.

The Twisted Gate

"Your Luminescence." Advisor Deidok interrupted her internal lament. "Should we pursue the demon lord?"

After the Assault on Light's Haven sixteen years ago, when the iymed had all retreated, the scouts reported finding the body of the unconscious demon lord. With Ayristark by her side, Mashira had journeyed across the barren field to the small circle of grass where the beast slept. She had already cleansed the Zaidon earlier in the day, and the demon lord would be next. Back then, there were no demons left to contend with, and certainly no giant wolves. This time was different. Survival was their priority. The pitch-black of the night seemed to offer her no hope when some movement caught her eye. The spring was pushing water back to the Surface.

"No," she finally answered. "Our job right now is to protect the rest of the city and heal the wounded."

"Perhaps a word to the fighters," Deidok suggested. "Let them know it's over."

With Sundancer's help, Mashira created a makeshift platform. She climbed up and cleared her throat. "May I have your attention, please."

One by one, the fighters faced her. In the light of the street lanterns, she saw the blood, dirt, and fatigue on their faces. For most of them, this was their first real battle, and the trauma of its memory would stay with them forever. They looked to her for guidance, for inspiration.

"You should all be very proud of yourselves," the Prima said. "I know when you look across that field of darkness, you find half of Royal Oak torn and burned from the Surface. When you look out there, no longer can you see the mighty tree that symbolized the foundation for our kingdom. But I tell you this now. If you're looking out there to determine who has won tonight, you will not find the answer. No, my friends, look to yourselves. Look at the tens of thousands of people you've saved, citizens kept safe from any harm. Tonight, we faced the power of a demon lord. We saw the myth of the Denhauli come to life. We endured the full force of the iymed army. Look to yourselves with pride for we fought them back and survived!

"A city can be rebuilt. A tree can be replanted. What matters in this moment, and what will always matter, is life. We have taken an oath to protect the innocent. We have sworn to defend our fellow humans from the evil that infects our lands. And tonight, we have upheld that promise!

"And while we've returned many demons to the traitorous Verago, some are still lurking in the shadows. The battle is over for now as they retreat to tend to their wounds, but our duties are not complete. We must stay strong and keep everyone safe through the remainder of the night. We'll start by creating a barrier across the open end of the city. Find anything you can. We need to build some semblance of a wall to keep those fiends out!"

Sundancer helped Mashira down from her stage, and before long, vendor carts, crates, barrels, and random pieces of wood and stone were set along the exposed edge of the city. Exhausted, the Prima searched for a place to rest and noticed Archdon Scarit sitting alone. "How are you feeling?"

Scarit sniffled as a tear rolled down his cheek. "Fine, Your Luminescence."

Mashira plopped down beside him. "Is something the matter?"

The head archdon covered his face. "She's gone, isn't she? Omana?"

"It seems so. Omana and Millan were the last two out there when the purge went off. If they don't turn up by morning, we have to assume they were killed in the attack."

"She was my right hand, indulging the wishes of a stubborn and selfish old man. I trusted her judgment on everything. She made all the decisions. She was the real head archdon. I need her to run this city. I can't do it alone."

Mashira consoled Scarit as he whimpered uncontrollably. There were arduous times ahead for Royal Oak, but she remained optimistic.

****

Sprawled out on the ground, Erynion was delirious and exhausted. He couldn't move, even if he wanted to. His body begged for sleep, but his mind clung to the last bits of energy to stay awake. This was exactly what he wanted to avoid. This was the reason he wanted to be killed. Despite his use of dark energy, he couldn't escape his inevitable fate. Erynion had succumbed to the agony. Learning his identity hadn't helped in this regard, but rather, seemed to make it worse.

The silver lining was at least he knew who he was: Prince Altheus, royalty, the onetime future king. Married to the most beautiful woman, he had a young daughter whom he had named after his late sister. And lastly, he had a younger brother for whom he had cared for deeply, that is, until recent events. But all that was different now. Now, he was Erynion, the demon lord.

Erynion breathed heavily as he gazed into the starry night sky. He recalled only bits and pieces from the purge. The agony had lasted longer than usual. Maybe it was because he'd learned his identity, or maybe it was because of the archdon who had tried to break through his dome. The demon lord clenched his jaw as his mind conjured up the face of Archdon Omana. The same priest who restrained him earlier, and then cut off two of his fingers during the battle. Once the purge started, though, the agony rapidly receded. First came the metal spikes, then the raging fire. The corner of his mouth pushed up into a crooked smile. The purge must've swallowed Omana up.

Erynion noticed a large shadowy blur backlit with a red glow approaching him. The demon lord closed his eyes to blink, but they stayed shut until he heard someone speak.

He's out. Let's get him moved. The voice was gruff and definitely male. But two things struck the demon lord as odd. The first was that the words weren't demon speak. Whoever this was sounded human. But even more disturbing is that he didn't hear the voice with his ears. It was in his head.

Erynion's eyes shot open to find the black wolf looming over him.

What's this? A priest? This one's tone was gentle and pleasant. But like her companion, her words were not demonic, and her voice was not heard by ear.

Best to kill him and be done with it, the gruff voice said.

Erynion's head rolled to the side, and in the glow of the red wolf's fur, he spotted a brown robe covered in chains. The young priest had a fresh scar—three claw marks—on his right cheek that reminded the demon lord of his own self-inflicted wound. With a final effort before the sleep took him, Erynion managed to murmur, "No, I need him alive."

CHAPTER 32

Millan awoke on the floor of the forest. He winced as the pain in his ribs forced him into a seated position. The rustling of metal gave him pause. He attempted to reach for the sore spot on his side, but he was bound hand and foot. The restraints were too tight to wriggle free. With no one around, he rested his head on the tree behind him. Overhead, the birds darted back and forth, chirping at one another. As he watched their antics, he tried to reflect on the events of the previous night.

He had been trapped inside the demon's spell with Erynion. With its hideous metal teeth, the purge devoured the city. While Erynion expelled all his energy, Millan dipped into his pocket to fish out Don Skully's star. Mashira's warning echoed clearly in his head. He had promised not to use it. If he tried to slay Erynion with the blessing, he might die. But what choice did he have? He had no other weapon, he couldn't escape with the purge in effect, and the demons would return to reclaim their demon lord once it was over. He thought about Nesinu and the loss of his beloved mentor, and before long, Millan had made his decision.

Beyond that, his memory was hazy. As Millan sat in the

forest, two startling questions came to mind. *Where am I? How did I get here?* The birds that flitted about had made him feel somewhat at ease, but he lost sight of them. Their distant chirps faded to complete silence.

"Kjjevazi uh kul evlev."

Millan's heart sank. It only made sense he was held prisoner by demons, but he knew exactly which demon this was. The iymed was missing his jester hat, but the rest of his ensemble was unmistakable. A white cloth hung partially from his pocket, and he played with a dagger in his left hand.

"Did you have a good sleep, Don Millan?"

"Not particularly. So, you remember me then?"

The demon sauntered toward him. "I don't think I'll ever forget you."

"Did they stop teaching manners in the Depths?" Millan asked.

"What?"

"No introduction? After all, you know my name. Aren't you going to tell me yours?"

"Flinch," he said begrudgingly.

"Flinch? I'm assuming that's not your real name, but I suppose it'll do. So, Flinch, what am I doing here?"

"Good question." The iymed smirked. "If it were up to me, you wouldn't even have your hands."

Millan gulped. "Well, then thank the angels it's not up to you."

"Clever priest. Clever, clever, but dead as ever. You'll be mine soon."

"Holding a grudge? If I remember correctly, it was *you* who attacked *me*."

Flinch shrugged. "Well, to be fair, we were only trying to kill you. Not mutilate you and drag you back for interrogation."

"Oh, well, I guess that's better. Look, I was just defending myself."

"Yeah, yeah. That's the excuse all you humans use.

Why can't you just accept your fate and join us? Then, this war would be over."

"Accept our fate? Join you? Uh, we're winning this war."

"Hmm." Flinch pretended to be pensive. "I suppose you're right. Getting half your city obliterated sounds like winning to me. Besides, whether it's now or in fifty years, you'll join us once you die. At least most people will."

"Not if we destroy the Amulet. Then, there will finally be peace."

"Is that what they teach you? Your people had the chance to destroy the Amulet long ago."

Millan couldn't believe the audacity of this demon, throwing the validity of the priest's history lessons into question. What tall tale was this jester about to weave? "What are you talking about?"

"It's funny. You believe your path is righteous because you use *holy* energy. So you're good, and we're evil. But if it wasn't for the evil, greed, and selfishness of humans, this war would've ended centuries ago."

"Ha! Lies and treachery. I suppose I shouldn't expect anything less from a corrupt soul."

"Oh, I'm a *corrupt soul*," Flinch mocked. "What a convenient excuse to not listen to the truth. Dardan fool. Verago gave you the means centuries ago. He helped to create your precious Talisman of Zavi."

Millan had heard this story more than enough times. "Yeah, which was fused with the Amulet by King Vask, but later broken by Verago when he took the Amulet for himself and betrayed humanity."

"Wrong! Fused with the Amulet? Really? If you believe that then you're just blind, the whole lot of you."

"Demons can be blind too. Like your friend. What was his name? Sonojj?"

Flinch glared at the priest. "Don't talk about Sonojj."

"Why not? I saw him, you know. But, he probably didn't see me. He was swallowed up in the purge like an insignificant pawn."

The jester iymed squeezed the handle of his dagger and pointed the tip at Millan. "I don't care why Erynion spared you. If you mention my friend again, I *will* kill you."

The priest bit his tongue. He couldn't tell how serious Flinch was. "So, why did the demon lord spare me?"

"Depths if I know. He said you live, and so you live. For now."

"You, too, I suppose."

"What?"

"You live too. For now," Millan said.

Flinch lifted his eyebrow. "What the depths does that mean?"

"You're following a demon lord that leaves death in his wake. Humans, demons. It makes no difference. If you stay with him, you'll end up back in the Depths just like—" Millan caught himself.

A tic appeared above the jester's cheek. "Just…like…what?"

"Just like Sonojj."

Millan held his breath as the blade whooshed past his ear, but the dagger missed its mark. As Flinch moseyed toward the petrified priest, Millan noted how the demon's right arm hung at his side.

"Damn Maligus, my aim is useless with my left hand." The iymed wiggled the handle of his dagger. After he pulled the blade free from the tree, Flinch squatted in front of Millan. "Know this, pig. When this is over, and he no longer needs you, I will make you pay for all of this. Until then, I am loyal to the Devil. And if Verago says to follow Erynion, then that's what I do. Orders and all. Besides, with Ojjuk and Eyzora as his new guides, Erynion will be unstoppable."

"Who and who?" Millan had never heard the names before.

"Ojjuk and Eyzora, the Denhauli. You know, the giant wolves that freed him and helped decimate your city?"

"They're just demons like the rest of you, and they'll fall like the rest of you. That doesn't make Erynion unstoppable."

"You don't understand. They're a direct link to Verago. Through them, the Devil can speak to his demon lord and lead us all to victory," Flinch explained.

"How is that possible?"

"Never you mind that. Just know the demon lord will get what he came for."

"What? King Batar? I doubt a whisper in his ear is going to change anything. He'll never get into Light's Haven. He purges uncontrollably. He clearly doesn't have a good handle on his power. He's unstable. And who knows? Maybe the next time it happens, you'll be caught in it."

"Why are you trying to convince me of this?" The iymed walked away from Millan. "Why do you even care? I already told you my allegiance is unwavering. I am loyal to the end."

"*Hmph*. Loyal, huh? Didn't your leader tell you not to kill me?"

Flinch feigned confusion. "It looks like you're still alive to me."

"*Pfff*. Yeah, thanks to your shoddy aim."

Without another word, Flinch flung the dagger once more. Millan froze as the blade whizzed by him and buried itself in the exact same place on the tree trunk.

Flinch chortled. "I guess you're not as clever as I thought."

"Fan izted!" the demon lord shouted sternly.

There was no telling how long he'd been standing there. His long white hair was pulled back, and the Devil's Eye glowed magnificently. The sight of it refreshed Millan's memory of the previous night.

It was only a few moments. With Skully's gift in hand, Millan had prayed over Erynion. The energy had coursed through him. As the sword of light erupted from the conduit, the demon lord's eyes shot open, and Millan was caught in the gaze of the Devil's Eye. Something took hold of the priest and restricted his movement.

Bound by chains, Millan looked away from the Devil's Eye. Filled with shame, he knew what had stopped his attack the previous night. It was simply fear, and he had hesitated. And in those brief seconds, he had wasted so much energy that he had lost consciousness.

"I wasn't going to hurt him," Flinch grumbled as he retrieved his dagger.

"Leave us."

The jester pulled the cloth from his pocket and presented it to Erynion. "It's good to see you awake. You left this on the shoreline yesterday. I thought you might want it back."

The demon lord nodded as he accepted the fabric and placed it back over the Devil's Eye. He had the smallest hint of a smile as he patted the iymed on the shoulder.

"I'll be waiting for you," Flinch called to Millan as he left the area.

Alone with the demon lord, the young priest didn't move a muscle. With a lack of urgency, the beast approached and towered over his prisoner. The demon's presence was imposing, and Millan marveled at how human he appeared to be.

Erynion lowered himself to the ground. "I apologize if my guard frightened or harmed you in any way."

The young priest did his best to stay calm.

"Are you all right? You do understand what I'm saying, don't you?"

Millan barely managed to nod.

"Did Flinch harm you at all?" he pressed.

Another question related to Millan's well-being? Was this guy a demon or not? The young priest subtly shook his head.

"Hmm. How about we start off with something easy. What's your name?"

The Twisted Gate

"Don...Don Millan," he said after some hesitation.

"Don Millan? My name is—" The demon lord interrupted himself, and there was a long pause. "My name is Erynion."

"I know who you are. And, I know what you've done. Why did you bring me here?"

"Because, believe it or not, I need your help."

Millan knew helping a demon meant being a traitor to his fellow man. At first, he struggled to speak, but soon his budding resolve pushed the words out. "If you expect me to forsake my people, I suppose I won't be living much longer."

"I'm not asking you to forsake anyone. If anything, helping me will save the lives you wish to protect."

"Helping you will save lives? Whose lives? Everyone except the king?"

"What?"

"Well, I won't do it!" Millan insisted.

"I don't understand."

"Of course you do. You don't have to lie your way around it. I know what your purpose is. You want me to betray my kingdom and kill King Batar for you. And in exchange, you'll leave the rest of us alone. Tell me I'm wrong."

The demon lord stared blankly at the young priest. "You're wrong. The task of killing Batar is mine and mine alone."

"Well, fine then. Why don't you tell me what you and your army can't do yourselves?"

"Despite what you've been taught about demons, I bear no ill will toward humanity. I know convincing you is practically impossible, but the truth is that I have no more desire to kill innocent people than you do."

"It certainly doesn't seem that way," Millan said snidely, but immediately tightened his lips.

The demon lord seemed to ignore the comment. "You may not know this, but when I was found by your guild near my twisted gate, I didn't fight them. When your people found me on the shore of Lake Ivorus, I put up no resistance. Even though the person who sits before you is a demon, mindless violence is not in my nature."

The irony was that Millan had been present at both instances. He knew Erynion was speaking the truth, but it didn't explain the rest. "What about last night? What about Malarekita? What about—what about Nesinu and Don Skully? You wiped them from the Surface on your very first night."

"Malarekita was beyond my control. I was being used by the Seductress, a mistake that will never happen again. As for Royal Oak and Nesinu, those incidents do not sit well with me. This is why I need your help."

"What could I possibly do?" Millan asked.

"The purge is a danger to everyone in the kingdom. I have yet to gain full control of my power and suppress the agony. If the purge is released every night that I'm here, there won't be a kingdom left for anyone to live in."

The thought of a purge hitting a new city or town every night scared the young priest. Something had to be done to prevent that scenario from becoming reality, and Millan knew the perfect solution. "Then let me slay you and return you to the Depths. Isn't that what you wanted at the lake? That solves everything."

"Not everything, I'm afraid. Much was revealed to me last night. Memories that were locked behind my identity have shown me the truth."

"What truth?" Millan tried to act nonchalant as he probed Erynion for his secrets.

"I'm sure it comes as no surprise to you that I can't tell you. But, I can't allow myself to be killed or cleansed. If I'm slain before my objective is completed, there's no chance of redemption for me."

"Redemption?"

Erynion nodded. "Yes. I must right the wrong of my brother."

"Your brother?" Millan suddenly realized the demon lord may have just given up a vital piece of information regarding his identity. The young priest also understood if he pressed the issue any further and verified Erynion's true past, his chances of surviving this encounter would plummet. "What does your brother have to do with any of this? I thought we were trying to figure out how to stop the purges."

Erynion narrowed his eyes. Millan felt as though the demon was looking through him and reading his thoughts. The young priest did his best to maintain his composure, but his heart was trying to burst through his chest. The longer the demon stayed silent, the higher Millan's anxiety soared. His face felt like it was being held to a flame.

Finally, Erynion broke the horrifying silence. "I know of a way. When I was in Nolka, your priests created a barrier of light to contain me. It failed, but by crossing through it, I felt my own energy drop. The agony subsided momentarily. And again last night, when I was restrained by the priests, I didn't feel the agony when the sun fell. I had some energy, but it was curbed by the holy blessings. I need holy energy to prevent the purge."

"So, you need me for the holy energy. You think my energy will stop the purge? I'm just a regular priest. Last night, I saw someone much stronger than I am try to attack you before your purge went off. She couldn't even get past the barrier."

"Yes, the archdon. I remember you with her now. But what you don't understand is the barrier is part of the purge. The key is to prevent it from even starting, and for that I need your energy."

"Why don't you just use your power? Isn't that what's causing the agony?"

"My mind is just starting to open up. There's knowledge buried deep within, but with the agony plaguing me, there's no chance for me to retrieve it. So, will you help me?"

As the Nesinu priest mulled over the offer, he became mindful of the restraints digging into his arm. Millan wiggled his shoulders to get more comfortable, and the chains jingled as they collided with each other. "So you want me to stay your prisoner and follow you around everywhere as you destroy my kingdom, just so I can blast you with light and stop the purge each night?"

"Essentially, yes, something like that. But my goal is not to destroy your kingdom. The only person I wish to kill is the king," Erynion clarified. "You're a user of holy energy, and I need it to stop the purges, which benefits your people."

"And yours. No purge makes it safer for everybody and everything."

"Yes, that's exactly my point. This arrangement would help both sides. It can potentially save countless lives. So, do you accept?"

Millan had no idea what answer to give. If he refused, he'd most likely be killed and the purges would continue. If he accepted, he'd be sacrificing his life to become Erynion's permanent prisoner. How long would it be before he was rescued or able to escape? Would helping the demon lord mean he was also indirectly killing King Batar? But what if Erynion never got to the king?

The demon lord stood. "I understand this is not an easy decision. Why don't you take a bit and think it over?"

Millan desperately scoured the area for some clue as to what choice he should make. Was it selfish that he wanted to neither die nor be a prisoner? And what prevented Erynion from killing him later when he no longer needed Millan's holy energy?

The young priest glanced down at the metal links that kept him bound. The answer was literally all around him. "Hey. I have another idea."

"You do?"

"Well, it's actually quite ingenious." Millan was proud of himself, but didn't wish to appear boastful.

The Twisted Gate

"Go on. I'm listening."

"You see, I think for an arrangement to be truly successful, both parties have to get what they want."

Erynion dropped to one knee. "And what do you want?"

"Well, um, I really don't want to be here, but I also want to be alive."

"Impossible. How will I get holy energy without a priest? Are you planning to have someone take your place?"

"No, no, nothing like that. There's another way, though. What do you know about enchantments?" Millan asked.

"Not much. Enlighten me."

"A long time ago, a man named Archdon Bamby discovered we can store energy within objects, regardless of whether the energy is light, dark, or elemental. It's called an enchantment. Your iymed all have weapons imbued with dark energy, just like these chains. Now, you're in luck because a don typically doesn't know the first thing about enchanting. But because my teacher was so great, I do."

"You do?"

Millan grinned. "Yes. Yes, I do."

"So, what are you suggesting?"

"I'm suggesting you take these chains off me. I'll disenchant them to remove the dark energy and then enchant them with holy energy. It'll have a similar effect to the Blessing of Divine Restraint, except I don't have to physically be here."

"And what do you require to do all this?"

Millan sucked in air between his teeth. "Unfortunately, I'm not wonderful at it, so it's going to take time. However long I spend casting the spell, the enchantment will last about three times longer."

"So, let me get this straight. You're going to spend all day casting this enchantment blessing, and it only gives me three days?"

Millan rocked his head side to side. "Well, I still have to disenchant them. And even if I spend the rest of today, that's only about eight hours. Plus, I'll need to eat and rest."

Erynion snorted. "It looks like even this way, you stay my prisoner."

"Hmm." Millan stayed positive as he worked to resolve the time issue. If only his skill was on the level of an archdon. "Well, I may not be great at it, but I know someone who is. So, here's my offer. I'll stay with you and build up the enchantment until it lasts for a few days. That should give you more than enough time to go back north to Nolka."

"Back to Nolka?"

"Yes, the head priest there is Archdon Feranis. He's a master at enchantment. If he spends a day on these, you'll be set for a whole year."

"And if you and I have already parted ways, how will I get him to do this?"

"Good question. You don't. I do. This is to ensure you don't go back on your word and kill me when my part is complete."

The demon lord leaned back. "You think I would do that?"

"I'm sorry, but regardless of what you say, you're still a demon, and so I'm inclined to distrust you."

"Fair enough, but know this. If you're being honest with me, you have my word I won't harm you."

Even though his words were in Kisejjad, they put Millan at ease. "Thank you."

"So, how do you propose we do this?"

"I enchant the chains during the day, and you wear them at night. This will serve as a proper test to make sure the energy is strong enough to keep your agony and the purge at bay. When our time together comes to an end, just make sure you show up at Nolka before the third day. I'll take care of the rest, assuming you let me live."

Erynion groaned. "You've made it abundantly clear that you don't trust me. But tell me, how can I be sure I can trust you once you're free?"

"What reason would I have to not fulfill my end of the deal? If I don't play my part, more cities will fall to the purge."

"Starting with Nolka."

The young priest thought of his parents, refugees in the city he had just put in the path of the demon lord. This was the only solution Millan could think of, and he knew failure was not an acceptable outcome. "So, what do you think? Do we have an arrangement?"

Erynion took his time, and the silence made Millan nervous. The demon lord stood up and towered over the priest. "Yes, I believe we do."

CHAPTER 33

Sundancer was greeted by the first morning light. She opened her eyes cautiously, unable to recall when she fell asleep. Hers was one of many beds that lined both long sides of a rectangular room. Most of the beds were occupied, but no one else appeared to be awake. A few stray strands of her hair hovered in front of her face. She pinched them and studied the dark-red hue. Her hair, no longer braided, hung freely along her shoulders. She grabbed a tuft to get a better view when she realized something was amiss. With the blanket crumpled around her waist, her upper body was completely exposed. Someone had undressed her.

Sundancer yanked the cover up to her neck to hide her naked torso and checked the room again. From behind the safety of her blanket, she searched for some clothing. A middle-aged woman entered the large room and patrolled the aisle between the rows of beds. She wore a pink robe with a pattern of green leaves on spiraling, golden vines. As she neared the foot of the bloodseeker's bed, the woman made eye contact and smiled kindly. "Good morning, Lady Sundancer. I'm glad to see you're feeling better."

"What am I doing here? Where are my clothes?" The bloodseeker raised her voice. "Where's Prima Mashira?"

"Please, be at peace. Her Luminescence is in the building down the street. There's supposed to be a meeting in a few hours. Advisor Ayristark and Advisor Cole are already on their way from Light's Haven. I was told to inform you that you may join them when you and Advisor Razza Merona are feeling better. The advisor is near the entrance"—she motioned to the door—"I believe she's still asleep."

Sundancer casually scouted the end of the room, but there was no way for her to tell who was who from this distance. "I'm fine."

"I see."

The bloodseeker examined the intricate design on the woman's robe. "So, you're a pinkleaf?"

"That's right. My name is Bolya."

"Huh, I thought Summa Arcana left Royal Oak with Drevarius."

Bolya clasped her hands together. "Well, though our sect is a part of Summa Arcana, it was mainly the *war-mages* of Royal Oak that followed Drevarius to Alovajj. We pan-mages consider ourselves a different breed, much like guardians and bloodseekers, I'm sure."

"Different skills, of course, but we're still one guild." Sundancer stretched her neck. "So, why am I here?"

"Oh, you don't remember?"

"Remember what?"

The pinkleaf walked to the side of the bed. "You had an acute syncopal episode."

"I had what?"

"I'm sorry. I've been around healers all night. Um, in simple terms, you blacked out for a short time. Don't worry, though, you're recovering nicely."

Sundancer was disturbed by the thought of losing consciousness while on duty. "Any idea how that happened?"

"Oh, sure. It's very common when someone overexerts themselves post-invasive accelerated mending."

The words jumbled together in the paladin's ears. "Post-invasive…what?"

"Accelerated mending. More commonly known as rapid recovery. I suppose that's easier to say though not entirely accurate. You were healed quite a bit during the battle last night, correct?"

The bloodseeker nodded. "When I encountered the demon lord, he siphoned most of my energy. I could barely stand on my own. When we evacuated the rectory courtyard, Prima Mashira and Archdon Vikard both healed me until I was able to run on my own."

"Well, there you have it."

"I don't understand."

"Invasive accelerated mending is an unnatural form of healing. In cases where a large amount of energy is transferred, like yours, it typically leads to a misperception of one's own strength, a false sense of rejuvenation."

"Unnatural? False?"

"Yes." Bolya smiled wryly. "That's not to say it's a bad thing. In fact, it probably saved your life. This type of healing is ideal for emergency situations, like potentially mortal injuries or trying to escape a purge. But, therein lies the fundamental difference between priest and pan-mage healers."

"Uh-huh. And so, why am I here exactly?"

"Energy realignment. The energy the priests put into your body was scattered and unorganized. It didn't flow properly with your own natural energy. Under normal conditions, you probably would've experienced some minor fatigue as your body aligned the foreign energy with your own. However, you overexerted yourself far too soon after the mending process."

"Because I had a false sense of rejuvenation."

"Correct."

"Got it." The bloodseeker briefly peered under the

blanket before clutching it to her chest again. "Now can you tell me why you undressed me?"

"Disrobing a patient is a common healing practice in our sect. To assist the energy in flowing properly, we had to remove your armor and allow you to lie naturally."

"Lie naturally? You couldn't even leave me with my undergarments? How much resistance could they have posed?"

"I apologize. It's simply our way. Some may seek priestly healing because of it, but no one can deny the effectiveness of our methods. This is also why we let down your hair. I must say it's a lovely shade of red. I've never seen it before."

"Thank you. It's a first for me as well."

Bolya cocked her head. "I'm sorry?"

"Never mind. So, now that I'm all better, may I get dressed?"

"Of course. Allow me to fetch your belongings right away."

"Uh, excuse me, miss." One of the wounded sat up in a bed across the room.

"Yes?" the pinkleaf asked.

"I came in with another guy last night. He was stabbed in the neck." The man pointed to his throat. "He was bleeding real bad."

"Sounds like a punctured carotid. I'm sorry, we've had many patients come in. I'll check with the other healers and see if anyone knows your friend."

"Thank you."

After Bolya left, the man stared at Sundancer. The bloodseeker held the blanket firmly to her chest, her shoulders exposed, and glared back at him. To her disbelief, he continued to ogle.

"Unless you wish to lose your sight, I suggest you stop staring," she threatened.

"Oh—uh—my apologies," he stammered. He averted his gaze, and his cheeks lit up like ripe apples. "I didn't mean to eavesdrop, but you're Lady Sundancer, aren't you? The Champion of the Light? The Prima's bodyguard?"

"That's right."

The man beamed as he made eye contact with her. "Depths! I saw when you and the Prima took down those six brutes. Oh man, the way you flew through the air and came down on that one demon. That was fangling unbelievable. How the depths did you do that?"

"What do you mean?"

He scoffed. "I know paladins are amazing fighters, especially champions, but that was something else. You moved so smoothly, so gracefully. It was like you knew what was going to happen before it happened."

"I can't really explain it."

"Oh, I…I see." An awkward silence filled the room as the man looked away.

How was she supposed to explain years of training in something this guy had probably never even heard of? Sundancer did her best anyway. "I can see it before it happens. But not…not in my mind. It's not like a vision. It's more like…like a feeling. But more than a feeling. Does that make any sense?"

"Sounds incredible."

Sundancer cleared her throat. "So, you're not a paladin?"

"Me? Oh, no. I'm just a watcher. I actually applied to join the Paladin Order a few years back, but—you know what, it doesn't matter."

"And you were at the oak?"

"Yup. We were guarding the east edge. You know, blocking the streets so no demons could get away from the fight. After you all left to chase down those demonic wolves, we were ordered to secure the twisted gate."

"And what happened to your friend? The one with the neck wound?"

"Oh, I'm not really sure," the watcher said. "When we took over the plaza, Pips and I—uh, Pips is his nickname."

"Ah."

"Pips and I were patrolling the perimeter when we came across this civilian in one of the alleys. I guess she somehow wandered near the twisted gate by mistake. So, we approach her, you know, to advise her to return to her home or just stay away from the area. And when she faces us, she's just the most beautiful woman you've ever seen. Oh, well, at least *I've* ever seen. I mean, until this morning, because you're very beautiful too."

Sundancer furrowed her brow as she tried to understand the story, but the watcher only seemed concerned with making a fool of himself.

"So anyway, I ask her where she lives, and she just gives me this look of horror, like she's wandered into the Den. She doesn't say a single word. We figure she's in shock. Neither of us recognized her, so we decided the best thing to do was to take her to the inn. As we're heading toward the Golden Branch, the ground starts to shake real bad."

"The purge?"

"Exactly. This woman falls over and clings to Pips. So, we take shelter next to a building to keep our balance. This goes on for a couple minutes, I guess, and when it's over, she's grinning. She's rubbing his arm, you know, acting all friendly. She's got this sly smile on her face, and she gives him a wink. Any Dardan fool could figure out what she was getting at."

The bloodseeker rolled her eyes. "Mm-hmm."

"Now, Pips is a good guy, but he's got no girl, and now he's got a gorgeous one hanging on his arm. And I know we're on duty, but I feel for the guy. So, before we continue on, I wait while she leads him down a side street. Next thing I hear is this choking sound. When I turn around, this woman charges at me with a knife. She slashes me across the chest and knocks me to the ground. If it wasn't for my height, I'm sure she would've gone for my fangling throat."

The watcher pulled his covers down to reveal the scar from the bottom of his sternum to his right shoulder. "Next thing I know, people are calling for help. The woman drops the knife and just takes off running. I look over, and there's Pips walking toward me, holding his neck with blood just pouring down his arm. Depths, I hope he's all right."

"This woman. She didn't speak at all?"

"No, I asked her her name, where she lived. Nothing. She didn't say anything the whole time. I just assumed she was too scared to."

"Hmm. Do you at least remember what she looked like?" Sundancer asked.

"I don't think I could ever forget." The watcher closed his eyes and rested his head against the wall. "She had long, straight hair, pitch-black. It did a fantastic job framing her face as it snaked elegantly down her neck. Her eyes were so inviting, the kind that just put you at ease. Dark blue, like the sky at dusk. Her lips were a pale red. She wore this dress that clung to her body in such a way that you saw everything without seeing anything. I don't know how to describe it. I did think it was a little long, though. The bottom dragged along the ground, but who cares. That red dress fit her perfectly."

****

The room bustled as nine of the archdons from Royal Oak stood in an area no larger than a small classroom. At the front, Mashira sat on a plain chair with two others on either side of her. On her right were the two advisors who had just arrived from Light's Haven. Advisor Ayristark, a man of great importance, looked the part. Though not exceedingly tall, his presence still dominated. His hair was graying, but he looked quite young for someone in his sixties. The Talisman had treated him well during his reign as Primus. Advisor Cole, in the next seat over, was in his fifties with no sign of hair atop his head. With a scowl stamped across his lips, he appeared perpetually displeased.

On the Prima's left rested Advisor Deidok and an empty chair. Deidok was nearly twenty years older than Ayristark and looked exactly his age. His eyes were closed but fluttered open when a sharp knock came at the wooden door. Sundancer and Advisor Razza Merona entered the room.

"How are you both feeling?" Mashira asked.

"Fine," the paladin said flatly.

"I'm feeling well, thank you, Your Luminescence." Razza took her seat next to Deidok.

"I think we're ready to begin then," the Prima said.

The archdons from Royal Oak quieted down and lined up in a row before their leader.

"I want to thank you all for coming this morning. I know you were all helping with the barricade or the wounded and probably didn't get much sleep, if any. I'm pleased and grateful that everyone is helping where they can. However, there are matters we must resolve before I return to Light's Haven.

"Some of you may or may not have heard that Archdon Scarit has resigned as head archdon of Royal Oak. Over the past few years, his health has been in decline, and the attack last night made him realize it's time for someone else to take his place. Considering the state of Royal Oak, I do not wish to leave here today without putting a leader in charge, so we'll skip the formal interviews. Since Archdon Westan is still seriously hurt from his burns, he will not be included in this process. And as for Archdon Omana..."

Mashira inconspicuously observed Ayristark. His worn face showed no sign of sorrow, but the Prima sensed his pain over the loss of his former advisor. Though Mashira herself had never been close to the archdon, Omana had been a dear friend of the family. She had taught Mortis the Blessing of the Fallen Angel.

The Prima returned her focus to the row of archdons. "Archdon Omana and Don Millan were caught in the purge last night and are presumed dead. The Council has assembled here so we can choose a new head archdon. If any of you wish to be considered, please step forward now."

The priests in the black robes and white scarves looked among themselves, but none moved out of line. Typically, when choosing a new head, there were many candidates vying for the spot. However, given the state of Royal Oak, Mashira wasn't at all surprised with their reaction.

"If it's fear or modesty that holds you back, that is not what this city needs right now. They need someone to take charge, someone to look to for help. Do not abandon your own city in this time of peril. They need a leader."

"They need a healer." Vikard broke formation and bowed before the Prima and her advisors. "If it pleases the Council, I offer myself for consideration to become the next head archdon of Royal Oak."

Deidok perked up. "Archdon Vikard is correct. What this city needs most is to be healed, to be rebuilt. It needs someone with a caring heart."

"Does no one else wish to be considered? Let no one say the opportunity wasn't given." After a long pause, the Prima addressed the sole candidate. "Very well. Come forward, Archdon Vikard. As is the custom, will you allow the Council to evaluate you?"

Vikard inched forward and dropped to one knee. "I will."

"My trusted advisors, if you have any questions for Archdon Vikard, please ask them and give me your final say."

Deidok spoke first. "In these perilous times, it seems we do not have the luxury of time. I know of Archdon Vikard through his father and through his own reputation. I have no questions to ask, and I have already given my say. The city needs a healer. Maybe he cannot use his power to rebuild, but he has the right mentality. Archdon Vikard has insight and intellect. He will make a fine head archdon."

With Deidok's opinion given, Ayristark started his line of questioning. "How do you plan to safely rebuild the city?"

"Like closing an open wound, we must complete the barricade," Vikard explained. "Our top priority will be to keep the people safe. After that, we'll rebuild the wall during the day. And at night, I'll assign priests to join the watch, including an archdon. I'll also petition the paladins to help as well."

"And what are your plans for the people that have lost everything in the purge? Will you help them?"

"We'll help if we can. People in dire situations will be encouraged to look to friends and family outside the city for help until Royal Oak is restored."

"And if they have none?" Ayristark asked.

"Then we'll do the best we can to accommodate them, but we ourselves have lost the rectory. I won't force anyone to open their homes to strangers, but I would hope that some will follow my lead."

"You intend to open your home to people you don't know?"

"Not exactly," Vikard said. "I know these people. I've lived with them for the last ten years. I wouldn't consider anyone in this city a stranger."

"And what happens after the city is rebuilt, and everything returns to how it once was? Will you still take strays into your home and care for them?"

"As a last resort, perhaps. No one should be turned away. But when the city is whole again, the rectory will be there for those who need it."

"Hmm, you are your father's son," Ayristark said with little emotion. "A bit idealistic, but that will slowly change. As no one else will step forward, this shows me you have courage and you'll do what needs to be done. And not for yourself either. I offer this piece of advice, though. Human life is sacred and should not be devalued ever. But be mindful of those who constantly seek help because they are too lazy to help themselves. These are the lowest of our society because by believing your time is best spent helping them, they are in fact devaluing *your* life. I would also recommend you work closely with the nobility of the city. The help of the duchess may prove invaluable. I am in agreement with Advisor Deidok."

"Thank you, Advisor Ayristark. I won't forget your words."

"Advisor Razza Merona, would you like to go next?" Mashira asked.

"My apologies, Your Luminescence," Razza said. "I haven't had time to think this over, and I'm still recovering from my injury. Advisors Deidok and Ayristark speak well, and I trust in their wisdom. But I also trust yours as well. I'm in agreement with your final decision."

"Very well." Mashira pivoted in her chair to face her final advisor. "Advisor Cole?"

Slouched with his head propped up by his fist, Cole said, "No one else stepped forward, so you're the only choice. There's nothing to add."

Mashira was disappointed in the comment. At a critical moment like this, the Council needed to show strength and confidence in their decision, not apathy. She pushed on the arms of her chair and rose to her feet. "Archdon Vikard, I have seen you in battle. You are always where you're needed most. You have a quick mind, and you've seen firsthand the terror our kingdom must now face. I concur with my advisors. And so, I, Prima Mashira, witnessed by the Council and all others present, hereby bestow upon you, Archdon Vikard, the title of head archdon for the city of Royal Oak. May the angels give us strength and guide us. May the angels watch over you."

"And you as well," Vikard said.

"Arise, Head Archdon Vikard. There's much work to

be done. We'll be in constant contact with you during these trying times. Please don't hesitate to petition for aid from other cities."

"I won't."

"Unfortunately, we'll have to postpone the celebration for now," Mashira said. "I ask that you go and tend to your city. The Council has another matter we must discuss in private."

"Of course. Thank you." Vikard bowed, then stood to face his colleagues. The Royal Oak archdons swarmed around him to offer their congratulations. The group steadily moved as a cluster toward the door and squeezed past the threshold.

Mashira turned to her bodyguard. "I'm glad to see you're doing well, Lady Sundancer. Would you please excuse us and close the door when you leave?"

The paladin obliged and departed. As the door to the small room banged against its frame and latched into place, the four advisors rearranged their chairs and angled them toward the Prima.

Mashira's eyes darted between each of her advisors. She knew the next topic would be far more difficult to discuss than selecting a new head archdon. The Prima inhaled deeply and allowed the air out slowly. "In light of recent events, a thought comes to mind. I'm deeply conflicted over this, and so I need your help. Do we seek help from the Death Gods?"

"Absolutely not," Advisor Cole stated decisively.

Deidok wagged his finger. "Now, now, let's not be hasty. Archdon Omana made the suggestion yesterday, and it was promptly dismissed. Perhaps she would be alive if we had listened."

"How dare you?" Razza Merona blurted out. "How dare you insinuate that we're responsible for her death because we didn't agree with her idea?"

"I don't believe that's what I said."

"And I don't see how last night justifies the idea now."

"Really?" In the entire time he served as Mashira's advisor, the old man never showed the slightest animosity toward anyone. "Then what course of action is justified after a demon lord obliterates half of the second-largest city in our kingdom?"

"Nothing justifies working with those murderers!"

Mashira intervened. "Razza, please."

"She's right, though," Cole said. "Or have you forgotten how many innocent watchers they killed at Deimor Outpost?"

The Prima placed her hands on her hips. "I have not forgotten."

"Then how could you propose such a *ridiculous* notion?"

"That's enough! I knew this wasn't going to be an easy discussion, but I will not let this turn into some charade where we sit around belittling one another and ignoring the issue at hand. This is serious. Did you even look at where the royal oak once stood? Did you see the wasteland that demon lord left behind?"

Cole's face tightened like he had just bitten into a lemon. "But the Death Gods?"

"If you think I make this suggestion lightly or I'm happy about it, you're sorely mistaken. It hasn't even been three years since Deimor Outpost. If you think I've forgotten about what they did or that I've forgiven them, think again. But listen to me when I tell you this is not about them."

There was only silence from her advisors, even Cole made no attempt to interrupt her. The fire burned in Mashira's chest. "They may be the subject of this discussion, but this decision is not about them. It's about *us*. About *our* survival. The survival of *our* kingdom and the people we have sworn to protect. There's a level of understanding and knowledge we must admit we just don't have. And I fear if we delay much longer, there won't be much of a kingdom left for us to defend. I know why they were exiled to Alovajj, or have you forgotten I was the one who sent them there?"

The Prima sat down and took a few deep breaths. "I am trying to look past my personal feelings on the matter and think about what is best for our people. I hope you can do the same."

"Your Luminescence, there is an answer," Ayristark said. "You can take back the Talisman of Zavi from the king. You can kill the demon lord with it."

"And leave the king completely vulnerable? No, it's clear Verago wants Batar dead, and as long as he wears the Talisman, at least we know he's safe."

"Then we increase his guard. Bloodseekers, guardians, priests, whatever it takes. But, the kingdom will fall if Batar keeps the Talisman. We cannot stop the demon lord without it."

Mashira rubbed her forehead. "I'm sorry, but this is not up for discussion. Batar keeps the Talisman."

Deidok squinted and the wrinkles around his eyes became more pronounced. "Is your answer based on your feelings for the boy?"

Over the past few years, the Prima's affection for Batar had dwindled and finally vanished. He wasn't the same person she had met nearly a decade ago. She had made this clear to her advisors on numerous occasions, and the fact that it was coming up again only frustrated her further. "No, as I've already explained several times, there's nothing between us anymore. My answer is based solely on the fact that Verago wants him. The Devil doesn't target a single person unless he has a very good reason. Do you understand what I'm trying to tell you? Batar is the focus of some plan. Verago wants him and only him, and we don't know why."

"And how are we supposed to find out?" Ayristark asked.

"Excellent question. I was thinking we might ask for help from the people who have answers. Which brings us back to the reason I called this meeting."

"So, you believe the Death Gods know why Verago wants Batar?"

"Of course. You remember the letter we received three years ago from Rendomin, right? He found a journal that indicated the Death Gods knew Verago was going to try to capture and kill Batar."

"But instead, he captured and killed Altheus." Deidok clicked his tongue. "What a terrible night."

"Yes, but that's beside the point," the Prima said. "They knew Devil's Breach was going to happen."

Razza jumped back in. "But that doesn't mean they knew why. I see no reason why we should trust them after what they did."

The opposition was mounting against her idea. Mashira studied the faces of each of her advisors and couldn't determine if their expressions were showing pity or concern. And, perhaps they were right about the Death Gods. Maybe pursuing this idea was a mistake, but before she conceded, she needed to lay all her cards on the table.

"Look. We all know Deimor Outpost was not an unprovoked incident. Yes, they crossed the line. What they did was inexcusable. But we know the events that led up to it, don't we? We can pretend our hands are clean, but the truth is we enlisted the help of Anoctis. We hired Rendomin to spy on the Death Gods."

Ayristark drummed his fingers on the arm of his chair. "Rendomin acted on his own accord. What happened was outside our agreement and outside our control."

"But we put him there, in Alovajj, under false pretenses. Like it or not, that psychotic Dardan fool of a thief was our responsibility."

"May I say something?" Cole asked politely.

Mashira was startled by how courteous the advisor spoke. "Um, of course."

"You believe the Death Gods know why it's so important for Verago to kill Batar, correct?"

"Without a doubt."

"I see. Well, to that, I say, so what?"

"I'm sorry?"

"So what? So what if they know? Is knowing that bit of information going to magically stop the demon lord from destroying other cities?"

"You've completely missed the point," Mashira said. "They know things that we don't. They have dedicated their lives to learning as much as they can about demons, dark energy, and Verago. For angel's sake, Shinigami was the Grand Overseer of the Brotherhood for how many years? Twenty-five? Thirty? Do you think anyone on the Surface knows Verago better than he does? If they know why the Devil wants Batar, think what else they might know. Maybe they can stop Erynion."

"And what about their methods?" Deidok asked. "By enlisting their help, are we not condoning their methods of obtaining this information?"

"We know they torture demons," Ayristark added. "Vile beasts to be sure, but their souls are still human. We'd be walking a fine line."

"Please, Your Luminescence," Razza begged. "Leave them in exile."

"Where they belong," Cole muttered.

Mashira scowled, and the fire in her chest flickered. It seemed clear where her advisors stood regarding the Death Gods. She thought back to the previous night and how helpless she'd felt as Erynion annihilated half of the city. If she had the Talisman of Zavi—

No, she couldn't think like that. She couldn't take the Talisman from Batar. The risk was too great. But, what other course of action existed? Was she really prepared to go against the advice of her Council? In the end, that's all they were there for: advice. It was her decision to make and hers alone.

"No," she said softly.

Cole raised his eyebrow. "No?"

Mashira fanned the flames in her heart. "That's right.

No."

"You can't be serious. You're going to ignore the advice of your entire Council?"

"I don't know. I guess we'll see." Mashira sprang to her feet as her internal fire roared to life. "It's pretty presumptuous of you to speak for all advisors when no one has given me their final say."

"Well, that's easy," Cole said. "I say no, not now, not ever."

"And I think you've made that quite clear, but let me just say this. If we keep insisting on taking this high road, the kingdom is done. Do you get that? We're not even fighting Verago! We're fighting one of his playthings. And if by the grace of the angels, we kill this demon lord, what stops the Devil from making another? And what happens when he kills Batar? What unspeakable event will happen then? Yes, I agree consulting with the Death Gods is not the perfect solution, but at least it's a fangling solution!" Mashira stomped on the floor so hard she felt pain shoot up her leg. "We need to know what they know."

Cole sneered. "But at what price?"

"Are we to keep going in circles then? We all know what's at stake. And if no one has anything new to offer, then I want your final say. Do you think we should reestablish contact with Alovajj and make peace with the Death Gods in order to stop Erynion and Verago?"

Advisor Deidok shrugged. "Truth be told, I've always favored this decision."

Cole nearly fell out of his chair. *"What?"*

Mashira's jaw dropped. "You have?"

"Oh, yes. But, this course of action is not one to be taken lightly. I believe we all need to be aware of the challenges that will accompany it. I can understand why you might think I was opposed to it, but I absolutely agree we should do this."

Advisor Cole glared at Deidok. "You senile—"

Ayristark intervened. "Your Luminescence, it was by

your order that King Cato exiled the Death Gods in the first place. We all know the history. There's no reason to rehash it. But at the time, we were not faced with such a threat. I want to reiterate what Deidok said. If we are to pursue this course of action, we need to go into it with open eyes and an open mind. We have to take the good with the bad, and pray that in the end, we have made the right decision. And so, given these unfortunate circumstances, I find myself in agreement with you. While not ideal, this is our best option, and so I favor this decision."

Mashira's eyes widened as she struggled to catch her breath. In an instant, her fears melted away and a huge weight was lifted from her shoulders. She had just received support from two of her four advisors, including Ayristark, whose opinion she valued most. "Thank you."

"However," the former Primus continued, "we must be cautious. There has been a lot of bad blood between the Death Gods and the rest of the kingdom. It would be unwise to place all of our trust and hope in them."

Razza Merona shook her head. "I have to disagree with what's been said. I'm doubtful the Death Gods can offer us salvation from this nightmare. In fact, I believe working with them can be just as harmful as it is helpful. I cannot agree that this is the best path to follow."

"Finally, some reason," Cole said.

"*However*, since it appears to be the only path we can follow, I cannot in good conscience reject this idea either. And so, until a time at which I can provide a suitable alternative, I will withhold my criticism. For now—whatever your decision—you will have my cooperation."

The Prima felt as if she could float. Only moments ago, she was prepared to act in defiance of the Council's advice, but now the opposite would be true. The fire within her calmed and burned steadily. Mashira strolled toward Advisor Cole. "Although I'm sure we all know what your opinion is, everyone should be given the same opportunity to offer their final say. So, let's hear it."

Cole's hands slid back and forth over his thighs. With a grunt, he stood beside the Prima and addressed the Council. He spoke slowly, as if meticulously selecting each word before he said it. "What I'm experiencing at this moment can only be described as profound disbelief. I can't believe what I'm hearing. I can't believe what you all are agreeing to. So quick to forget."

Mashira kept her lips sealed. She had to allow him to speak.

"I don't care what you say. You've all forgotten what those people did to us. They nearly tore the kingdom in two. I reject this decision with every fiber of my being. And what's more, I cannot be on this Council if this is the course of action you mean to take."

"Advisor Cole, what are you saying?" Mashira asked.

"I know we haven't always seen eye to eye on many topics, but I've still stood by you. This is different, though. Shinigami may be human by our definition, but he's just as bad as the Devil. And you don't make peace with one demon to destroy another."

"Your opinion of the Death God leader is noted. You claim we're quick to forget, but it seems you've forgotten how Shinigami's help at the Assault on Light's Haven ensured our victory."

"So you say. I suppose that reconciles everything else. Well, don't let me stop you. I see you've received a favorable answer from the Council. I wonder if any of them hold an opinion of their own, or do they agree with you on everything."

"You're out of line, Advisor," Mashira scolded.

"Advisor? Don't make me laugh. What's the point of such a title if you never heed my advice."

"I don't have to agree with you to heed your words."

Cole threw his hands up. "It doesn't matter now anyway. I take it you plan to proceed with this idea and petition the Death Gods for help?"

"I do."

"Then allow me to take this final opportunity to tell you all you're making a grave mistake. Once you throw your lot in with the Death Gods, everything will change, and trust me when I say, it will not get better. I refuse to play any part in this." Cole removed the white scarf with the red stripes and threw it on the ground. "I resign from my position as your advisor."

The scarf on the floor irritated Mashira to no end. She had no issues with the act of resignation, in general. But, what she found unacceptable was how he was doing it so disrespectfully, discarding the symbol of his rank.

"This is not something you can take back later," the Prima warned. "I'll give you a moment to reconsider, and I suggest you think very carefully before you speak again."

Cole brought his face so close to hers that their noses were nearly touching. "It's obvious I'm thinking more clearly than any of you. And I'm not sure how much clearer I can be. You're a disgrace to the rank, to the Talisman, and to the guild. Your Council is a joke, and I won't be a part of it any longer. I resign my position, and that is final."

The words stung, but they were just words. There was no truth behind them. Cole was trying to get a rise out of her. Mashira grimaced as she tried to douse the flames that were blazing on the inside. Cole knocked his chair aside on his way out. He gripped the handle and swung open the door.

"That's it then?" the Prima asked. "You intend to just leave your seat empty?"

Cole paused in the threshold. "No, have your brother fill it."

CHAPTER 34

Eriph inspected his reflection. His naturally feathered blond hair clung to his shoulders, and his brown robe hung plainly over his body. Behind him, his bag lay on the bed with a black scarf peeking out. He hadn't put it on since his Exclusion. He corralled his hair with both hands and tied it back into a tail. Today was going to be his first official day as a Death God. Alovajj was his new home. His heartbeat was powerful but steady. The Death God founders held his fate in their hands. If Eriph wasn't accepted as an officer and provided a place in Moultia Palace, he would be just like the thousands of citizens who lived in Alovajj without a real voice. But whatever the founders' decision, today would be the last day he wore the brown robe. Eriph took a deep breath before he scooped up the bag with his belongings and hoisted his shield over his shoulder. He descended the stairs and entered the tavern portion of the lodge.

The owner's son, a boy who could barely grow hair on his face, greeted him. "Good morning, sir. Would you like to eat?"

"Good morning."

Another voice interrupted the polite exchange.

"Morning? Ha! Eleven strikes has already passed. It's nearly afternoon!"

Eriph smiled. "Cross, what are you doing up? After last night, I thought you'd still be asleep."

"Me? Never. I have to head back to Memorial City today. No time for sleep. Come, put that fangling shield down and join me."

Eriph slipped by the owner's son and sat at the table. Cross, a large fellow with the personality to match, was a traveling merchant who made frequent trips to Alovajj from Memorial City. An orange beard in need of serious trimming shrouded most of his face, but anyone could tell when he smiled.

"So, the food any good?" the excluded priest asked.

"Nothing quite like it after how much I drank last night. You don't seem too bad, though."

"Oh, well, that's because you were already ten pints in when I walked through the gate."

Cross squinted as if trying to remember the events of the previous night. "Oh yeah. You came from Royal Oak, right? Depths of a ride. You hear the news?"

"News? No, what's that?"

"Fangling demons messed it up pretty bad. They say the purge took out half the fangling city."

Eriph had chills. "Purge? Half the city? Was it occupied?"

"Mmm, no, it doesn't sound like it. I think most of the civilians were out of range. But word is plenty of fighters fell. It was this huge battle. Apparently, there was a twisted gate in the royal oak."

"A twisted gate? In the oak? How's that possible? Was there no sacred ground?"

The merchant shrugged. "No fangling clue. I'm just telling you what I heard."

"And who told you about this?"

"Boss. Got the letter this morning. She's recalling all of us back to Memorial City until further notice. Apparently,

Prima Mashira even called Ayristark and Cole out to Royal Oak early this morning. Some emergency Council meeting."

"Really? The Council met this morning?"

"That's what the letter said."

The possibilities swarmed in Eriph's mind. If Candelux ever planned to reconnect with the Death Gods, the Prima would want the support of the Council. And if the attack on Royal Oak was as devastating as Cross indicated, then it might lead the Council to this drastic decision.

"Hey!" Cross broke Eriph's concentration. "My head's still a little fuzzy, but did you say you were going up to Moultia Palace today?"

"That's right." The excluded priest stood and picked up his shield. "Listen, I'm sorry to leave so abruptly, but I really need to go. I guess I'm skipping breakfast today."

"Skipping breakfast? Ha! That's the dumbest fangling thing I've ever heard. At least take some bread."

Eriph snagged a roll from the merchant's plate.

Cross threw his hands up. "Hey! I said *some* bread, not *my* bread!"

"Thanks, I owe you one."

The merchant grumbled as the excluded priest slung the shield across his back. Eriph devoured the roll as he exited the inn. Outside, he basked in the warmth of the sun. He prayed he was right about the Prima's desire to work with the Death Gods. This could be the start of something incredible. He glanced up and down the street. Prior to his Exclusion, he had lived in Alovajj for an entire year, training with Founder Brahawee, and so he knew the city well. As he crossed the street and made his way to the Scriptorum, Eriph thought back to the previous morning in Royal Oak.

He had planned to wake up at daybreak, but his encounter with the two iymed by the royal oak had forced him to sleep for an extra couple of hours. He had just donned his brown robe when a knock came at the door.

"Who is it?"

"Mashira."

The excluded priest was silent. There was no way he heard that correctly. "Sorry? Who is it?"

"Mashira. Prima Mashira."

The man practically leapt toward the door to open it. Standing on the opposite side of the threshold was the Candelux leader.

"Your Luminescence, I wasn't expecting you."

"I know." Mashira stretched her lips into some semblance of a smile. "I heard you were still in the city and wanted to come see you before you left."

"Uh, sure. Come in." Once the Prima had passed through, Eriph went to close the door, but something blocked the way. A paladin forced the door back open and entered after Mashira.

"I see you brought company." The excluded priest checked for any other guests before shutting the door.

Mashira gestured toward the paladin. "This is my bodyguard, Lady Sundancer, Champion of the Light."

"Wait. *The* Lady Sundancer? You brought a champion bloodseeker to protect you from me? Wow! You don't trust me that much?"

"Amusing, but she's not for you."

Eriph wondered about the reason for the visit. Even though he wasn't expecting a positive answer, he needed to ask anyway. "Have you reconsidered my Exclusion?"

Mashira pursed her lips. "No, unfortunately, that is final. But, despite all of that, you've been very helpful to us. Archdon Feranis told me of your actions when the Marksman attacked you all near Nesinu."

"Really? I thought he left that out of his report."

"Officially, yes, he did. But, he made sure I knew. Also, Archdon Omana explained to me what happened last night by the oak. I wanted to thank you."

"No problem."

Mashira chuckled nervously. "I'm not sure what to do

with Don Millan, though. I mean, the Blessing of the Fallen Angel?"

Eriph matched her laugh. "Yeah, I was a little surprised myself. If you want my advice, go easy on him. He's a good kid. Actually, I'm surprised he's so faithful to Candelux considering Don Skully was his mentor."

"I suppose you're right. It'd be unfair to hold him accountable for the actions of his teacher. He just needs a push in the right direction."

Eriph sensed there was something more to her visit. "Was there anything else?"

Mashira didn't answer right away, almost as if she was conflicted about answering the question honestly. "No, I guess not. I thought I'd come to see you and offer my thanks in person. And, to wish you well."

"I appreciate that. Though I may have broken the rules in your eyes, I still hold the philosophies of our guild...of *your* guild close to my heart."

"May the angels watch over you, Eriph."

"And you as well, Your Luminescence."

The Prima, with Lady Sundancer close behind, opened the door and stepped into the hallway. Eriph knew this might be the last time he'd be able to speak with her. "They can help, you know."

Mashira peered over her shoulder.

The excluded priest leaned against the doorframe. "The Death Gods. That's why you really came to see me this morning, isn't it?"

The Prima didn't appear to be upset, and she wasn't leaving, so he continued. "They can help. Deep down, you know they can help. They know things you couldn't possibly imagine."

"A little premature, don't you think?"

"You tell me. Nesinu? Nolka? Malarekita? Maybe the major cities can stay safe, but what about all the other towns out there?"

"Even if the Council decided to take such a drastic

measure, why would the Death Gods help us after everything that's happened between us?" Mashira asked.

"To stop Verago. Yes, mistakes have happened on both sides, but they can be forgiven. They need to be forgiven. We need to move on, together."

"Perhaps, one day. But so far, we've done just fine without them."

Before Mashira could leave, Eriph hopped into the hallway and blocked her path. Sundancer advanced on the excluded priest, but the Prima held up her hand and halted the bloodseeker.

"Eriph, what are you doing?"

"Please, Your Luminescence. Hear me out."

"I'm sorry, but I'm afraid there's nothing more to discuss."

"Fine, I understand. Just let me say this. If you change your mind, I'd be honored to request their help on your behalf. You know where I'll be. You know how to reach me."

****

Two guards greeted Eriph at the entrance to Moultia Palace and escorted him toward the throne room. Seven hundred years ago, as Thoris united the four tribes into one kingdom, Alova remained separate. The city-state was ruled by their only monarch, Queen Ezmirelda, and this palace had been built for her. After her death, though, she left no heirs, and so the nobility of Alova decided to join the kingdom and use the palace as their home. Centuries later, the Amulet of Yezda mysteriously appeared in the forests outside the city, infecting wanderers and transforming them into demons. It wasn't long before the dark creatures set their sights on Alova. With no knowledge yet of holy energy, the city was defenseless against the constant attacks. The palace was the last part to fall. It was then that this cursed place was renamed Alovajj, the city of demons.

All evidence of the brutal massacre had been erased after the Death Gods reclaimed the city and made it impervious to demon attacks. As Eriph marched down the long corridor leading to the old throne room, it felt as if he had returned home. The doors opened to reveal the massive space and three figures, adorned in robes, seated at the far end.

As the excluded priest neared the three men, the guards indicated for him to stop. Eriph placed his shield on the ground and dropped to one knee. He bowed to the man in the middle. "Founder Shinigami."

Shinigami's robe was black with red trim. A red figure-eight pattern covered the majority of the vestment, and a stitching of a white skull adorned each of his shoulders. His features mimicked his robe with hair just as black and eyes with a hint of red. Once the Grand Overseer of the Brotherhood of Prevarra, Shinigami betrayed Verago during the Assault on Light's Haven. In the aftermath, he became the head of the newly formed Sect Eighty-Eight.

"Eriph, welcome back."

The excluded priest bowed to the man seated on Shinigami's right. "Founder Drevarius."

Drevarius's extravagant robe was pleasing to the eye with its multiple shades of blue. His dark hair stuck out in all directions like an untamed bush. The only thing that kept it out of his face was a pair of spectacles on the top of his forehead. Before the Assault, Drevarius carried the title of High War-Mage and shared control over the Summa Arcana guild with High Pan-Mage Yewa.

"Eriph, it's good to see you again. Have you come to stay with us for good?"

"I have, if you'll have me."

The war-mage nodded. "I'm glad to hear it. I'm sure Brahawee will be pleased most of all."

"Thank you." Eriph shifted and bowed to the man on Shinigami's left. "Founder Mortis."

Mortis wore a dark-purple robe with a hood that kept most of his face in the shadows. His left sleeve was oversized, and an ornate dagger with a black-and-white handle protruded from his side. Not only was Mortis the brother of Prima Mashira, but he had been selected to join her Council following the Assault on Light's Haven. A few months later, when Mashira condemned Sect Eighty-Eight's practices and ordered the exile, Mortis was forced to decide where his allegiance would reside.

"Eriph," Mortis said unenthusiastically.

"Esteemed founders, I come before you today because I would like to join the Death Gods, not just as a citizen of Alovajj, but as an officer. In the time I've trained here, my eyes have been opened. I've seen pieces of the truth, and I wish to learn more. I also wish to bring an end to this war against the demons that has been raging for centuries. I believe the Death Gods have the best chance of doing just that."

"Very well," Shinigami said. "As you're no doubt aware, in order to become an officer in our sect, one of the founders must sponsor you and vouch for you. And once you're accepted, *if* you're accepted, you are under the command of your sponsor. He or she will have the authority to strip you of your rank without question. Is that clear?"

Eriph's heart raced. "Yes, it is."

"I will let the other founders know about your intentions, and you'll be contacted when a decision is made."

"I understand. I was wondering if I might be able to speak with—"

"One moment." Mortis interjected. "I would like to be Eriph's sponsor."

"Seriously?" Drevarius exclaimed.

Mortis glared at the war-mage.

Eriph knew where Drevarius was coming from because he himself was surprised. In his entire time training with

Founder Brahawee, Eriph had barely heard a complete sentence from Mortis. "Uh, thank you, thank you."

Shinigami smirked. "Well, that was easy. Excellent! Mortis, from now on, Eriph is in your care and under your watch."

"The guards will show you the empty rooms in my wing of the palace," Mortis said. "Pick whichever you like."

Eriph was dumbfounded. He'd been told stories about candidates having to wait weeks to hear back from the founders, only to end up rejected. But for some reason, Mortis jumped at the opportunity to sponsor him, and Eriph had no idea why.

"Thank you. That's very kind. But before I go, I have one other matter to discuss."

"Go on," Shinigami said.

Eriph relaxed since the hard part was over. "No doubt you've heard about Royal Oak, the most recent in a string of attacks surrounding this new demon lord. Malarekita endured Corruption. Nesinu was erased from the map. The kingdom is in peril while the demon lord runs free. They need our help."

"I agree. They certainly need help."

"Then we should help them."

Shinigami arched his eyebrow. "Should we? I'm not so sure. Prima Mashira and King Cato made it abundantly clear they want nothing to do with us. We were forced out of the kingdom. We had no choice but to take up residence in a demon-infested city. Even when there was an open line of communication, there was little benefit to it. They won't listen to us, and they don't agree with our methods."

"And they weren't exactly happy after Deimor Outpost," Drevarius added.

Mortis groaned and folded his arms across his chest.

"Yes, yes, you're right," Eriph conceded. "And I'm aware of all of that. But it's different now. When they lost half of Royal Oak, they realized they don't know their enemy as well as they thought. They're willing to put past events behind them, work with you—with *us*—for the greater good of stopping Erynion and Verago."

Shinigami tilted his head. "What makes you say that?"

Eriph slid his hand into his pocket and retrieved a letter. "I come with a message from Prima Mashira."

Printed in Poland
by Amazon Fulfillment
Poland Sp. z o.o., Wrocław
04 July 2023